THE LAST WAVE

THE LAST WAVE

GILLIAN BEST

ANANSI

First published in the UK by Freight Books
Published in Canada in 2017 and the USA in 2018 by House of Anansi Press Inc.
www.houseofanansi.com

House of Anansi Press is committed to protecting our natural environment.
As part of our efforts, the interior of this book is printed on paper that contains
100% post-consumer recycled fibres, is acid-free, and is processed chlorine-free.

21 20 19 18 17 1 2 3 4 5

Library and Archives Canada Cataloguing in Publication

Best, Gillian, 1975–, author
The last wave / Gillian Best.

Issued in print and electronic formats.
ISBN 978-1-4870-0293-0 (softcover).—ISBN 978-1-4870-0294-7 (EPUB).—
ISBN 978-1-4870-0295-4 (Kindle)

I. Title.

PS8603.E77498L37 2017   C813'.6   C2017-902290-3
                    C2017-902291-1

Library of Congress Control Number: 2017945107

Book design: Alysia Shewchuk

 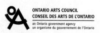

Canada Council Conseil des Arts
for the Arts du Canada

ONTARIO ARTS COUNCIL
CONSEIL DES ARTS DE L'ONTARIO
an Ontario government agency
un organisme du gouvernement de l'Ontario

*We acknowledge for their financial support of our publishing program
the Canada Council for the Arts, the Ontario Arts Council, and the Government of
Canada through the Canada Book Fund.*

Printed and bound in Canada

MIX
Paper from
responsible sources
FSC® C016245

For Mom, Dave, and Kerri
The best Bests.

And for the artist Richard Stone,
who put a novel in his painting
and read the first draft on the installment plan.

THE LAST WAVE

JOHN, 2014

I REACHED OUT for my wife and my hand touched the place where her shoulder should have been. I buried my face in her pillow and felt a few stray grains of sand brush against my cheek. Her body was absent, but I knew exactly where her hips should lie.

I did not know where she was, but it was easy enough to guess. She always did prefer the seabed.

The mental snapshots I kept of her were full of water. Her hair was never dry, damp towels always covered the radiators, and for an hour or so after a swim, her nose dripped as though the seawater was trying to get back to its rightful place.

The swimming costumes — all dark, all practical — the bathing caps, and the lanolin to keep the chafing down followed her wherever she went. She only deigned to swim in the sea: never a pool and never heated. The sea is alive, expansive; a pool is dead and confining. The sea is freedom. There is nothing in a pool: no current, no tide, no waves, and most of all

1

no history. Antiseptic and cold in their perfection, swimming pools. Horrible things.

She swam at every opportunity, regardless of weather or temperature. On the coldest days, I worried if she was gone too long, because hypothermia had once forced her back onto the land. If it was too cold, in the depths of winter, to keep herself from going mad she sat shivering on the beach, staring out at the froth, desperate to be engulfed in it.

She would say: The sea has always been here. It's seen everything.

"Martha," I called.

Downstairs, the sink was full of dishes, cups and crumbs covered the counter, and I thought to myself that this was a bit much even by her standards. Her dedication to the water rarely prevented her from keeping a clean house. I piled the rest of the dirty crockery into the sink and brushed the crumbs onto the floor as Webb loped over. The window was open and the wind was up; the flowered curtains snapped like the lifeguard flags at the beach in summer, threatening to push the shells off the windowsill.

Webb budged my leg with his head and I patted his head. "Good boy."

"We'll miss the tide," I said to the closed bathroom door.

Webb barked and I gave him half a slice of stale toast from the countertop, which he gobbled down, barely slowing to chew. He grinned at me, drool oozing from the sides of his mouth.

"Come on, Martha," I said. "You won't have time to eat." I waited at the door for a reply, but she was silent, so I looked through the pantry for the porridge she ate each morning. I couldn't find it.

A gust blew through the window again, and as I turned around I saw the old tea box where I kept my tobacco on the top shelf. I took it down, and just as I was ready to roll the paper up tightly, another whoosh of wind came through the kitchen and the unmade cigarette flew onto the floor. Webb sniffed around my feet.

"No," I said, moving his snout away with my foot. "Bad dog." But he was relentless and I had to shove him harder, which caused him to lose his balance. He fell down yelping and I felt like a beast. He was older than me and had a harder time of it, balancing on three legs.

I rolled it up again but it was a struggle: my fingers were not as limber as they had once been.

"Martha, we'll miss the tide," I said to the closed bathroom door.

It was early September, but the weather was closer to November and the sky was dull like wedding silver that hadn't been used in years.

I went out into the front garden to have my fag and saw the neighbour, Henry. A real curtain-twitcher. He waved but I didn't. Martha would say I'd been rude, but I did not want to get involved in a conversation with him. He had too many questions and I was not interested in answering any of them.

I gave up on the cigarette and went upstairs to our room to find Martha, who should have been getting her swimming kit sorted. But there was no sign of her.

As I passed the window I saw the front gate was open, though I'd thought it was closed when I was outside moments earlier, and I rushed outside to look for her. It was then that I realized I was in my slippers, the rain coming down in earnest.

Who would go swimming on a day like this?

Martha.

But there was no sign of her. I walked to the gate and strained to see through the wet, past the bend in the road, which was the route she always took down to the sea.

Henry shouted to me from his window and I asked, "Have you seen Martha?"

He replied but it got lost between the window and my ears, the rain pounding the ground and mist dampening the sound of his voice. These days, most things sound as though I am underwater.

Good, Martha would say. That's how I ought to sound.

Henry stood in the doorway, his track jacket collar flipped up against the weather. "John," he said. "Are you all right?"

I worried about him: no wife, no children, a middle-aged man living by himself. There was an eagerness to help that was off-putting. Henry was the type of man you saw checking his hair in the reflection whilst he pumped the petrol, the sort of man who was either on the brink of a midlife crisis or in the midst of one, I could never be certain.

"Fine," I said, shutting the door quickly. He was in the habit of inviting himself over for a cup of tea, and though I disliked rudeness, I did not have the time to deal with him.

"Martha?" I shouted. "Darling?" I called, opening the bathroom door. "My love?" I said as I went upstairs.

But she wasn't there. Her dresses had been laid out across the white duvet: black with long sleeves, navy with a fuller skirt, and green tweed. I could not picture her wearing any of them; they were not the sort of thing she wore every day. They lacked a certain practicality.

I heard knocking at the door and expected to see Martha standing on the front step, sheepishly admitting she had forgotten her keys and ready to apologize for leaving without Webb and me. I was hoping she would regret trying to steal a bit more time in the sea by going without us.

But when I leaned out the window, it was Henry. I ducked back in quickly.

"John," he called. "Open the door."

I slammed the window shut and pulled the curtains closed, hoping he'd take the hint. I had never met someone so pushy. How had Martha managed to slip past him? If he'd seen her, she would have felt obligated to invite him in and they'd still be in the kitchen, Henry prattling on about the leaks in his roof, or foxes or badgers.

The hinges on our front door creak in a distinctive way and have done since the day we bought the house. I would know the sound that door made anywhere.

"John," he called from inside our house.

"Go away," I shouted.

Henry's footsteps on the stairs sounded confident, as if he believed he had a right to do as he pleased and enter our house as though it were his own.

"What's going on?" He stood at the edge of our room, where the hardwood flooring in the corridor meets the dove grey carpeting in our bedroom, with one hand in his pocket and the other resting on the doorframe. It was the sort of pose one might take at a pub while trying to affect an air of nonchalance.

I turned my back to him. "Do you make a habit of home invasion?"

"John," he said.

I turned my head in his direction, and as I did I glanced at the wardrobe and that's when I saw it: the case I always brought along for her attempts. This was not its proper place. I kept it downstairs next to her swimming bag. Martha must have moved it during one of her cleaning sprees.

I picked it up and ran my hands over its worn leather, creased and cracked from frequent exposure to salt water. It was the size of a briefcase and soft, with no hard edges — and though the clasps had lost their shine and there were the beginnings of a hole in one of the corners, it was perfect. Some things get better with age, their history eclipsing the shine of shop-bought virtue.

I opened it to make sure everything was in the right place: the jar of pebbles, the maps and charts, the tide table, the tins of grease. A flask for chicken broth and a half a packet of stale biscuits. Had Henry not been hovering over my shoulder I would have opened the pebble jar. There is something tenacious about the smell of the sea; it seeps into everything it touches, including stone, and on days when she wanted to go in but couldn't, the smell took her there instead. When she inhaled the scent, she always did so with her eyes closed.

"Webb," I called, pushing past Henry in the doorway. I went downstairs and the dog met me in the kitchen, where I found a piece of rope to tie to his collar for appearances' sake.

I heard Henry coming down the stairs and picked up my pace. Case in one hand, dog in the other, I threw the front door open and set out down the path. But he was behind me.

"Please, John, you'll regret it."

I looked over my shoulder and met his gaze, giving him a moment to explain himself. He was silent. Webb and I carried on.

As we passed through the front gate, I felt his hand clamp down on my shoulder.

"Get your hands off me! We're late enough as it is."

"Late for what, John?"

Every day it was the same thing. Where are you going? What are you doing? Care to come over for supper? Can I come round for a cuppa later? Do you need any help? Always snooping around, too, in the cupboards, the refrigerator. He thought I didn't notice.

"It's a training day," I said.

"Training for what?"

It was like talking to a three-year-old.

"It's raining," he said. "Why not leave it for today?"

I was standing in the rain so I knew it was raining. He must have thought I was an idiot.

"Have to get moving," I said, turning toward the road. "Mustn't keep her waiting."

Webb barked his agreement. He was irritated by Henry's intrusiveness too.

I pictured her in the sea: strong arms churning through the water, elbows raised high, and glimpses of her face — masked by goggles — when she turned to breathe as she swam parallel to the shore. It was better when she swam across and not out because I could go with her then, in a way. I was her lighthouse, but rather than protecting her from harm I was what called her back to the land.

"John, I don't think you should go."

I turned and he was behind me. "Frankly, Henry, I'm not at all interested in what you think."

He put his hand firmly on my shoulder again. "She isn't there."

"How would you know? Are you psychic now?"

"Why don't you come over? I'll put a fire on. There's a bit of Battenberg cake left that my sister brought at the weekend."

"How kind," I said through gritted teeth.

"John, she passed away."

The rain clouded my glasses but I saw the pity in his face. "Why would you say something like that!"

I yanked Webb's makeshift leash and we walked off as Henry's shouts became lost in the rain.

When we arrived, I noticed two things: that the wind was offshore, which meant that Martha would have to fight the currents as well as the air, and that I was still wearing my slippers. I squinted to see her yellow swimming cap.

Though it was mid-afternoon it looked like dusk, but that was all right. Martha preferred overcast days for swimming. The sun turned the water into a mirror. I want to see under the surface, she said. I want to know what I'm getting into.

Ever since we were young I had watched her disappear into the foam and the froth, returning two or more hours later, utterly spent. I would wrap my arms around her as we sat on the pebble beach while she gave me her numbers: first half-hour, breathing every five strokes; second half-hour every three; breaststroke for twenty minutes. It was mathematical, calculated, and repetitive. She said it was meditative, the endless counting. One, two, three, breathe. Kick, pull, glide, breathe. Focus. Don't think about how cold it is, how far there is to go, the aching in your shoulders, or the stinging of the salt. Just swim.

It was difficult watching her out there in the sea, as she was pummelled by waves breaking over her. I wanted to keep her with me on dry land, but I knew that to try would only push her toward the sea. Instead I looked forward to the moment she emerged from the water, enjoyed watching her figure arise from the deep and walk straight to me. And were it not for her aquatic adventures, I would not have had the pleasure of wrapping my arms around her as she leaned back, her wet hair soaking me through. I was glad to be included in some way, to have a job: what the sea took from her, her heat and strength, I gave back.

On the beach the pebbles were cold and hard; the rain, too. The place was deserted except for a group of teenagers halfway down, shielded by an outcropping of rock. They were all anoraks, cans of something, and tinny music muted by the wet.

I sat on the ground, and as Webb barked in circles I tried to work out where Martha could be.

"Cut it out," I said. He wasn't usually like this.

I looked at the teenagers and there was something familiar about the scene. I felt I'd been here before, with a group of people, but perhaps closer to the pier. I felt an echo — nothing as solid as a memory — of miserable weather, Marmite, and cheese.

The motion of the sea was calming in a way, even though the wind was blowing the tops of the waves off into mist, and I thought perhaps that was why I couldn't see her, that the water was hiding her, keeping her from me. I scanned the horizon, looking out toward France, my eyes open and unblinking, but she wasn't there.

But if she wasn't there and she wasn't at home, where was she? Those were her places. She could be counted on to be in either one of them at almost any given moment. It was unlike her to miss a swim, and even more unlike her to disappear.

Walking in the direction of the teenagers, I continued to search. What if something had happened? What if she had overestimated herself? Underestimated the conditions? What if she needed help?

"Have you seen her?" I shouted. "My wife, Martha? Was she here?"

A girl about fourteen years old walked over and smiled, as though she recognized me.

"You again?"

"Have you seen her? Short bob, about five and a half feet tall. Yellow bathing cap."

She looked at the ground. "Not today."

"That's impossible. She has to be here."

"Are you sure?"

"Why would I have come if I wasn't?"

She took her hood down as though she were looking for something, but I wasn't sure what it might be. "I've seen you here before."

"Martha comes every day. She'll attempt the Channel again in early September."

"It's nearly October," she said.

I looked inland. The point where spectators stand is an outcropping covered in matted-down grass. I wouldn't have ever had cause to be up there because if Martha was swimming then I was in the support boat, but I could picture the view from up there, or rather I felt what it was like to stand there.

And then I was sitting at home with the three dresses laid out and there were people with me in our bedroom. Our daughter, maybe. I blinked and I was standing in the rain listening to Henry. Everything was now and then, before and after, past and present all jumbled together, crashing into one another.

The pebbles made me wince as I tottered over them in my slippered feet, my toes numb from the cold. I knew then where she was. I dropped to my knees and opened the case. Everything that was Martha was there: the grease, the earplugs, the bathing caps, old goggles, and the pebbles. I counted them, ten in total. One for each attempt.

I stared at them in my palm and they were the same as the rust-coloured ones I was kneeling on, speckled with whirls of white and slate grey. I traced my finger over them as Webb rushed toward me, bounding out of the sea.

His fur, which was the same colour as some of the pebbles, was drenched, and when he shook himself off, sandy water covered everything. I pushed him away as he tried to lick my face, but he sensed something wasn't right and kept nudging me until I spilled the pebbles.

I shouted at him and tried to pick the right ones up again, but there was no way to tell which ones were hers and which ones weren't.

I looked in the case. It was all that was left of her now. It was everything and nothing. Webb barked at me from the shoreline, and with the case in my hand I chased him into the sea. It was the only place left where we could find her and the only place we could be with her.

The water was so cold it burned. The sea was in motion. It was a living thing, she used to say. More alive than any of us.

It was unsettling. The rocky bottom shifted with each wave and the currents pulled me forward and backward until I lost all balance and plunged under water. My arms and legs flailed as I tried to right myself, and I lost my grip on the case getting my head above water. I cried out when I saw the case floating away.

I gasped for air but got a lungful of water. I couldn't swim. It was foolish to live so close to it and never have learned, but it was my personal superstition: for her to swim well, I could not.

It felt as though the sea would take me to her if I let it, and then I felt arms around me and barking. I was being dragged to shore and once I was on land again I sat with my head between my knees, coughing, gasping, spitting out water. The girl was beside me, soaked through.

"What are you trying to do?" she said. "Kill yourself?"

I saw her looking at the case.

"Leave it. It belongs to her."

"Who?" she asked. "There's no one out there," she said gently.

"There is," I said.

I turned away and looked at the outcropping and bits came back to me. She had requested a burial at sea and I had promised. I pictured my daughter or my son, and remembered something about danger, about wandering off, things being close enough.

I had thrown her ashes into the waves, shining like mackerel scales.

The girl sat on my right and Webb settled himself at my feet and we looked out across the Channel.

I thought of Martha's voice, the way she used to say my name. The words had all become crumpled in my mind, heavy like wet towels. I tried to remember the first time I had heard her say it. Was it as she stood straddling her bicycle when I had introduced myself? I wasn't sure, but I could picture it as though it had happened yesterday. "John," I heard her say. It was like so many other things that I couldn't remember, that I just felt. I knew exactly what it felt like to hear her say it. I had never thought hearing my own name could have thrilled me so much, but it did. How her different tones told me everything I needed to know. Short and clipped when she was cross; lengthened in the middle when she was being tender.

The harder I tried to hear it again, the further away it receded, like the tide.

"Did she ever get there?" the girl asked.

"Where?"

"Across."

"Cap Gris Nez," I said.

In the support boat I had poured chicken broth into a cup attached to a long pole and tried to hold it steady for her while she struggled against the waves. She had trod water, propelling herself up above the chop. No good drinking the sea, she'd said. The power in her legs was undeniable. I saw the sores on her shoulders, around her neck and under her arms, chafing from the salt. She had joked that if the officials wouldn't have been upset she would have swum naked.

"Why'd she do it?" the girl asked.

"To see," I said.

Webb lifted his head as though he were about to bark, but instead managed a muffled ruff, and I looked over toward the cliff where the girl's friends were motioning to her.

She squinted into the distance, which, given the weather, wasn't far. There wasn't much to look at: the muddy water sloshing in and out, the white horses the icing on the edge of horizon line, everything in motion, frothing and churning.

She stood up and walked toward it, head held high and her chin up against the weather. She didn't hesitate when she stepped into the water. She took a few steps out, only up past her knees, and reached down, fishing the case out before turning back.

The distance between us was ten feet, maybe fifteen, and my eyesight was not bad. It could have been anything: the way she walked, her purpose, her confidence, or just seeing her holding the case. It could have been so many other things besides.

There are moments when why no longer matters. Why do we fall in love? Why do we live and why do we die? There comes a moment when we know the point is simply that we are: in love, alive, or even dead. The young are gifted the luxury of why, the old the wisdom to realize why doesn't matter in the end.

"You can't leave it. No littering," she said as she placed the case next to Webb.

"How was the water?" I asked.

She blinked. "Wet."

I smiled despite myself and thought of the bathtub, the cold water, and the salt I'd brought for her. You can't deny me this, Martha had said.

Shouts came from her friends in the distance and she turned to look at them. The girl's hands were jammed into her pockets, her teeth chattering and stray pieces of hair stuck to her cheeks.

"I'll be fine," I told her, releasing her from her perception of obligation, but she didn't leave.

"Why are you looking at me like that?" she asked.

I wanted to say that she looked like my wife. The way she stared out at the sea, squinting slightly when she scrutinized something intently, and the way her wet hair was plastered to her cheeks. I wanted to say that she was unintentionally teasing me and that through no fault of her own she was making the hollow feeling I kept with me now grow. I often forgot the cause of that feeling, and when I was reminded of it, it was as sharp as the first time. It was a feeling that sucked the breath out of my lungs, a feeling that felt like drowning.

"Go," I said. "Please."

When she was far enough down the beach, I turned to where she had been sitting and dug a small hole in the sand underneath the pebbles. When it looked big enough, I opened the case and took what was left: the biscuits, the maps and charts in it. I poured the pebbles I had saved from Webb's exuberance on top and then at the last minute reconsidered. I gathered up the ones I thought were hers and added a few more so that there were ten.

Ten for as many swims.

I looked at the handwriting on the map. There was a note about the currents and Martha had added the words "Strait of Dover" at the narrowest point between England and France.

Our kitchen table had often been covered in these maps. When planning an attempt, Martha would trace the route she wanted to swim endless times with her finger — small grains of sand caught under her nails lent them an egg-speckled veneer — running over the course, adding the smallest details gleaned from frequent chats to fishermen. Rocks here, seaweed blooms there. Everything had been noted in plain blue ink and her precise, joined-up script, the same writing that was on the cards she gave me for birthdays, anniversaries, and non-occasions — surprise reminders of her affection. Her cursive was on endless lists and reminders, notes scribbled on the backs of envelopes or left on the table, and when I thought of them what I saw was Dear John. John, dear.

I clawed at the sand and the pebbles and threw handfuls at the hole in the ground. I kicked more sand and pebbles onto what was left of her, blocking her out.

"You have to stay here," I said.

When I stood up, Webb followed my lead and we walked home together. I didn't bother retying the rope to his collar; we were two old men trudging home in the rain.

It was nearly dark when we turned onto our street, and Webb barked impatiently as I stood in front of the door, searching for the keys. They weren't in my coat or trouser pockets and I won-dered how I had managed to go out without them. And then I looked down and saw that I was still in my slippers.

Slippers: slippery, slipping.

I looked next door and prayed that the lights would be on and that Henry would have a spare set. The idea of having to engage in conversation exhausted me, but I had no other choice; it was that or I would have to sleep in the garden.

The pale blue flickering light of the television was on, accom-panied only by a faint glow from somewhere in the kitchen.

I rang the bell and when he answered the door all I said was, "Keys?"

"Come in out of the rain," he said, stepping aside. "Go through to the living room, John, and I'll bring you a cup of tea."

I did not want to sit down, nor did I want a cup of tea, but Webb seemed keen on the offer of a warm, dry room in which to settle and he pushed past me into the dark. Though our houses were laid out in the same way, there was a lightness in our house that was not shared with Henry's: his rooms gave the impres-sion that even on the brightest days they would still feel dark. It was that kind of place: cramped, cold, and uncomfortable.

I looked but found no pictures of a wife, children, or other proof of familial ties. There were no photographs at all. Martha made sure that the faces of our family were never far away. Henry had a large mirror over the mantelpiece where I caught sight of myself. I was more hunched than I had remembered. If I thought of myself, I pictured my face as a combination of when Martha and I were first married and when the children were still in school, but the reflection told me otherwise: my eyebrows had taken on a life of their own, springing up over my spectacles like unruly hedgerows; the few hairs left on my head were plastered down on my scalp from rain, and the natural slimness I had always had now made my face look gaunt and hollow.

Henry came into the room with a tray full of tea things and set it down on the side. He looked at me expectantly.

"Let me take your coat," he said, moving toward me as though to help me out of it.

"Leave it, I'm fine."

"It's soaked right the way through."

He was right, but I didn't have the strength to take it off myself and I wasn't about to let him help me. I sat in an armchair and he sat on the sofa.

"I take it you made it to the seaside, then," he said.

I must have looked puzzled because he pointed to my slippers, which were covered in sand. It is one thing to embarrass yourself, but quite another to do it in front of someone like him.

"Done it myself," Henry said. "Walked to the little shop during halftime to get a couple more cans. Wouldn't have noticed if I hadn't stepped in gum. Nearly ruined the carpet, but at least Arsenal won."

The way he laughed made me think he'd made it up. I did not want to sit there in his house. I couldn't. I had the feeling there was something pressing I had to do. I gripped the arms of the chair as the room closed in on me.

"Stay," he said.

"I have to go."

"Why's that?"

"There's something I need to do."

"Which is?"

I sputtered, searching for the right words that would release me from his clutches. "Martha needs me."

Henry poured two cups of tea and added milk. "Sugar?"

I made no reply and he offered me a mug.

"John," he said. "She's not…" He sighed and leaned back on the sofa. "Drink your tea."

"I'm sure she's got our dinner on the stove by now." I straightened my tie. "I'm needed at home."

"I don't want to have to tell you again."

"Tell me what? How dare you speak to me like this."

He put his tea down and rubbed his face with both hands as though I had given him a headache. As if I was hard work.

"I didn't demand to be dragged in here to keep you company."

"You weren't dragged in here. You knocked on my door. You've locked yourself out again."

"If I have misplaced my keys, which is not at all like me, then my wife will let me in." I stood up and clapped my thigh, signalling for Webb to follow. The room was so small and dark that it was difficult to see where the way out was, but Webb knew and I followed him down the path and back up again until we were at our front door.

I rang the bell and Webb barked.

"I don't think anyone's home," Henry said from behind me in a smug tone. "There aren't any lights on, you see."

"It must be late. She's probably gone to sleep." I stepped back and picked up a pebble, which I threw at the bedroom window. It missed its mark. "Martha!" I waited a few seconds and called again. "Martha!"

The windows remained dark. She didn't come to the door.

"What's happened?" I asked Henry. "Something must have happened. You were in. Did you not see?" I looked around, searching for a clue, but all I saw was our house, our garden, and our street standing empty and motionless in the night.

He put his hand on my shoulder and put the key in the lock, opening the door. "Let's go inside," he said.

We did and it was cold and dark. Henry turned on the lights, revealing dirty dishes on the counter, half-eaten bowls of soup, and a level of disarray that was unlike Martha.

"Darling?" I called.

"John," he said. "She's not here."

I turned away from him and searched the ground-floor rooms, turning on lights and calling her name. Henry waited in the kitchen until I returned empty-handed.

"She died," he said. "She was ill, she had cancer. You took care of her. She passed away here, John, with you, last month. There was a small funeral where she used to swim. You scattered her ashes in the sea."

"Liar!" I said, pushing him away. "Get out of here!"

"It's a hard thing to have to remember."

"You're lying!"

He met my gaze and a moment passed between us, and in my mind's eye I saw the three dresses on the bed and tasted the Marmite and cheese sandwiches. I stumbled, pulling out the chair as it sank in again.

Henry helped me off with my coat. "Are you hungry?"

"No."

"Have you eaten today?"

"Where is Martha? She should be here, it's late. She doesn't swim after dark. What if something's happened? What if she needs me?" I went to the door and pressed my face up to the glass.

"John, please. Calm down."

"It's the middle of the night and my wife is missing. I will not calm down!"

He reached out for my arm and tried to guide me back to the table.

"Let go of me!"

"You're getting upset."

"Where is Martha?" I shouted at him as loud as I could.

He closed his eyes. "Martha passed away, John."

I floundered backward, into the chair. He opened the cupboard and took down a tin of beans. "I'll heat this up."

As he washed a saucepan I looked around the kitchen. How could she have passed? She'd been in the bath this morning. The door had slammed shut. The seashells had been on the windowsill. The Marigold washing-up gloves had hung over the side of the sink.

"Martha must have gone out. Popped out to the shops for something."

Henry was silent. The running tap was the only sound in the house until he turned it off, and then there were only the faded, distant voices unfurling in my head. He opened the tin, emptied its contents into the pan, and put it on the stove.

"Toast?" he asked.

I made no reply, and as he turned around I saw that his eyes were watering. He turned back quickly and looked up at the ceiling.

The sound of a ceramic dish moving across the tiles broke the silence as Webb pushed his bowl toward me. "You're out of water," I said.

Henry put the beans on two plates and brought them to the table, handing me a fork. "You need to eat."

"I'll wait for my wife, she won't be much longer."

If she came home and he was still here, there would be no getting rid of him. He would insist on saying hello, which would turn into a conversation around what had kept her out so late, what she had done, and who she had been with. And that would follow on to the sort of banal chat that people had about gardens and other neighbours. Henry was a man who would do anything to keep from going back to his empty house.

He hung his head and stared at the beans. "You've gone to the seaside a lot recently."

"Martha is training."

I pushed my plate away untouched and went to the window. I craned my neck to look down the road but the rain was coming down harder and I couldn't see anything, least of all the figure I most desperately wanted to see.

"It's not like her to be so late," I said.

When I turned around, Henry was tapping away at his phone.

"Will I call someone? Harriet maybe?"

I shook my head. "Martha won't be with her."

"Would you like me to stay?"

"What for?"

I felt his eyes boring a hole in the back of my head as I stared out the window, and I could not understand why he thought I was the one in need of help.

His mobile buzzed and I left him to read his message as I put the dishes in the sink.

"Best to have these cleaned up by the time she gets home," I said.

Henry sighed and I knew I wasn't a good host but I didn't care about what he thought. All that mattered was for the kitchen not to look like a tip when my wife arrived home.

"I don't know what to do," he said, as much to me as to the phone.

I put the Marigold gloves on. "It's late. I'll tell her you dropped by."

Finally he went to the door. "Will you be all right?"

"Of course." I worried about him, all alone over there. It wasn't right and he didn't strike me as the most capable of men.

"Remember to lock the door," he said.

"Goodnight, Henry."

I washed and dried the plates, and I felt badly for him with no family, going home to an empty house. There was nothing I could do. I left the kitchen light on for Martha and went upstairs. Webb followed me, which was unlike him; normally, he waited by the door until everyone was home. I dismissed it, though. Henry must have put the dog on edge — he has that effect.

I took one last look out the window — but our street was empty, so I got into bed and pulled the duvet up to my chin. I rolled over and put my hand in the empty space where Martha should have been; and when I closed my eyes I caught the faintest bit of her smell, that distinct combination of soap, fresh laundry, and the sea. I inhaled deeply — and it was almost as if she were there.

FALLING DOWN

MARTHA, 1947

"RICHARD," I heard my mother say in the kitchen, in that tone she had that did not encourage questions. "Take her with you."

"Martha has no interest in fishing," my father replied. "She's a ten-year-old girl. The last time —"

"She's been cooped up in this house for far longer than is good for her. And she's doing my head in."

My mother's head was a frequent source of trouble. Her moods could easily fluctuate and it was difficult to tell which side you might end up on. But there were signs that my father and I had learned to read. If she gripped the countertop for support as she bore the frustration of our annoyances, or if the pitch of her voice was higher than usual — as it often was when she came home from visiting one of her better-off friends — we knew the chances of winding up on her bad side were as predictable as rain on a bank holiday. More often than not, my father and I seemed capable only of reinforcing what she saw as our collective shortcomings. When we were particularly irksome, my father and I could generally be found sitting quietly in the living room, reading.

"Send her out to play in the garden," my father said.

"Richard," my mother cautioned, in a tone I had come to know very well.

I pictured my father hanging his head as he replied. "Fine, dear."

Though I was not pleased with the way my mother had told my father to take me with him, I was keen on the outing. My bare feet on the wood floors barely made a sound as I skipped back to my room from my listening post at the top of the stairs — the source of much of my insight into my parents' thoughts. The ones they shared with each other, at least. I suppose their most private thoughts were kept in darker recesses, in places they hardly went themselves.

"Martha!" I heard my father call from the foot of the stairs. "Put your shoes on and grab a cardigan, love."

I looked out my bedroom window across the rooftops that stretched toward the flash of sea on the horizon. Though it wasn't the bright blue of picture postcards, the sky was clear. It was early summer, and it seemed like the day was warm enough to go without another layer, which stood every chance of being lost or forgotten. But I did as I was told, taking my least favourite one — mint green with a Peter Pan collar that I despised because it looked like a lime sherbet sweet — in the hopes that the outing might provide a believable excuse for me to be rid of it.

I had no interest in fishing. But the prospect of leaving the confines of our house, garden, and road was thrilling. Such escapes were few and far between, even now after the war had ended. Invitations like this did not come around often and I knew that the better I behaved myself, the better the chance there'd be for another one.

My father stood by the door with his fishing line and a metal lunchbox that I knew contained the hooks and worms he would need my help with, though I didn't know what he did without my help. I suspected that going fishing was just a way to get out of the house. I presented myself to him with a salute: feet together, back straight. It was a habit I had gotten into since he had come back from the fighting; my hope was it would convince him that I was respectful and knowledgeable enough to hear about his adventures in France. What I especially wanted to hear, of course, was the story of how he had lost his right arm. It was something that I had never heard my mother mention. That she was quiet about it was noteworthy: she considered nothing else outside her bounds.

"You carry the tackle," he said, as he stood aside so I could open the door for him.

I turned the handle and stepped aside. He walked past me, not even stopping to make sure I had closed the door properly. His message was perfectly clear: he and I were not going fishing together; rather, I was an interloper and would have to pull my own weight and do my best to keep up.

I walked as quickly as I could, but it soon turned into an ungainly run as I struggled to keep pace with him, the metal tackle box dangling from my hand and crashing into my bare knees with each step. I would have fresh bruises when we got home — my mother would no doubt feel compelled to remind me that my clumsiness was wilful. She did not believe it was possible for a girl to be so unfeminine, and in this way — and many others — I was cast as a disappointment. I knew she would have preferred a daughter like my friend Cath, who could not only plait her hair properly, but preferred the types of dresses that I felt were restrictive and adorned with unnecessary ruffles and frills.

We lived at the top of the hill. From the kitchen window at the side of the house, if I stood on my toes, I was able to catch a glimpse of the ferries that were in operation again, now the war was over. From my window, I could see parts of the winding road that led down to the sea that weren't hidden by oaks and plane trees. It was a snake-like road, looping back and forth, adding distance to any journey. But its twists and turns gave the boring street with nothing more than nearly identical houses a sense of jollity.

The harbour at the bottom of the hill was mostly blocked from view, keeping my father and his fishing friends hidden, should my mother decide to pry. But I knew there was a breakwater that jutted out from the other side of the harbour, nearer the dock, curving around slightly, looking like a finger pointing at the pier. Sometimes I saw men fishing there, too, but never my father's friends.

"There is to be no talking," my father said, when I had caught up to him.

I nodded in agreement. This was serious business.

"You're to put one worm on each hook. No more, no less."

I nodded.

"Take care not to drop the worm. I don't want to be surrounded by dead worm bodies the rest of the afternoon."

I kept nodding my head.

"And you're not to jump and dance around. Not like last time."

Last time I had not been at my best. I had been listening to the radio quite intensely the week before and worked out an elaborate dance I insisted on demonstrating for my father and his friends. My father was not impressed, but it hadn't mattered. I'd been captivated by the sound of my footsteps on the pier as they mixed with the water lapping against it, more than enough excitement to fill my mind to near bursting, leaving little room for his lectures on proper behaviour.

"Keep out of the way," he said. "And be quiet."

This last instruction was the most important. Coming down to the pier was a rare chance for my father to meet up with his friends — especially the ones my mother did not care for — and to talk about the sorts of things that young girls should not know about. His instruction to be quiet extended not only to the day that spread out before us, but also to the evening when we returned home. As far as my mother was concerned, we had gone fishing and nothing else. There would be no talk of which of his friends we had seen, and certainly no mention of a mid-afternoon trip to the lawn bowling club, where my father and some of his chums might enjoy a cheeky drink from a spirit flask. That part of the afternoon was such a delicate matter that we did not even speak of it between ourselves.

My father, I assumed, had many secrets, and to be cast as reliable enough to keep things to myself, even if the secret wasn't much more than a cheeky drink, was something I cherished. When he gave me the signal that we were going to go and see the boys at the bowling club, he met my gaze and held it for a while and I felt as though he recognized something in me that my mother would never see.

We rounded the last corner and my father put his hand out, barring me from running across the road. The junction was where recent arrivals from France could be counted on to get confused, where driving on the left somehow got the better of them — my father preferred more caution to less. He checked once and then again, and when he was certain it was safe we crossed the road and walked up behind the Dover Seaview Hotel with its cream walls and black wrought-iron balconies that suggested exotic places I had never been to.

Facing the sea, I turned to my left and saw the promenade stretching all the way to the docks with their cranes and ships. On our end, everything was on a small scale, person to person, and gradually, as you got nearer the docks, things grew until you felt dwarfed by the ferries and the steamers. They held no interest for me, and I felt a loyalty to my father, who didn't often look in that direction. There were bombed buildings there still, rubble and dust, holes in everything. We didn't go down that way. The reasons had never been explained to me, but I understood that part of town was not for people like us. And anyhow, it was nicer where we stood and you could pretend things were getting back to normal. If you squinted a bit, you could see the way the Seaview Hotel was meant to look; you could see past the bits where it was broken like my father. And out in the water a ways, the breakwater that was meant to protect us from winter storms, among other things.

But the most fascinating thing was the pier, dotted with men and their fishing poles. For as long as I could remember, the pier had been off limits, but now that the fighting was done, the pier was ours. The men clustered in some areas — better chances or personal preferences, I couldn't tell — a group nearer the shore, and another toward the end.

The pier had a sturdiness to it, a trustworthiness that I liked. Even during the air raids when we'd had to go into the caves, I'd felt that if nothing was left when we emerged then at least the pier would be there. And now it was put back to its proper use; now it was a pleasure pier again.

I had learned enough by then to know that being admitted into this circle of masculinity was a rare moment, not to be taken lightly. I had often been privy to my mother's world, listened to her and her friends natter on about hairstyles and slimming regimes and little tricks to get rid of persistent mould, but they were the sorts of conversations that were so dull that even pretending to be interested was impossible. Now and again there would be something halfway worthwhile, something that hinted at the possibility of intrigue or a life more appealing than what I knew awaited me when I grew up and began my so-called life of Domestic Bliss. But even a whiff of something truly scandalous, like a suspected affair, was rarer than Christmas.

The men on the pier told stories that took place in locations far away from Dover, from England and our day-to-day lives. The most frequent tales were about the war, but they weren't half as grim as my mother made them out to be. The stories of Peter the Pigeon Man, who'd worked for the army messenger ministry, were some of my favourites.

And it wasn't just the other men who talked on the pier; it was my father, too. If the men forgot about me, and felt they were in private, then I learned some of what he had been through, what he had seen and done in the war. My ears were sharp, in a constant state of readiness for clues as to what had happened to his arm.

As we walked along, the pavement gave way to the wooden planks that were weathered by storms coming across the Channel. My father began to look for a suitable place, searching for familiar faces and pals he might want to catch up with. Depending on his mood we might sit next to younger, chattier men; or if he felt the need for peace and quiet then we would take our place next to the older, silent ones. Both were good in my mind: the younger ones could be counted on to tell amusing stories that were utterly unsuitable for my young ears, and the older ones told tales that I could never have imagined.

My father nodded to two younger men, and I took it as a sign that he was in a good mood. We stopped next to them and they chatted briefly before my father leaned his line against the railing. That was my cue.

I opened the metal lunchbox, removing the bread and butter sandwiches my mother had packed for us before taking the bucket of worms out, and while my father got caught up on the latest fishing news I threaded the first worm on the hook and handed the pole back to him.

He turned and nodded to me, saying nothing. It was our signal that I was to make myself scarce.

There was a rhythm to it, and it was important to get into it as quickly as possible. Prepare the hook, hand the pole back to my father, and then fade into the background for a while as he tried his luck. I was to get on with whatever caught my fancy while also remaining attentive so that he never had to wait for another worm.

I was sure his friends helped him, while sparing him the embarrassment of having to ask, in the same way he had shown me over and over how to tie my shoelaces, stepping in when he saw I was struggling. But when I was there, we all played along: it was a child's job and helping him was a favour done for me, a skill he was teaching me that I might be able to put to use later.

He cast the line over the edge and I backed away, satisfied that my job was done and I had some time to myself. I skipped off down to the very end of the pier.

The end of the pier was one of my favourite places. Nobody fished there so I was free to sing and dance as I liked, knowing I would not be bothering anyone but myself. Here I could talk aloud to my imaginary friend Charlotte and act out some of my more elaborate fantasies. Fantasies that were based on places I had read about in the set of encyclopedias my mother had purchased for me, hoping to keep me busy during the long years when we were all but trapped in the house, waiting for the war to finish. I read them with varying levels of interest: I preferred the exotic to the mundane, the faraway to the familiar; the aardvarks and armadillos to the ants and albatross. Most recently I had started the volume for "H," skipping over the entry for Hadrian's Wall, instead reading and rereading the entry for Hawaii. It was magical: an island, like the one I lived on, it had once had a queen, and a large continent was situated to the east. Though the similarities ended there, I enjoyed imagining a different set of possibilities for myself as the weeks and months passed.

There was something about the water that day that caught my eye. The sun had emerged, which was unexpected and delightful, and the light reflected off the sea in such a way that made parts of the water almost too dazzling to look at. It was calm, the waves loping forward leisurely, but there was a spot I noticed off the edge of the pier where there was a little whirlpool. I'd never seen anything like it before: the water changed from a metallic blue to a muddy brown and the ripples came and went in different directions. I imagined that underneath it was a roiling, boiling cauldron and possibly the entrance to a secret world, maybe the gateway to Atlantis or King Neptune's realm.

I leaned forward but I was at an awkward height: too short to see over the top railing but tall enough that the second railing beneath it blocked my view. I crouched down on all fours and crawled under the second bar nearer the edge, my eyes fixated on the currents below. I wondered if my father or his friends knew about this whirlpool and whether or not they could provide more in the way of factual information. I wanted to know what it felt like to run my hands across the surface of the water where it bubbled up, to know what the currents might feel like against my body, but there was little chance of that, as I couldn't swim.

I crawled forward, my bare, bruised knees tender against the splintering old wood. Lost in my own thoughts, when I heard my father calling for me I sat up quickly and the back of my head crashed into the metal railing. My hand flew out behind me to push the bar away on instinct and, as I did that, I lost my balance.

Even when I replayed it in my memory, it seemed to happen in slow motion. When I played it back in my mind that night, tucked up in my bed, it felt as though there should have been plenty of time for me to grab on to something to save myself; that I ought, as my mother reproached me when we got home, to have managed to keep myself dry.

But I didn't manage it. That was the first day I got wet.

I fell head first toward the water, but it happened so quickly that I didn't even have time to think to take a breath. I remember hitting the water and thinking that it was strange that it hurt so much; it felt as though I had hit something solid and hard. That moment changed the way I looked at the sea forever. Before, it had been a vastness that had nothing to do with me: it was there and I knew it was cold, and other than a few apathetic splashes to humour my friends, my disinterest in the water remained firmly in place. Once or twice, when I had gone in as far as my knees, I had felt the water move around me and make way for me. But when I hit the water that day, I understood that it was able to be more than one thing.

I must have called out or screamed for help because just before I hit the surface I heard someone call my name.

I hit it so hard — and I only found this out later — that I could have easily been concussed, or worse. At the time, though, all I knew was that I was being engulfed in the cold, dark sea. It was everywhere and I was terrified and what was worse was that I didn't know which way was up because it was so black. Darker than a moonless night. And the salty, briny murk was everywhere: up my nose and in my ears. I desperately wanted a breath but somehow I managed to keep my mouth shut.

As I flailed my arms and legs around wildly, clawing for the surface or anything that might save me, I had the sense of being trapped inside a box that was growing smaller with every passing moment. The sea felt as though it were getting darker all the time, closing in on me; my chest felt as though it was about to burst. I was angry with myself for leaning over the edge, for doing something so foolish. But my thoughts were not for myself, rather they were for my father, who would have to go home and explain everything.

I was being pushed parallel to the shoreline and after what felt like ages but was probably close to a minute, I felt my body relax and I was able to open my eyes. In that moment, I was no longer afraid. Instead of feeling trapped by the sea I felt supported by it, drifting with its currents. And before I could notice that I was colder than I had ever been in my life, I saw something coming toward me. I didn't know what it was or what form it took; all I saw was the water moving differently, in a way that I believed meant I was being approached. I didn't know what it might be or what it might want from me, but I didn't feel afraid. Submerged, I was held by the sea, watching.

The next thing I knew there were arms around me and I knew it was not my father and not a mermaid. I was dragged upward, and before I knew it my head had broken the surface and I could breathe again. I gulped down breath after breath as I faced the sky and was swum back to land, and once I was on dry land I burst into tears, sobbing and coughing up water.

I was carried up the beach to where my father and his friends were all waiting for me. I had never before seen that expression on my father's face and I never saw it again. He clutched me to his chest, unconcerned that I was getting his clothes wet, and held me so tightly that it was hard to breathe.

When he finally released me from his grip, he draped his light jacket over my shoulders and a few of the other men piled theirs on, too, and we walked like that up to the bowling club. No one said a thing.

Once we were inside, someone made a fire even though it was June and they sat me down in front of it. Someone brought me an old horse blanket and wrapped it around my legs.

"Drink this," a man said to me. His hair was wet.

I took the mug and studied him. "Are you...?"

He nodded. "You scared your father half to death."

I took a sip of the drink and turned my nose up at it.

He chuckled. "There's only a drop of whisky in it. It'll warm you up."

I nodded and wondered why my father was not administering hot drinks to me.

"I'm Jim," he said, holding out his hand.

I shook it, unsure of why the circumstances required such formalities.

"Sit closer to the fire," he said. "You're freezing."

I did as I was told.

He stared at me and I didn't understand why — it felt as though he was looking through me for something or someone else. He was soaked through; his shirt clung to his thin frame and his trousers were drooping from the weight of the water. His skin was as white as the chicken we ate for every Sunday lunch but it had an unusual quality to it that made him appear see-through. Had he been shirtless, I felt I would have been able to see his heart beating.

I turned away, hoping to catch sight of my father, but there was no sign of him. The place was eerily quiet and still; everyone but me and my rescuer had disappeared.

"My father?" I said through chattering teeth.

"He's just out back," he said, and motioned for me to drink.

The blanket that covered my legs slid to the floor and Jim reached down quickly to replace it. He smoothed it down and looked up at me as he crouched at my feet. He wasn't that old, Jim, probably not even twenty, yet I could tell that he now felt a personal responsibility for me. As we looked at one another I thought that even though he wasn't handsome he seemed sweet and kind.

He stood up after a moment or two. "Will I go and find your father?"

I nodded and off he went to the back garden, leaving me in the clubhouse all by myself. I had never been in there when it was empty, and the things I normally found interesting and comforting took on a sinister tone. Especially since I knew it was a warm summer's day outside while I was huddled up inside as if it were the middle of February. The sound of the floorboards creaking, in the way old buildings have, startled me, and the shadows cast by the flickering flames moved unevenly and set my nerves on edge.

Failing to keep my wits about me, I bolted toward the back door; even if my father wasn't there, I would at least be in the daylight again. I was about to push the door open when I heard voices through the open window. I paused and listened. There was my father's voice, but it was crying. Until that moment I hadn't considered that my father would ever cry — or that there might be anything in the world awful enough to upset him so.

I stood concealed in the shadows, crouching under the thick windowsill, listening to him cry. His shoulders did not move as I imagined they might have if he'd been truly sobbing, but his expression in profile was as heartbroken as any I had ever seen, which included the mourners at my great aunt's funeral the year before. I looked on for as long as I dared before retreating back to my spot in front of the fire. The shame my father would feel if he knew I had seen him in such a state was the sort of thing that he would never overcome. I could not carry the weight of that responsibility.

I settled in again and cupped my drink, which had gone cold, as I propped my feet up as close as I could get them to the fire. I kept my back to the garden. The thought of any of the men even suspecting I had seen anything was awful, but the thought that I was the cause of all this misery was too much to bear.

Soon enough, the club took on a cozy afternoon feeling that reminded me of winter days curled up on the sofa in a tangle of blankets. I let my head drop a little to one side so I could scrunch further down in the chair and I noticed that there was an echo in my ear. I stuck my baby finger in, trying to dislodge whatever was trapped in there.

"Won't work," Jim said.

His voice startled me, torpedoing through the still air.

"Tilt your head to one side and hop up and down." He demonstrated but I didn't move. He smiled in such a way that I thought he was playing a trick.

"Try it, you'll see."

I shook my head half-heartedly with no result.

"Harder," he said.

I followed his instructions, certain that it couldn't possibly work and then, suddenly, there was a feeling of pressure being released, followed by a slow trickle of water that made me shiver. I jammed my finger back in my ear.

"Don't," he said. "Damages the eardrum."

I wiped my finger on my leg and looked past him. "Where's —"

He turned to his right, back toward the garden, and there was my father. I wanted to run to him and wrap my arms around his waist, holding on as tightly as possible so that he would know I was fine, but I knew that sort of behaviour — from anyone — was not encouraged.

"Come on, Martha," he said, putting his arm around my shoulders and guiding me up. "Your mother will be waiting."

I leaned into his body, pressing my side into his, and we walked out into the afternoon sun. We walked slowly, dreading having to tell the tale to my mother — who would surely punish both of us in unknown and unexpected ways. I had hoped that he might offer some words of advice on how we might best deal with the situation, but our walk home was a quiet one and I enjoyed it.

My hair was nearly dry by the time we arrived back at the house, though my clothes were not. I looked like I had gotten caught in a sharp shower and since my father was dry as a bone, there would be no explaining my appearance due to the weather.

We walked in the front door and heard the radio on, my mother humming along from her spot on the sofa in the living room. Humming was a promising sign.

I followed my father as he headed toward the living room, but just before we crossed the threshold he stopped abruptly, turning to me.

"You must be cold — why don't you go upstairs and change?" he said, in a tone that was both tender and inaudible to my mother.

I crept up the stairs to my room and put on a fresh frock, choosing one that I loathed, covered as it was in frills and other abominations. One of my mother's favourites. Once I was dressed I headed back to the staircase but didn't go downstairs. I had not yet been summoned to present myself and it occurred to me that I might be better off if I waited until I was forced to give my version of the events. I strained to hear what was going on downstairs. Their voices weren't loud enough to reach me, which I took as a good sign. If there had been shouting, I would have heard it loud and clear.

After listening for a while and hearing nothing, I retreated to my room and lay on my bed to replay all that had happened. Briefly I thought of how close I'd come to death, but what really captured my imagination, what kept my mind busy until dinner that evening, was the sea. I kept remembering the moments just before Jim rescued me, when I recognized the water as something magical. I was surprised that I didn't break out in a cold sweat just thinking about it.

Dinner passed quietly and there was no mention of the incident from either of my parents. Did that mean my father hadn't told her about it? If so, that made it a secret between us — my father and me and the sea. I was a part of his world, of his group of friends that my mother did not know and had no interest in knowing. The possibilities of this new development were as exciting as my new understanding of the sea.

THE NEXT MORNING there was a knock at the front door. My mother had gone out to the shops and my father was in the back garden. He wasn't gardening as such, though that's what we called it; rather, he was sitting with his back to the house, staring out into the distance. He hadn't heard the knock, so I opened the door.

Jim smiled broadly. "Managed to keep out of harm's way so far?"

The possibilities Jim's arrival presented were thrilling. "Dad's out back," I said.

"Good. There's something I wanted to talk with you about."

I took a step back. People did not come to call on me in general — and certainly not my father's friends. But here he was. Maybe he wanted nothing more than to make sure I was all right, but there was a hint, a gleam in his eye.

Jim crouched down. "About yesterday."

My body tensed, bracing for a lecture about health and safety and how I ought not do things that caused my father so much worry and pain. Jim's face was deadly serious.

"You can't swim, can you?"

The answer to this seemed obvious, so I said nothing.

"Would you like to learn?"

I nodded vigorously, unable to believe my own good fortune. "Dad's in the garden," I said.

"We'll go and tell him then, will we?"

"Tell him what?"

"That I'm going to teach you to swim."

That this was a good idea and that I was interested was not in doubt — what I could not quite understand was what had motivated him to appear, now, at our front door. Had my father phoned him last night and asked him to teach me? And if so, why had he not thought to mention it?

"You've got a swimming costume?"

I nodded my head yes. Though I had not wanted it — with its silly tropical floral pattern in a dizzying array of bright colours — I was glad of it now.

"Go and put it on then," Jim said, stepping around me and into the foyer. I left him standing there and nipped upstairs to rummage in my wardrobe, searching through the box with my summer things that had not been taken out for use yet.

I had expected that Jim would have gone outside to see my father while I was changing but he was exactly where I had left him when I returned. I held my towel up for him to see in the same way I had seen the men hold up a big fish they'd caught.

He smiled and then finally started out to the garden. I was relieved — I knew full well I could not just leave the house with this man without telling anyone where I was going — and, towel dangling from my hand, I followed him. Jim paused at the back door and looked through the window at my father, who was sitting on the ground a few feet from the house. I looked up at Jim, at his thin cheeks and his eyes, which were blue but had the same thinness in their colour that his skin did. It was the same starved quality the sunlight had in the depths of winter. His jaw twitched and his expression was one I had not seen before: all the feeling of it seemed wrapped up in his eyes. For a moment then, he looked as though he were staring at the same thing as my father, something off in the distance of their memories, unreachable.

Jim stepped into the garden and I followed.

"Richard," he said quietly.

My father's shoulders tensed briefly and I heard a short, sharp intake of breath before he turned in our direction.

"Jim," he replied.

They looked at each other and a private recognition passed between them.

"Swimming lessons for this one, I think," Jim said.

"That's a good idea," my father said.

"Take her off your hands for a couple of hours."

"Exercise will do her good."

My lack of exercise had been mentioned before, but in the context of my being out of doors. There was something about being forced to endure the elements that my mother felt might straighten out my wilfulness, the idea being, I supposed, that having someone else issue orders might be instructive.

"I'll teach her the basics, what she needs to know about the sea," Jim said.

"Good," my father said, turning back to look at whatever it was that required his intense focus.

Jim took the hint and we retreated into the house.

"GET A PULLOVER for afterwards," he said.

Jim matched his pace to mine, appearing content to enjoy the walk. He was completely different to my father, who looked straight ahead or down at his feet as we went. Jim looked about, his attention turned when he saw a wood pigeon wobbling on a thin branch, or he cocked his head to one side as a car passed, as though he were trying to remember where he'd seen the driver last.

"We'll go to the harbour, but when you're ready, I can show you a better place. Less crowded. Just over there," he said as he pointed westward. "Bit of a hike, mind. But worth it."

I looked but couldn't see much past the houses. Even though we were still near enough the top of the hill that I could see the water.

"Where?" I asked.

He looked down and then up again, and upon realizing the problem, picked me up by my waist, holding me so I faced the right direction. "There," he said. "Shakespeare's Bay."

He turned the other way, so that I could see the docks in the distance. "And over there, at the foot of the cliffs, you might find a way down to the water, if you're so inclined. Just remember the tides. Don't get caught out by them."

After he set me down, we continued to walk in a comfortable silence and I wanted to ask him more about the way down that I might find, and how he knew, but he began to whistle and I decided against it. Instead, I looked ahead of me, and wondered what lay in the water out there past the breakwater that I could now see, and what I might learn of the sea, once I could swim.

When we arrived on the harbour with the beach in front of us, he stopped and he put his hand on my shoulder. "Now," he said. "You'll have to move fast, work at it. The hardest thing is getting used to the cold, but you will get used to it."

That sounded like an order.

"Breathing is key. Even breaths, that's the secret. Inhale for as long as you exhale. At first, it'll feel like the water is pushing down on your chest, forcing the air out of your lungs. Don't fight it. Learn to understand it."

I didn't see what he meant. I could only remember the feeling of the sea closing in on me and as I remembered it, and as the water came into view, my breathing sped up.

"The currents aren't bad here but still we'll get to them later. Another day."

I nodded and tripped over the toes of my shoes, which was a common enough occurrence that I hardly noticed, but Jim's hand shot out and grabbed my arm, holding me up. It was firm, and I knew he was in charge. He could be counted on.

We passed through the crowds on the promenade and as we crossed onto the pebbles, I noticed two ladies giving us a curious look as they ate their sandwiches. I turned away from them and jutted my chin forward as I had seen my mother do before, hoping to affect a look of purpose as we made our way through the people stretched out on their towels, the children running about noisily, and the groups of men with their trousers rolled up who looked to me as if they hadn't planned on coming along to the seaside at all.

The promenade encircled the harbour the way I curled my hand around a hot cup of tea, and though it was behind me now, I felt it there, cradling the water as though it were in need of protection. The view from this point was different to the one I had when I accompanied my father; then I looked out and saw nothing, which was, I now realized, incorrect. Now the sea had a starting point, and it gave me a different perspective: the coast stretched past what I considered the boundary of the pier on either side of me, the castle on one side and I didn't know what on the other. I paused and turned back and saw that even the town looked like it was staring out at the water — everything was facing the sea. The town seemed to me to be addressing the sea, as though everyone knew something that I was about to find out.

We walked across the copper-coloured pebbles on the beach and I wished we had gone somewhere else that was less crowded and more concealed. The harbour was in full view of everyone, and the nearer we got to the water's edge the more self-conscious I became. Normally I paid no attention to what people thought of me, but I worried that I might be recognized from yesterday's accident, that my return might be met with disapproval.

"Right," Jim said, taking his shirt off and folding it neatly on the ground.

He stood there, looking at me expectantly.

"You went in yesterday with your clothes on and you can do the same again today if you like, but it's much easier in your bathing suit." He pulled his trousers down to reveal his swimming trunks and stood there, hands on his hips, waiting.

I removed my shoes and clothes and we stood side by side facing the water. I felt as if everyone else was staring at us. Dover was a small town and people talked. What would they think? That I was being as bold as brass, putting myself in harm's way by going back in the sea, and with a strange man no less. And what would my mother think when word got back to her that I had been to the seaside with only one of my father's unsuitable friends for company?

Jim waded in and I watched. He didn't react at all to the drop in temperature, though my skin remembered the cold from the day before and I winced on his behalf. He continued to walk until he was waist deep, at which point he turned around and motioned for me to follow. Even getting to the edge was difficult; the pebbles moved under my bare feet as I walked, and some were quite sharp, not yet worn smooth by the sea. I felt his eyes on me and I had the suspicion that I was letting him down, so I straightened my posture and tried to look confident. I got two steps in and stopped.

The cold burned. It felt even colder than it had yesterday, and my instinct was to turn and run. But I didn't want Jim to think I wasn't up to the task.

The ripples lapped gently around my knees and then my thighs, and the deeper I went the colder it got until I could no longer feel my feet. The familiar sensation had gone and in its place was something strange: my feet moved as they had always done, but I felt disconnected from them. When the water was up to my waist I stopped, though Jim was still several feet away.

He moved nearer and said, "Take a breath. Put your head under."

I didn't do any such thing. There was no way that I could summon the courage to do that.

He dunked his head under quickly and came back up with a look of shock on his face. This was crazy.

"The longer you wait, the worse it's going to be. You can't let your mind talk you out of it. Don't think, act. You're retraining your muscles, starting with your brain. You're learning to act differently."

I reasoned with myself. I had done it yesterday, although by accident, and therefore I could do it again today. I took a deep breath and plunged my head under.

When I surfaced, Jim smiled proudly. "See?" he said. "Not that bad at all."

I got used to the sea in the same way one might get used to a new friend or a puppy. I began to learn what I could expect from the water, what it tasted like — which I did not care for much — and how it moved. It was too cold to stay in for long, but it was enough for me to be captivated.

Once we were back on land, we took our things to the pier, and there under the cover of the trestles he held a towel to shield me from view as I changed. He wrapped his towel round his waist and I turned my back to give him some privacy. When we were finished, he said, "Martha, every morning I'll be here. If you'd like to come swimming again."

He folded his swimming trunks up in his towel.

"It will make your father feel better, knowing you can swim. Do you understand?"

I didn't, but the tone of his voice led me to believe it had something to do with the war. It was a tone I had heard my father use occasionally, and one that my mother knew meant to leave well enough alone. I didn't need to know why. All I needed to know was that yesterday my father had cried in front of his friends, and if my learning to swim could prevent that from happening again, then I would learn.

"So, will I see you tomorrow?"

"Yes," I said.

I walked home by myself, skirting the edge of town, past the council estate and then through neighbourhoods where some of my schoolmates lived. The sun dried my hair and the salt formed a thin crust on my skin that tickled whenever the breeze blew. The nearer I got, the more frequently I turned to look back at the sea. In the course of two days it had changed into something completely different than what I'd thought it had always been. Before, it had just been something that was there, and I'd had no reason to take notice of it. But all that had changed.

I stood at the top of road looking down through the hazy light. The sea flowed out to the horizon and didn't stop, moving past that line as though it went on forever, flooding over the edge. I wanted to know exactly how far it could be followed and where it would lead. For the first time in my life I felt surrounded by water — I physically felt that England was an island, with the sea every which way I might turn.

When I arrived home my mother was stirring something in the kitchen, her hair wrapped in a scarf, and she was singing along with the radio. The smell of what would be our dinner filled the house. It was the usual: grease, with a hint of meat and potatoes.

I opened the breadbox — startling her, because she gasped and turned around, nearly knocking the pot off the stove.

"What have I told you about sneaking up on people?"

This was a common accusation and I knew better than to reply. I reached for the bread knife and she frowned.

"You're eating us out of house and home," she said.

I cut the slice thinner than I would have liked but was generous in my application of butter.

"Your father said you went swimming," she said. It was a question and a statement and an accusation all in one, a specialty of hers.

I nodded and took a bite, chewing slowly to make the small snack last longer.

"You're not to go again," she said.

"Why?" I was used to her informing me that the new thing I had discovered I enjoyed was no longer on her list of approved activities. I knew better than to let her watch me get into a strop about it.

"I don't want you spending time with a stranger."

"He's one of Dad's friends."

She turned to me and put her hands on her hips. "You're not a little girl anymore, Martha."

I would be eleven in a few months but didn't see what any of that had to do with it.

"It's inappropriate. I don't want you going down to the harbour anymore."

I took what was left of my snack and went off in search of my father, who would — I hoped — help me convince her that my learning to swim was a good idea. The list of things my mother found inappropriate grew with each passing day and seemed to include everything that I might possibly enjoy. The corresponding list of correct things to do included such delights as going to church, helping the aged, and reading books about cooking and good household management.

My father was not in the living room and the sun was still out, so I checked in the garden. He was sitting under the yew tree, leaning his back against it for support. Its shadows had crept onto his legs and looked as if they were closing in on him. I made sure to shut the door loudly so he would not think I was sneaking up on him.

I sat next to him and stared at my legs stretched out next to his. I glanced up at his face and looked away quickly — it looked like he had been crying again, which was upsetting enough, but what was worse was that my mother was not here with him, comforting him. Why was she inside stirring a pot none of us wanted to eat from?

I picked nervously at the grass, hoping he would ask me how it had gone so I wouldn't have to be the one to break the silence. After what felt like ages but was probably only a few minutes I said, "It was cold."

I turned slightly to see what his reaction would be, but his face didn't change.

"I wasn't scared," I added, hoping that might rouse him.

He took his handkerchief from his breast pocket and dabbed at his eyes.

"Jim said he would be there again tomorrow and I could go along if I liked."

Finally I got a reaction. He put his hand on my knee and squeezed it.

"Mum says I shouldn't go, that it's not right. To go with Jim."

My father took my chin gently in his hand and turned my face toward his own.

"Swimming will keep you safe," he said.

I nodded gravely and waited for him to continue, but he didn't. He turned back to whatever it was that he had been looking at, his hand resting firmly on my knee, and we sat like that until my mother dragged us in for dinner.

WE ATE PROMPTLY at five o'clock so that afterward my mother could listen to her favourite radio programmes or go round to the neighbour's house and play cards. She dished the mush onto our plates and said grace. She was the first to pick up her fork; I actually think she was rather fond of her own cooking.

Dinner was where we received our instructions for the following day.

"Richard," she said. "The tap in the kitchen is dripping again."

"I'll have a look," my father said.

"Martha, Sally has agreed to run you up a dress, so we'll need to be at hers for eleven tomorrow morning."

Which was about the same time as I had planned to go swimming with Jim.

"You know her daughter Ellie, don't you?"

I did, and I disliked her intensely. The idea of spending the day in her house, which was dark and filled with cigarette smoke, was just about the worst thing I could think of, but it was useless to protest.

I glanced at my father, hoping to catch his eye, but he was staring at the grey mound he had to get through before dinner could come to a close.

My mother always finished her food quickly as though it were a race — a habit made easier by the fact that none of the dishes she prepared required much in the way of chewing. Once she had set her fork down she would make it known that she was waiting for the rest of us to hurry up: she drummed her nails on the table, talked about how much she was looking forward to her programme, which came on in precisely fifteen minutes, or how there would be little point in eating the meal she had slaved over if we were going to let it get cold.

The moment the last fork was set on a plate — tonight, my father's — she swept the plates into the sink, tuning in to the Light Programme of music on the radio as she washed them. It was when she had her hands in the soapy water, with the music flowing, that she hummed a little bit, and moved her feet along to the rhythm. It was not something we commented on, but my father and I shared a look. And I knew that we were both happy for her to have a private place she could go.

Before I went to sleep that night, I looked out my window and the last bits of sunlight were clawing at the horizon — the sun wasn't ready to sleep yet, either. They hit the water in a way that made it shimmer like the scales of the mackerel my father and his friends caught.

And as I lay in my bed the water came back to me. But the sea did not rush around me as it had done when I fell in — it did not swarm or threaten to overwhelm me, but instead was calm and inviting, coaxing me toward it.

The next morning, I listened carefully for my mother's heels against the wood floors. As I tracked her progress I put my bathing suit on and a towel into my bag, and the moment I heard the front door shut I knew she had popped out to the shops, going in the opposite direction from the water. The new dress was not my concern. I put my shoes on and ran to the sea.

THE SPRING TIDE

MARTHA, 1965

THE GLARING KITCHEN light illuminated everything that I had tried to keep hidden: the unwashed dishes in the sink, the pile of laundry that needed ironing, the socks and underwear that dangled over the radiators, and the seashells on the window-sill collecting dust that I had neither time nor energy to clean.

I put a load of laundry in the machine, put a saucepan on to boil the eggs, and popped two slices of bread in the toaster, ready for when the children came downstairs. Then I put the clean dishes away and washed the ones left in the sink. The water gushed from the tap and I stared straight ahead, mechanically scrubbing and rinsing.

There was a rhythm to it and I noticed that I was counting: one, two, three, rinse, one, two, three, over and over again, and I heard Jim's voice all those years ago in the sea as he taught me to breathe. One, two, three, breathe. The soapy water was a frothing sea: peaks of dish soap were white horses as the cutlery swam for shore.

In the dark half-light, the freezing fog hanging thick outside the window, I put the kettle on. Those few morning minutes before my family awoke were the only ones I had to myself, and I thought of them as morning minutes because each morning started exactly as it had done for the previous ten years: I eased myself out of bed at half past six, put on my worn dressing gown, and began making breakfast.

Though I washed enough dishes to be a scullery maid, I had never before made the connection to the sea. It had been so long since I had last crawled through the breakers that I didn't know if I would remember now, and though it must have been ingrained in my muscles, the memory held in my limbs, the physical wasn't the only part of it. To swim in the sea required a mental focus that I could no longer summon.

The house was a shambolic, chaotic mess, which would take me the better part of the morning if not longer to sort out in time to host John's manager that evening for dinner. The idea of it was daunting and demoralizing; I would have loved nothing more than to sit down and feel sorry for myself for a few minutes. But I did not hear the sounds of my children getting dressed and ready for school, so self-pity would have to wait.

"Harriet," I called, climbing the stairs. "Time to get up, love." I waited for a response, and when none was forthcoming I switched on the lights and heard her groan. "Dressed, hair brushed, and downstairs for breakfast in ten minutes."

I opened Iain's door as I knocked on it, and there he was, playing with his Scalextric car set. "Put that away now and get dressed, please. Breakfast in ten minutes."

He ignored me. "Iain," I said, "if you don't put that away now, I'm going to confiscate it."

"Mum," he whined.

"I mean it."

"I don't want breakfast."

"Yes, you do. You'll be hungry."

"I want to play with this."

"Iain, I don't want to have to ask you again."

He scowled at me and stomped over to his wardrobe. "I hate you. Why do you have to be so mean?"

I shut the door, impervious to his words — I had no time to be hurt by them. Besides, I knew he'd have forgotten the whole thing by the time he got to the table. Back in our bedroom I moved quietly, but not too quietly, so that John would be woken gently. Opening the curtains provided enough light for me to grab the same clothes I had worn the day before and dress. Before I went back downstairs I gave John a nudge. His reply was a snort as he rolled over.

In a few minutes, the eggs were boiling and I was slicing toast into soldiers and shouting for the children to hurry up.

"I can't find my tie," Iain said as he sat down at the table.

I put his plate in front of him. "Is it on your dresser? Don't you have another in the wardrobe?"

"I hate eggs," he replied.

"They hate you too, darling."

"I want toast and Marmite."

"That's disgusting," Harriet said as she scraped her chair across the tiles.

"Harry, please. The floor. Lift the chair. How many times have we talked about this?"

"Can I go Canterbury at the weekend with Katie? Her mum invited me. They're going shopping."

"We'll talk about it later." I put her breakfast on the table.

She pushed the plate away. "I'm not hungry."

"Would you both please just eat your breakfasts?"

"Do as your mother says," John said. He took his spot at the head of the table and opened the paper. "George and I will be home at six, Martha. I've asked around and he enjoys a drop of Scotch after dinner." Without looking up from the paper he reached his hand out, searching for the cup of tea I had forgotten to make.

I put the kettle on and knocked over my own unfinished and now-cold tea, the brown liquid covering the counter and dripping onto the floor. No one offered to help clean it up.

John peered over his newspaper. "This is a very important dinner," he said.

"I know," I replied as I mopped up the spilt tea.

Breakfast passed quickly, the children bickering amongst themselves at a low enough level that my intervention was unnecessary, and John immersed in his own world, leaving me free to consider how best to organize my list of chores.

"He'll be expecting a first-rate meal," he said on his way out the door. I watched him walk through the garden and then turn around. He popped his head back through the doorway and said, "If you get a chance, see if you can't do something about the garden?"

It was an ordinary day: routine after routine, the way the days and months and years passed, the way my twenties had escaped me in a blur, the way in which we are lulled into forgetting the details of the promises we make.

While Iain and Harriet were at school, I found time in between rounds of laundry and cleaning and decided to take a look at the garden. It wasn't a good day for it: the mist was threatening to turn into sleet or worse. The weather could go either way — which, I suppose, could have also been said about everything that followed.

I put my wellies on and wrapped up against the weather: my old fisherman's pullover that was missing the top button, a wool scarf of indeterminate origin, and a plastic outer layer in a particularly vulgar shade of green. When I stepped outside, the bleak weather beat the stupefaction of housework out of me. There was something inspiring about the scene: the decaying mess of leaves covering the frosty mud; the smell of the earth. I felt as though I could change things here if I made an effort. With two young children and a husband to take care of there were days when I existed only within the confines of our four walls, and to be outside renewed my vigour. The moisture, visible in the air, provoked something deep within me that had been in hibernation.

My luck with gardening had never been good, but at least I was outside, which would please John, especially if any of our neighbours passed by. Results were superseded by a show of effort in our house.

I started with the myrtle bush, cutting back the branches at what was probably the wrong time of year; but it was an obvious place to start and my accomplishments would be immediately visible. It was too early in the spring for any buds, let alone blossoms, but the leaves were pretty and I took a small clipping inside with me.

It's hard to say exactly what jostled me then. It could have been the warmth of the house, which was suffocating in contrast to the chill outside. It could have been the difference in smells: inside, the remains of hundreds of dinners that clung to everything; outside, the freshness of earth — and, hidden in the air coming off the sea, that familiar scent of the kelp and salt.

Outside I felt that I was escaping something, the feeling of everything being close, closer, closing in. My mind wandered back to the comfort of counting my strokes as I swam.

The myrtle bush was a souvenir of days long past. A reminder of when I was first married and had yet to lose myself inside this house. I had planted it to remind both John and I of a moment of love — but more and more it reminded me of what I had given up.

In the kitchen, I filled a glass with water and put the clipping in it and saw there was one delicate pink blossom clinging to the branch. I looked at the breakfast dishes stacked on the side, waiting to be washed. There was a pile of ironing and the washing machine needed emptying. John's manager was coming to dinner that evening, which meant the whole house needed to be scrubbed, polished, and shined to within an inch of its life. The beef joint needed to be put in the oven sooner rather than later, the potatoes peeled, and the children fed, washed, and sent upstairs as soon as they got home from school.

I set the myrtle on the table and turned it around so the blossom faced me. Memories are sparked in different ways: a smell, a sound, a phrase. Maybe it was the shape of the clouds, which looked that day like billowing waves, rearing up, toppling over themselves; or it could have been the wind sweeping inland, carrying with it salt and kelp. I returned to the door, flung it open, and inhaled deeply. It was faint but I remembered it. I would have known it anywhere: that distinct smell of the sea.

We lived only a few miles from the shore, and during their summer holidays we took the children to the harbour where I had learned to swim so they could splash and paddle, but that was not the sea that had got into my bones. It was the difference between a swimming suit and a bathing suit: our children wore bathing suits, and dabbled at the water's edge, while I wore a swimming suit and went as far from land as I could. We took them to the beach, but I went swimming. Their idea of the seashore was a picture postcard. The sea I knew was big and in constant motion, changing as and when its moods dictated. It was cold and wet and strong, a part of the world in a way that I was not, tucked up inside my house, living the life of a dutiful wife and good mother.

That winter had been the coldest in decades. White snow had flown off the chalk cliffs, covering the pebbles and the castle, muffling the sounds around us. It had been a pretty novelty at first, but the bitter chill did not pass for weeks. Now that the temperature had finally risen, if only slightly, the need to embrace the promise of spring tugged at me.

When I was younger; when I was young. The sea, the sea, it called to me. I had learned to swim side by side with the Channel swimmers. Summer holidays saw the rest of my friends primping on the pebble beach, modelling the latest styles in swimwear, but I couldn't sit there sunning myself when the water was so tantalizingly close.

My mother had chided me, saying I ought to spend less time in the water and reminding me that muscular shoulders and arms on a young woman were unattractive at best, repellent at worst. It was a constant battle, my strength against dress seams.

The moisture in the air invigorated me and I recalled something I had heard at the church service John and I attended for no other reason than to be seen to be decent members of the community. We were not religious, but our attendance was.

For there is hope of a tree, if it be cut down, that it will sprout again, and that the tender branch thereof will not cease. Though the root thereof wax old in the earth, and the stock thereof die in the ground; yet through the scent of water it will bud and bring forth boughs like a plant.

I did not expect to sprout boughs but I found myself walking with increasing speed toward the sea. When I got to the water's edge near Shakespeare's Bay it was all froth, foaming up onto the beach with each set of waves. The surf inched higher and higher up the beach, covering my boots, and I knew the tide was coming in to greet me as though I were a long-lost friend.

In the months before we were married I swam nearly every day and so did everyone else, or at least it seemed to me at the time. People came from all over the world — from America, Europe, and even Egypt — to have a go at the Channel, but thankfully for the most part they trained in the open-air pool in the next village up the coast, only practising in the sea when the windows for their swims approached.

The season officially started in July and went on through to the end of September, and there was such a frenzy about it that I remember my father complaining that all the most reliable fisherman didn't fish anymore; instead, they were piloting boats that stood watch over swimmers. Dover had not been prepared for the onslaught of swimmers, but it was so much more preferable than the soldiers and bombs that they were welcomed with open arms.

It was impossible to avoid: the shore was cluttered with gawkers and press and well-wishers. But I wasn't involved in it — I was just a girl who swam. To have thought seriously about a Channel crossing was ludicrous. The way I overheard other people talking about it — swimmers included — confirmed this. Their talk was of conquering the Channel, beating the sea, of doing something extraordinary. I contented myself with entertaining the idea in the privacy of my own imagination, and bristled at the idea of asserting dominance. That was not what the water was for.

I emerged one morning and headed right to my towel, which I kept under a myrtle bush a ways back from the shoreline. As I was drying off I noticed a man in a crumpled jacket staring at me; I covered myself and turned away, hoping he would leave quickly so I could change. I needed to make it home in time to go to a fitting for my wedding dress — which had to be let out in the back again. "If you would just stop this incessant swimming, Martha," I could hear my mother say. "You ought to be focusing on planning for your future as Mrs. Roberts. Being a good wife isn't as easy as it looks."

I glanced over my shoulder and the man was still there. Had there been bushes other than the one I was standing in front of, I would have accused him of lurking in them. He looked utterly out of place there, pretending he didn't want something, and I lost patience.

"Can I help you?" I said.

He looked around as though he weren't certain if I was addressing him or someone else.

"Yes, you. Is there something I can do for you?"

He edged closer and took off his hat. "Are you a swimmer?"

I was standing in my swimming suit, having just returned from a swim in the sea, and so I didn't answer his question; rather, I looked down at my dripping-wet legs.

"Oh, of course. Excuse me, of course you are."

"So what if I am?"

"I'm with the *Post*, Miss, and I just wondered if you're one of the women who will be swimming the Channel this year."

I couldn't help myself; the laugh that burst out of me was not an intentional comment on his obvious ineptitude: it was merely a physical reaction, which I tried to hide by covering my mouth.

"It's just that, I, uh, I saw you, out there," he said, pointing to the water.

"I was out there."

"Have you got a deal with another paper or something? I don't want to get you in trouble or anything, it's just, uh, I was hoping that, if you are a Channel swimmer and you aren't already sponsored by one of the other papers, maybe you might have time to talk to me? About the swimming," he said.

"I'm sorry to disappoint you, but I have no intention of swimming to France. When I go, I'll take a more traditional means of transportation."

I watched as he scribbled something in his notebook. "Can I quote you on that?"

"Sorry?"

"I have to file five hundred words by tonight and no one will talk to me."

"Do you make a habit of lurking? Perhaps that might have something to do with the reluctance."

He smiled awkwardly and stared at his shoes. I waited for him to make his excuses and leave but he did nothing and I was getting cold, so I dried myself off as best I could and put my pullover and shorts back on. I hated wearing a wet swimsuit under dry clothes — so clammy and cold, never mind the fact that I would drip the entire way back to my parents' house.

"Why not?"

"Excuse me?" I said as my head popped out through my top.

"Why aren't you going to swim the Channel? Don't take this the wrong way, but I was watching you out there and you look pretty strong. Stronger than some of the other girls."

"I've no interest in it."

Which was of course a lie. Channel swimming was everywhere you looked that summer and in the back of my mind, where I kept my most secret of secrets, I had imagined swimming all twenty-one miles of it. And that's where it had to stay. It was safer there, in my thoughts.

What would it have proved, anyhow? What would it change? A few minutes in the limelight would have no bearing on the life that lay ahead of me; it would simply bring greater disappointment — and that's if I managed to complete the crossing at all. My life was laid out in front of me in the same way that my wedding dress would soon be laid out on my childhood bed: it was tailored to me, all I had to do was put it on. What would be the sense of changing my mind, of dreaming of a different future? As much as I struggled with the confines of the life I had accepted, I knew that it was better to try and be grateful for what I had, instead of hoping for something different.

"Don't you think you could make it?"

"Of course I could."

"Then why aren't you gonna try?"

I smiled curtly. "I'm sorry, but I have to be going."

His question was so American, I thought as I picked up my towel, swimming cap, and goggles, and stuffed them in my bag. And I remembered a conversation I had overheard when I was younger. One of my mother's friends had taken up with an American solider after the war. She had been taken out and shown off, carrying on to a degree my mother and her friends found shameful. This woman had talked of going to America, of getting out of Dover, and had made no secret of how small and provincial she thought their lives were. Then out of nowhere — to hear them tell it — the soldier up and left, abandoning her, leaving her with nothing. Her mistake of course wasn't taking up with the soldier. It was deciding that she wanted more, that what was available to her here was not good enough. It was a snub, pure and simple. I knew better than to publicly bet on something that wasn't a sure thing. Harbouring dreams was fine, but to keep them whole, they had to remain private.

I heard the reporter's footsteps on the pebbles behind me. "Where're you going?"

I had never before met such an intrusive person. Around town, there had been no small amount of grumbling about how impertinent the Americans were but I had decided to disbelieve it, until now.

"I don't see how it's any business of yours."

"So you're not off to meet your pilot?"

"What?" I stopped dead in my tracks.

"Your pilot. You don't really think I'm buying the idea that you're not in training with the rest of them. How do I know you're not some English ringer, some secret weapon the Brits have to show the rest of us up?"

His flattery was well placed and I'm sure I blushed. "I'm going to see my dressmaker."

"Dressmaker?"

"Yes."

"Well, I suppose you'd have to."

"And why is that?"

"It's a small town you've got here. Not that it's not pretty, a castle overlooking the sea, that's impressive. And the white cliffs, they're beautiful. But there's not much else going on. Not like New York City."

"I'm sure it seems small in comparison."

"Everything does."

I continued to walk toward home and he continued to follow me. "Look," I said. "I don't mean to be rude, but as you've noticed, this is a small town. I'm afraid I'm going to have to ask you to stop following me."

He shrugged. "If you change your mind, I'm at the White Horse Inn."

I HADN'T THOUGHT about that day in years — but on that early spring day, as the froth covered my boots and the sea wrapped itself around my ankles, my body remembered that time in my life more acutely than my mind did. My body wasn't hindered by what my mind knew to be fact. There were the habits I had developed over the years spent in the water: shaking my hands to loosen my wrists as I waded in, rolling my shoulders to unlock the muscles that would inevitably tighten once I was back on dry land. I found myself unconsciously repeating those movements now, as if the sea had some kind of hold on me that I was helpless to resist.

I took my boots off and threw them beyond the tidal line, and let the icy water chill my toes to the point where I no longer felt them — and consequently no longer felt tied to the earth. I felt the waves calling me, beckoning me into the frigid depths with the offer of a promise made long ago.

A little later that summer, as my wedding date grew nearer, I had put common sense to one side and gone to the White Horse Inn with the intention of striking a deal with the journalist's newspaper. I would grant them exclusive coverage and they would pay for the costs associated with my crossing — the pilot, the Channel Swimming & Piloting Federation's fees for overseeing an official attempt, the petrol for the boat. But the girl at the front desk said he had checked out a week ago; I had lost my chance. I was still reminded of it each time I passed the White Horse. We are not all destined to be tall poppies.

Ten years later, ten years out of the water and fully clothed, I walked into the waves and was knocked down almost immediately. I had forgotten the power they held as they crashed down, and the strength of the undertow as the water retreated from the shore. The air was knocked out of my chest and I went down hard, my knees hitting the shifting stones on the seabed. The water churned as though it were angry with me for getting in its way; or maybe it was upset that I had been away for so very long. My heart pounded and echoed in my ears as my hands searched through the flood, my clothes weighted me down and I was desperate to grab hold of something, anything that might save me.

I did not feel safe in the sea then. I felt the same way I had in that first moment when I fell off the pier so many years ago: terrified, choking with fear. My chest was tight and I fought the urge to open my mouth and cry for help. I tried to remain as calm as possible and planted my feet to stand up, bracing myself against the next set of waves. My head breached the waterline and I gasped for air, only to be knocked down again by another surge of the sea, throwing me on the ground.

It was a fight, a test.

I dragged myself toward land — half crawling, half swimming — out of harm's way, but it was a battle and the sea would not let me go easily, pulling me away from the shore. The water's violence toward me was because of the choice I'd made years ago; the sea could not tolerate taking second place. Its wrath was worse because I had chosen John right here, in this spot, while the sea had licked our feet.

That summer I had been given all the things one is told to aspire to; the problem was that in saying yes, I had also said no. I had said yes to John, after he had waited here, on this very beach, for me to finish my swim. He had asked me to come out of the water for him and though he had not meant it literally, the results were the same.

It had been a beautiful afternoon. I had not known with certainty that he would ask me that day, but it had been in the air. It was the logical conclusion to the months we had spent together and it was expected, never questioned. There I was, having only just finished school, about to embark upon a wonderful life and I didn't question it. It did not occur to me that I would have to choose between loves or that I ever could.

John was taking me out to dinner that night, somewhere fancy, he had said. But as I waded into the sea that afternoon for a swim, it was not the question he might ask that was on my mind, but the one the journalist had asked me. Instead of swimming parallel to the shore, as I normally did, I found myself heading eastward, making my way toward France.

Gliding through the water almost completely submerged had always been a retreat to a different world for me. Swimming front crawl allowed me to focus inward, blocking everything else out — and the absolute quiet it afforded was unique. No other solitude — not going to the library, not sitting on a bench by myself — allowed my mind to wander so freely, roaming the wilds of my fantasies and the hundreds of other lives I imagined for myself. It was something I could only ever do when properly wet.

That afternoon I had not intended to think about the Channel; I had only meant to clear my head and enjoy an hour or so by myself. I knew John had made a reservation at the restaurant and he'd said we couldn't be late. But, not for the first time, I lost my sense of time as I swam; and there was something inspiring about going toward a destination. With every stroke I got a little bit closer to France, and with every breath the idea that I could swim the Channel began to seem possible. It began to feel necessary.

I don't know how long John waited for me as I indulged in my fantasies and he in his worries, because he has never told me. But I do know that when I waded out of the sea and I saw him there — he was easy to spot as I walked through the shallows, suited and booted, looking as out of place as he must have felt — the look on his face was sheer relief. He came out as far as he could, and we met when we were both knee-deep.

He put his arm around my shoulders to guide me back onto dry land.

"Martha," he said. "Come out of the water."

And I did. I came out of the water for him that day and once we were married, I stayed on dry land for nearly ten years. It wasn't that I didn't want to go back. But life got in the way, as is its habit. A wedding, a house, a baby and then another, and soon enough a decade had passed.

I SURVIVED THE assault of the sea on that bitter spring afternoon. But as I sat in the foam, watching the water seethe around me, I knew ten years had been too long, and that the beating was punishment I deserved.

The easiest thing to do would have been to go home and pretend none of it had happened. My skin was dead-chicken white, my fingertips were blue, and my teeth had not stopped chattering; I knew that to stay out there any longer would be as dangerous as it was reckless. I couldn't feel anything, but in another way I felt it all.

It was impossible to explain. I didn't know where the urge came from — if it was the hope of the trees, as I had heard in our church service, or some other force. But I knew I felt it strongly in my arms, shoulders, and hands. To swim required physical strength, but the act itself provided mental energy.

The beach was empty, and I tore off my sopping wet clothes and stripped down to my bra and knickers, and for the first time in years, I went swimming. This time my body moved through the water as it always had, and in some ways I felt as though I had never been out of the water. I listened to the familiar sloshing in my ears, tasted the salt as it stung my tongue and burned my eyes, and let the strength of the sea cradle me.

What I felt more than the cold and more than the aching burn of unused muscles was that I was free here.

When I arrived home I followed the sound of voices into the front room, where my husband was sitting with George, his manager. I am certain I looked as if I had just been drowned, and I greeted them with the giddy smile of an addict who has finally gotten the fix she craved.

"Where have you been?" John asked.

I stood there dripping. "Swimming," I said. I couldn't help but grin.

He took me by the arm and led me into the kitchen. "Won't be a minute, George," he said.

He shut the door. "Please tell me there is a good reason for this," he said, gesturing at my mermaid-like state. "Please tell me you have just saved someone from drowning."

I was about to say no, but then it occurred to me that maybe I had. "Actually," I said, "I did save someone this afternoon."

His expression changed instantly. "Really? Who?"

I was about to speak when he cut me off.

"No, never mind, go and change and then come and tell us both at the same time. That might be the only thing that can turn this night around."

"I saved myself, John," I said, just before he opened the door to the front room.

"Say again?"

"I saved myself."

"Martha, I have had a long day and don't care to play games. Now, either you've saved someone or you haven't. Which is it?"

It was not the right time to have this conversation but there were things that needed to be said and things that needed to be heard.

"The Channel, John. I'm going to swim the Channel."

"What has that got to do with anything?"

"I have made dinner every night for the past ten years, and lunch and breakfast. That's . . ." I paused to do the calculations. "That's nearly eleven thousand meals."

He looked puzzled.

"I have scrubbed and swept and washed and dried and ironed. Every day for ten years."

He looked over his shoulder anxiously. "And you decided to stop, without warning, today? Martha, my manager, that man in the next room, should be considering how he's going to tell me I'll be getting a promotion as we share a glass of Scotch while digesting a very good meal. As it is, he's probably starving and wondering how I was ever hired in the first place."

I wrapped my arms around myself, suddenly unable to focus on anything beyond how cold I was.

"I've had enough, John. I have."

"Enough of what?"

"Of being a wife and a mother and a housekeeper. I need more."

"More of what? What could you possibly want for? I have given you a nice house, two children. We have all the mod cons." He pointed at the washing machine. "That, that right there is brand new, top of the line. Who else do you know who has a machine like that?"

"I don't make a habit of asking after other people's appliances."

"You have everything you could possibly want or need, right here."

"There's something missing."

"For God's sake, what could that possibly be? Beyond the obvious, which is the dinner you were meant to prepare."

"I'm trying to have a serious conversation."

"I can see that, but it's neither the time nor the place." He shook his head.

And then his tone dropped, the anger was sucked out of his voice, and he turned what I loved against me.

"You told me once, on the beach, after a swim, you told me about how important the timing was in your breathing. How you had to get it right, go with the rhythm of the waves in choppy water. Otherwise you'd get a mouthful of water, not air. Do you remember?"

I nodded. And I remembered, too, an account of a tsunami in Hawaii that I had read about as a girl. I had marvelled at the idea of a wall of water rising up from the Pacific as high as a thirteen-storey building. At how the water had been sucked out to sea, away from the shore, before the great wave hit.

"We can have all the serious conversations you want, but not now. We can talk until we're both blue in the face about whatever you feel you're missing in life — we can discuss it, in full, tomorrow." He gripped the back of the chair in front of him tightly. He was exasperated, frustrated — all the things I was feeling. "When my manager is not sitting in the next room wondering what in the hell is going on in here," he said.

When the wave at Hilo hit, it cut through everything in its path, and there in my kitchen I understood the force it had, better than I had before. There was something in me that cut through the cold and exhaustion. "You're right," I said. "It's entirely inappropriate to have this very important chat while George is sitting in the next room. The timing is all wrong." I locked eyes with my husband. "Perhaps you ought to ask him to leave. I don't feel up to entertaining this evening."

His eyes widened and he grabbed my arm and I winced as he pulled me close, his fingertips digging into my muscle that used to be strong. This was not how the man I knew behaved. "Whatever you're upset about will have to wait. Go fix yourself up and I will try and salvage what is left of the evening you've seen fit to ruin."

It was believed to have been an underwater earthquake that set the Hawaiian tsunami in motion, the grating of earth plates against one another, vying for dominance.

"At least it's only one dinner," I said.

"One dinner? It's the most important dinner we've ever had. Our entire future rests on me getting this promotion and you've managed to ruin that beyond all repair."

His grip tightened until I wrenched my arm away.

"What about my promotion?"

"Promoted? To what? You don't have a job, Martha."

"I don't want to be known only as Mrs. John Roberts. Or Mummy." My voice was rising with each word, gaining speed and height like a wave, and his face screwed up into a scowl of incomprehension.

"I don't want to be the person who makes dinner and cleans the house and does the school run and goes to school plays and takes care of people when they're unwell and hosts dinner parties."

"And I don't want to go to my job day in and day out to support this family," he said, seething with anger. "But I do. Life isn't about doing what you want. It's about doing what needs to be done."

"John," I said, looking up at him, all six foot four inches of him, with his squinting eyes and clenched jaw. "I want to do something extraordinary. I want to swim the Channel."

"What has that got to do with any of this? Did you not hear me? None of this is about want!" He gestured wildly, his arms drawing in our kitchen, our house, and our life. "What in the hell has gotten into you?"

He turned to look at George pretending he couldn't hear us through the glass doors. "There's no way he'll give me that promotion now. How can I control an entire department of men if I can't even control my own wife?"

"A wife isn't for controlling," I said. "I have to do more than laundry. I want to do something bigger." I stepped forward, intending to change out of my dripping clothes, but he would not let me pass.

He looked furious — with me or himself I couldn't tell.

"I'm going to put some dry clothes on. Then I will come down and cook you and George your dinner. And then, John, I am going to swim the Channel."

"What is so bloody important about swimming the Channel?" he shouted.

"My life depends on it."

The sea has a multitude of faces, and once you know what to look for you can tell when it becomes enraged. John's expression in that moment was similar to the pictures of the waves that destroyed Hilo and Haena: boiling with rage that had gathered speed and energy over time and distance. That energy had to go somewhere.

But the sound is what you remember. The Hawaiians told reporters the approaching waves sounded like a freight train. The sound of his hand against my face sounded like the crack I made when I fell off the pier and into the sea as a girl.

He stared at me as if he couldn't believe what he had just done. I touched my face; the spot where he had hit me was hot.

I went upstairs and changed. In the mirror I thought I saw the beginnings of a bruise and wondered how he would explain it to George. Briefly I thought of covering it with makeup — but we were past that point. We were not Victorians wading into the sea hidden in bathing machines; we were naturists parading around, warts and all.

Once the wave had gone, dragging half of Hilo with it, the people rebuilt and life carried on. Normally the change was incremental, the sea wearing down the cliffs until they became sand. But in our house, the cliff had fallen into the sea in an instant.

I went back to the kitchen. I took the cutting board out and by force of habit started chopping peppers and onions, whisking eggs and lighting the flame on the gas hob. As I was pouring the eggs into the hot pan, John came into the kitchen and sat down at the table.

"There's no need. He's gone."

I kept my back to him. "I'm hungry. I expect you are as well."

I brought the food over to the table and sat down next to him in my usual spot.

"Shall I say grace?" he asked.

I shook my head no as I dished up the meal. "No one's here to see."

When my mouth was full I realized how hungry I was, and I barely chewed as I shovelled and swallowed in the awkward silence that hung between us. The silence in a kitchen isn't absolute; there are background noises. The hum of the refrigerator, the boiler clicking on and off, the sound of forks scraping across plates.

Halfway through, John cleared his throat. "What is this?" he asked, looking at the cutting I'd placed on the table that morning.

"Myrtle," I said. "From the garden."

He brought it close to his face. "It looks familiar."

"It grows by the seaside."

I had hoped he might remember. "The day you proposed. You tore off one of these branches, from where I hid my towel," I said.

The faint smile appeared. "It was hard to break."

"It gets its strength from the sea."

He twirled it between his fingers. "You've never said anything about the Channel before."

I pictured myself in the water and felt my expression soften.

"Why?" he asked.

I leaned back in my chair and sighed. Despite what had passed between us, the food had warmed me and the heaviness of sleep was creeping through my limbs. "Because I miss it."

"You can swim without having to cross the Channel."

"I used to not mind the sea wall in the harbour. I thought it was protecting me. But today, I went to the bay and swam straight out. There was nothing in front of me but water, right on to the horizon. I have never felt so free."

He picked at the grit under his fingernails. "Free? You're not being held captive here, you know."

And I had the strangest sensation that he and I were, if not the same, then similar. That he had found a saving grace in me.

"Ten years ago I got out of the water for you. That was my choice. But I need to go back now." I picked up the dinner plates. "I can't go on otherwise."

It was not my intention to frighten him, though I believe I did. It was difficult to express my need in words because it wasn't something I thought, it was something I felt. But when I looked at him I think he understood — if not the reason, then at least the fact that it was going to happen, with or without his support.

In the morning the usual routine played out, and when the children were finally dressed and at the table, I served them their breakfasts.

"Mummy," Iain said. "What's happened to your face?"

I put my hand to my cheek and realized that looking in the mirror was something that, if I did it at all, happened much later in the day, after they were gone.

"Eat your eggs and soldiers before they get cold," I said.

"Your mother went swimming yesterday," John said as he took his seat. "There must have been a piece of driftwood that she didn't see." He didn't look at me when he spoke and I thought less of him for it.

But then he got up from the table and stood beside me, his arm around my shoulders. "And she'll be going again today."

"But it's still cold," Harriet said.

"It is," John said. "But your mother will not let anything stand in her way."

The children looked at him, utterly baffled.

"Your mother," he said with a mixture of pride and fear, "is going to swim the English Channel."

Their eyes grew wide. They had an idea of what that meant, having seen others training in the harbour during the summer break.

"Aren't you, Martha?" he said.

I nodded in reply; his encouragement had caught me off guard. I wondered if it was guilt speaking, or an apology, or if it was his way of saying he loved me.

As I took my swimming costume out of the bottom drawer in the dresser — where I kept the things I no longer had much use for but couldn't bring myself to throw away — I wondered if it was even possible. The navy suit I had worn when I was a young woman had lost most of its shape, and what was left of the elastic fabric was sagging. My second skin had lost its strength, as had my arms, shoulders, and legs. Seeing the suit in that sorry state blew a whiff of fear through my resolve. Once I started I would have to finish. There would be no stopping until I reached France.

COMING OUT

HARRIET, 1999

THERE ARE SECRETS in every family, stories that are held tightly to your chest, spirited away into the recesses of a house or a life and not thought of until years later. Some fade and soften, becoming almost unbelievable, to the point where they float somewhere between the truth and legend. But some grow sharp, their facts maturing into perfect points: kitchen knives, blades up, lying in wait in the drawer.

"I'd like to meet them," Iris said as she passed the salad across the table.

I reached for the salt, shaking my head.

She moved the shaker just out of reach.

"They don't approve of…" I opened my arms wide to include our home, our life, and everything else that mattered.

"Time heals." She wiped up a spot of oil from the salad, so small that I hadn't noticed it.

I moved the brown rice and lentil stew around on my plate, hoping she would drop the subject.

"Are you ashamed of me?" she said.

"Yes, deeply, that's why I married you and am carrying our baby."

"You've met my parents."

"Your parents are lovely."

She stabbed a spear of asparagus and chewed slowly without breaking eye contact, which was her version of the silent treatment.

"Are you ever going to give up on this?" I asked.

She swallowed and did not blink. I knew she could outlast me and I looked down at my food.

"Iris," I said. "It won't be what you're hoping for. They won't change and can't admit they're in the wrong."

"I'm your wife. In-laws are part of the deal."

"Technically you're not actually my wife," I said.

Iris glared at me before reaching across the table to slap my hand.

"Sorry," I said, smiling as I leaned back and put my hand on my belly.

"I want them to know who I am," she said softly.

We went to bed at different times, and when she climbed under the duvet I waited for her arm to wrap around me, her wrist settling into its favourite spot between my breasts, but she turned her back to me and the space between us remained.

Later, as the night worked its way toward morning, I had the unnerving feeling that I was dreaming but unable to wake up. It wasn't exactly a nightmare, but it was frightening. I thought I was moving my mouth and speaking to someone — though who that might be was not clear: myself in the dream, my mother and father, or all of us together. The sensation was familiar: I was being dragged away and under, deeper into the dream by the currents I was trying to escape.

The dream dissipated but — along with my wife's insistence on meeting my parents — it had unsettled memories.

It was Boxing Day; my brother Iain and I had driven from London together on Christmas Eve. We had been awash in the hope and happiness of just starting out in life: I had managed to get a few articles printed in the London papers, and Iain had wormed his way into a promising role at HSBC. The atmosphere in the car as we drove home was one of victory: we had made good, had given our parents reasons to be proud.

Iain had wanted to stay in the city over the holidays and go to the pub, but I insisted he come to Dover with me. It had been a few years since I'd been to visit and I felt guilty. The distance had given me space in which to recast my parents in a more tolerant light, but what was more pressing was that I had met Iris.

Iain made no secret of feeling put out, but once we were in the car we turned the music up loud and sang along, just like the old days, which only fuelled my determination. It was Christmas, I reasoned, and everyone would be happier than usual, ready to make an effort and be welcoming — so what could possibly go wrong?

That I even had those thoughts shows how wilfully naive I was. To think that I could swan into my parents' home and announce that I was in love with a woman and be greeted with affection and acceptance was a desperate fantasy.

We were finishing dinner and I had fortified myself with the liberal application of wine. I took a deep breath and when a natural lull in conversation presented itself I blurted out the words lesbian, girlfriend, living with, and some time now. I paused briefly, and before anyone could speak I finished with can't change and it's who I am.

In my deluded vision this was the moment when my mother should have thrown her arms around my shoulders and proclaimed on behalf of the entire family that I was loved regardless. Even Iain's shrug, given years ago in the pub, was better than this. To make my imaginary family more realistic I had pictured my father grumbling for a few moments before my mother shamed him into acceptance.

In reality, everything stopped. The silence was absolute. My words had created a vacuum, an awful, soundless shock not unlike the moment you learn a loved one has died, when nothing can be said because letting the absence take over is the only possible reaction.

My father broke the silence by saying unnatural, disgusting, and wrong. His face grew red and spittle collected at the side of his mouth as he said, a real man, the right man, and you'll never be happy. He ended his diatribe with a choice selection: married, children, and normal life, and then he looked at me with an expression I'd only seen once before.

I must have been nine years old when Mum ruined an important dinner. I remembered the day well because she wasn't there when we got home from school and Dad, when he arrived home, was with someone from work. He gave Iain and me some toast and ushered us upstairs. He told us to be quiet and asked where Mum was. When I heard her voice in the kitchen I crept to the top of the stairs and listened, expecting some bit of gossip but getting instead a horrible row. What I saw from my vantage point was my father's face and it was full of a cold judgement that I knew I never wanted to receive. But it wasn't just his expression; it was everything about him: the way he held himself over my mother, unable to consider a different perspective.

As he shouted at me across the table that Boxing Day I

looked to my mother for support or encouragement, anything that showed a recognition of our mutual need to go beyond what was possible within the confines of these four walls, but she betrayed me that day, too. She looked at the cold turkey, the day-old gravy, and reheated sprouts while my father ranted until he reached the apex of his rage and pounded his fist on the table, shaking the glasses. "No daughter of mine!" he bellowed as he stood up with such force that he knocked his chair over.

When I told Iris how it had all played out, with my head in her lap on the couch we had bought together, in the flat we shared, I said truthfully that in the moment I had felt nothing. Emotions are secondary in some situations, and my reaction to my father's words was physical: I thought I would be sick.

My father threw his rage at me and I remembered the night in the kitchen when he and Mum had fought and I heard his hand hit her cheek, her head jerking sideways. His face was twisted into the same scowl, his lips peeled back from his teeth, nostrils flared, and his eyes were tiny little slits. It's hard to say what he was most offended by: the fact that I was gay or that I had been so brazen as to announce it. I have wondered in the intervening years whether we could have carried on as we always had done if it had remained a secret.

Shaking, I left the table and went to my room, which was unchanged. My belongings and what was left of the person I had been were museum pieces, covered in dust.

Everything about the house was stale. Time had passed in the years since I had last been there and nothing had changed, which was depressing and comforting in unequal measure. Time had passed, nothing more and nothing less, and what was obvious was that life's incremental changes were not welcome here. Progress was excluded and so was I.

I sat on the edge of the bed and cursed myself for having gone further into this house where I was not wanted, when what I should have done was storm out the front door and go directly back to London. The walls were closing in on me and I felt trapped. And I knew why my mother had fled to the sea.

It took me a while to summon up the courage to leave, but once I was ready I walked down the stairs with no intention of even saying goodbye. The creaky stairs that had given me away when I came in late as a teenager betrayed me again as I tried to creep out of the house, because my father appeared as I reached for the doorknob.

Calmly he said, "This is not easy to say, but if you insist upon continuing this lifestyle you give me no choice." He paused, and looked down at his feet. Then, meeting my stare again he said, "Goodbye. Leave your key on the table before you go."

When he finished he simply turned his back to me and returned to his chair in the living room. I was paralyzed, my feet would not move and I didn't know what to do. I was too stunned to react.

I opened the door and lifted my bag over my shoulder and then I walked slowly down the path to the pavement. Before I turned into the road I looked back once more and saw my mother in the doorway, cardigan pulled tightly around her body, staring at me. I waited for her to say something and I hoped it would be that she loved me and always would, even though we weren't the sort of people who said things like that. I wanted her to tell me that I was always welcome, even though she couldn't because it wasn't her home, not really. A home, for us, was a man's castle, and in our home the women did the laundry. My mother had been granted one exception and whenever she had something important to talk about she insisted on a walk by the sea.

My mother turned and went into the house and I thought that was it, that she was disgusted by me to such an extent that she couldn't even say goodbye. Iain was already in the car at this point and he tooted the horn. I opened the passenger door and threw my bag in the back seat.

"Harry!" my mother called.

I turned around and she had the garden shears in her hands and was trimming the bush at the end of the garden. I watched her clip off a branch and wondered what she was doing.

She brought it over and handed it to me. It was a damp brown twig dotted with rotted blossoms.

"Myrtle," she said. "It gave me strength when I needed it most."

ON SUNDAY, WE awoke to an unusually sunny day and Iris — a pathologically cheery early riser — was bursting with plans.

"Come on," she said, pulling the duvet off me. "Let's go somewhere. A drive in the country, nice pub lunch."

She stood there in a T-shirt and knickers in our bedroom, and the sun streaming in from the windows made her skin glow. She noticed me looking at her and she smiled, letting me look for as long as I wanted.

"Come back to bed," I said. "It's not even nine in the morning."

"Day's a-wasting." She crumpled the duvet in the far corner of the room.

It took us over an hour to get out of London, but once we were drifting along through the green fields, dotted with trees and bushes and nature showing off, I was lulled into sleep. When the car stopped, all I remembered as I struggled out of sleep was a sheep standing perilously close to the motorway. Iris had her hand on my shoulder, so the first place I looked when I opened my eyes wasn't out the window, but at her face as she beamed back at me, the woman I'd fallen in love with years ago.

"We're here," she said.

"Where's here?" I asked. Then I looked. "Turn around," I said.

"We're already here. What's the harm?"

"I don't want to do this."

"Fine, I'll go introduce myself."

"Iris, don't."

She put her hand on the car door release and glanced at me. I shook my head but that didn't stop her. She opened the door and walked up the path. I didn't follow immediately, hoping that without me she would turn around and we could get away unnoticed. But she didn't stop and so I had no choice. That's the thing about family: it's not about want. Want has nothing to do with it.

The front door was painted a high-gloss lacquer black, exactly the same as it had been the last time I was here, though the Christmas wreath was not there. The myrtle bush looked bigger and was actually beautiful in full bloom. Everything looked — as I had known it would — neat as a pin, because that's how my father preferred it. Left to her own devices, I always thought my mother would ignore everything but the myrtle.

Iris put her finger on the bell and just before she rang it I whispered, "We can still turn around." She pressed it regardless and it echoed through the foyer.

I prayed they were out at church or at a friend's house playing cards or anywhere else, as long as they weren't in.

I heard a kerfuffle coming from the kitchen and looked through the window next to the door. There was my father, holding a cup of tea as my mother looked on with what I thought of as her usual mixture of irritation and sadness. I saw her wipe her hands on a kitchen towel and shake her head as she came to the door. She didn't look through the window to see who it might be — though she would not have seen me if she had, since I had shrunk behind Iris.

She opened the door and my wife smiled the biggest, warmest smile she could. I knew it wouldn't be enough.

"Yes?" Mum said.

Her voice. I didn't realize how much I had missed it. With just one word I was taken back to her table and my childhood, to a time before I had learned to make my own decisions, and after she had been brave enough to make hers.

I put my hand on my belly instinctively as I looked at my mother's face. She had aged but not much: her shoulders were still broad and strong, and her posture was still aggressively good. The skin on her jowls was looser and her face looked softer but she still looked the way I pictured her. I wanted to wrap my arms around her and hold on tightly. I wanted to burst into tears and for her to smooth my hair down and make me a cup of hot chocolate and tell me everything would be okay. I wanted to be the little girl she loved, curled up on her lap.

"I'm Iris." My wife held out her hand.

Mum took it and then she looked at me and when she put it together she dropped Iris's hand.

"Hi," I said.

Dad appeared behind her and my body bristled. He looked at Iris and then at me.

"Have I forgotten you were coming?" he said.

His face was a mirror. I took after him physically: tall with a narrow face, and a complexion prone to burning upon any exposure to sun — quite unlike my mother, who turned a lovely, toasted olive colour.

"Go inside," my mother told him.

"Or did you forget to tell me?" He looked at her accusingly.

"John, go inside. Drink one of the cups of tea you've made for yourself." She gave him a gentle shove.

"I'm sorry it's taken us so long to visit," Iris said.

Mum ignored her and looked at me. "It's not a good time."

"I'm sorry. I didn't realize you were busy," I said.

"How could you? You don't phone."

"But we're here now," Iris said in the relentlessly cheery voice she saved for her students. "We're so pleased to have caught you at home. We just thought we'd pop by for a cup of tea."

"You don't pop by from London," Mum said.

I suppressed a smile.

"But you're here now." She stepped aside. "You may as well come in."

We settled into the living room that hadn't changed. The brown sofa was flanked by two brown chairs, the throw pillows were still beige and looked as if no one had ever thought to use them, their shape still perfect. The wallpaper, which had always looked as though it had come from a pub, was peeling back at the seams, but that obviously wasn't a concern. Interior decorating was not an interest my mother had ever had.

Furniture sees everything: it is where we fall in and out of love, where we share bad news and good, where we hold hands and each other. It sits silently, watching, and makes no judgements but holds memories in its fabric. The red wine stain when arms were thrown up in celebration, the gravy stain from the last Christmas when everyone was home, and the cigarette burn from the secret party we had thrown as teenagers. It was all still here. A still life.

My father sat in his chair, which is where I always pictured him when I thought of him. He was a living photograph, wearing the same uniform of wool trousers, corduroy waistcoat, check shirt and tie, all in earth tones. My father didn't wear blue, because it was my mother's colour. He was the hills, and she the sea. The difference in his appearance that day was his feet. Where before he had always had Oxfords on, now he wore carpet slippers. It was an admission more than anything else that though things inside the house had not changed, their lives had, at least in some way. The slippers meant that life outside these four walls was no longer for him. Mum, I noticed, had her shoes on.

Iris took my hand in hers and my body tensed. I had never held hands with anyone in this house. My parents, married for over forty years, were not physically affectionate with one another, and I could have counted on one hand the number of times I'd seen them kiss. Contact of any kind was for other people.

"You have a lovely garden," Iris said to my father.

He stared at our intertwined fingers.

Mum brought the tea things through and nearly dropped the tray when she saw us. I tried to release myself from Iris's grasp but she squeezed my hand tightly. To let go would have been much worse.

"Milk?" Mum asked.

"Thanks," Iris replied.

"You still take yours black, I assume?" she said to me.

It was such a small, everyday question that it hardly counted as a question at all, but it was my childhood. In that one sentence I heard her say she was hurt that I didn't call, that she missed me and still remembered me.

The minutes that passed as tea was offered round felt longer than any of Mum's Channel swims had ever been.

Mum perched on the edge of her chair. This was not the first awkward, impromptu afternoon tea she'd hosted and it probably wouldn't be the last. My father had always had a habit of bringing people home after church; not because he wanted to spend time with them, but so he could be seen with them.

"How is London?" my mother asked.

"Yeah, good," I said.

Iris shot me a look. "It's wonderful. We went to the theatre last week, and we have tickets to the new exhibition at the Tate next month."

"I've never been to the theatre," my mother said.

"That's terrible! You should come, we'll make a weekend of it. We'd love to have you."

My mother forced a smile. "How kind of you to offer."

"Never cared much for the theatre," Dad said. "Don't see the point in it."

"Some people enjoy it," I muttered.

"Sorry?" he said.

"Nothing," I replied.

"And what sort of things do you enjoy?" Iris asked, in her best schoolteacher voice.

"I don't think we've been introduced." His voice was like ice.

"Iris," she said.

"And how do you know Harriet?"

Before either of us could reply, my mother said, "She's a friend of Harriet's from London."

"She's my —"

"Friend from work," Mum interjected. She closed her eyes and shook her head. "John, would you get the biscuits, please?"

"What?" he said, unable to take his eyes off Iris, who tightened her grip on my hand.

I'd forgotten what it was like to be on the receiving end of his stare.

"John, the biscuits. Just put them on a plate."

He scowled — bristling, no doubt, at being asked to do women's work — and though I expected him to say something, he went into the kitchen without a word.

When he was gone my mother turned and looked me in the eye. "Why now?" she said.

It was a good question but I couldn't tell her that Iris had essentially kidnapped me and I couldn't tell her the reasons why it had to be that way, because I could barely admit to myself the thoughts that I was having. I looked at my mother and gave myself permission to acknowledge how I would answer her, if I could: It has been years, Mum, my wife has never met you and I'm pregnant with our first child, and the distance has faded my bad memories and I wonder if you still think of me. I wonder if you still love me and think of me as your daughter because sometimes in a random moment, I'm reminded of you and I wish I could tell you that I miss you. Regardless of the fact that she had stood by my father when he cast me out, I still loved her.

But even if I had been able to say those things to her, and even if she had wanted to hear them, saying them in the living room would have been wrong. Those answers were for the sea.

Dad came into the room with a fresh cup of tea and seemed startled to see us but tried not to show it.

"Where are the biscuits, John?"

"Sorry?"

Sighing, Mum went over to him and whispered, "Biscuits. I sent you to the kitchen for biscuits." She tugged at the cup but he wouldn't let go.

"What are you doing?" he said.

"You have a cup already." She pointed to the side table.

He looked at it and then at the cup in his hand. "That's gone cold."

"No it hasn't."

"How would you know?"

"John, please." She brushed the hair off her forehead. "The biscuits."

He tried to laugh it off. "How thoughtless. Can I get more hot water for anyone else?"

I shook my head and Mum turned him toward the kitchen. It's the little details that give us away.

"What's going on?" I asked.

"Nothing. Everything is fine."

The sound of things falling out of the cupboards came from the kitchen followed by my father's voice. I got up but Mum stopped me.

"Leave him."

"I'm just going to see if he needs any help." It was a sentence I never thought I would say. But just then he came back into the living room. Seemingly oblivious to us, he kept walking, starting up the stairs. I ignored my mother and followed him.

"Everything all right, Dad?" I said from the foot of the stairs as he gripped the banister.

He grumbled something in reply that I didn't catch.

I turned and my mother's eyes were closed, her shoulders hunched forward, and she looked old and tired. This was the woman who had raised my brother and me, who had swum the Channel. Her body language made her unrecognizable.

From the corner of my eye, I saw Iris turn, watching my father's movements with greater scrutiny than before.

"What's he doing?" I asked.

Mum leaned back for support. "I don't know."

I looked away and wished we hadn't come.

Mum pulled her lumpy grey cardigan tighter. "He's not always himself these days. I came home from a swim the other day to find he'd used all the cups in the house. And the first thing he did was ask why there were no clean mugs. They were everywhere." As she spoke she looked out at the garden.

Iris drew a breath in and I knew she was going to try and offer my mother some words of comfort, but I went to her side and squeezed her hand tightly. As I did I realized this was probably the longest we had ever held hands in all the years we had been together.

"This house is getting too big," Mum said. "With you in London and now Iain in Sydney . . ." She went to the mantel and ran her fingers over the picture frame that held one of the few family photos we had. It had been taken down at Shakespeare's Bay, the day after Mum had first tried to swim to France and hadn't succeeded. My brother and I were smiling but you could tell our expressions were put on for the camera. My father looked protective with his arm around Mum's shoulder and my mother looked crushed.

"Why is this here?" I asked.

"Your father likes to remember the good old days," she said.

I didn't know whether to be touched by the fact it was there, or hurt and angry that my father was only able to miss the old me.

"How is Iain?" I asked, to make conversation and distract myself from a line of thinking that would make the afternoon harder than it already was.

"Fine, I suppose. He hasn't phoned recently."

And that was the problem. They stayed here and waited for news to come to them. They were not people who picked up the phone to chat and keep in touch. That was not their job. If there was something newsworthy to relay, you called them.

"He's busy with work," she said.

She turned away from the picture, and as she was sitting down there was a horrible crash from upstairs.

She was off like a shot, shouting my father's name as she went. We followed her and there was something reassuring about seeing her run up the stairs.

Dad was on the floor of their bedroom surrounded by bags, boxes, and suitcases.

"What is wrong with you?" Mum hissed.

"I was looking for something."

She scooped things up and shoved them back in the wardrobe quickly, which was unlike her. "This has to stop. We've talked about this. If you want something just ask and I'll get it."

"Don't talk to me as though I'm a child."

"Stop acting like one."

Witnessing this private moment that passed between my parents made me want to run back to London as quickly as possible. It made me question what else she did for him and would have to do in the future. I was not ready for my parents to unravel.

My father appeared embarrassed and tried to laugh it off. "I suppose this is the way you'll remember me from now on, isn't it?"

I couldn't answer.

Mum helped him off the floor. "Who's your friend?"

"Iris, Dad."

He smiled. "Lovely name." He was acting as though the preceding hour had not occurred. "Now, who wants a nice cup of tea?" Without waiting for the reply, he went downstairs.

I put my hand on my mother's arm. "What's wrong with him?"

She was silent until Iris excused herself to help with the tea.

"Stress," she said.

"Is it?"

She folded up the old blue blanket and put it at the foot of the bed. It was the same blanket I remembered wrapping around her shoulders when we dragged her back into the boat after that first Channel attempt.

"All he has to say is that she has a lovely name?"

Mum nodded. "This is the first time I can see the benefits of this."

Without thinking I snapped, "Of what?" Daring her to put a name on it.

But she must have known what a name would mean and simply said, "Growing old."

"Is he all right?"

She shrugged in the same way she used to when I'd ask her what it was like to swim so far — in a nonchalant way that meant I was focused on the wrong thing.

"Pregnant?" she said.

My cheeks flushed and I put my hand on my belly. I wasn't even showing.

Everything was overwhelming and I felt as if I would burst into tears as she watched me, waiting for a reply. I wanted the impossible: for us to go back to that Boxing Day lunch and for them to react differently.

She slid the boxes into the closet side by side and her hand rested there briefly, as though she were steeling herself for what came next.

"Folic acid. You'll need supplements."

"I'm taking a multivitamin."

I picked up a worn leather case and paused. "Is this what he was looking for?"

She smiled. "It's one of his things."

"What?"

"It's mostly cups of tea, but it's driving me to distraction." She sighed. "I worry now, when I leave him for too long."

"Why?"

She straightened her cardigan and smoothed down her skirt. "You just never know what you might come home to." Her voice was tight and she was shoving things into the wardrobe now, not putting them away properly. Her haste made it obvious that this was something she would have to do again in the very near future.

I thought of Iris and her family and the weekly phone calls and the way her face lit up when she heard their voices. The way they laughed together and teased each other and knew each other in the deepest sense. I knew my parents' phone number and little else.

My mother took the case onto her lap and ran her hands over the salt-stained leather as though it were an old friend.

"He always brings it. In the boat, when I swim." She opened it and rummaged through the assortment of things that to the untrained eye looked like rubbish, removing an old jam jar of pebbles, which she held up to the light from the window.

"One pebble for one swim," she said to herself.

I would never forget her first Channel attempt. I had begged to be allowed to come along in the support boat with my father. I wanted to be part of it — she had spent so much time in the sea that I was convinced she preferred it to us. I wanted to see what it was out there, away from Dover, that called to her.

In the middle of the night, an hour before high tide, we had driven down to Shakespeare's Bay and my mother made her final preparations: double-checking things with the pilot, reassuring my father, and coating her skin in foul-smelling grease. I stood at the water's edge and looked across the Channel and all I saw was blackness — the water and the night sky blended into one another and seemed to swallow everything. I had no idea how we were going to keep an eye trained on my mother when it was impossible to see anything.

I got in the boat with my father, the pilot, and an official from the Federation and we motored maybe fifty metres away from the water's edge. When we were in place, my mother slipped into the water and we waited for her to swim to shore. When she was ten paces up from the waterline, she waved and the official waved back, which meant the swim had officially begun.

I heard her moving through the water, her body making a rhythmic sound as she began her swim. It was similar to the sound that the water made lapping at the sides of the boat but more consistent: her arms moved steadily, and when she turned toward the boat to breathe she looked happy, peaceful. In the shadowy morning I sat with my back against the railing of the boat and listened to her swim until the sky began to fade into daylight and I could see her in the sea.

She was a different person in the water. On land she could be clumsy but in the water she had grace and strength. Iain used to tell me he thought she was a mermaid, and the way she slipped through the water made me wonder if he might actually be right.

But it turned out that the practicalities of assisting on a Channel swim were not as interesting as my twelve-year-old imagination had hoped. Most of what needed doing amounted to sticking a bottle with tea or broth to the end of a pole, and offering it to her as though she were a trained seal. The only other thing to do was make sure she wasn't getting too tired or too cold, things I thought would be easy enough to do after the pilot had briefed my father and me on what we were looking for.

I religiously checked the wristwatch that my mother had given me specifically for that purpose. We had been on the boat for hours when the sun came up, and I marvelled at the large tankers on the horizon.

"Mum!" I shouted over the railing as I waved my arms.

She came nearer the boat, being careful to avoid touching any part of it because if she did the swim would be over and she would be disqualified.

It was beautiful out there, with nothing but water stretching out in every direction and the sun colouring the bottoms of the clouds all the oranges, pinks, and yellows I normally only saw in the evening.

"What's it like?" I asked.

She pushed her goggles up and floated on her back. The goggles had suctioned the skin inside their protective seal with so much force that the most prominent feature of her face were deep purple bruises.

"How are you?" my father asked her, standing next to me. "It's time to eat."

She was not in a hurry to meet our demands, happily floating in the light chop, but eventually she righted herself and stroked over to the pole.

"What is the name of the street you grew up on?" he asked.

"I'm fine, John."

"Name the street."

I watched her sculling slowly and knew we were not foremost in her mind.

"Ardent Road."

"When did we get married?"

"In the afternoon."

"Martha."

She said, "You were there, you don't remember?"

"I'm not asking for my own edification," he said. "I'm asking to make sure you're fit to continue."

"I'll be the judge of that."

My father gripped the railing of the boat, leaning over as far as he could, squinting to see her face as he offered her the flask of broth. But my mother ignored it all, looking straight ahead toward France.

"Martha," my father said in the tone he usually reserved for my brother and me when we were being especially trying. He waved the pole, trying to attract her attention.

"John," she replied. "We got married in the autumn and you wore a navy suit with a yellow tie and new shoes that gave you blisters, and as we drove from the church to the reception hall, you took off your socks and shoes and I put plasters on the backs of your heels. And we laughed because you had holes in your socks."

"What year?" he shouted across the railing.

She reached for the flask but missed, her fingers touching it briefly before it slipped out of reach. I held it as steady as I could but the sea was changing and the gentle chop was growing up.

"Mum!" I called as loud as I could.

She reached her arm out again and it was as if she was stuck in slow motion. Earlier on in the swim her hand had shot out from the water like a shark attacking its prey and the broth was down her mouth in moments, but now she swam slowly and carelessly, the efficiency gone from her movements.

I called her name again, and when she didn't reply I turned to my father who was as white as the chalk cliffs that watched over the shore. Even if both of us had not been intimately familiar with the elegance my mother had when she swam, it still would have been obvious that something was wrong.

A pair of gulls circled the boat and screeched their demands for food as I watched my mother's head — protected only by a yellow swimming cap — dip under the water. I waited for it to reappear, silently counting the seconds that passed, and realized that her feet had stopped kicking, too.

"Mum!" I screamed.

I felt the acid coming up from my belly and thought I would be sick. I stared at the water and tried not to think about the worst but I could not keep from imagining my mother disappearing into the sea.

"Do something!" I shouted at my father, who stood glued to his spot, glaring at the water.

The spray whipped across the deck, soaking us through and making it impossible to see anything. But what was more terrifying was that between the sound of our boat's motor and the sloshing of the sea, even if my mother were calling out for help there would be no way for us to hear her.

"We have to save Mum!"

"Go and get the pilot."

I did as I was told and soon we were all lined up along the side of the boat, looking and calling for my mother. And then I saw the yellow top of her head.

"Mum!" I screamed, pointing.

The pilot grabbed the life preserver and threw it out to her, but instead of moving toward it, she paddled away.

"Martha, grab hold!"

When she continued to ignore us, my father started throwing the various bottles of tea and broth at her but she didn't stop until one of them nearly hit her on the head.

"What are you doing?" she said, slurring her words.

"Get out," he said.

She shook her head.

"You nearly drowned."

She gasped for breath then put her face back in the water and kept on swimming, but it didn't look like she was actually moving; rather, it seemed as though she was swimming in place.

"Martha, stop!"

He looked for something else to throw at her but nothing was close to hand, and after a few more strokes my mother finally stopped and waited for him to speak.

This time he chose his words carefully. "You're going too slowly."

"Awfully critical."

He studied her, looking for a reason she would accept for getting out and giving up. "Are you cold?"

"I'm fine."

Her voice sounded drunk and it was obvious she wasn't able to keep her attention focused on any one thing.

My father bent down to me and said, "Tell the pilot she's getting out and to bring the boat as close as he can to her."

I did and the boat slowly edged its way closer.

"Martha, you have to get out now."

She shook her head.

"This is dangerous."

She looked at us with a dazed expression, and Dad bent down and reached his arms out to her. She lurched to and fro with no control and I had a horrible premonition that she would slip under the water and drift away from us. I didn't think she would have the strength to pull herself out even if she wanted to.

Dad couldn't swim and the pilot had to steer the boat, so I did what I thought was the only thing left to do. I took off my life jacket, shoes, and jumper — but just as I began to climb over the railing, my father grabbed my T-shirt and pulled me back onto the deck.

"What are you doing?"

"She needs help!"

Then we heard her shouting from the bottom of the ladder. Dad reached down and grabbed her underneath her arms, hauling her onto the deck as if she were a prize fish he had just done battle with. He fell backward and half of her body landed on top of him. She was gasping for breath and I helped him drag her the rest of the way onto the boat. I had never felt skin so cold. Touching her hands felt like taking ice from the freezer.

What I was not prepared for was the chafing. Where the straps of her costume touched her shoulders there were horrible red sores that looked like knees that had been skinned over and over again without having the chance to heal. Her lips were swollen and there were marks on her face, which I learned later were from some jellyfish she had encountered only a few miles into the swim.

Together, Dad and I helped her to the mound of fishing nets where we lay her down and wrapped her in blankets. I snuggled in next to her, wrapping my arm around her shoulders as best I could.

The first thing she said to us was not thank you. "How far did I make it?"

"A third of the way," my father said.

She said nothing, but as we motored back home and I lay with my head on her chest, happy to listen to her heartbeat and the whirr of the engine, I felt her body shaking and knew she was crying.

A few days later she was plaiting my hair and I asked her why she'd done it.

"To see," she said, as though it were obvious, as though whatever lay hidden in those two small words was simple enough to understand, even for someone my age.

"But you almost drowned," I said.

"But I didn't."

"But what if you did?" I said, yanking my hair away from her. "What if you did?"

She turned me around so I was facing her, put her hands on my bare knees, and locked eyes with me.

"Harry," she said. "I hope one day you know what it feels like to be completely and utterly compelled to see about something."

WHEN ALL OF the things Dad had pulled out of the wardrobe had been put back, my mother leaned against the bed.

"Did you ever see?" I asked.

"Sorry?"

"Do you remember, after the first time you tried, I asked you why you did it and you said, 'to see'?"

Poking out from underneath the wardrobe was an old post-card with French words on it that she picked up and looked at, smiling for a moment. "Yes. I did."

I wanted to ask what she had seen and if it had been worth it, but the voices from downstairs were getting louder so we went down and found Iris and Dad laughing as they looked at old photos.

"Here's Harriet on her bicycle," Dad said.

Mum and I stood on the edge of the living room and I don't think either of us could believe what we were seeing. It was obvious Iris had found her calling as a primary school teacher, the way she was listening to my father's stories as if they were the most fascinating things she had ever heard. The scene was so beautifully dangerous — it allowed me to imagine him holding our baby as Iris flipped through photo albums after Sunday lunch.

It was a fragile moment and I knew the right thing to do was savour it for what it was. It looked like the honest, mod-ern truth of a family. Without thinking, I believed in it and I threw my arms around Iris and kissed her cheek. She must have been caught up in it too, because she turned to me and we kissed on the mouth.

It was reckless. It was the best kiss I've ever had.

The sound of my father gasping and sputtering, stuck for the right words to say, shattered the glow of the moment and turned it into something familiar. Dad got up and stumbled backward and Iris reached out to catch him but he pushed her hand away and fell. The look of surprise, shock, and hurt on his face was not on account of the fall.

I knew what to expect next and I would not put Iris through it so I grabbed her hand and dragged her toward the front door.

"Harriet!" my father shouted as I opened the door.

We walked down the garden path to the car and I kept my arm around Iris's shoulders, protecting her from everything I had vowed I would never endure again.

I opened the passenger's side. "Get in."

"Harry," she said softly.

I didn't reply. Instead, I turned back to the house and took what I thought would be my last look at it. I forced myself to remember the happy times, when we had laughed and enjoyed each other for who we were, when I was too young to have been a disappointment.

My mother came flying out the front door waving a plastic carrier bag and trowel. "Wait!"

She bent down at the foot of the myrtle bush and dug.

"Mum," I said, going over to her.

She yanked a branch with small pink blossoms out of the ground, and its roots dripped dirt onto the grass as she held it up to me. She gave me the bag and motioned for me to hold it open.

"What are you doing?"

"Iris is who you went to see, isn't she?"

"I don't know what you're talking about."

"When you were a little girl and you asked me why I wanted to swim the Channel." She bit her lip. "It's her, isn't it?"

It took me a moment, but I worked out what she was trying to say: it wasn't the sea she was going to see, so much as a part of herself. All I could do was nod my head yes. She fiddled with one of the blossoms on the bush. "So you know, don't you?"

"Martha!" my father bellowed from the doorway.

I looked in his direction and she put her hand gently on my chin, refocusing my attention.

"Each time I swim, I leave my things under the same myrtle bush. It gets its strength from the sea."

"So do you," I said.

Her eyes were tearing up. "And you get yours from her."

I nodded.

"This," she said. "Take it in case you ever wonder if it's worth it."

We stood with the plant between us, between my father and my wife and the past and the future and just then, for a brief moment, my mother and I were in the present with each other, two women who understood what it was to feel compelled.

"When are you due?"

"September."

"Harriet," she said and hugged me quickly. I felt the tiny bulge of my stomach press into her and I held her tightly.

I forced myself not to cry as I got in the driver's seat. I heard her say something to my father but I couldn't work out what, and I remembered that night when I sat on the landing and saw them in the kitchen, the night before she started swimming again, when she had stood up for herself and the thing she needed most.

My parents stood in the doorway of my childhood home, watching and waiting for us to leave. If anyone had driven by they would have seen a normal family, waving goodbye. Only we knew that the unusual was secreted away in the recesses of our wardrobes, buried in the dirt at the end of the garden.

I had my hand on the clutch and I was ready to drive away but something made me stop. I felt I owed it to my mother after all these years to stand with her against my father's ideas of what was right and what was wrong.

I got out and leaned across the roof of our car. "Remember," I said. "That we came to see."

As we drove down the road, I looked over at Iris and put my hand on hers, squeezing it. "Thank you," I said.

When we arrived home it was dark and we were hungry and exhausted, and while Iris busied herself cobbling something together for dinner, I potted the plant, hoping it would grow and carry on the tradition I decided the women in our family would hold dear.

My hands were covered in dirt and all I could see in the plant was my mother's face as we pulled away that afternoon, wearing the same expression she wore whenever she looked at the sea.

JOHN ASKS

JOHN, 1955

THE GIRL BEHIND the counter at the florist's grinned as I collected the corsage.

"Special day?" she asked. She had that knowing excitement unique to women in certain situations. It unnerved me — it was as though they were all connected through some invisible wiring, or tuned into a frequency that was unavailable to men; in circumstances like these they knew precisely what to do, what to wear, and what would happen. Whereas men — myself more than most — seemed to bumble along as best we could, finding ourselves in confusing positions, unable to telegraph the most basic social graces. This, I had learned from my father, was one of the benefits of marriage.

"Be careful when you pin it on her dress. My boyfriend's pricked me before."

I stared at my shoes and prayed that she would stop talking so I could leave.

"What's the occasion?"

I put my wallet on the counter and she handed me the corsage: a red rose surrounded by a tasteful amount of white baby's breath. My first instinct was to smell it, and it was then that I realized this evening would be the first memory I would have of Martha when she smelled like something other than the sea.

The walk to Martha's parents' house would not need as much time as I had given myself, even if I dragged it out by taking the long way and moving as slowly as possible. It was only four in the afternoon, and already the walls of my flat had felt as if they were closing in on me; I couldn't go back there. So I went along to Martha's, trying my best to remain unconcerned that it might make me appear too eager or too keen.

I walked up the road to the house and looked at things with more interest than usual — if things went as planned, then this walk would no longer be part of my life. I forced myself to notice things I thought Martha might: the washing hung out to dry on the Thomases' house, which must mean that Mrs. Thomas was over her illness and they would not be requiring so much help. The newspapers had piled up at the foot of the Andersons' front door, which could mean that he was away for a filthy weekend up in Blackpool again. What gossip did Martha and I have in our future? What would our new neighbourhood bring for us once we were married and settled into our own home?

The very idea of it was thrilling. To know, as I walked home from my administrative job down at the port, that I was walking toward something instead of away; that waiting for me at home was the woman I was in love with.

When her mother opened the door she looked surprised. "John," she said. "We weren't expecting you just yet."

It was unusual that she didn't invite me in immediately,

but I tried not to take that as a bad omen. "It's such a beautiful evening, Mrs. Munro. I thought maybe we might take a walk before our reservation at six thirty."

Martha's mother bit her lip and looked nervously over her shoulder.

"Is everything all right?" I asked.

"Mmm, yes," she said, fiddling with her bracelet. "Everything is fine. Unfortunately, Martha isn't back yet."

"Sorry?"

Mrs. Munro forced a pleasant smile. "She's just popped out."

"Popped out?"

"I'm sure she won't be much longer. Come inside." She opened the door and waited for me to walk into the living room, where I knew Martha's father would be on the couch, staring at something just out of reach.

I followed her into the room with its closed curtains and stale air, and sat on the end of the brown corduroy sofa.

"Richard," her mother said. "John's early."

Martha's mother had different tones for me and for her husband: I knew when she was speaking to me because she had a singsong voice that always made me feel like a child. But when she spoke to Richard, her inflection changed and all I heard were years of admonishment and frustration.

Richard looked at me and nodded his head with the economy of movement of a man unwilling to expend any more energy than absolutely necessary. Martha had told me that he spent a great deal of time sitting in this room, looking out at the garden through a small crack in the curtains. These he had recently, with the warm weather, changed from heavy wool to lace, which let a specific and dreamy kind of light into the room.

The living room was his domain. Martha's mother had taken charge of everything else, but she did not dare to come in here and disturb her husband's thoughts. When I came to pick Martha up the first time, she introduced me to her parents in the neutral territory of the front corridor; over time, I learned that in their silent domestic wars, Richard had seceded all ground with the exception of this room. It alone was no longer subject to his wife's relentless improvements. The refinements, as she preferred them to be called, included walls that had been painted a blistering, high-gloss white and required constant monitoring to ensure maximum brightness at all times, along with the banishment of anything that might be referred to as dark, sombre, dour, or joyless. This gave the impression that the house — barring Richard's personal refuge — existed in a state of perpetual readiness for a party that, as far as I knew, had never happened and never would.

The room was more constricting than my flat. As I sat there on the sofa, my chest tightened until I felt as though my lungs were a vacuum, hoovering up all the air and selfishly keeping it to themselves, while my heart pumped aggressively in my chest, desperate for oxygen.

"Early?" Richard said. "For what?"

"Martha," I replied. I took the dark green velvet box out of my breast pocket and placed it on the cushion between us.

He turned his head slightly and rested his fingertips on the box. "Martha," he said.

"It's such a lovely day, seems a shame to waste it."

"I expect that's what she thought."

"Is she —"

He nodded. "Where else?" The way he said it needed no visual clues. It was clear he was proud.

Forgetting myself, I sighed loudly. She was always in the water. And if she wasn't, then she had just come from the sea, water dripping slowly out of her ears and making it difficult for her to hear me; or else she was about to go to the sea because the winds were perfect or the tide was in. Other men I knew worried about their girlfriends meeting someone more attractive, or with more money.

"Good," I said, trying to salvage things.

"Is it?" He cocked his eyebrow.

"Of course. She needs to get it out of her system. Soon enough, there won't be much time for it."

"Is that so?"

"I'd like to start a family and I'm sure that Martha —"

"Did she ever tell you about her first swim?"

I shook my head. To me, Martha swimming was something that happened in the continuous present; it was an ongoing process with no beginning point. I had never imagined a moment in her life when she hadn't been a swimmer. Yet I also believed that her swimming was a way of temporarily filling the void that our marriage and subsequent young family would soon replace.

"I heard a shriek," Richard said. "And then a slap as she hit the water. I didn't see her fall, but a friend of mine did. He said she hit the surface flat." He held his hand out to demonstrate, palm down. "It was a miracle she didn't break any bones. Falling flat onto the water, ten, maybe fifteen feet down from the pier."

The room had become stifling. I couldn't sit there any longer, waiting for Martha to come home. I stood up and held my hand out.

"I think I'll go and see if I can drag her onto dry land," I said.

He shook my hand and gave me a funny smile. "Best of luck, son."

As I walked down to the water, I wondered if she was putting me through a test, to see if I was worthy. I would pass such a test easily, I decided; but then I began to wonder if it wasn't a test after all. Maybe Martha wasn't swimming parallel to the shore; maybe she was swimming away from me.

It was beautiful; the sun was shining and there was hardly any breeze to speak of. I went to Martha's usual spot, which was marked by a myrtle bush. I found her bag, clothes, and towel neatly folded on top of one another and sat down to wait. All around me were the happy sounds of a summer evening: children laughing and running, barbecues, and radios. It was clear enough that in the distance you could almost see France. I felt completely out of place in my navy suit, necktie, and polished black shoes — clothes I wore only for the most important situations. The last time I had worn them was when my manager made the announcement that I had been given a promotion. They were serious clothes for serious things and I could not have been more serious about wanting to marry her.

I must have looked ridiculous sitting on the ground, sweating in my suit, because I caught people near to me staring. Though the seaside was open to everyone, that's not where I felt I was then; I was at Martha's private beach, looking at her sea and her water.

It was her special spot, and as I sat there I was able to see it through her eyes.

She had described it to me on our first date, despite my protestations of "I grew up here, I know what the shore looks like."

Martha had laughed, saying, "Okay, tell me what you see, then."

"The white cliffs, the pier, the ships. The sea."

"That's it? That's all you see?"

"What else is there? It's scenery. It's what you show people who visit from out of town."

She had shaken her head as though pitying me. "Maybe you should have your eyes checked."

"My eyes are just fine, thank you."

"The pebbles sing when the water washes over them," she said. "And the way the currents swirl at the end of the pier where the water has to move differently, where it gets thrown off course. There's the seabed, which holds all of history right there in the sediment. Everything that ever was and ever will be — part of it ends up there, on the ocean floor. The waves that lap at your toes when you stand on the water's edge have come a very long way and they've seen more than you and I ever will." Her expression as she spoke made me want to freeze her face in that exact way forever.

Now I squinted at the horizon, hoping to catch a glimpse of her in her yellow cap. The shallows were crowded with children swimming and splashing though, and it was hard to see past them. I took off my socks and shoes, rolled up my trousers, and waded into the water, steering clear of the children in an effort to keep my suit in good condition. But part of me wondered if I might increase the chances of her saying yes if, when I asked, there was sand under my nails as I slipped the ring on her finger.

Scanning the horizon for the little yellow dot revealed only the sea stretching out into the distance, which made it seem as if the world ended just there, just out of reach. The ferry looked like it was about to fall off the edge of the known world and I felt my chest tighten again. If the ferry could fall off, then so could Martha.

THE FIRST TIME I had seen her in her element was on our third date. We were a group of three couples — her best friend Doreen along with her boyfriend, and my mate from work Thom and his girlfriend — and we had taken a picnic to the headland atop the cliffs, overlooking the sea below. It was a beautiful day and we walked a ways up the headland searching for somewhere secluded. The girls walked ahead of us and Martha walked slightly ahead of them.

"Martha, you've had my custard, what did you think?" Doreen was saying.

I waited for her to look over her shoulder and reply.

"It wasn't that bad, was it?" Doreen said.

When Martha still didn't turn around, Doreen reached out and touched her arm.

Martha jumped. "What?"

Doreen laughed. "Where do you go? And where are you rushing off to?"

"The tide's going out. If we hurry we can still go for a swim before it's too rocky."

"You're not going to climb down the side of the cliffs just to go swimming, are you?"

"Of course not. There are stairs carved into the rock. Up ahead. So we need to keep moving."

Doreen shook her head and put her hand on her friend's shoulder. "It's not that kind of outing."

But Martha was different from the other two girls. They'd had their hair done for the afternoon and were wearing nice sundresses, while Martha wore shorts and her hair — cut in a short crop — looked like it was in need of a thorough brushing. The others giggled and gossiped but Martha was completely oblivious. When she turned to me a moment later I felt myself stand slightly taller, smile a bit broader.

"You'll go swimming with me, won't you?"

"Of course," I said. What else could I have said?

"Since when do you swim?" Thom said.

I glared at him. "I'll be fine."

"Why wouldn't you be?" Martha said.

Thom watched her, trying to gauge her knowledge from her expression. "John can't swim," he said.

I blushed as she looked at me with disbelief, and prayed that my lack of aquatic abilities would not draw our afternoon to a close.

"Martha," Doreen said. "No one else wants to go swimming. Let's just have a nice lunch." She held up the basket, trying to tempt her, and Martha looked straight at me.

"Let's go swimming," I said.

She beamed and jogged up ahead and I ran to catch up. We walked further on and then Martha turned off into the scrub grass on the edge of the cliff. It was extraordinary: the white cliff face was shaved off, a sheer drop down to the froth below, which from this height seemed as gentle as soap suds. All I saw as I looked out was Martha and then the sea and then a haze that dissolved into the horizon. It looked like she was the last person, standing at the edge of the world. She looked over her shoulder and I couldn't be certain, but I thought she winked before stepping over the edge, disappearing from sight. I followed quickly, wanting her back in my sight again, and found her picking her way down steps carved into the side of the cliff. She was dwarfed by it all, but she was confident in each step, racing excitedly toward the sea as though it was calling her name.

The nearer to the sea we got, the more slippery the steps became, the algae and seawater making the surface slick.

"Be careful," Martha said, placing her hand on the rock face, pausing to look back at me.

At the bottom, there were several flat slabs and Martha stood atop the largest one to the right of the steps. She tugged her pullover off in one quick motion and for the first time I saw how bronzed her back was; the straps of her swimming costume were not lined up as they would usually be, letting me see the tan lines that criss-crossed her back.

She was not afraid or ashamed or thinking of anything other than a swim. She stared out at the sea with such devotion and desire that I knew then I would only be happy if she looked at me with the same expression.

"Do you swim often?" I asked.

"Every day."

"It's a lovely way to spend summers."

"I swim in winter too."

"Here? Isn't it too cold?"

She smiled. "I don't always stay in very long, but the thing to do is avoid drying up."

The sea lapped gently at the edge of the rock and she slipped into the water, which was waist-high. She held her hand out to me. I removed my socks and shoes, and hesitated. I hadn't anticipated this and was unprepared. I felt her watching me, and in one swift motion I undid my trousers and let them fall to the ground. Then I edged my way to the brink of the rock. I looked at the water and couldn't see the bottom. Martha stood there swaying softly in the current with her arm outstretched, waiting for me. My eagerness was stronger than my fear. I took her hand and stepped in, fumbling and slipping forward, until finally steadying myself with my hands on her broad shoulders.

"You really can't swim?" she asked.

I shook my head and committed to memory the spot where each fingertip touched my skin as she held onto my arm.

"I'll teach you," she said, before she dove headfirst into an oncoming wave, which crested into me, knocking me backward. Perhaps she thought that I would learn simply by watching. Coughing, I steadied myself and watched her swim away. All I could do was wait and hope she would come back to me.

WHEN I FINALLY saw the yellow blip of her bathing cap out there in the shark-grey water, I shouted instinctively, even though I knew there was no way she could hear me. I went toward her, wading in up to my knees — as far as I dared to go without her nearby. Though she had promised to teach me, I still had not learned to swim and perhaps there was something in that — perhaps she had thought better of it, preferring to keep the sea to herself. And so I remained connected to the underwater world through the superstitions of fishing boats and ferries, where women were unwelcome unless they were about to give birth and no one learned to swim. At first the idea of a sailor being unable to swim sounds like madness, but when you realize that swimming will only prolong death and bring false hope to dire circumstances, it begins to make more sense.

I waved my arms over my head, drawing the attention of everyone on the shore and in the sea but Martha. Once again, the water had put itself between us. It was a protective barrier that encircled her, guarding her and keeping me at bay.

I went back to her towel and sat down to wait. I had learned months ago that when she was in the water she could not see me or hear me. When she was in the water what remained on the land did not exist.

But she must have known today was the day. Her mother was terrible at keeping secrets, and some had been rather vocal about the fact that I was taking too much time in asking. We had been dancing around the idea for the better part of a month. If it was time for the big question, then why was she hiding in the sea?

The yellow dot of her head came in and out of view as she swam against the current, parallel to shore. With each pull of her arms she made subtle progress; I could see it was hard going against the wishes of the water, and I was jealous. I didn't understand what it was, precisely, that the sea had over me — when I looked at it all I saw was a cold, foreboding, and vast thing with its own language, rhythm, and form.

It was nearly six and she showed no signs of coming in; our reservation would certainly be missed. Was she taking her time on purpose? Or was she avoiding me completely, sparing me the agony of a face-to-face rejection?

All around me were pebbles, stones, and rocks. Martha's beach was not sandy — it was ill-suited to sitting about relaxing; it required one to make an effort to enjoy it. I folded her towel in half and then in half again, and it offered enough cushioning for the moment. I looked at the sea, at my watch, and back out to sea. The yellow dot had moved sideways and no closer to shore.

What if she didn't say yes? Then what? What could I do?

I picked up one pebble and placed it atop another, both shot through with rust-coloured lines on a bright background washed white over hundreds of years by the sea's force, the gentle and constant repetition of the waves erasing what was once there. Washed smooth with the salt like Martha's skin. I put those pebbles on another, larger one with lines ground into it, like the calcification of a fossil, the sea proving to me that it would do what it wanted with what it had, whenever it so pleased.

I chose a flat pebble — balancing it atop the others — as grey as the winter sky when I first set eyes on her. She had been riding her bicycle in the pouring rain, pedalling standing up wearing an old white fisherman's pullover. She was looking up to the sky, face radiant with rainwater, short brown fringe plastered to her forehead. I had been under the awning of the butcher's shop holding a bag of mince. What caught my attention was her smile, beaming as she soaked up all the moisture from the sky.

Another pebble, another flash of how it started between us. Near the beginning, when I was still trying to learn to swim and I felt her hands on my bare back as she held me up in the sea. I had looked up and seen the clouds and water splashed over me, and when I opened my eyes again there she was, looking down at me, her face in place of the sun.

At a dance, trying to lead her around the floor as she tripped over her feet, apologizing for every misstep. She had walked unevenly, as though expecting the ground to shift at any moment.

In a beer garden on a warm afternoon, staring at her bare knees covered in bruises and marks — a catalogue of all the tables and chairs she had walked into that week.

Seven pebbles now, and seven reasons why I needed her to say yes. The way she made me feel calm the moment I saw her, another reason. How she made me want to show her what I was really like, that I struggled to find my place in the world, to understand the way things worked. How I wanted to tell her everything and babbled, yammered, and chuntered on through afternoons and evenings spent together walking and dancing. The way she had of turning whatever anger or frustration I had developed during the day into nothing, with only a smile. Being near her was all I needed to lift the fog from my moods.

More pebbles: one white, one brown and mottled like an egg.

I imagined our future: a white house with a smart little garden out back; dining together each evening, and breakfasting in the conservatory on stormy mornings; at Christmas, a tree with presents and a roast duck on the table; birthdays and anniversaries. All the moments that would blend together to build a blur of happiness. We could easily make this future ours if only she would come out of the water. I imagined going to sleep with my arms around her and waking up similarly entangled. Dangerous thoughts to have on a warm evening.

I thought of cups of tea between the folds of the Saturday papers, the voices of our children laughing in the fading autumn light. A family would be mine and it would be a reflection of my worth as a man. I would go home to the people who loved me and the people I loved the most. It was all I wanted and everything that mattered.

I looked up to check on the progress my yellow dot was making and I was surprised to see it swimming back to me. I straightened my tie.

When she emerged from the water I watched her walk through the surf and the sea ran off her skin. It was touching her shoulders, arms, waist, and thighs, as if daring me to try and win her away.

She saw me immediately when I stood and her face lit up. Her gaze made me feel as if I were shimmering.

She took off her yellow cap as she weaved through the families, barbecues, and children. I could tell by the way she walked that she liked that I was watching. I had no choice; I couldn't take my eyes off her. Everyone else on the beach faded away and all I could see was Martha in a dripping-wet navy costume with wide straps across her shoulders and, when she turned around, the bottom seams creeping upward as though purely to tempt me, as though the suit itself understood its purpose was to show her off.

"John," she said. "What are you doing here?"

My chest contracted. She wasn't expecting me.

"Dinner," I said. "I booked us a table."

"But that's not for ages yet."

I held out my arm and she held my wrist so she could see the time.

She clamped her hands over her mouth in shock. "I lose track," she said.

I wrapped the towel around her shoulders.

"I'm sorry," she said.

I took advantage of the situation and held her tightly through the towel as her hair dripped on my face.

"Have you been waiting long?"

"No," I lied.

I would wait as long as it took.

Later, after she had changed and we had eaten chips instead of the fancy dinner I had planned for us, the crowds along the promenade in which we so often lost ourselves felt too close. In need of space, we walked up to the top of the cliffs, past the port, and along the headland, surrounded only by the grass and the night sky and the sea. I still had not asked, and I thought of postponing it and inviting her out the next evening. It would be the only way to salvage the evening. We had missed our reservation, the corsage had wilted, and I was losing my nerve. The night I proposed had to be worthy. The beginning had to be right.

"Let's go down there," she said, pointing to the water at the bottom of the cliffs.

"It's dark."

"I know."

"Do you ever want to go anywhere but the sea?"

She didn't hear me, or if she did then she didn't answer because she was already scrambling down the stairs cut into the rock.

"Do you remember? One of our first dates?" I called to her as I stepped cautiously forward, grateful for the nearly full moon.

"It was our third," she replied. "Careful, nearer the bottom the steps are covered with algae."

The sound of the sea in the dark is one of the most frightening sounds I have ever heard. In front of me was the water but all I saw was a yawning black hole. At my feet I heard the waves singing over the pebbles, and further out that song turned into a roar more terrifying than a lion's. It was impossible for me to tell how big the surf was — all I knew was that away from the harbour, we were not protected by the sea wall. Randomly, the moonlight illuminated the crests of certain waves as they peaked and folded in on top of themselves, flattening out and racing toward us.

"What are you doing?" I shouted.

Martha was knee-deep in the water, the foam rushing backward and forward, making her sway as though a branch in a breeze. She turned toward me and said, "I've always wanted to swim at night."

I said, "You can't go in now."

She looked me in the eye as she undressed, and when she was just in her bra and knickers it was as though she was daring me to do the same. The look in her eye quickened my pulse, and I reached my hand out for her bare stomach and she pulled me to her.

"The waves won't be big here," she said. "While the tide's still out, there's a long, shallow seabed. You've got to go at least a hundred yards out to get anything close to little breakers." She put her hand over mine. "Don't worry."

The sea sounded like a jet engine and I imagined it coming closer and closer until a rogue wave simply reared up and crushed us both. The water was unpredictable; things could change quickly that could not be changed back.

I drew my other hand around her waist, up her back, around her shoulder, and down her arm before taking her hand in mine.

"Please," I said.

She squeezed my hand and pulled me closer, further into the water. To one side I felt the force of the sea, to the other side was the unbreakable face of the white cliffs. But it was what was in front of me that I was interested in as she moved closer and kissed my neck, cheek, and mouth.

We kept walking as the water curled around our legs, but the rocks shifted under my feet and I lost my balance, ruining the mood and my suit as I fell onto my hands and knees in the sea.

"Are you all right?" Martha asked, her face next to mine in seconds.

It was the right moment.

"Martha," I said.

"Yes?" she said.

In an instant I forgot everything I had planned to say and I fumbled with my words. What if she says no, screamed again through my mind; what if she says no, then what? We would stop seeing each other. I would never see her again. I would go back to my work, to Friday nights in the pub with the boys, and weekends spent avoiding my landlady and her prying questions. Humiliated and forced to pretend otherwise, compelled to project an outward appearance of happiness.

"Martha," I said. I leaned back on my knees, the water swirling around my waist, and I looked at her face as the moonlight cast a glow across one cheek.

"It's beautiful," she said.

I put my hand on my breast pocket to check for the ring and then I noticed she was looking at the water. Though our focus was different she wasn't wrong; everything was beautiful.

"Martha," I said as I took the ring from my pocket. The sea moved in to protect her, the currents tugging her toward the open water while they pushed me back toward dry land. The water was like a puppy nudging his master's leg for attention. It wasn't overtly forceful, but it was clear it planned to overpower me slowly, in the same way that it would eventually turn rocks into fine grains of sand.

Being down on both knees was not traditional, but I told myself it was one for her, and one for the sea. I held the ring up. "Will you marry me?" The sea snaked around my waist.

"John," she said softly.

I watched her face in the moonlight as she absorbed the question.

The water grew stronger and more determined, and I was reaching for her ring finger when a small wave hit me at the wrong angle and I was knocked off balance. My hands flew out to my sides to provide anchor.

She grabbed hold of my shoulders, steadying me. "Yes," she said.

But the sea disagreed and the surf rushed in with tidal force, knocking me down again. I flapped around like a stray piece of seaweed.

Martha took hold of my hands and pulled me up. She cupped my chin and gently wiped the water off my face.

"Yes," she said, before she kissed me.

Her hands ran along my shoulders, back, and waist and I pulled her as close as possible, her body pressing into mine, and then when she paused to take a breath, I reached for her left hand.

"The ring?" I said, feeling nothing new on her finger.

"What?" she asked.

"Where is it?"

We looked at her hand and then at the water.

We searched through the water as the tide pushed inland, taking back the ground that had been relinquished during low tide, but we didn't find the ring. I wanted to know if she sided with the sea but I couldn't risk knowing the answer.

"John," she said. "The tide's coming in. We need to go."

"We need to find it."

"We won't be able to."

"We have to look harder."

"There's no point. If we're meant to have it, it will come back to us."

"Do you really believe that?" I asked.

She nodded.

"I don't share your trust."

"That doesn't matter," she said.

"It doesn't?"

"Of course not."

"What does?"

She held her hand out and when I took it she led me toward the back of the narrow beach, where the cliffs met the ground. We gathered our clothes and at the foot of the cliffs I saw a shrub or bush, it was hard to tell. I pulled at it, wrestling with a small end that did not want to snap, until finally I tore a section free. The sea was chasing us, licking at our heels as we made a break for dry land. It was so dark that I had to rely on Martha to guide me safely back to the stairs. She felt her way along the cliff face and I followed, my hands running over the rough chalky stones, and when she paused at the foot of the staircase, I did not look up. It did not matter to me where we went, because I would follow her anywhere.

She squeezed my hand tightly. "You asked."

I took her hand and wrapped the piece of torn shrub around her finger. "You said yes."

LA MANCHE

HENRY, 2010

I PUSHED THE open door further so I could pop my head into the house.

"Martha?" I called. My feet remained planted outside the doorway. Technically, I wasn't yet walking uninvited into their home.

"Hello?" I said.

Webb galumphed over to me and pushed his head into my thigh. I petted him, then nudged him out of the way.

"Where is everyone, old boy?" I asked the dog. By way of reply he hobbled into the kitchen and stood at her side.

"Sorry. The door was open."

She didn't say anything.

"Martha? The door was open."

She said, "Oh, yes."

The kitchen was in a terrible state by her standards. Two days' worth of breakfast dishes cluttered the table, the drying rack was full and poorly organized, the cupboard above the stove was open and, worst of all, the washing-up gloves were crumpled on the side of the counter, heaped on top of a dirty pot.

"Is everything all right?"

She nodded but didn't look up from the picture she was holding. I couldn't make out who was in the photo, but the frame was a style I remembered as being popular decades earlier, when the fashion was for things to be ornate. It was oak with gold trim and it made the picture feel historical, like a snapshot that had captured the moment of a lifetime.

"Where's John?"

"Newcastle. Golfing weekend."

"I didn't see you out this morning." I sat down next to her at the table.

"Were you spying on me, Henry?"

"No."

She ran her fingers over the frame. "Henry."

"I happened to be doing some gardening this morning and I didn't see you," I said. I had been hiding my loneliness behind the shrubbery since I had met them, and they had always been kind enough to play along.

"You felt driven to see to that disaster you call a garden first thing this morning?"

"I take inspiration when it comes."

Martha gave me a sideways glance. "Henry, you have lived here for eight years. In that time have you not managed to make any other friends?"

"You didn't come."

I saw her sigh and knew I was wearing on her nerves more than usual.

"I was busy," she said.

"With what?" I put my hand on her arm, but she shrugged it off.

"The care and maintenance of my life."

"Sounds thrilling."

"Blew my hair straight back."

"So why was the door open?"

"Don't you have something you ought to be doing? Something that can only be properly seen to at your house?"

"It's my day off."

"I wish it was mine."

Webb put his chin on my leg and whimpered. "Has he been out?"

The photo clattered loudly as she set it on the table. "Yes, Henry, he's been out."

"Is everything all right?"

"Please go." She turned the photo over, so it lay face down.

"The door was open."

"Henry."

"I just want to be sure."

"Why does it matter? An open door. Who cares?"

She turned her head toward me and she looked tired, with black bags under her eyes and a weariness about her whole body.

"Martha."

"Knowing won't change a thing."

"So tell me."

"It's a door."

"It was open."

"I left it open so Webb could go out." She pulled her cardigan tightly around her waist and went to the sink.

"No you didn't."

"I'm in no mood."

"You're only prolonging this," I said, going to stand beside her.

She moved a few paces away and began organizing the dishes: stacking the plates underneath a bowl, turning the cutlery all in one direction. "Prolonging this? Henry. This is my house and I'm afraid I'm going to have to ask you to leave."

"This is a neighbourhood watch area. I'm your neighbour. I'm watching."

"Do it from the comfort of your own home."

"I'm worried about you."

"For God's sake! It's just a bloody door, Henry! Not everything in this life has to end in tragedy!" She turned on the tap and poured dish soap into the sink. "Maybe I'm coming down with what John has."

"Alzheimer's isn't catching."

"We don't say that word in this house." She pulled on the washing-up gloves.

"The door was open. The word flew out."

She threw the sponge into the sink. "Stop it." Water splashed on her cardigan, but didn't sink into the wool; instead, it dripped onto the floor.

"You don't have dementia."

"No," she said. "I don't."

I went to the sideboard where the phone and the calendar were and I looked to see if anything was listed under today's date. It was blank. But the day before, there was an appointment scheduled for half past three. I went back to the table and picked up the picture.

"Where was this taken?" I asked.

It was her in the picture. She wore a modest swimsuit, several decades out of fashion now, and stood on a sandy beach looking over her shoulder at the sea.

"Cap Gris Nez," she said as she tied the threadbare floral apron on.

"When you arrived?"

A clean spoon crashed onto the draining board. "Before I left."

Another spoon clattered against the aluminum. "Was that your best swim?"

I grabbed her hand as she was about to drop another. "What do you mean?" she asked, as I prised the last piece of cutlery from her and set it quietly in its place.

"Your fastest."

"I don't know," she said, arranging the plates on the side to drip dry.

"How can you not know?"

She turned off the tap and brushed the crumbs off the counter onto the floor for Webb. Pointing at the freshly washed dishes, she simply instructed: "Dry."

I took the old frayed cloth that hung in front of the stove and stood to her left, following directions.

"The time was never the point."

"But it's what you wrote on the walls."

Her focus moved from the dishes to the counter, which she cleaned with such intensity I thought she might actually remove the finish. "Do you go to the White Horse Inn often?"

"Just once. But I saw your name, and the dates and times."

"I hope Brian made you pay for your drinks."

"I told him you were my neighbour."

"Did he believe you?"

I shrugged. "Who knows? I had to pay for my drinks, though."

"You only get a free drink after you've swum the Channel. One drink per swim. Those are the rules."

"How many free drinks has he given you?"

"Nine."

"That many?"

She cocked her eyebrow at me. "And how many times have you swum the Channel?"

I dried a spoon and set it down carefully on the counter.

"That's what I thought," she said.

"Did you only swim from France the once?"

"Henry, why all the questions?"

"The door was open."

"Most doors do."

"Yours is never left open. Webb might run out into traffic again."

"He's learned."

"What if he hasn't?"

"Then he'll lose another leg."

"Martha, why was your door open? Someone could have just walked in."

"Someone did," she said. She ran her gloved fingers over the bottom of the saucepan and, satisfied that it was clean, she rinsed it once more in the sink before handing it to me.

"I was caught up in other things," she said.

"What things?"

"Have you always been this nosy?"

"No."

"Don't feel it's a skill you need to pursue for my sake." She removed the washing-up gloves and dropped them in the sink.

I looked at them, floating on top of the soapsuds, and then I looked at her.

"Something's not right," I said.

She smiled politely.

"Is it John?"

She shook her head.

"The children? Iain? Harriet?"

She shook her head again.

"Who, then?"

Martha shook her head and looked at the floor.

I lowered my voice. "Is it you, Martha?"

She closed her eyes and looked away. Before she spoke, she drew in a large breath and exhaled loudly.

"If you must know, Henry, I've just had some news from the doctor."

"What did he say?"

"She."

"What?"

"The doctor. He's a she."

I rolled my eyes. "What did she say?"

Martha pressed her lips together and smoothed her cardigan down. She looked out onto the street, through the window that was the same in my house and was my prime twitching location when I was waiting for her.

She lowered her voice. "She said…"

Pausing, putting her hands in her pockets and lifting her chin.

"She said I have cancer."

That word filled up every inch of space in the kitchen. It floated into the living room and settled with the dust onto the picture frames that sat on the mantel. It ran up the stairs and flung itself into the bedrooms, burrowing deep under the duvets until it settled back down in the kitchen, in the space between Martha and me.

"You can't have cancer. You're in good health. You swim the Channel, for Christ's sake."

She glared at my language and I blushed.

"Apparently, cancer doesn't care."

There were a multitude of questions I wanted to ask, but all I could manage was, "Is the doctor sure?"

She scowled at me. "Why would she say such a thing if she was anything less than absolutely certain?"

"I'm sorry."

"So am I."

She looked at me then, chin jutting out in the late-morning sun that streamed through the window, and I thought I saw something behind her usual defiance. It was not fear, and it was not weakness, but it might well have been an idea forming in the back of her mind, an acknowledgement perhaps, that she was not quite as invincible as she thought.

THAT WAS ONLY the second time I had ever heard Martha come close to apologizing.

The first time was when I met John.

All that had separated me from the end of my shift was another loop and a half around the centre of town. As I drove down the high street I focused not on trying to find another boarded-up shop, but on what I might eat for my supper. Driving a bus was monotonous but it suited me.

Nothing out of the ordinary had happened that day. Mrs. Baullard had gotten off in front of the supermarket and had advised me of the low prices I ought to be taking advantage of. Dottie and her two boys had been waiting after school and had all smiled and waved to me as they got on.

Down near the harbour is where I picked John up, though I didn't know his name at the time. He was standing at the stop but it wasn't immediately clear to me whether he was waiting for the bus or just standing there. He didn't look like the sort who took the bus: grey suit, waistcoat, nice tie. Maybe it was his posture. He didn't look expectant, which is what you normally get from people waiting for the bus. I had been driving a bus since I moved to Dover, over five years before, and I had learned where people fit into the grand scheme of things. John looked like someone who had a motor and drove.

Since he was at the stop, I pulled up to the curb and opened the doors.

"Hi," I said as he stepped on-board. "Car in the garage, then?"

He grew upset as I spoke to him. As if he had spent a lifetime driving and was suddenly demoted to the bus.

He smiled awkwardly. "Sorry."

"It's ninety pence."

John fumbled with his wallet and then shoved his free hand into his jacket pocket, producing a mess of coins that he moved around a bit, looking for the right combination.

"Here," I said, picking out the correct fare. "It's easier with two hands."

He looked at me and for a moment I thought he was going to say something. But he must have changed his mind, because he simply nodded curtly and took a seat toward the back.

The bus was filling up with the afternoon crowds of schoolchildren and childminders but it was by no means crowded. I watched him in the mirror and he looked anxious, staring out the window. It was as if he were searching for something he had lost.

The last loop of the day can be the hardest. I wanted to be at home and away from the repetition. I was at the point when all I heard in my head was that nursery rhyme, *The wheels on the bus go round and round, round and round*, and not even the loud music coming from a group of teens could drown it out. My thoughts were going in circles, and John, who was sat near the back, was out of the loop.

When I was a child my father always made me say hello to the bus driver when we got on, and thank him as we were leaving. I had thought it a ridiculous affectation then, something he did to show anyone within earshot that he was better than they were. Now, though, I think he was trying to teach me to be kind. There is a peculiar type of loneliness that comes from being surrounded by people who ignore you.

I stopped the bus at the harbour where John had originally gotten on and I looked out at the water, which was calm even though there were steely grey skies hanging low over it. The clouds kept coming, piling up on top of one another, and it felt like a storm was brewing out in the Channel. I glanced in my mirror and saw that John was still there. He was looking at the sea, too.

I waited to see if he was going to get off but he stayed put. From then on, each time we neared a stop I slowed down even if no one was waiting, but he didn't get out of his seat. A couple of times he looked around as though his stop were coming up, wringing his hands and edging nearer to the aisle, but he didn't press the request button and he didn't get off my bus.

When I arrived at the changeover spot, the next driver waved at me and I wondered what to do about John. I turned the engine off, and before I left the bus I looked at him and there was something about the way he was staring out the window.

I went over to him. "Did you miss your stop?"

His attention snapped back to me. "Sorry?"

"Your stop. You've done a full loop around town now, I thought maybe you missed the right one?" I wanted to ask if he was all right.

He smiled tentatively. "I'm not familiar with this."

I nodded, expecting him to go on, but he didn't.

"You live locally then?"

"Yes," he said. "Yes. Just over on…" He glanced out the window and his lips looked like they'd found the words he was searching for but his voice was silent. "Up the hill a ways," he said, tapping at the window.

"You're on the wrong bus. You need to head back into town and change onto the 5A bus."

He nodded along as I spoke but I wasn't certain he followed me.

"You know, it's on my way, let me run you up there. My car's just round the corner."

"No, I'm fine, thank you."

"It's no bother, really. I'm going that way."

He seemed uneasy at the offer of a drive but he got up and walked off the bus with me. The state of my car was an embarrassment; I pushed the empty crisp packets and chocolate bar wrappers off the seat for him.

"What street?" I said as I put the car in gear.

"Sorry?" John said. He squinted out the window as if he were trying to get his bearings. Like he was a tourist who had visited Dover before and was now relying on a faded memory to navigate.

"Don't come into town much?"

"My wife tends to the myrtle bush in the front garden," he said.

I glanced at him and the man I had thought he was, smartly dressed on an afternoon out in town, faded away, and in his place was an old man fidgeting with the buttons on his jacket.

"Myrtle?"

He nodded, suddenly appearing more confident in the conversation. "Doesn't look like much, scraggly branches this time of year, but soon enough there will be blossoms. Pink."

"You see them down by the shore mostly," I said as I drove up the hill. "Just let me know when to turn off."

His fingers went at his buttons.

"My neighbour has a bush like that," I said.

"Sorry?"

"The myrtle."

"My wife has a myrtle bush in our garden," he said again. "Not much to look at, this time of year."

"You find them down by the shore for the most part," I said, wondering if he would notice the repetition.

"That's where my wife's plant came from, the shore." He turned to me and beamed. "She swims."

"Is that so," I said.

"Every day. She's training."

"Is she?"

"The Channel, of course."

"Is your wife's name Martha?"

His face lit up. "Martha."

"I think I'm your neighbour," I said. "I'm Henry, I live at 105."

He smiled and nodded as he watched the rest of the houses go by, and he had the strangest expression on his face; it was as if he wasn't actually there with me in the car.

"Henry," he said. "Yes."

When I pulled into my driveway Martha was standing at the foot of their garden. I parked the car and John fumbled with his seatbelt until I released it for him. The moment his foot hit the pavement, I heard Martha shouting to him.

"John! What took you so long?" She rushed over and rested her arms on top of the fence.

He shook his head and ignored her.

"Have you got the milk?" she asked.

He brushed her words away with his hands as if her question was designed exclusively to irritate him, and walked past her into their house.

"Thank you," she said to me. "For driving him home from the shops."

"I didn't."

"Say again?"

"I didn't pick him up at the shops; he was down by the harbour."

"He was?"

"He was."

"He went out for milk."

"Right."

"Hours ago. Just to the corner shop."

"Maybe they ran out," I said.

"Maybe." She feigned a smile.

"You're always welcome to pop round to mine if you run out of something. No sense going all the way to the shops."

"Thank you." She ran her fingers across the cracked white paint on the fence. "We didn't run out of milk."

"I thought you said that's why he went to the shops."

"It is."

She pointed to the ground at my feet. "You really ought to cut that periwinkle back before it takes over."

"Periwinkle?"

"There, the bluish-purple flower."

"Right, thanks," I said. I put my hands in my pockets and looked at her. She seemed to not want to go inside just yet. "Everything all right?"

"Mmm," she said. "I'm sorry, I hope John wasn't too much trouble. Thank you again for driving him home." She turned toward their front door and started walking away slowly.

"Anytime," I said.

I HAD NOT imagined we would become friends that day, and I had not imagined there would come a time when it was her health we would need to discuss. I sat in her kitchen unable to move as she ran her fingers around and around the oversized buttons on her cardigan. I wanted to do something useful, but there was nothing I could do to reverse the diagnosis. Cancer was cancer and life had changed irrevocably.

"When are you expecting John home?"

The kitchen was still, as though it was waiting for the news we had already had. Or maybe it was as though the kitchen was sitting in a stunned silence, unable to digest everything we had heard. The calendar pinned to the wall above the phone counted the days until the end of the year with no guarantee of who would be around to see them all.

"He'll be back the day after tomorrow," she said.

"Not sooner?"

"Why would he come home sooner?"

The way she said it made me feel that what I was missing was obvious. "You haven't told him, have you?"

"Why would I?" She got up and filled the kettle, putting a teabag in the mug I always used when I came over, a white-and-blue pattern that made me think of tropical seas.

"Why would you not?"

"Because he's having a lovely weekend away."

"But this is awful."

Her back was to me but I saw her lay her hands flat on the counter. I saw her adjust her plain gold wedding band.

"It will still be awful when he gets back." She turned to face me and crossed her arms over her chest. "Don't you think it would be worse to ruin his weekend?"

The space in the kitchen was filled with the shriek of the kettle.

"No," I said as she poured the water.

"Let him enjoy another couple of days. It's kind."

"It's cruel."

"What would you know about it? Over there, all by yourself."

Her voice was sharp. I got up from the table and stood in front of her. I wanted to say something that would make everything okay, though I suspected that if she knew I was even considering the possibility of there being words enough to fix this she would shout and curse me for being so impractical and naive. So I didn't try and find those words.

"You know where I am if you need anything."

I shut the door firmly and went back to mine. I promised myself that I would not do anything rash, that I would not give in to my anger. I sat on the right-hand side of the sofa because that was my side, even though there was no one in this house who would lay claim to the other one. It was a habit and, I suppose, the way I prayed.

The sofa was from a charity shop, covered in a brown tartan fabric that had looked comforting when I bought it. There was one cigarette burn on the underside of the left-hand seat cushion, which I had flipped and swapped with the right, just in case.

Though I knew that "just in case" would never happen. Not now. Not since I'd come back to our family home and there had been an open door that I hadn't taken enough notice of.

It had been a Wednesday in November. It was late enough to be dark, but not dark enough to be late. Around dinnertime. You could have walked into any of the homes on our street at that time and opened the front door to be greeted by the flavour of chicken, beef, or lamb. I walked into our house and was met by the familiar smell of a roasting chicken.

I had hardly noticed that the door was open. I was in a rush. I had other things on my mind. I called hello as I walked into the foyer but got no answer. There was no time to register the quiet emptiness of the house because the phone in the foyer rang and I had to take it. It was an urgent work matter, in a period of my life when going around in circles meant something completely different, back when I had a desk, and a family picture took pride of place. But the phone had rung, insisting it was more important. It took priority.

Now, from the depths of the old tartan sofa, I dialled the number I had memorized ages ago, and it rang and rang until I heard the familiar recording.

Hello, this is Beth. I'm sorry to have missed your call, but if you leave me a message I'll get back to you as soon as I can.

Then there was a squealing beep and silence. I held the handset to my ear, listening to nothing and wondering whether, if I stayed on the line long enough, it was possible to reset history. The dull, electrical buzz in my ear continued until I was satisfied that there was nothing I could do to change things.

That phone call meant that I had to go back to the office; without giving it any more thought, I'd gotten back into my car and left. I was there and home in less than an hour, including the time it took for me to resolve the issue — which, honestly, could have waited until morning if not for the fact that I had wanted to look good to a new client.

And in that time, without my knowing, my daughter had been taken from her room upstairs in our house to the A&E at our local hospital. She was suffering from an allergic reaction — anaphylaxis, I learned later — brought on by exposure to shellfish, which was strange because my Ellie wasn't keen on seafood of any kind.

Her mother had found her, and had been the one to drive speeding through the streets with our daughter on the seat next to her, struggling to breathe. Sometime that night, once I'd caught up with them, once the unanswered phone calls had been answered and I had gotten in my car again and driven across town to the hospital, to find Beth shaking and weeping in a corridor with flickering fluorescent lights and the stomach-churning smell of disinfectant and urine, I learned that there had been a special class at the school that day that had been intended to broaden the children's tastes. A chef had been brought in from town to tempt the students into eating something other than cheesy chips and brown sauce.

Beth said, "I found her upstairs, unconscious."

"But everything looked fine."

"I saw her rucksack in the corridor, her jacket on the stairs."

I didn't know if I had seen those things, too; all I remembered was that the phone had rung.

"I called out, to see if anyone was home," I said, my voice flat, as though on autopilot.

"She couldn't breathe. How could she have said anything?"

"I didn't know." All I could do was reiterate facts.

"You didn't think to check?"

"I didn't think anything was wrong."

"Nothing seemed out of the ordinary?"

And I pictured the door. It had been open. Ajar, more like. A tiny crack which, had things turned out differently, would have been one of those things that become family in-jokes after a while. Our Ellie, always leaving doors open. And it was true: the cupboards in the kitchen were always slightly ajar. Things on the stairs or in the corridor didn't even tug at the corners of my attention because ours was not an overly tidy house; it was a home full of people coming and going, leading busy lives, and as such there were often things on the floor.

All it would have taken was one minute, possibly less, for me to have gone upstairs and looked in her room. But I didn't.

LATER THAT DAY, as I was thinking about lunch, the doorbell shattered the silence and I jumped when I heard it. When I opened the door to find Martha standing there, my heart was pounding in my chest.

"Have you got a passport?" she asked.

I don't know what I was expecting her to say but it wasn't that.

"Yes," I said. "Is everything all right?" It was a stupid question to ask, and I knew it might provoke her, but I asked anyhow.

"Go and get it.'

"Why?"

"Because you won't be able to get off the ferry without it."

"Where are we going?"

"France."

"Why?"

"We don't have time for all these questions. The next ferry leaves in forty-five minutes." She adjusted the strap of her handbag on her shoulder.

She made quite a strange character, standing there on my doorstep demanding I accompany her to France. It was certainly the first time in a long time anyone had demanded I go anywhere, and something about the way she held herself — back straight, chin up, not breaking eye contact for one minute — made it clear that she would not be taking no for an answer.

"What about Webb?"

"He'll be fine. We won't be long."

We managed to make the ferry and as we stood on the deck, the wind whipping around us, I stole a glance at Martha. It was hard to say exactly how old she was. Her skin was weathered by her time spent in the water — the sun, wind, and sea had gotten into her face, etching delicate lines around her eyes and mouth, but they hadn't stolen her youthfulness, which for me was held in the tan lines that lurked in unexpected places, like the back of her neck and her temples. When she had her hair cut after the summer season, a line, like a waterline, was revealed on the back of her neck; it was the same on her temples where, if you knew what you were looking for, you could make out a faint line left by the strap of her goggles. Her laugh was the most youthful thing about her, though. It was a girl's laugh, high-pitched and full of surprised delight.

"Martha," I said.

She turned toward me and the wind scattered her hair across her face.

"France?"

She grinned. "*Mais oui*."

"Could you be more specific?"

She smiled by way of reply, before turning her attention back to the water.

I'd learned in the years we had known each other that if the sea was in sight, that's where her eyes would be drawn. Some days it was impossible to have a conversation unless it related to the tides or swell or wind. Her body was the only part of her that ever came onto dry land; everything else — everything that mattered — did not.

The ferry crossing would take an hour and a half, so I left Martha to her thoughts. I went inside and took a seat away from the tourists and holidaymakers trying to cling to the last vestiges of summer. I hadn't brought a book with me, which put me at the mercy of my own thoughts. Soon enough, the shapes on the carpeting under my feet plunged me back to that awful night in the hospital.

I had spent a long time examining the pattern of the flooring, trying to outsmart it and discover where it repeated itself in the wrong order. I had scrutinized a one-foot square area until I knew it by heart: a series of blue, grey, and green diamonds, all touching and fanning out in circles. I searched for the rules to the pattern, devising them as quickly as I rejected them. I did this because it was easier than talking to Beth about what had happened.

We were waiting because that's what hospitals are for. Everyone in them is waiting for something: to see the doctor, to get well, to go home. When I saw another couple leaving in tears, I was cheered slightly, even though I knew I was being horrible. There was only so much bad news to go around; if these other families bore the brunt of it, then there was still a chance we might escape — not unscathed, but in one piece.

Was another dreary hospital corridor in my future? Would I be the one to take Martha to her appointments, as John's unravelling mind could not consistently be counted on for the mundane basics of life like driving and knowing the days of the week? Would I be promoted from neighbour to carer?

When the ferry arrived, we got back in the car and drove awkwardly through Calais. We were without a map and Martha navigated from the memory of her last visit, some forty years before. "Head toward the sea. Follow the road that hugs the coast," were the only words she could offer me by way of instruction. They could easily have been the motto she used for every situation life had ever thrown at her, I thought.

It felt strange to drive on the right-hand side of the road, and I was grateful the motorway wasn't busy. The Channel stretched out on the passenger side like an oil slick, and Martha rolled down the window and the sea air swept in, filling the car with its distinctive smell of summer holidays and ice cream picnics.

From time to time I glanced at the water. It lapped onto the shore here, too, and I wondered if somewhere out there, in the middle of the Channel, it parted like a schoolboy's haircut. Was there a line down the middle where the water was given its orders?

Her eyes were shut when we reached the little village.

"We're here," I said softly.

She looked around and pointed to the left. "Down that road just there."

She adjusted her position in the seat, sitting up taller and leaning forward, and I would not have been surprised if she had thrown the door open before I came to a complete stop, running full throttle toward the sea. "You know, I only swam from France once. It's not allowed anymore."

"Why?"

"We had to wait for the weather."

"No, I mean why isn't it allowed?"

She shrugged. "The French authorities made a decision."

"Based on what?"

"Who knows? It's a shame: it gave you an advantage. The currents are miserable here. Better to get them out of the way at the beginning of a swim, when you've got the most energy."

The village of Cap Gris Nez was not that different from a small coastal village back home: there was a butcher, fishmonger, greengrocer, hardware store, and a handful of cafés and bistros. It gave me that slightly sad, end-of-holidays feeling as we drove through the half-empty streets. It was a summer town and we were at the end of the season, so the day-after-the-night-before atmosphere was heavy in the air.

I parked and followed Martha down to the shore, which was completely different to ours on the other side. Where ours was formidable, with the white cliffs standing guard, looming over the sea as though to remind it that they had risen above its depths, here there was a sandy beach, windswept and rugged, with dunes to hide away in that stretched along the coast as far as I could see. It was a difference in national identity: the English coast buttoned up and formal, and the French coast relaxed and ready for a bit of sunbathing.

I held out my hand to steady her as we tripped down the dunes, but she didn't take it. The sand shifted under our feet and I wasn't prepared for it, but she was. Her body must have remembered it: this place, these dunes, and this sand. I hoped the place remembered her as fondly as she did it.

She made a beeline for the sea. Once she was at the water's edge she crouched down and put her hands in, cupping up a handful of water that she then splashed on her face.

"What are you doing that for?" I asked.

Seawater dripped off the tip of her nose. "If we were Catholic, and went into church, we would bless ourselves with holy water."

"We're not Catholic and we're not in church."

"Only one of those things is true, Henry."

She dabbed the drips off her face with the cuff of her jacket as she stared out at the deep.

"What are you looking at?" I asked.

The wind blew the spray onshore.

"Myself," Martha said.

She stayed like that, crouched at the foot of the sea, while I looked on, feeling very much like an unwanted intruder. She touched the sand, ran her fingers through it, drew lines and circles in it, and rinsed her hands over and over again in the cold, grey water. Eventually she stood up and we continued walking south.

"You swam from this beach?"

She pointed to land that jutted out into the sea up ahead. "Further down, past that marker. The currents are a bit easier."

We walked toward it and Martha said, "Would have been almost forty years ago. I was planning to cross on the thirtieth of August, but there was weather. I waited here until the fourth of September." She brushed her hair off her face. "All my successful swims were in September."

"What do you mean, waited?"

"Your pilot gives you a week-long window. You go when he says it's time. I didn't get the green light immediately, so I waited."

"I bet John wasn't happy about that."

"No, but he and the children managed."

"He wasn't with you?"

"No," she said. "I came across on my own."

I couldn't have been sure, but it sounded like there was a hint of pride in her voice just then.

"Why?" I asked.

"Why what?"

"Did you swim it?"

She stopped walking and smiled. "Because I wanted to see if I could, and I wanted to know what it was like, being out there in the middle of the open water."

I looked at the sea. To me, it was a cauldron of froth, foaming at the mouth, ready to devour anyone foolish enough to tempt it. You couldn't see the bottom, you couldn't see the end of it, and it was cold and smelled like fish.

"Weren't you ever frightened?"

She traced a curve in the wet sand with her foot. "Only once, and only briefly."

I waited for her to go on.

"I fell in when I was a girl. Nearly drowned."

"And you went back in?"

"The next day."

"Why?"

She put her hand on my shoulder and tucked her hair behind her ear as she looked at me. "Because..." She paused and looked at the water as if it knew the answer. "Because it was one of the few things that made my father...feel better."

We continued to walk down the beach while the tide came in, and the surf grazed her shoes. I angled inland, wary of the salt.

"Must have been nice, to know you were swimming home."

She murmured something that sounded like agreement.

"Have you been back since?"

Martha shook her head. "It was the only time I've ever been to France. For more than a few minutes."

I must have looked puzzled.

"You're only allowed to stay a few minutes when you finish a swim. Then it's back in the boat." She stopped walking. "It's the only time I ever left England."

"Apart from now."

"Apart from now," she said, and then she turned around and walked back in the direction from which we came.

We walked into the wind. Our footsteps were lost to the incoming tide and the sand looked untouched, as though we had never been there.

Farther up ahead, there was a row of plain cottages overlooking the water that had obviously been built in a more modest time. Perched on the threshold of the sea, they appeared to stand guard as the water consumed the earth, inch by inch. Martha walked toward the buttery one with the red tile roof; once she reached the wooden steps, she climbed them with the familiarity of someone who lived there.

"Martha?"

I hesitated at the foot of the stairs.

"The food was very good," she said. She put her hand on the door and seemed to pause briefly as she looked in. Then she slid the glass door open without so much as knocking and went inside. There was nothing left for me to do but follow.

The interior was small, basically a large living room redecorated in the style of a dining room. There were a total of five pine tables, with one fresh flower in an identical vase in the centre of each. The decor was provided — primarily — by the sea: the entire back wall was one big window, and the rest of the room, with its cream walls and tastefully generic artwork, knew its place.

We stood on the edge of the entranceway, waiting for someone to appear. Martha seemed as comfortable there as she was at hers, while I expected to have an angry Frenchman chasing us down the dunes within minutes.

"Are you sure about this?" I asked.

Before she could reply, a waitress appeared and we were told to take whichever table suited us. Martha chose the one with the best view.

"I stayed here," she said, once we were settled. "They've redecorated since, but…"

We ordered our meal, and then Martha seemed to become restless. She fiddled around with the salt and pepper shakers, then it was the small vase that was the object of her attention. She twirled it between her fingers absently, as she might have done with her hair had it been longer, while she looked around the room. She seemed to be searching for something just out of sight.

The waitress brought a bottle of white wine, and once it was poured Martha went to the bar in the very back, which looked like a more tasteful version of the average dad's bar, and leaned over the counter.

"Henry," she said. "Look!"

I went to stand next to her and there, on the wall behind the bar, were some old photographs curled at the edges and a few newspaper clippings — some written in English, but most in French — that were yellowed with age.

"Second from the bottom," she said, pointing.

I squinted. "Is that you?" It was a picture of a woman on a beach in an old swimming costume, modest in cut, staring — almost glaring — at the camera.

She nodded. "He really did put it up."

"Sorry?"

She went back to the table and took a drink. "I promised I'd send him the article, from the local paper back home. And in return he promised to put it up."

She rested her chin in her hand and her expression suggested that she was somewhere else.

"How many times have you swum it now?"

"Nine, successfully. Ten attempts."

"Once more?"

She shook her head. "I don't think I'll manage it. Not now."

"You don't know that for sure."

"Henry." She looked at me gravely.

"Other people have."

"I'm not other people."

No, I thought. You aren't.

Dinner arrived and we ate in a comfortable silence.

Beth and I had stood with Ellie's hospital bed between us as we watched her, waiting for her to wake up. The silence that filled the room was tense and sharp. Our hope was that, during the time she had been deprived of oxygen, her brain hadn't suffered too much long-term damage. But there was no way of telling until she woke up.

"I'm sorry," I said.

Beth ignored me.

"I didn't know."

She wouldn't look me in the eye.

"I love her."

Beth's expression told me that she didn't believe me.

"She's my daughter too."

Her eyes narrowed and she leaned across the bed where our

little girl lay. "This wouldn't have happened if you had only paid attention."

"This isn't my fault."

"Who walks into a house without noticing the door's been left open?"

"You would've done the same thing."

She scoffed.

"Beth, it was an accident," I pleaded.

She shook her head, her eyes watering. "I noticed," she said, stabbing her finger into her chest. "How could you have been so careless?"

"Penny for your thoughts," Martha said, jolting me back to the present and the table at which we sat. I had hardly touched my food.

"Is this your first time in France?" Martha asked.

I shook my head. "Years ago. Paris."

"Was it as romantic as they say?"

"Quite the opposite, actually."

She raised her eyebrow. "Is that so?"

"Not the memory I was hoping for."

"They can't all be good."

"No, they can't," I said, feigning interest in my now-cold fish supper.

She waited politely for as long as she could, but by the time I had made a noticeable dent in my meal, I could tell that she had lost her patience.

I set my knife and fork down. "We can go whenever you like."

"No, you finish that up. If you don't mind, I think I'll see if I can take a look around."

She put her napkin on top of her plate and went off in search of the waitress. I drank the rest of my wine and tried to picture

Martha sitting here on her own, waiting to swim. It was difficult because their garden, and the sea, were where I always pictured her. There was something about her that was ill-suited to the confines of the indoors; rooms did not seem big enough to contain her.

Overhead, I heard creaking floorboards.

I took one last bite of the fish and its congealed sauce, then pushed the plate away. What was she hoping to find here? What had she left behind that was so important to come back to now?

In Paris, I had left my wife behind. Metaphorically, not factually. We took the same flight home, crammed into the tiny seats side by side — but our marriage was finished, left with the crumpled towels in the bath, waiting for someone else to come along and clean up the mess. Beth and I had been civil to one another, but nothing had been the same since Ellie.

I had hoped the City of Light would become the City of Second Chances, and that what had brought Beth and I together in the beginning would reassert itself over that weekend. But it was blame and recrimination instead of passion and romance.

There was no going back and there was no chance of fixing things that had been broken for longer than they had been functional. I hoped that whatever it was Martha wanted to find didn't need to be repaired.

I heard the footsteps moving overhead again and I was watching for her as she came downstairs. She turned the corner, sniffed, and wiped her nose, and I saw that her eyes were red. Given her circumstances, it was a relief.

"Did you find what you were looking for?"

"I wasn't looking for anything," she said.

It was my turn to raise an eyebrow. "Is that so?"

"The food is very good here, which you would know if you had eaten yours."

I got up from the table and offered her my arm, which she brushed away.

"It's cancer, Henry, I'm not crippled."

"Time to go home, then?"

She looked out the window once more and I thought I heard a sigh. I couldn't tell if it was wistful, nostalgic, or mournful, but she seemed to have made her peace with something.

"Yes," she said. "It's time."

FROM FRANCE TO ENGLAND

MARTHA, 2010

ON THE FERRY back to Dover, I sat by myself. Henry preferred the bow and I the stern; it was a difference in perspective.

Crossing the Channel by ferry on a mild evening with the sun setting in the distance is romantic regardless of circumstances. It's a slow way to travel, and even if you aren't fond of the sea there is a dreamy quality about being in the middle of open water that is difficult to resist. It's the ebb and flow of the tides gently rocking the ship, or maybe the vastness that comes from the age of the oceans, and that they are permanent while we are not.

The permanence was comforting, as was the fact that I shared something with the sea: the human body has the same ratio of water to salt. I have always loved knowing that I share something fundamental with the water.

It was a mackerel sky that evening. The clouds were lit from underneath in a blood-red hue, and the sun bloomed pink like my myrtle blossoms. I felt that somehow the sea — my sea — knew about my diagnosis and was trying to console me.

The colours had been this dramatic for me only once before, and I hadn't been able to appreciate them then because I had been swimming. I had been steadily churning my way toward the white cliffs and trying to get Monsieur Sylvain out of my head. It seemed reasonable to think that a twenty-one-hour swim would be sufficient to get through all possible thoughts, so that by the time my feet were once again on the rust-coloured pebbles at Dover, he would be confined to distant memory.

I remember turning my head to breathe and the colour of the sky filling my goggles as though they had sprung a leak. My initial impulse had been to stop and take it all in — but I knew that if I did, the momentum I had built up would vanish. I was nearing the end of my first successful swim — though I didn't know that at the time — and I felt there was something special occurring. My shoulders ached in ways I had never imagined, deep within their sockets. So deep, in fact, that it was hard to precisely place the pain. All I knew was that it hurt when I lifted my arm, and on the follow-through, as my hand grazed my thigh.

I kept swimming, and the nearer I got to Dover the more jubilant I became. But I was torn: as much as I wanted to finish the swim, I didn't want it to end. I didn't want to get out of the water.

Five days earlier, I had taken the ferry across on my own. I had been married for fifteen years and had two children, friends, and the makings of a good life. But I could not have been happier to wave goodbye to all of that and simply start swimming.

John had been gripped with a panic that something horrible would happen to me in the water. That I might succumb to hypothermia or exhaustion, or even drown. Those were things I hardly thought about and certainly did not bother considering in any more depth than absolutely necessary. I felt safe in the sea and I have never been able to properly explain that to anyone.

I said goodbye to my family, to England, and the moment I got on the ferry I allowed myself to think of nothing but swimming in order to prepare for what lay ahead.

As far as training went, my meagre preparations would be scandalous by today's standards. But back then, it was more about the individual and what he or she could do; it wasn't the way it is now, where success is determined by the team a swimmer has assembled.

I had chosen a good pilot, though, and when the taxi dropped me at my gîte in Cap Gris Nez, I phoned Charlie to check on the weather.

"Martha," he said. "It doesn't look good."

I slumped into the hard wooden chair in the reception hall where the only phone for guests was located.

"Generally, or specifically?" I asked.

"There's weather coming down from the North Sea. And the isobars on the Atlantic are worrying."

"Have I come for nothing?"

There was a pause, and all I heard was the buzz of the line.

"No. But it'll be tight. I might not be able to give you much notice."

"I don't need notice. I need to swim."

"I know."

"Charlie, this is —"

"I know."

"It doesn't have to be great or good. Just possible."

"I'm not putting anyone at risk."

"I'm not asking you to. But understand that I'll swim through chop, waves, wind, rain."

I heard him take a drag from his roll-up and imagined him sitting in his front room, the pink and yellow flowers on the wallpaper in stark contrast to his unshaven beard and bristly demeanour.

"I have to try," I said.

"You have to make it."

"I will."

"Will you? It'll be harder in rough seas. It'll take everything, and once you've given what you have, it will demand more. And you'll have to have those reserves."

"I can do this."

My voice — I thought — conveyed confidence that I wasn't entirely sure I had, but prayed I would develop the moment I was horizontal and moving through the water.

"Phone again tomorrow," he said.

I put the receiver down and wondered if I had squandered the money my church had raised to allow me to pay for, among other things, the Federation's fees so that the swim was recorded as official. It was one thing for me to fail on a personal level — it would be a blow to my self-esteem, and I would never hear the end of it from John, not after the fight it had taken for me to get back in the water. But it was quite another thing to let an entire congregation down.

I knew Charlie would do his best, but he couldn't control the weather any more than I could. He knew this part of the sea as though it were his most intimate friend, having fished on it for over thirty years. He knew its moods and whims, tricks and traps, better than most. And he could be counted upon. He was my pilot and I trusted him to let me try if it was at all possible.

I did my best to settle in as the rain streamed down the window in my room. The gîte itself was not bad, and though I had expected to feel excited to be on my own for a few days, I found that without swimming and my family, I was at a loose end.

After unpacking the few items I had brought along — two changes of clothes, two swimsuits, and a book — I set out for the shore. The gîte was sandwiched between similar houses in a row that overlooked the beach and it offered a quick escape to the water should that be necessary. I walked through the dining room and let myself out onto the deck, where the wind caught me off guard and I stumbled.

The swell had grown since I had gotten off the ferry, and looked to be around five feet, with an onshore wind and ominous grey clouds hanging low to the north. The rain had lessened from pelting to solid drizzle and, possibly for the first time, I almost felt disappointed to be on the beach. Everywhere I looked, it seemed that the elements were against me; I realized that the chances of not completing the swim were far greater than those of succeeding.

I believed I had learned to read the sea over the years, to listen to what it was telling me and to act accordingly. If the wind back home was coming onshore, I swam parallel to the beach. If it was offshore then I swam perpendicular, steering myself in the direction of France and repeating to myself that this was what it would be like on the day I did it for real. After a bad storm, I kept a careful watch for jellyfish and bits of detritus that might lead to injury. I watched for changing currents, knew the tides, and understood how to time my breathing according to the height and strength of the waves.

What I saw then, as the ocean hurled itself onto the beach and jabbed at the coastline, was that the water was angry; it was no time to be going in. I had read stories of surfers, desperate for waves after a dry spell, who would go to the beach at night and light bonfires, sacrificing boards to Neptune in the hopes that he might provide what they needed. I had never read of anything similar for swimmers. I knew that pouring oil onto water could calm stormy seas, but this assault wouldn't be calmed by a few drops, and I didn't fancy swimming through an oil spill in a few days' time.

To make getting soaked through as useful as it could be, I walked along the water's edge, trying to learn where the currents mixed and where the water fought against itself. The three miles off the French coast were the hardest of any Channel swim; they were the truest test of one's strength and determination, which was why I would start from this foreign coast. Getting through this water when I was still fresh would make my chances of succeeding that much better.

I tried to pinpoint exactly where it was that most people must fail, so that I would know whether or not my chances were good. If the weather calmed down even slightly, I promised myself I would get in and swim those three miles over and over again. In the event that I wasn't able to make an attempt this time, then I could at least console myself with the knowledge that I had conquered some of it.

I trudged through the wet sand until I could go no further, the wind buffeting my right side and the drizzle chilling me deep into my bones. Turning to face the sea, I shouted, "I will swim the Channel. I will not get out until I reach England."

In return, the water threw salty spray in my face.

I squared my shoulders and stood up to it as though it were a schoolyard bully. "I need to do this. I need to prove to myself that I can. I need to show everyone at home that I am more than a wife and a mother. They need to see that…"

I paused. I had never said any of these things aloud before, and though the beach was empty and the only things that could hear me were the wind, the rain, and the sea, the mere fact that I had uttered them gave them a reality I wasn't prepared for. It's one thing knowing your own mind and heart, quietly to yourself, but it's a very different thing to announce to the world that you need to be seen to be extraordinary.

Was it a good reason to swim? I didn't know and I didn't care. All I was focused on was doing it.

I WAS SO cold when I returned to the gîte that day, I thought I would never warm up. But just as I was beginning to feel truly sorry for myself, I realized that there was an unintended benefit to being this cold: this was training of a kind. I was still working toward my swim. By staying outside for hours in the cold and the wet I was conditioning myself. Teaching my body to overcome the elements.

After I had changed into dry clothes, I lay down on the bed, unsure of what else to do. Dinner was to be served in a few hours and I hadn't felt like reading. As I stared at the ceiling, going over the swim in my mind, there was a knock on the door.

Monsieur Sylvain, the owner, spoke very little English, but he beckoned me to follow him. He said words like *pleur* and *froid* as he mimed being cold. He trundled down the corridor, and when he turned and saw that I was still standing in the doorway to my room, he came back and led me by the hand downstairs to the sitting room, where he indicated that I should take the chair he had pulled up in front of a roaring fire.

I let go of his hand as soon as I could without seeming rude. The minute I was settled in my seat, he rushed off and reappeared moments later with a small glass of pastis, which I had never tasted before. I did not immediately take to it.

He smiled warmly and drew up a chair, crossing his legs and happily chattering away in rapid-fire French. I understood none of what he said, unable to pick out even one word of it. His motive was unclear: was he simply trying to be a good host to his only guest? I couldn't tell. I wanted to be alone with my thoughts, to prepare myself for my swim and think about everything in between here and there.

Dinner was served — unexpectedly — in front of the fire, and just when I thought Monsieur Sylvain had run out of things to say and we would eat in silence, he switched the radio on and I was bombarded with his commentary on whatever the news of the day was, coming over the wires.

The next day I awoke and didn't know where I was. I was not accustomed to sleeping anywhere but home. To steady myself I opened the curtains, hoping to see a calm sea and clear sky, but instead I saw a red sky and white horses covering the water.

I phoned Charlie regardless, hoping he might have better news.

"When are you setting out?" I asked.

I heard him draw on his cigarette. "Not today."

"It's just a bit of chop."

"Weather's coming. It'll meet you when you're halfway."

"I'll swim faster, then."

"If you want to risk your life, you're more than welcome. But I'm not risking mine, and I'm not risking my boat."

"But I've come all this way."

I heard him exhale, and then there was a pause and I thought the line had gone dead. Just as I was about to hang up I heard him clear his throat. "I know you have. I do. But weather's com-ing, and it's bad."

It was my turn to pause.

"I suppose we're always at the mercy of the Furies," I said.

I hung up the phone and the sound of it clattered through the foyer. The day stretched out before me, empty.

I decided to walk along the shore and see if I could find someplace calm enough to swim. My body and mind were ach-ing for a wet; just to be immersed in the salty brine would have been enough.

I buttoned my overcoat as I opened the back door, and Monsieur Sylvain appeared as though from nowhere, which led me to wonder if he, too, was searching for something with which to occupy his time, now that holiday season was finished and I was his only guest.

He waved his hands at me and pointed at the outdoors, say-ing words I couldn't understand. Eventually he mimed that I should wait, and since I had no intention of heeding him, when he disappeared down the corridor I opened the door and the wind blew through the house.

When my feet touched the sand at the foot of the stairs I heard my name being called and turned to find him shaking an all-weather jacket at me. Gratefully, I accepted it.

He pointed to the sea and shook his head. "*Non*," he said.

I smiled, finally able to understand something.

"*Oui*," I replied. And off I went.

I stomped down the dunes, hating all of France for having worse weather than England.

I watched the wind whip up breakers on the water's surface and wondered how far away these waves had started. Was the wind bringing them down from the North Sea or further afield?

Were they coming from the North Atlantic, having somehow made their way around Ireland and the UK? I imagined some hateful giant dropping stones in the sea on the edge of the Arctic, chuckling at my misfortune.

The miserable weather increased my desire to swim and it also made my fear of a reprise of my earlier, unsuccessful attempt swell. I remembered almost everything from that day five years ago. I had lost the feeling in my fingers and toes quite early on but promised myself I would not tell anyone in the boat, and the searing pain of the sores on my skin — made by a combination of salt water and chafing from my swimsuit — was burned into my memory. The entire time I had been in the water, all I'd thought about was getting out, but I was stubborn. Only when my lips and tongue had become swollen from salt, only when I saw my daughter shouting from the side of the boat, only when my husband had to pull me out did I consider admitting defeat. What had kept me going was my singular desire to have an accomplishment that I could claim as my own. Eventually, though, sense won and I had been pulled out — delirious — back into the boat.

I had felt humiliated. My pride, and the sense I had of myself, had been rubbed off by the salt and water, left behind with a layer of my skin.

But this time would be different; this time I had years of training, hundreds of miles logged in the water. This time would be a success, I promised myself, as I returned from my walk to the gîte, cold and wet, to be greeted by Monsieur Sylvain who was waiting anxiously by the door. He chattered excitedly as he ushered me into the sitting room, where the fire was going strong. He brought me a bowl of bouillabaisse and I ate while drying off.

Later that evening, I sat in the reception hall and phoned home.

Harriet answered the phone exactly the way we had taught her, and momentarily my mood lifted.

"Hello, Roberts residence, Harriet speaking," she said.

"Hi Harry, it's Mum," I said. "How are you?"

"Yeah, good."

"Everything okay over there?"

"Iain's being a moron."

"Don't say things like that about your brother."

"Sorry, but he is. He spilled brown sauce on my school uniform and wouldn't clean it up, and then Dad got really cross with him until he started crying, which made Dad even crosser."

"How did he spill something on your uniform?"

"He was waving the bottle around his head like an airplane."

"What did I tell you about being on your best behaviour?"

"I am, Mum, it's Iain's fault," she whined.

I sighed. "Is your father home?"

"Yeah," she said, and I heard the phone banging against the table and her voice shouting through the house.

"Martha," John said. "Is it as bad over there as it is over here?"

"I should think so."

"You won't take any undue risks, will you?"

"It's all right, John, Charlie's quite concerned about his boat." My husband might not trust me, but he knew Charlie well enough to know the man would not risk his boat for anything.

"Shipping forecast isn't optimistic," he said.

"I am. The window is seven days," I replied.

He cleared his throat and changed the conversation. "How is everything over there?" he asked. "Food not too bad? You're keeping your strength up?"

"Yes, it's all fine."

"I spoke to Charlie earlier. He said it's low pressure off the Atlantic, wind coming down from the North Sea. Something about isobars."

"You called him?"

"He rang the house."

"It's a conspiracy."

"The whole congregation is praying for you."

"Tell them to pray for weather. I'll be fine on my own."

John sighed. "Will you?"

"John," I said, as I prayed the rosary with the phone cord.

"I'll see you soon enough," he said.

"You coping all right with the children? Harriet said something about brown sauce."

"Minor fracas. I've sorted it."

"Good," I said.

"Take care of yourself. Charlie and I will see you soon."

I went back to spend the rest of the evening in front of the fire, listening to Monsieur Sylvain natter on in French. Though we had no common language, we shared, I thought, a comfort taken from adherence to rituals, which gave us a way to pass the time. I couldn't understand what he was saying, but his company made it cozy and I started replying to him in English. Side by side in our leather armchairs, feet warmed by the embers, we went through the motions of an average evening, each of us deafened by an unfamiliar vocabulary.

I knew next to nothing about him beyond that he lived here by himself — which meant either that he was unmarried or that Madame Sylvain had met with an untimely end — and that he enjoyed listening to the sort of music my father had listened to on the radio when I was a girl. Old music that featured violins and clarinets and, in this case, accordions, limped out of an old record player kept in the corner of the room. Sometimes a particular movement would grab his attention and he would stop speaking, holding his index finger aloft as though the music were making his point for him.

But he didn't seem to mind my presence, and what was more unusual was that he didn't appear bothered when I stared. It was not my habit to be so rude, but as I couldn't decipher his words, I looked to his face for some clue.

It was hard to guess how old he was and I would not have been surprised to learn that he was in his mid-thirties, as I was — but he could have just as easily been fifty. He was not unattractive, with olive skin, brown eyes, and a greying but well-manicured beard. His deep voice was accompanied by hands that were constantly in motion, occasionally landing on my own wrist or hand. My initial reaction was to withdraw my arm, but eventually I got used to it, thinking of it less as an inappropriate gesture and more a part of the story he was telling.

The wonderful thing about Monsieur Sylvain's lack of English was that I could speak with freedom, saying whatever I wanted regardless of who might be hurt. It was almost as good as being in the water.

"The other thing," I found myself saying as he refilled my glass with pastis, "is that he clips his toenails whilst he's sat on the edge of our bed. Whenever I hear the sound of the clippers, I make a note to vacuum the next day."

He nodded gravely, as though he were following every word, and then it was his turn to speak. I pretended that he was expressing his complete agreement with me.

"It's utterly ridiculous," I said. "I have mentioned it to him, but John insists that a house is a man's castle and that he'll do as he pleases. When I get in a proper strop — which is infrequent, mind — he rolls his eyes and pretends as though I'm overreacting." I paused. "It's unhygienic. And I don't care to feel the crunch of someone's toenails underfoot."

I leaned back in my chair, enjoying the warmth. Monsieur Sylvain spoke at length as I nodded along.

"I don't know what made me decide to do it," I said. "Quite impulsive, really. I suppose it's vanity. I could've paid more attention to the garden, or joined the Women's Institute, done charitable work — but I wanted to do something different. When I was a young woman, a reporter approached me on the beach and asked me if I was going to swim the Channel. It was all the rage for a while: the Americans came over, the Egyptians sent men every summer. Oh, they were wonderful to watch.

"Anyhow, this reporter asked me if I was going to swim it and of course I said no — I mean, it was completely ridiculous to think that I could do such a thing. Only a few other women had done it. Trudy Ederle was the one all the Americans raved about. But he got me thinking."

I paused to catch my breath, and when I realized what I had said — aloud — I felt my cheeks redden. I turned to Monsieur Sylvain, trying to work out how best to mime my apologies, and when I saw his face, smiling gently at me, I nearly burst out laughing. The freedom we were enjoying had again caught me off guard.

I continued. "Nothing I could have done about it then. John and I were getting married and I had responsibilities. There were expectations to meet. My mother insisted that no wedding dress had ever looked as awful as mine did, because it had to cover my tan lines and my muscular arms." I traced the lines on my shoulder and puffed myself up as a wrestler might — to much unintended comedic effect, apparently, as Monsieur Sylvain did his best to stifle a laugh. But it was a warm laugh, followed by a warm smile. "John, well, he didn't come right out and say it, but I could tell he wasn't keen. Bad enough a young woman prancing around half-naked for all the world to see, but a married woman? It was a different era."

This time when I paused, he said something that sounded sympathetic. It was in the slight tilt of his head, the softness in his voice, the way I felt when he looked at me as he got up to put another log on the fire. He offered me more to drink but I brushed him away, doing a breaststroke mime through the air.

"Now," I said, pointing my fingers down, hoping to describe the present. "Things are a bit different. I'm not a foolish young woman anymore." I made a silly face, hoping that might convey youthful silliness, and then immediately afterward shook my head no.

In the morning he accompanied me on my daily walk up and down the beach. I was in better spirits the moment my feet hit the sand because the rain had finally stopped and the wind had shrunk from a howl to a gentle yelp. We walked side by side and as he pointed, I learned about the nature of the sea on our doorstep. Not the sort of precise information that I would have been able to relay to Charlie — more a sense of things. He moved his hands in one way that I understood to be currents, another for rocks, and another — in a slightly hysterical-looking gesture — for danger.

On the fourth day, I was not desperate to swim home. It occurred to me as we sat — as was our custom now — in front of the fire, that maybe the storm had been meant to steer me off course, and in so doing put me onto the right course.

I allowed myself to imagine another life. What if I were to never leave France? No rule said I had to. There were responsibilities and it would not be easy, but it was within the realm of the possible. These few days spent weathering a storm could be taken as a glimpse into an alternate version of my life, one in which I could be Marthe instead of Martha. Better judgement was quick to return: what difference would it make, swapping a small town for a smaller village? An Englishman for a Frenchman? Days still needed to be filled, houses cleaned, meals prepared and eaten. The difference was that it was different.

Monsieur Sylvain retired at the same time as I did that evening, which was unusual: he seemed to be a night owl, and normally put another log on the fire when I excused myself for the night. He walked with me to my room, both of us still talking, and I paused at the door, waiting for him to finish his thought. When he was done he said a few more things, short phrases that I took to be goodnights and sleep wells, and then he did something unexpected: he kissed both my cheeks. I did my best to avoid appearing shocked. He was French and we were in France, waiting out the weather.

I told myself to think nothing of it, but throughout the night my thoughts returned to that moment. It was an echo of how I'd felt when John and I first met, but stronger, intensified perhaps because it was impossible to know the meaning of words I didn't understand. Enjoyable because I was in control of the fantasy.

The dawn of the next morning turned my thoughts back to the sea: the storm had subsided and the wind had died down, though in its place was a heavy fog. And down the phone Charlie said the conditions still weren't right for a cross-Channel swim, but I was at least able to get in the water and swim alongside the shoreline.

Monsieur Sylvain and I continued our habit of walking, and he paced back and forth on the hard sand while I swam parallel to the shore. When I turned to my left to breathe, I saw his figure on the beach, his heavy navy cardigan standing out against the dunes.

My body came back to me as I got used to a different part of the sea and learned its subtle differences. My shoulders, weakened slightly from a few days marooned on dry land, sprang back into shape, and it felt good to remind myself that I was strong. The problem was my mind. I was unable to keep my focus on the water as my thoughts returned, without consent, to my French host.

I knew nothing about him beyond the cursory facts, but that did not stop me as I imagined him to be adept at all kinds of things, from tennis to playing an instrument, and possessing a long-standing interest in cinema and opera. I gave him a small apartment in Paris filled with books and a conservatory filled with plants.

That evening I looked forward to dinner, though I wished I had packed with more foresight. I was not a woman who would ever be described as chic, but I would have liked to have worn something different that night.

Monsieur Sylvain — I still didn't even know his first name — sat across the table from me and we chatted intensely. We had come to the unspoken agreement to base our reactions on one another's facial expressions: we laughed in between bites, and frowned where it seemed appropriate. I spoke freely, even more so than on previous evenings, and it was invigorating.

He escorted me to my room again and grasped my arms and kissed my cheeks, which I was prepared for. What I was not ready for was my reaction. My hand was on the door and I opened it halfway. Then I paused, only briefly, but noticeably. In that moment I looked at him, at his lovely brown eyes the colour of dark oak, and I was shocked to feel interest in the smallest of possibilities.

I smiled warmly and squeezed his hand. He looked down and then kissed me once more, his mouth grazing mine as he aimed for my cheek.

As I lay in bed I felt I had missed a chance; that I had not been strong when strength was required.

AFTER A TERRIBLE, sleepless night, I awoke early and went for a swim by myself. When I returned, Monsieur Sylvain was gesticulating at the phone and shouting in French.

"Charlie!" he yelled.

"Pardon?" I said, dripping water on the floor.

"*Téléphone*!"

He pointed to the foyer with one hand and with the other mimed speaking on the phone. I changed quickly and rang back.

"It's going to be tight," Charlie told me. "But it's our best chance."

"How tight is tight?"

"You'll have to start before first light. John and I will be at the beach at four a.m."

"Should we wait?"

"There's a storm in the North Sea. It'll come down this way."

"So we're going?"

He paused. "You don't have to. If you've changed your mind."

"I haven't."

"Then we're going tonight," he said. "I'll let the Federation Official know to be ready."

A week ago I would not have suggested waiting even one more minute: I would have run to the water's edge and thrown myself in the sea. But I was there then and not here.

I set the phone down and saw Monsieur Sylvain waiting anxiously.

"*Nager*?" he said, miming breaststroke.

I smiled. "*Oui*."

We shared one more meal together, Monsieur Sylvain and I, under a subdued mood. I went to bed well before the sun went down. I had expected to feel excited, anxious, even nervous before the swim; but all I felt was sadness tinged with regret.

My alarm woke me at midnight. The bill had been paid and I had tried to explain to Monsieur Sylvain that I would be leaving in the early hours, in case he thought I had slipped away without saying goodbye intentionally. I put my swimsuit on and carried my case downstairs as quietly as possible and when I passed through the sitting room I was surprised to see him stretched out, dozing, with a small lamp casting him in a warm glow.

I opened the door quietly, praying it would not creak and wake him. I turned back for one last look before I shut the door for good and struck out for the beach. I left behind the possibility of another life and set out in the pitch-black night to look for the blinking lights on an old fishing boat, ferrying my pilot and husband to me.

There was a light breeze coming off the water and it was colder than I had expected, but all together the conditions seemed as good as I could have hoped for. The sky, tempered with pinpricks of stars, was as dark as the depths of the ocean, and the moon cast a white glow over the calm water.

I jumped up and down, swinging my arms back and forth

to limber up, and after ten minutes I thought I heard the sound of the motor.

"Marthe!"

His voice startled me and I looked back toward the gîte.

"Marthe!" he called again.

"Here!" I shouted. "I'm here!"

He jogged up to me and I felt the spark of his hand on my bare back. A small searchlight scanned the shore and I knew that meant Charlie, the Federation official, and John were near.

I cupped his face in my hands and he wrapped his arms around me. I let him warm me. Though I should have been, I was not in a rush to let go. He leaned back, not releasing me from his embrace, and brushed the hair off my face, looking at me in a way no one had ever done before. Then, as the light from the boat searched for me, he kissed me. Not on either cheek, but on the mouth.

My heart was pounding and I drew him closer, desperate to remember everything about him, every sensation, every thrilling tingle. And then we let each other go.

He stepped back. "*Bonne chance, chérie.*"

I waved to him and then, hearing my husband's familiar voice coming from the water, I turned away from Monsieur Sylvain, from France, and gave the task at hand my full attention.

The moment my toes touched the water something in my brain switched on — or possibly off — and I was focused. I walked into the sea and felt my muscles stiffen at the cold. When the water was above my knees, my hands went over my head and I dove straight in, feet flutter-kicking the instant they left the ground, arms stretching as far as possible out in front of me, pulling my body stroke by stroke back to England. A swimmer's motor is her legs: the kick is where the energy lies. Charlie had cautioned me against going flat out from the get-go, warning that it was essential to keep something back for when the tide changed, for when the chop picked up, for when things got hard, but the pent-up energy I'd accumulated in France was difficult to contain. And I didn't want to hold on to it anymore. In the dark, unable to see much more than the lights on Charlie's boat, I swam hard and fast.

THAT AFTERNOON WITH Henry, I went upstairs to the room I had stayed in and looked for something I had left behind. As with an old friend, the haircut and clothes were different but the character and bones remained: different curtains and bedding, but the wood frames were as I remembered them.

Behind the mirror that hung over the dresser, I had tucked a small note. One of the few French phrases I had learned was *au revoir*, which literally meant "until I see you again." I had scribbled it on a slip of paper and hidden it away, telling myself that it would be enough.

In the many years since that swim, I had imagined what it would be like to return for a visit as I had thought I might, in case the opening was still there. But like so many things, it was too late now.

I turned the mirror and held my breath. I don't know what I was hoping for but, as I had expected, the scrap of paper, yellowed over decades, fluttered to the ground. He had never found it.

I had planned that swim as much as possible, setting out the procedure for feedings, for communicating, for dealing with the unforeseen, determined not to fail a second time. I had imagined how it might go. I had imagined pausing to enjoy the sun rising when I hit midway, not realizing or refusing to remember that the pain would push even just carrying on to the edge of possibility. Hour after hour, I repeated the same basic motions: arms windmilling, legs kicking, head turning to breathe.

My mind went blank, going into some kind of hibernation that was similar to sleep; I was aware of everything, but as an observer, not a participant. I remembered noticing when the sores from my straps opened up to the acid burn of the salt, and I remembered answering questions correctly, proving that hypothermia had not set in. But these were markers: exceptions, not the norm. The swim was an immersion into trust — the trust I had in Charlie and John to keep me safe, the trust I had in myself to make it to the other side.

When I finally made it onto the shore in England, I collapsed and John rushed out of the boat to pick me up, carrying me proudly to the car before driving us home. As we pulled up to the house, the children were waiting outside holding a hand-painted sign that read "Congratulations." They were cheering and shouting for me, and I couldn't help but get swept up in the excitement of it all. It was my first successful swim and I was exhausted, swollen, and covered in sores — fit only for several days of bed rest. But I had done it.

As I returned from France the second time, my sores internal now and more than a few days of bed rest in my future, I remembered that hard-won sense of exhaustion, the pride I had felt upon returning home, and a feeling of things having just begun.

Henry drove us home and our house as it had looked that day forty years ago came back to me in detail: I pictured Iain and Harriet jumping for joy and thought of how happy we had all been then. I missed my family and wished for more time.

The evening air was full of hawthorn. Henry offered to come in and sit with me for a while but I didn't accept. Instead, I went into my dark house alone and sat in the kitchen and cried. I cried for lost chances and for all the people who were no longer in my life.

JOHN DEAR

JOHN, 2010

IT WAS A Sunday afternoon when I returned from a weekend golfing in Newcastle. Webb limped up to greet me, his excitement in no way diminished by his uneven gait. I put my clubs down next to the front door along with my carryall, and went through to the kitchen.

"Who's coming to dinner?" I asked as I kissed my wife.

"No one," Martha replied, her attention focused on peeling potatoes.

"A roast just for us?"

She nodded.

"Bit much, don't you think?"

"It's a special occasion."

"Really?"

The knife hit the wooden cutting board with more force than necessary. "Really."

"Have I forgotten something?"

She shook her head.

We were no longer young, my wife and I, but we were not the old I had pictured as a child, of elderly people with stooped backs and walking sticks and feebleness of mind and body. We were in the process of becoming old but we had not yet fully settled into old age, or so I thought. There were signs of impending changes, some of which we saw and acknowledged for what they were. Others we swept quickly under the rug in the hopes that they were unfortunate and unusual.

"Dinner won't be long," she said.

I went upstairs to unpack. Our bed was unmade, which was unusual, but I didn't think anything of it. I straightened the white duvet and put my things away. I laid out my comb and cologne on the dresser, put my dirty clothes in the hamper, and then bent to return my bag to the bottom of the wardrobe. It wouldn't fit in the space, so I had to drag a few things out in order to squeeze it in. First my dress shoes, which hadn't been worn in so long they had accumulated a thin film of dust; as I brushed them off absently I noticed what had been nestled behind them. It was the old case I used to bring in the boat when I accompanied Martha on her cross-Channel swims.

I smiled as I ran my hands over its worn leather and rusting clasps. It was a well-travelled bag. Opening it, my fingers searched until they felt the smooth glass of the jar I was looking for.

I tilted the jar back and forth to see if the pebbles would make the same sound as they did on the beach when the sea receded, but they did not. On the beach it sounded as though they were singing in a way, a light tinkling noise that was linked in my mind to Martha. Most people would have thought the sea sounded like waves cresting onto a beach, but for me it sounded like a child's toy piano.

I was just about to open the jar to see if the stones still held the smell of the water when Martha called me to dinner.

She was sitting at the table when I went downstairs, the roast dinner laid out in front of her. I took my seat and my stomach rumbled in anticipation.

"How was the weekend?"

"Fine. Glad I went."

"You didn't…"

I shook my head. "I drew no more attention to myself than Leith did after five pints."

She passed me the gravy boat.

"How was your weekend?" I asked.

"Quiet, mostly."

Martha cut her lamb with surgical precision. Her plate achieved a level of organization that the armed forces could have aspired to: nothing touched anything else. I knew that this was a tell. She was in charge of that plate and the food would follow her instructions.

"Martha?"

She speared a carrot and chewed deliberately.

"Yes, John?"

I put my cutlery down and waited. She continued to eat but would not look at me.

"Is there something? Did something happen at the weekend?"

I thought of the unmade bed, which led me to notice, in hindsight, the newspapers piled on the side, and the fact that Henry had not immediately appeared when my taxi pulled up to the house earlier.

She paused as her fork was about to go into her mouth. She returned it to the side of the plate, lamb sticking to the tines.

"Yes, actually."

I waited. She took a deep breath.

"I need to go in for some medical treatments."

"Medical treatments?"

"Yes."

"For what?"

"For something I have."

"Which is?"

She looked up from her plate and met my gaze. "Cancer," she said, and picked up the fork, eating the lamb.

"Cancer?" I whispered. I could barely bring myself to say the word.

She nodded.

"How serious is it?"

"It's cancer, John. When is it not serious?"

That she answered in her usual clipped tone — the one she saved for things that beggared belief — meant she was the woman I had waved goodbye to on Thursday, and that though this was awful news, her character remained intact.

"Eat your dinner before it goes cold," she said.

I stayed at the table after we were finished to keep her company as she did the washing-up. It was the same kitchen table we'd had since we were first married; the marks and gouges in the wood were mementoes of our family's life together.

When you're first married and just starting out, you don't think of things like cancer. When you buy things like sofas and beds, sheets and crockery, tables and chairs, you don't think about things beyond what's immediately practical. Your mind is focused on the present and maybe the near future — and the price — but nothing more. When we were picking this table out I never thought about what it would have to see us through over the years. I didn't think to wonder then if it would be able to endure the awkward Christmases, the silent dinners, and the teary breakfasts.

I didn't ask, is this table strong enough to hold me up when my wife tells me she has cancer?

THE LAST TIME this table had withstood anything on a similar level was the last Christmas that Harriet came home.

It was Boxing Day and we were all in our traditional spots: Martha and me at the heads, Iain to my left, and Harriet to my right. It was the sort of dinner we had had every night when they were growing up, a simple family meal. It was my favourite part of the day. I looked around at them and was astonished at the people our children had become: competent, successful adults. They had done so many things that their mother and I had never dreamed of. Both had gone to university and both had moved to London to fight it out amongst the great and the good. Promising careers looked set to see them through their adult lives.

"How long are you two with us?" I asked.

"I've taken until New Year's off," Iain said. "But I'm thinking I'll head back to London tomorrow or possibly the day after. Depends if Eric can get away tomorrow evening."

"I haven't heard that name in a while," Martha said.

"He's been busy. They have two girls now."

"Two children already?"

Iain nodded. "Their youngest, Abbey, has come down with the flu. If she's better and his missus doesn't mind, we're hoping to catch up over a few drinks tomorrow."

"And you, Harry? Seeing any old chums while you're here?" I asked.

"No, not really," she said. "Haven't kept in touch."

"I saw Amy's mum last week in the Post Office. She expected her back here for the holidays. I'm sure she'd love a phone from you," Martha said.

"I bet she would," Harriet said under her breath.

"Sorry?" Martha said, cupping her hand to her ear.

"Nothing," Harriet said, before she drained her glass. "Is there any more wine?"

"John, see if there's anything in the kitchen, would you?"

I brought another bottle back to the table. "Good job I stocked up," I said, jokingly.

Glasses were topped up all around.

"I have some news," Harriet said.

"Go on then," I said.

"Harry," Iain cautioned.

They exchanged looks and I wondered what they were up to.

"I have good news," she said, unable to contain her smile. "I'm seeing someone." She was worrying the edge of the table-cloth and I was expecting her to announce her engagement next.

"That's wonderful news," I said.

"I'm glad you think so."

"What's the lucky man's name, then?" I said.

"Iris."

"That's a very unusual name for a man. Is he foreign?"

"No, from Devon. But he's a she."

My daughter stared at her brother and a grim silence fell over us.

"Sorry?" I said.

I looked at Martha's face for clarity but her expression was as blank as my own must have been.

"Iris is a woman. She's a schoolteacher."

"I don't follow you," I said.

"John," my wife tempered, as though I were being wilfully ignorant.

"I don't understand why this man is a woman."

I thought I saw Harriet roll her eyes at her brother.

"Because I'm a lesbian, Dad."

She said it in a clear, authoritative voice as if it were the most natural thing in the world. Everyone at the table looked at me and what I remember most is the smell of the Brussels sprouts, wilted and sour, that we hadn't finished.

"Don't be ridiculous, Harriet. You're not a lesbian," I said.

Iain looked away.

"That's preposterous. You were raised in a good home. Properly. There's no reason you would have become a deviant."

"I'm not a deviant."

"Of course you're not. You'll find the right man soon enough."

"No I won't. I've found the right woman."

"Harriet, stop this immediately." I heard my own voice grow louder.

"John," Martha said.

"What?" I replied.

"Let's not do this," she said.

"Do what? I'm simply pointing out that she cannot possibly be involved with a woman."

"I am," Harriet said. "I'm very much involved with her. In fact, we're moving in together as soon as we can find a place we can afford."

"You'll do no such thing."

"What? Are you going to stop me? Come to London and forbid it?"

"If I have to, yes."

"Dad, can't you just be happy for her?" Iain said.

"There's nothing to be happy about. It's against everything that's right and good in the world. It's against God and it's against nature and I won't hear any more about it."

"'Against nature'? You do know that homosexuality can be found in animals, birds… even the Ancient Greeks, they were queer."

"Do not use that kind of language in my house," I growled.

"What kind of language?" She locked eyes with me. "Oh, did you mean saying the word sex? Because that's what couples generally do, Dad. You've even done it, at least twice."

"Harriet Elizabeth Roberts!" I stood up and knocked my chair backward. "That is enough! If you cannot behave in a decent, reasonable manner then you will have to leave."

"You're kicking me out? On Christmas?"

"It's Boxing Day. And I will not have someone under my roof —"

"It's Mum's house too," she said smugly. "And mine, and Iain's."

"It is most certainly not your house!"

Harriet looked to her mother then — for help or comfort, I didn't know — but whatever it was she was hoping to find, it wasn't there. My wife stared at her plate.

"And you are not my daughter. As long as you continue to behave in this manner —"

"What? Falling in love? You'd rather I was with a man I didn't love? You'd rather I lived a life of quiet desperation, like you? Whiling away the days in a passionless life, content to appear happy rather than actually be happy?"

"Harriet," Martha said. "Calm down." She reached out for our daughter's hand.

"And you'll be happy?" I demanded. "This life will make you happy? You'll never have children. You'll never get married. You won't be able to lead a normal life!"

I thought of how much I had loved watching her grow as a little girl, how much enjoyment she had given me as I taught her to ride a bicycle, helped her to zip up her jacket; I thought of the thin wisps of hair that used to tickle my face when she sat on my knee as I read the paper to her.

Her expression changed when I said "happy." The stubborn fight in her flushed cheeks and her fiery eyes — that headstrong look that she and I shared — vanished. In its place was a Harriet I didn't recognize. Her eyes welled up with tears and she ran upstairs to her room, as though she were a little girl and I had just scolded her for leaving the heating on or hitting her brother.

"Get out!" I couldn't believe what I was saying but I was saying it. "Get out of this house this instant and don't you come back until you see sense. I will not have you staying here one minute longer!"

Harriet returned to London that evening, to where she felt loved and accepted and happy. Her home, our home, shrunk again.

Weeks later, in the doldrums of February when the wind and rain were competing and the sky was showing off all the variations of grey it knew, I came home from work to find a copy of the *Guardian* on the kitchen table at my spot.

Martha was in the kitchen, busy with something on the stove, her swimsuit drying near the radiator and steaming up the windows. Webb was asleep under the table. The evening's routine was unbroken except for the new addition of the newspaper.

I kissed Martha on the cheek and she nodded toward the paper.

"Life and Style section, page two," she said.

"What's happening?"

"Life and Style section, page two," she repeated.

"Why won't you just tell me what's going on?"

She put her hands on her hips and gave me a look I knew well enough. It was a look that meant I was to do as I was told.

I opened the paper and didn't see anything particularly noteworthy.

"What am I looking at?"

"Toward the bottom, right-hand side."

"Martha, I'm tired. Just tell me what you want me to see."

She wiped her hands on a tea towel and came over beside me.

"There," she said, pointing as though it were obvious.

And there in the byline was Harriet's name, in black and white. I felt Martha's hand on my shoulder.

"The *Guardian*," I said. "Of course."

"What do you mean, 'of course'?"

She pressed her hand into my shoulder in a way that was not entirely loving.

"Well," I said, choosing my words carefully. "Someone like her wouldn't be writing for the *Daily Mail*."

She took her hand off my shoulder and swatted the back of my head.

"John," she said.

"It's true."

"'Someone like her,'" she mimicked. "She's your daughter."

My instinct was to correct her, but that would have been foolish. And would have only served to reinforce something I wished I could take back.

"Is she?" I said. "Is she still my daughter?"

"Don't be daft."

"It's an honest question."

"Is it?" she said, going back to the pot on the stove that was bubbling vigorously.

"What do you mean by that?"

She stirred the pot. "You were the one who disowned her."

"I didn't mean it."

"Sounded like you were quite serious at the time."

"Well, that was then."

"And this is now?"

Martha had that tone that subtly implied I was being ridiculous.

"What do you want me to do?" I asked.

She added salt to what smelled like lamb stew. Her back was to me and I wished I was able to see her face.

"Martha?"

She put the wooden spoon down slowly on the saucer to the left of the hob. Then she turned around, her face a tangle of emotions.

"You can start by reading the article she wrote and being proud of her."

I read the article, twice. While I was reading it, all I could think of were not the recommendations the government had devised to encourage better eating habits amongst its citizens, but the girl I had helped raise. I remembered how impatient she had been to learn to read. She would sit on my knee after dinner as I read to her from the paper, her finger following along, her mouth working as though somehow chewing the words to get a sense of them.

When we'd finished eating that evening, Martha cleared the plates quickly and set out her Channel charts.

"You're thinking of doing another swim?" I asked.

She mumbled something in a non-committal way and I took the hint.

"Think I'll take Webb out for his constitutional," I said.

"Fine," she replied, without looking up.

The dog and I had a few well-trodden routes that we took on our evening walks; but that night, I didn't feel the pull of the castle's grounds or any of the woods on the eastern side of town. Instead we walked without a specific destination or path in mind, letting our feet make the decisions.

Eventually we ended up on what was technically called the Marine Parade even though the locals all just referred to it as the harbourfront, if they were that specific at all. We walked parallel to the shoreline and listened to the wind whip the water into waves that threw themselves against the breakwater a few hundred metres out. Nights like this made me wary of the sea — tonight, more so than usual — though Webb didn't appear bothered.

We walked away from the pier, toward the foot of the castle, and when the weather overwhelmed us I decided we should call into the White Horse Inn for a swift one. It wasn't my habit to frequent pubs — I wasn't much of a drinker — but there were times when the idea of a cozy, warm pub on a dark, wintery evening seemed the most sensible course of action. And this pub in particular always felt welcoming.

Away from the drafts of the door, we settled in and my thoughts drifted to London and my daughter. I pictured her life as best I could but it was difficult, having never once gone to London myself. I knew it purely from pictures — and even then it was only the newsworthy areas or places popular with tourists that I had seen. Piccadilly Circus, Oxford Street, the

Houses of Parliament and Big Ben. Trafalgar Square. I had no idea what the residential areas looked like, so in my mind they looked like Dover but on a much grander scale.

I tried my best to imagine Harriet going to the butcher's and the greengrocer's, doing her weekly shop as Martha had always done, but I realized that I was just substituting our experiences for hers. Knowing the insignificant details of her life felt important; even though I knew that wasn't the point, it was easier to focus on the inconsequential, the trivial. It brought my attention to the fact that my assumptions about our relationship had been inaccurate for years. I had thought that I knew her well, knew her character and personality in the way that only a parent could. But the revelations of Boxing Day had proven otherwise. When had it happened? When had we grown apart? Because it felt like it had happened much less recently than Christmas.

I sunk a pint and tried to work out how I might bring myself to overlook my daughter's choices — because that seemed like the only solution if I wanted to be part of her life again. What would have been preferable, of course, was her not having mentioned it in the first place. What could we have possibly gained from knowing?

These were not helpful thoughts and so I pushed them from my mind. What would it take to bring her back into the fold?

I went to the bar and got another pint and as I was sitting down I knew exactly what I would have to do. Apologize. There was simply nothing else for it.

An apology. It was so simple. I'm sorry, Harriet. That was all I needed to say; but the difficult part was, I would have to mean it. By uttering those few, small words I would sanction her actions and negate my beliefs. And I didn't know if I had it in me to do it, though I knew it was the right thing to do.

I got up and asked the barman for a piece of paper and a pen. I didn't trust myself to have the courage to say it over the phone.

My hand was poised at the top of the paper for a long time. I thought of her face at the dinner table that Boxing Day evening. How wretched she must have felt. When my thoughts wandered to my own feelings, I pushed them away.

Focus on her, I told myself. Focus on everything else about her that you love. She is an accumulation of hundreds and thousands of other things. She is not just someone who has made the wrong choice. It's not your choice, it's hers. It's her life.

Eventually, I was able to begin.

Dear Harry, I wrote.

And then I didn't know what to say. All I had to do was write *I'm sorry*. It should not have been hard.

I thought of Martha, a few miles off the French coast, right where the currents were strongest. I remembered watching her exhaust herself swimming just to keep in place as the wind picked up and the chop increased to the point where the bright yellow of her swimming cap appeared intermittently. She did not give up, though I'm certain part of her wanted to.

Dear Harry,

I read your article that was in today's Guardian. *It was very good, well-written, balanced, informed. I'm so proud of you. You're a talented young woman and you have accomplished a lot.*

I remember when you were a little girl and you sat on my lap and we read the paper together. I hope I have had a positive influence on you and the choices you've made in your career.

I can't pretend to understand all the decisions you've made in your life and I can't say I agree with them either.

But what I can say is that you are my daughter and I love you.

I read the short note back and had no idea if it would be enough.

When Webb and I got home, the lights were off except for the one over the front door. It was late — for us — and I knew Martha would have gone to bed. I shuffled through the drawers in the kitchen and the living room, looking for the address book, an envelope, and a postage stamp. It was important to have it ready to send in the morning in case I lost my nerve. I found what I needed and put the letter in the breast pocket of my jacket.

In the morning, the nearer I got to the postbox, the more nervous I became. But the letter slipped through the slot with ease and that was that. In the days and weeks that followed I waited, hoping for a reply, but nothing came. I had been rebuffed.

Now, as Martha and I sat acting out a normal Sunday, pretending to eat our roast dinner, I promised myself that I would not make the same mistake again. I would not wait until it was too late to do anything.

"Martha," I said. "I love you."

She was in the middle of chewing and nearly choked on her food.

"John, are you all right?"

I put my hand on her arm. "What makes you think I'm not?"

"It's a bit out of the blue."

It's a strange thing to be pleased and dismayed simultaneously. Her shock at my outburst led me to wonder if I ought to remind her of how much she meant to me more often.

"I don't say that enough, do I?"

"You don't need to tell me something I already know."

"Don't you like hearing it?"

"I do, it's just … unusual."

I pushed the plate with my uneaten dinner away. "I don't know what to do."

"Eat your dinner."

"That's not what I meant."

"I know, but it's what I want," she said. "This cannot take over our lives."

"How can it not? You're ill."

"I'll get better."

"How do you know?"

"I don't."

"What happens if you don't?"

"You'll carry on."

"Not without you."

"Don't be ridiculous. You know perfectly well you will."

I thought of the moment when I had first seen her. She had been riding her bicycle down by the sea. I had promised myself I would find out who she was. I had gone to great lengths to meet her and convince her to go out with me.

As I listened to the water sloshing about in the sink as she washed the plates, I thought about the moments in my life when more had been expected of me. They were small moments, mostly, but there were a few bigger ones, too.

I remembered dragging her out of the sea when I thought she might not make it and I remembered asking her to come out — voluntarily — for me. I had asked her to give up a part of herself and I remembered when she had one day asked for it back.

There she was in a white dress saying yes, then in hospital holding Harriet — our firstborn — and then again with Iain. People said they looked like me, Harriet in particular, but to my eye they both took after Martha: hazel eyes, pronounced cupid's bows above their mouths, and freckles when they were younger. I remembered the way Martha looked at me when I first held our daughter. It was as if she couldn't believe it.

I saw her left hand when I tied the myrtle on her finger and then, finally, the ring; and I could feel the smoothness of the pebbles I had collected for each swim she did. And the tan lines, oh, the tan lines. If ever there was anything more alluring than those, I had not seen it. They criss-crossed her back and were such a constant that I came to forget their uniqueness.

I thought of Martha and of all the things she had done for me in the course of our life together. And I imagined what it would be like if she were gone.

No one would make my dinner and sit with me while I ate. It was a selfish thought, but an honest one. I was completely capable of making it myself; it was not my lack of cooking ability that was upsetting. And it was not why she cooked for me. Part of it was because she cared for me. It was why she washed and ironed my clothes, why she held my hand, and why she had stayed with me all these years even when I was unbearable. The bed would be empty if she were gone. She wouldn't pull my arm around her as she waited for sleep. No one would kiss me first thing in the morning and last thing at night.

Without Martha what would our home be? Just four walls and a roof, and the idea of it made me sick. I went up behind her and wrapped my arms around her, snuggling my head in the crook of her neck.

"John," she said. "I'm busy."

I spun her around slowly and admired her face. I took a breath, as though to speak, but found that I couldn't. I couldn't tell her how scared I was.

She put her hand — covered in a soapy, wet Marigold glove — on my shoulder, closed her eyes, and leaned into me, her head resting on my chest. I smelled the almond-scented shampoo she used and knew that it would always be her shampoo in my mind.

"I'll fight it," she said.

"Of course."

"I'll think of it like a swim. Focus, commitment."

"No," I said. "Don't confuse it with something you love."

"It will take the same amount of strength and determination."

"It will ruin the sea."

"Since when did you side with the sea?"

"Always," I said.

"You have not."

"I have always sided with you, and you have always sided with the sea."

It was true.

The letter I had written to Harriet had provoked nothing in the way of a response; after a month, I had forgotten about it. So I'd been surprised, three months later, when the grey sky had taught itself some new colours and the rain had worn itself out, to see an envelope waiting for me on the kitchen table.

It was unopened, with the words "no longer at this address" scrawled across the front. I remembered wishing Martha hadn't seen it. I decided that either Harriet had moved or — more likely — she had refused to open it in silent protest. In sending it back she was forcing me to bear witness to my own failures.

I had picked it up and turned it over in my hands. Martha said nothing, but she went to the sideboard and got the address book out. She set it on the table, open to the right page, and pointed.

"Try again," she said, her finger stabbing at what I assumed was Harriet's most recent address.

I shook my head. "What's the point? She knows everything I've said in here."

"Knowing isn't the same thing as hearing."

So I had put the unopened envelope into a larger envelope and addressed it correctly. I put it in the postbox and hoped for the very, very best.

The dishwater from the Marigold gloves had soaked through my shirt but I didn't let go of Martha. I leaned back and looked at her, recommitting to memory all the things I had already stored about her face, and I said the things that we both knew and that we both needed to hear.

"I love you," I said.

"I won't let this hurt you," she said.

"I promised to protect you and I will. I promised I would love you forever and I will."

Her eyes got wet and she nodded. "I know, John."

THE TIDE TURNED

MARTHA, 2011

THERE WERE GOOD days and bad days, but it was impossible to predict when either would arrive. All we could do was muddle through as best we could. It was a shared life that we navigated together and I don't know if it was the one John had imagined for us, if it had changed in ways he hadn't anticipated or if — when we were young and first married — he had considered our future at all beyond the perfunctory basics: marriage, home, children. A checklist that would grow into a life.

No, that's unkind. In truth, I didn't know what he wanted and hoped for, what the contents of his dreams for us were, because I had never asked. I hadn't thought he would need to be asked. But as with many things with my husband, the truth was not at all what I had imagined.

I heard him creaking down the stairs as I rested my head on the gloriously cold bathroom tiles and I wondered which John would be joining me that morning: the lucid one or the more recent version of himself — a man who had lately proven rather adept at time travel, skipping backward and forward through the years at uneven speeds.

Webb had taken it as his duty to stay with me through the night; his nose a familiar comfort seen through the crack of the door. He finally roused himself when he heard John's footsteps. The pair of them shuffled with uneven gaits as they crossed the kitchen, angling toward one another and meeting at the counter where the dog would be hoping for the crusts, which he saw as payment for a hard night's work.

The kitchen tap ran, and a few moments later I heard John put what I knew to be the empty glass on the counter. I counted to five and when he cleared his throat I smiled and took comfort in knowing someone else's habits so deeply.

I tested the waters and slowly lifted my head off the tiles, the aches in my body seeking out recesses in my joints that I had never known existed. When my head was level with my shoulders I paused, waiting to see if the nausea would strike again. I thought of all the times I'd been in the pilot's boat, speeding back across the chop for three hours from Cap Gris Nez, and how I had never once been seasick. I thought darkly of this new development as a way of making up for lost time, my days and nights spent here next to the toilet, holding on for dear life as my stomach convulsed and my insides burned.

There was a gentle knock on the door. "Martha?" John asked.

I managed a feeble reply. "Yes."

I could imagine my daughter and her wife seeing this sort of behaviour as antithetical to a marriage. I would not have been surprised if they left the bathroom door open at all times and believed privacy was a barrier to be overcome.

"Are you all right?" he asked.

Questions that were once banal had become imperative overnight. "Yes," I said.

I had no idea if it was true or not. Along with my left breast, I had lost the ability to tell.

"I'm putting the kettle on," he said.

"Good."

"Will I make two?"

"Hot water, lemon, and honey," I said. The trick to being sick was to avoid dehydration, and that I knew how to do.

While the kettle boiled I hoisted myself into a seated position, pushing my top half up to lean my back against the tub. I was dismayed to see how shrivelled and weak my arms had become. The skin hung off what used to be biceps, and the deltoids that had always caused so much trouble when I had tried to squeeze them into women's blouses now looked beaten and withered.

John knocked on the door again. "You decent?"

"Yes, come in."

He opened the door and I laughed at the sight of him: worn flannel pyjamas, tartan dressing gown, white hair stood on end like a mad professor, carrying a tray full of tea things.

"You needn't have made such a fuss," I said as he shuffled in.

He balanced the tray on the edge of the sink. "Nonsense. If you're going to do something . . ."

"You may as well do it properly," I finished.

He set my drink on the floor.

Webb wormed his way into the room, coming up to me and sniffing my feet, legs, and arms and then, apparently unable to resist, licking my face. When I pushed him away he looked crushed.

"Good dog," I said, and he settled himself in the doorway, guarding the threshold from potential intruders.

John looked around for a place to sit. "Crowded in here."

I motioned to the toilet. "Sit there," I suggested.

He shook his head and climbed into the tub. "You might need that."

I shook my head. "I don't see how I could, there's nothing left."

Blowing steam off my drink, I sipped at it slowly. It was a relief to feel liquid on my lips and tongue. "I would have thought the sickness would have passed by now."

"It can't last much longer, now the treatment's finished."

We stayed like that until mid-morning, communing in the commode as the sun shone brightly through the window, talking intermittently. It had all the makings of a good day.

John said, "I'd like to take you out."

I turned to look at him, his head resting between the soaps and shampoos, to see if he was having me on. "Take me out where?"

"It's been ages since we went out together."

"We went to the doctor last week."

"That's not what I mean," he said.

"I know."

"We don't have to, if you don't feel up to it."

Sometimes, it's the unpredictability of life that makes it wonderful. The expression on my husband's face was irresistible and reminded me of his more youthful self: the sharp cheekbones and the sly look in his grey eyes that meant he was ready to have a little fun.

I felt awful but the winter had lasted too long and I had felt like death warmed over for ages.

"Yes," I said. "Let's."

"Good."

"Where will we go?"

"I have an idea."

I smiled: it was my John who was here today.

"Fine, I'll get dressed and put my hair on."

An hour later we were standing in front of the door, ready to go.

"You look lovely," he said.

I had pulled from the depths of my wardrobe an old navy dress that reminded me of one I used to wear when we started to date.

He grinned and moved closer, putting a sprig of myrtle through my buttonhole, then he held my shoulders and kissed me on the mouth, as though we were still young.

"Do you remember?" he whispered.

"I could never forget."

He sighed happily. "I haven't, yet."

"I'll remember for both of us."

"I had planned it so much better."

"It was a perfect night."

"Was it?"

I took his hand in mine. "I said yes, didn't I?"

He opened the door and led me outside where Henry was waiting by the car.

"You didn't think I'd make you walk, did you?" John said.

We got in the back seat and Henry pulled out of the drive, piloting the car toward the centre of town. I rolled my window down and felt the warm, late-spring breeze on my face, the smell of the sea pulling me close. I hadn't seen it since before the chemotherapy and I felt like I had abandoned an old friend. It had been nearly three months, but when we turned the corner and it came into view it was exactly as I had left it: gleaming, swirling, teeming with life.

Henry turned the car again and we entered the dull cement backstreets, which to me were capable only of being gloomy even on the sunniest days. We pulled up to the curb and John came round to help me out.

"We'll get a taxi back later," he said.

"Enjoy yourselves. Don't do anything I wouldn't do," Henry called as he drove away.

"Where are we going?" I asked.

John was obviously pleased with himself and wouldn't tell me. "It's not far," was all he said.

We walked slowly along the pavement and I was surprised at how much the town had changed. Normally if I came this far, it was only ever to see the sea. To me the city was full of shadows and dust, shops that shut early, and shops that had shut permanently, with boarded-up doorways covered in peeling paint. Where I remembered there being a greengrocer there was a betting shop, and where the sewing shop had once been, there was a charity shop that seemed down on its luck.

John stopped in front of a restaurant with a tattered white awning. In green lettering it said *Dino's established 1975*, but it did not look open. We peered in the window and all we saw was the dining room, empty except for one table with a stack of unopened post.

Though he tried not to show it I could tell he was upset, and I tried my best to keep the mood light. If he got too upset, the day could quickly slide into disaster.

He smiled weakly. "This is where I'd planned on going."

"How were you to have known it was shut?"

"No, I mean before. When I proposed. This is the place where we missed our reservation. It doesn't look like much now, but back then…"

"A friend of mine went once. She said it was the nicest place she'd ever been. Linen napkins."

"I thought . . ." he said.

"It's the thought that counts."

He looked around nervously and I could see he was getting anxious, but then he took my hand and asked if I could manage to walk a short ways. I said yes and so he led me down the street and back toward the sea.

The sea. My own true north.

We walked along the parade, arms linked, with the sun shining on our faces and it was glorious. The copper-coloured pebbles glowed, making the water even more brilliantly blue. It was not a tropical hue; the sea here was not a lazy colour, it was cold and sharp. The contrast with the pebbles made it look like a high winter sky in a northern climate: crisp, clean, and pure. And the longer I looked at it, the more inviting it felt.

Slowly we shuffled toward the pier. The promenade was dotted with benches and out of necessity we stopped frequently. The chemotherapy had weakened me and I was not myself.

I eased myself down onto a bench. John sat next to me and when I turned to him, intending to rest my head on his shoulder, I noticed something. Mounted on the wooden boards was a small, black plaque:

In memory of Mrs. Ann Martin
There'll be love and laughter and peace ever after

"John," I said, running my fingers over the words.

"I remember that song," he said with pride.

He put his hand on my knee.

"Do you remember?" he asked. "One summer, after Harriet was born, but before Iain. We danced here. I think it was here." He looked up and down the promenade. "There was a fete and a band. And I swung you around."

I closed my eyes and could see it all. "I wore that red blouse, with the bows on the sleeves."

"That was one of my favourites, the red."

"We had Harriet in the pram, and you put it to one side so we could have a dance."

"I always did like dancing with you."

"But I'm clumsy," I said. "Terrible dancer."

"You always held on tighter than the other girls."

I opened my eyes and his face was so close to mine our noses nearly touched. He was grinning like a schoolboy. I slapped his arm.

"How many other girls?"

"Loads," he said. "Too many to count."

We laughed.

"John," I said. "I want a bench, with a plaque."

"What on earth for?" he asked incredulously.

"To mourn me," I said. I gave him a sly look and he struggled to keep a straight face. "I absolve you of three months' wearing black, but I insist on a bench with a plaque," I said, with as much high-intensity drama as any of the actresses on *Coronation Street* could muster.

"What makes you think you'll go first?" He winked at me. "I could forget myself, cross the road without looking."

I undid the top buttons on my blouse and pointed to my mastectomy scars.

He squeezed my knee and looked up to the sky, and I looked ahead at the water. If I had to go, there was something fitting about leaving my name here, as a reminder to the two things I had known most intimately.

He stood up and held his hand out for me. I took it, thinking we were going to head back home, but he steered us toward the pier.

"The tea room will be open," he said with confidence.

We passed other couples as we strolled down the pier, including a pair of teenagers clutching one another, hands in each other's back pockets, looking furtively for a quiet spot where they would remain unseen.

I nodded my head at them.

"Do you remember?" I said.

John blushed.

It had been shortly before he proposed. Up to then, there had been some tame fumbling in his car, in the cinema, and on my parents' doorstep, but nothing more than that.

That summer, though, there had been a stretch of days when the weather had been so glorious it was almost as if we didn't live in England. The grey was gone and it was finally hot.

It was a Saturday, and I had elected to wear a dress other than one of the ones my mother usually insisted upon. With these ensembles she intended to convey to John, and any other potential suitor who might make himself known, that I was a young lady and would make a wonderful mother, delightful wife, and competent homemaker. How all of that could have possibly been transmitted through fabric and frills was a mystery to me, but then my mother looked at clothes with an eye I'd never developed. She said it was important to show off my best assets, so when I tried on a frock that hit just below the knee, where my calves had developed nicely — "shapely," my mother called it — that dress was purchased immediately.

The real issue was when we had to consider necklines and straps. My mother favoured thin, dainty straps, but those made my broad shoulders appear even more masculine. Coupled with the tan lines from my swimming costume, I wound up wearing a lot of dresses with sleeves and a high neck. They made me feel caged.

It was too warm that evening for anything of that sort, so I wore a navy blue dress I had selected myself. It was one of the few dresses I had ever had that I truly enjoyed wearing. It had a halter-neck tied with a bow at the nape and the shape was A-line, gently flowing out at the bottom, with what my mother called an empire waist. There was an eyelet detail along the hem. But what I liked was that it looked like the sort of thing a chic Parisian might wear. When I put that dress on I felt as though I could have been my mirror self, but French, not English.

When John pressed the bell that evening, I answered the door in that navy dress and a pair of yellow sandals. He was silent as he looked me up and down and it was the first time I had properly felt like a woman. I twirled around for him and was thrilled he was lost for words.

I called goodbye to my parents and linked my arm in his.

"Where shall we go?" I asked.

"Anywhere you like," he said.

Around the bend in the road, out of sight of my mother — who had a habit of peering out the front window — John took me by the waist and drew me close, kissing me the way he did when we didn't want the evening to end.

"You're terrible," I said when our noses were nearly touching.

"I'm not the one in the dress," he replied, grinning.

There was no one else on the road and he moved behind me.

"What are you doing?"

I felt his finger on my back and it sent a shiver through my body as he traced the outline of my swimming costume that the sun had made. He kissed my bare shoulder and I swatted him away — a pretence of modesty, I didn't want him to stop.

"What if someone sees us?"

I felt his lips brush my neck when he said, "I'm sure they've seen much worse."

We went to the White Horse Inn, our favourite pub due to its back garden. There we could sit in the shadows of the ruins of the old St. James the Apostle church and be assured of as much privacy as was possible in public in a small town. Dusk crept over the top of the crumbling yellow bricks of the church — a reminder that the toll of the war was still to be found. John and I had a drink and then another, but I was restless in the muggy air, so unusual for us on the coast. I wanted to walk so we went along the parade, which was full of people: couples, families, and children all out looking for a cool breeze to relieve the sticky stupor inflicted by the heat.

It seemed reasonable to think that the sea would have a cooling effect, but there was no breeze, not even a gust, off the water that night. The sea was calm, lapping gently away at the pebbles on the beach and providing a delicate, tinkling soundtrack.

Being in the midst of the crowds made me feel even warmer than before, so I hopped down onto the pebbles and turned to gesture for John to follow. I needn't have bothered, though: he was right behind me.

I went straight for the sea.

"But Martha," he called. "I can't swim."

I paid him no attention as I strode across the beach, heading under the pier where it was cool and dark and we could be alone.

Near the back, away from the shoreline, we were mostly

hidden from view and though there were people on the beach, we were secluded enough. John put his arms around me and we kissed the way people do when they're first in love: quickly and greedily. I couldn't get enough of him.

John was bolder than ever that night. His hand ran up my leg, lifting my dress, moving steadily up my thigh. I didn't think I could hold out much longer — we were young, it was a hot summer, and everything felt natural. If swimming had taught me anything — and it had taught me a great deal — it was that our bodies were made to be used. They had purpose beyond whatever our minds dictated.

I heard the pebbles moving around us and I thought it was our shifting feet as we tried to move closer and closer to each other. I had thought we were alone under the pier, and though I heard soft voices and a cough, I ignored them. John didn't appear to have noticed and all I was interested in was him.

But then we heard a whistle coming from the shoreline and John turned to see two men standing only a few feet away from us, cans of beer glinting in the moonlight. He didn't say anything to them, just grabbed my hand and we dashed off in the opposite direction.

"Come back!" one of them shouted. "We want to see the show!"

I giggled. John was mortified.

"I'm sorry," he said.

"For what?"

He gave me a look that I took to mean, for embarrassing you.

"They didn't ruin my evening," I said.

"They've ruined mine."

"Don't be like that."

He glanced nervously at his shoes. "My landlady is away."

"Is she?"

He nodded. "Would you like to come to mine, for a drink?"

He held out his hand and led me to his flat, and I stood in his bedroom as he untied the bow at the nape of my neck and my dress fell to the floor.

John traced my tan lines with his fingers. "You have a second skin," he said.

WE MANAGED TO shuffle to the end of the pier and John held the door to the tea room open for me. We selected a table and assumed our natural positions: I faced the water and John faced the land, and it occurred to me that if the tea room had been here when I was a girl, I might not have fallen in the sea; I might not have become myself.

"Cake?" he asked.

"No, just tea."

"You should try and eat something. Ice cream?"

I shook my head. "Tea is fine."

"Good job the restaurant was closed."

He brought two cups of builder's tea to the table and I curled my hands around the paper cup. The tea was warming and I was glad of it. Even though it was a beautiful day, I was still prone to chills.

We faced one another and as I stared at my husband's face, which was now the face of an old man, I remembered how I had wondered about people our age when I was young. I hadn't understood why they spent so much time sitting and not speaking. They had seemed to be everywhere: on benches, in pubs, and in teahouses like the one we were in now. I had thought it must be so sad to be them, sitting in silence, having run out of things to say. But now I realized that maybe they just enjoyed looking at one another, as we were — maybe that had actually been the point of it all along. Maybe the point of life was to get to the moment where all you needed was to gaze at another person's face, one you knew better than your own, reading the lines and wrinkles that marked out the years you had spent together.

The room was empty except for a family with small children who were perched near the door, the mother fighting exhaustion, the father hiding his irritation, and the children bursting with sugary energy, desperate to be allowed back outside where they were free to run.

"You know, the castle was built in the 1180s," John said, jutting his chin in its direction.

"Finally, something older than us."

"It's been standing watch and keeping us safe all these years." I sipped my tea.

"You know, everything here was built with one purpose: to protect us. Even the breakwater. It's kept you safe all these years, holding back the worst of the storms."

His talk of protecting was making me feel frail.

"What did you want to do?" I asked.

He closed his eyes, and shook his head the same way he always did when he didn't understand and felt I was being difficult for the sake of it.

"What do you mean, Martha?"

"What did you want from life?"

"What kind of a question is that?"

"One I'd like to know the answer to."

"You know the answer."

"Tell me."

"What's the point if you know what I'm going to say?"

"Because hearing is different than knowing," I said. "Hearing is better."

He reached across the table and put his hand on mine. "I got everything I wanted."

"Nothing was missed out?"

"No."

"Not one thing?"

He raised his eyebrows. "Well," he said, pausing. "I would have like to have owned a red MG."

I nearly spat my tea out, I laughed so hard. He was pleased with himself and it showed.

"I have to see a man about a dog," he said. "Meet you at the end of the pier?"

I nodded and finished what was left of my tea before following him outside, and there, near the public toilets, was a mother trying to wipe the chocolate off her son's hands, and I thought of my own children, whose younger days had been full of similar moments. Children were sticky, tricky things, needy and independent simultaneously, but there was something endearing about the way they clung to their mothers that I found myself missing. Their needs were pure and direct, with no subtext — unlike the needs of a husband.

I walked the few steps to the edge of the pier and leaned against the railing, looking down at the water where I had first fallen in. The whirl that had caught my eye when I was a girl was there below me and I took comfort in its consistency. If the currents were still here, twisting and turning, then there was no reason I shouldn't be.

The sun was warm on my face and I scratched my scalp under the edge of my wig. It was a nice enough wig, the hair fuller and of a nicer, more mahogany colour than my own had ever been, but it felt like wearing a woolly hat in summer — hot and unnecessary. I took it off and stuffed it in my pocket. To my surprise, when I ran my hand over my head I felt the tiniest bit of stubble growing back.

I walked across the width of the pier so that I could look into the harbour. On such a beautiful day, at this time of year, I knew there would be swimmers beginning their training for the forthcoming season. How I wished I could be in there with them, in the glassy sea.

Even from a distance, I could tell by the quality of their strokes who had the greatest chance of success. Some, with their elbows high, hands reaching and stretching far past their heads, looked like they might be able to finish, and in a very good time. But a Channel swim is not just about the quality of one's stroke. You have to keep going long past the point when your brain tells you it's lost all interest in swimming. You have to keep moving, continue to struggle, hour after hour and mile after mile. The body becomes a machine devoted to kicking and pulling. The key is to get beyond everything else and focus on the basic mechanics until your brain finally goes to the place where it's still. You shut everything out as much as possible.

I had always felt my swims were a chance to prove myself worthy of the sea. Some swimmers wanted to dominate it, to exert as much control as possible, but that was to miss the point. Those were people who were not going to enjoy their time in the water, and to me that was a waste. It was the same thing with the ones who were concerned with their time, who wanted to get to France as quickly as possible. Yes, by the time I had finished I was glad to be out of the water in almost every respect, but no matter how exhausted, sore, and cold I was, I knew I was privileged to have been able to spend so much time with it.

My swims were closer to conversations with an old friend — it would have been rude to rush. Though there was no chance of that: I was never a particularly fast swimmer, but I had tenacity. I stayed in for as long as it took.

Closing my eyes, I inhaled deeply. The salt air smelled like home. Town was on my left and I wondered if my life would have been better or worse if I had done things differently. What if I hadn't married and settled down? What if I had stayed in France, or taken the newsman's bait and made my first attempt before getting married? What if I hadn't had children? Would I have gotten cancer? Would I have been happy? What if, what if.

I felt the castle looming over me as it had always done. Protecting England, as John said, but what did it mean? Keeping us safe from what, exactly? There was no chance of a marauding army invading Dover these days, so what did we have to be frightened of? Was life outside the town's boundaries so dangerous? I didn't know and couldn't say because I had never gone to see.

Was it worth it? Some days I thought that swimming the twenty-one miles to France had been enough, enough of an accomplishment, enough of a challenge to set me apart. But other days I felt small, pulled under by a hollowness I could not escape. I had hoped the swims would be the thing I became known for, and they had, but did they make me more than Mrs. Roberts or Mum? Of course, I hadn't just become a mum; I had raised two brilliant, beautiful children. And I hadn't just become a wife: I had fallen in love with a good man who loved me back. Was that enough? And how could you tell?

John came up beside me and held his hand out.

"What?" I said.

He opened his fingers slowly and in his palm was a Tunnock's teacake. "Your favourite."

It was wrong to regret spending my life with him, but in that moment his kindness felt like pity and it was suffocating. He was too predictable — and what was worse was that he didn't see it that way or even care that our routine was so insufferably dull.

I thanked him and put it in my pocket.

"You need to go in?" he asked.

I nodded.

"Maybe you should. Just get your feet in, not a proper swim, but something to keep you from drying up."

My husband had somehow come to an understanding within himself.

"Just up to your knees. Give the trousers a good soaking. It might lift your spirits."

It would. I knew it, he knew it, and so did the sea: why else would it be so calm and inviting? But it wouldn't satisfy me. What I needed from the water was something private.

He put his arm around my shoulders. "Are you tired, dear? Shall we go?"

I ignored him.

"Martha?" he said.

"What, John?" I snapped.

"I'll call a taxi."

"Good. You do that. I'd like to stay a while longer."

"I won't ring for one just yet, then."

"No, I'd like to be by myself for a while."

I didn't look at him. I'd purposely ruined his very sweet romantic afternoon and I didn't care.

"I'll see you at home," I said, and marched off as quickly and stridently as possible. Which amounted to a few sharp paces before I lost my breath and had to slow down, beholden to my shuffly, cancer-ridden gait.

I stomped down to the water's edge, not watching to see if he left or not. I couldn't tear my eyes away from the swimmers. I desperately wanted to be in there with them. I should have been. Under normal circumstances I would have been; by this point in the year my tan lines would have been firmly in place. But as it was, my body had nearly returned to a uniform colour. There was a shadow — more of an echo — of my swimsuit's outline, and I wondered if that was due to my stubbornness, my refusal to accept that I may never again be amongst the swimmers in the harbour.

Maybe my last swim was already behind me.

I stared at the sea wall enclosing the harbour. I thought about how much of my life had taken place here within its confines. How I had sought out the security that came with being caged in this small piece of the sea, choosing the freedom offered by my starting point of Shakespeare's Bay only when I was surrounded by people whose presence ensured I would come back. There were other places, too, up and down the coast I could have gone to; but this is where I had learned to swim all those years ago, where I had trained, and there was something that always pulled me back here.

Eventually the late afternoon brought a breeze and I felt a chill. It was time to go home. In the taxi on the ride back I struggled to keep my eyes open. I went into our house, and when I shut the door, John came into the foyer.

Without saying a thing, he carried me upstairs, pulled back the duvet, and helped me to undress. I lay back against the pillows and felt him standing there, watching over me.

I held my hand out and he squeezed it. I burst into tears.

He stroked my hand and I let myself cry. For the first time since the diagnosis, since the operation, since the chemotherapy.

Then he let go and I felt adrift. It was as if holding on to him was the only thing tethering me to the world. He sat on the edge of the bed and took off his shoes; I heard them drop softly on the carpeting. And then he got under the duvet and wrapped his arm around me, hugging me tightly, almost clutching me to him.

"How was the water?"

"I don't know. I didn't go in."

I couldn't see him and didn't know if he smiled a little bit when I said that, but he held me even tighter then.

THE FIFTH OF SEPTEMBER

MYRTLE, PRESENT DAY

THE MORNING OF my fourteenth birthday, my alarm woke me at five a.m. as usual. I got dressed and checked to make sure I hadn't forgotten to pack anything important. My Speedo, cap, goggles, towel, paddles, and pull buoy were all present and accounted for but I couldn't leave anything to chance, so I did a quick scan of my room and then another one in the bathroom, where I found my earplugs on the counter behind a box of tissues. I chucked them in my bag and breathed a sigh of relief.

My mums couldn't know or even suspect what I was up to.

On my way out, I passed through the kitchen and saw a small box wrapped in birthday paper — glitter and multicoloured polka dots — on the counter with a note next to it.

Have a great day, hon, it read in Iris's handwriting. *Proper gifts tonight. See you at All Star Lanes at 6 p.m. We love you to bits.*

I opened it to find a cupcake oozing with frosting and covered in gold leaf, which I ate in three bites. The wrapper I left on the note as thanks.

Wiping frosting off my mouth with the back of my hand, I left the flat silently and went down the stairs. Normally I'd turn left to go to the York Hall pool, where the rest of my teammates would soon be gathering for our daily practice. But instead I carried on to the tube and to London Bridge station, where I intended to catch the 6:42 train to Dover Priory.

I should have been working on flip turns and starts but I wanted to give myself a present, something I had always wanted: I was going to introduce myself to my grandparents on my birth mother's side.

From the station, it was about fifteen minutes on foot to their house. I didn't have money for a taxi so I walked. It was nice, too, because it gave me time to rehearse what I was going to say. Not that I hadn't been doing that since I'd decided to make the trip — but going over my lines again calmed my nerves. I thought about what my coach always told me before a meet: commit and visualize. So that's what I did.

When I got to 107 Shakespeare Road I stopped, and I was a bit disappointed because their house looked pretty much like all the others. I had always believed there would be something distinctive about their house, a clue to the people who lived inside. But there was nothing more than a shiny black door and white-grey bricks. The front garden was lacklustre as well; the only thing that looked like it was thriving was an ordinary bush with tiny pink blossoms and spiky branches.

The front windows were covered with lace curtains that looked like standard-issue, old-dear drapes, the same kind you might see in a care home.

There was one positive sign: the lights were on, so someone was home. I took a deep breath, pressed the bell, and listened as it echoed in the foyer.

I heard muffled voices and I thought I saw the curtains move and then, finally, the lock turned and the door opened, revealing my grandmother.

"Yes?" she said.

All the things I had practised saying flew out of my mind. If this had been a race, I would have been disqualified immediately for falling off the starting blocks.

"Hi," was the only thing that came out of my mouth. Even my voice sounded weird: small and thin.

I couldn't take my eyes off her. She wasn't what I'd been picturing, which was your typical granny: all cardigans and cats and tissues in her sleeve. I'd known that version wasn't quite right either, because I knew what she could do. But I had never once seen a photo of her, so in my imagination she had assumed default granny status.

She was really tall, taller than me and I was nearly five foot five inches, so she must have been nearer to five foot seven, or even eight. Her shoulders were broad — though that really shouldn't have come as a surprise, because she was a swimmer. We all have broad shoulders.

"Can I help you?" she asked.

I bit my lip and stared at my feet for a few moments. "I hope so," I said, once I'd screwed up my courage. "I'm looking for Martha Roberts."

"You've found her," she replied.

A man's voice shouted from the depths of the house, "Webb!" And then a three-legged dog nearly knocked her down as it raced past me and out the front door.

"Webb!" Martha called, clapping her hands. "Come back here!" She ran toward him and the moment she was close, he dashed off just out of reach.

The man rushed out of the house and whistled. The dog perked up his ears. Martha motioned for me to walk in a large circle so I was behind the dog and then, when she nodded, I ran toward him and he bolted straight into the house. The man — who I was almost certain must be my grandfather — followed him without giving me another look.

"Thanks," she said. "Care to come in for a cup of tea?"

I nodded and followed her into the house, where the man was already seated at the kitchen table, reading the newspaper and eating a boiled egg.

"We talked about this. You can't get him all riled up like that," she said.

He ignored her.

"Sit down," she said, pointing to the kitchen table. "This is my husband, John."

He grunted without looking up.

"Sorry, I didn't catch your name." She reached into the cupboard for mugs.

I hated my name. It was so ridiculous and old-fashioned.

"Myrtle," I said.

The moment I said my name, the mug she'd been getting down fell, bouncing off the counter before shattering on the floor.

"What are you doing?" John roared.

Webb ran back into the kitchen and went straight to Martha.

"No," she said, pushing him away with her foot. "John, he's your dog. Do something."

"He's fine."

Webb sniffed at the broken china and took one of the larger pieces in his mouth, carrying it through to the living room.

We all watched as he hopped up on the sofa, setting the china down next to him as he settled in.

"Webb!" Martha shouted. "John, get that away from him!"

"Ignore him, he won't eat it. He knows it's not food."

"That's what you said about the chicken bones," Martha said. They were carrying on as if I wasn't in the room.

"Oh Lord, the chicken bones! Are we going back to that? Are we always going to go back to the ever-loving chicken bones? Because if we are, then please, I pray that I am struck down now!" He held his arms out and looked to the ceiling.

"Stop it," she said curtly.

"Stop what? Stop going back to a minor incident that you insist on blowing out of all reasonable proportion every time the dog does something you don't want him to do? Stop rehashing something that happened ages ago and wound up being fine in the end?"

"I don't want to argue with you, please —"

I made sure to avoid eye contact with both of them. Instead I stared at the pattern on the placemat. Was this how they always were together?

"The hell you don't! All you do is argue and shout and wind me up! You pick on everything I do. All I hear, day in and day out, is John do this, John don't do that, John did you remember to do this." He pushed his chair back with enough force that it fell over. "If the dog wants to sit on the sofa and chew a chipped piece of crockery then let him!"

He stood there, apparently uncertain of where to go next, but clearly full of an energetic rage. He looked at the kitchen table, then over at the couch, and decided that things looked better with the dog. He shuffled into the living room and tripped on the edge of the rug, falling forward to land with a thud.

"Goddamnit!" he shouted, pushing the worn carpet away from his face and easing himself into a seated position.

"This house is a death trap! I'm sick and tired of this."

His face was red and he was breathing heavily.

"Nothing is simple here, ever. Traps around every corner." He glared at Martha. "You probably propped this up somehow," he said, pointing at the carpet. "You probably spent the better part of yesterday afternoon figuring out how to get me to fall down, just to prove I can't function without you."

Martha's face was stone cold but I thought I could see her eyes welling up. She seemed suddenly aware that I was in the room and forced a smile, which made me feel even more awkward.

"I should probably go," I said, getting up quickly.

"I'll walk you out," she said.

I got my bag and noticed that she got hers, too. When we were in the road she paused.

"Wait here," she said.

She went to the next-door neighbour's house and rang the bell. I watched as she had a short chat with a middle-aged man with brown hair. He did a lot of nodding then put his hand on her shoulder and nodded once more, then she came back to me.

"Is everything all right?"

"Mmm, yes. Everything is fine," she said.

We kept on walking and I wanted to ask her about her bag, which was bigger than you'd expect someone to take just to go down the shops.

"Your name is Myrtle?"

I nodded. "I hate it."

She laughed. "Myrtle, would you like to come to the seaside with me?"

The way she was acting, it's almost like she knew me.

I nodded and followed her. She walked at a good pace, and when we arrived I saw the same sea that I'd seen from the train. It was calm, the sun was shining, and I'd expected the beach to be full of people by this time of day, trying to squeeze the last bit out of summer. But I suppose they had other things to do.

We got off the pavement and went onto the pebbles and I was surprised that it wasn't a sandy beach. I'd never been to a beach without sand. It was strange and I couldn't imagine it being much fun for sunbathers. Martha sat down when we were about twenty-five metres from the water. There weren't any waves crashing dramatically onto the shore and I was a bit disappointed. In my mind the sea was always dramatic. In the distance were the ferries that went across to Calais, and some other massive boats in the harbour, but where we were was sheltered by a breakwater, making another little harbour-like area that was not that different to an incredibly huge outdoor swimming pool.

Martha stared out at the water and flexed her fingers. "Are you going to tell me why you came all this way?"

"How do you know I've come a long way?"

"Your club," she said, pointing to my bag. "Bethnal Green Sharks."

"No one survives a shark attack," I said out of habit.

She chuckled. "London's quite far."

"Not really."

"So you swim?"

"200 free, 100 fly, IM relay."

"Impressive," she said, though she didn't seem particularly impressed.

"Do you...I mean, are you a swimmer?"

"I am."

"What's your race?"

"I don't race." She picked up a coppery pebble and considered it. "I just swim. It helps me…think."

"Me too, or, well, it helps me to stop thinking."

"It's cleansing."

"How often do you go to the pool?"

"I've never been in a swimming pool in all my life."

"What?"

"Loathsome things, pools. Cold, dead. Utterly devoid of life. But the sea, well, that I go in as often as possible. Which isn't so often anymore, but as luck would have it, my strength is coming back to me and I'd planned on going in today." She pointed to her bag. "I was about to head out when you arrived."

She gave me this conspiratorial look and suddenly I felt nervous. She must have known who I was. Maybe Iris or Harriet had figured out I'd planned to come here and phoned to tell her. But I hadn't left any traces.

Martha stood up and whipped off her trousers and shirt to reveal a swimming costume not that different from mine: a dark blue Speedo but with a more modest cut in the leg. I don't know what I was expecting, but it wasn't that. Part of me had assumed — and wanted — her to act like my granny on Iris's side of the family. It was like, even though I knew she was a swimmer, I'd never been able to picture it. I guess I thought she'd wear something more mumsy.

She pulled her cap and goggles out of her bag and stuffed them under her shoulder strap. I smiled because I did almost the same thing, except I tucked them under the bum of my costume. Then she did something I really hadn't expected. She pulled off her hair.

She put her hands on her hips. "Coming?"

I must have looked really shocked.

"Chemo," she said, rubbing the stubble.

I looked away. I wanted to know details, but it hardly seemed my place to ask.

"I don't have my suit on," I said.

"But you have it with you?"

"Yeah."

She held her towel out with open arms, as if she were going to hug me. "Come on then, get a move on."

I wedged myself between the towel and the promenade, with my back to her,. When I'd finished changing, I watched her fold her things up and put them in her bag, before tucking them under a bush.

"What's that?" I asked, pointing to it. "It's the same as the one in your front garden."

She smiled softly. "Myrtle," she said. "It's commonly found near the sea."

With that, she set off toward the water. Just before I got my feet wet, I stopped.

"It's not that cold," she said.

"I've never been in the sea," I replied, shrugging.

She closed her eyes, shaking her head. "Don't worry. It feels like coming home." She held out her hand for me, and I took it, and together we waded into the glassy water.

It didn't feel anything like home. For one thing, it was incredibly cold. The water I was used to was not warm, but it was nothing like this. The sea burned and it felt different, smoother against my skin. The rocky ground shifted underneath my feet and though instantly I couldn't feel my toes, I knew I was touching slimy, disgusting things: fish shit for one, probably human shit as well, and certainly urine. I watched Martha lick the insides of her goggles, adjust the strap so it sat in the sweet spot below the top of her head, and stretch her hands up as she dove forward into what I now considered to be one giant toilet.

I shivered, wanting to get out, desperate for a hot bath or even the chlorinated confines of York Hall — itself not the cleanest place I'd ever been but, in comparison, gleaming with high standards of hygiene.

Martha didn't look back. She didn't look anywhere, really. Her body moved through the water with speed and efficiency. It was good to see and made me feel connected to something — my family maybe — in a way I never had before. My cousins on Iris's side of the family were all really nice, but they were all girlie and gushing and certainly not keen on sports of any kind, opposed to sweat or any activity that might wreck their makeup or blowouts. But here was a woman who seemed to happily forego all of that.

I pulled my latex cap down over my ears and fastened my goggles, licking the insides as she had done to keep them from fogging up. Then, trying not to think about anything at all, I dove into the water and swam flat out.

The hardest thing was not being able to see. I was used to the comfort of the black line at the bottom of the pool guiding me forward and back as I zipped up and down the lane, but here there was nothing to show me the way, and the water — the sea — was in motion, throwing me off course. In some places, I felt the tug of the current. In others, the water's temperature changed dramatically; my feet, kicking just below the surface, stayed warm, but my hands went deeper and when they hit a patch of cold water it was difficult to avoid recoiling. I struggled to keep my stroke correct, thinking of all the days spent doing technique drills with my coach.

When I turned my head to the side to breathe, I swallowed some salt water; it was inevitable no matter how hard I tried not to. Whenever I did, I thought I would be sick.

Swimmers — at least, swimmers like me — have a habit of saying some pools are fast and some aren't. "Fast water or slow?" was something we said to each other at meets. "It's a slow pool, we're stuffed." Or, "This is a fast pool and we're going to dominate." Psychological bullshit, but in a competition you need to take advantage. To me, it always felt as if some pools, and the water they contained, either wanted you or didn't. In the sea that day with my grandmother, the water felt slow because I was working against it, trying to cut a straight path forward. I didn't realize that the water was something you entered into a negotiation with; that you had to work with it in order to get where you wanted to go.

I followed Martha as she swam in the direction of the sea wall. I began to see that there was something really nice about just going forward without stopping and turning around every fifty metres.

It reminded me of a film clip I'd seen somewhere of a runner in Africa. The sun was high and the ground dusty. In the distance were mountains covered in a smattering of green. It looked hot. The only person in the frame was this runner and he wasn't in a race or doing a marathon or anything — he might have been training but it wasn't the way you might train here: he wasn't surrounded by a coach or teammates or anyone. It was just him running across this semi-desert landscape.

It was the runner's face that made the deepest impression on me. He was serene, blissful. Sweat poured down his face but he wasn't straining and it didn't seem like this was hard for him, or if it was he was certainly enjoying it. He was a man running because it felt good and he knew what his body could do.

That's how Martha and I swam that day. My birthday, the day I was christened by the sea.

We didn't stay in for too long, under half an hour, and when we were finished and sat on the beach in our dry clothes, hair dripping, noses running, she handed me a pebble.

"Thanks," I said, not sure why she'd given it to me.

There was a window of opportunity, a chance to ask her the things I had been wondering about for years, but I couldn't. I didn't have the nerve and I was enjoying the comfortable silence we shared as we looked at the sea, absorbed in our own separate thoughts. I wanted to tell her that I was her granddaughter, but the way she was with me made me think she already knew. And I didn't want to ruin the moment by asking her why, if she knew who I was, she had never come to visit.

She didn't seem like she wanted to talk, either. She stared out at the sea and I didn't understand what she was looking at, because nothing was happening. The water was flat. The sun was shining. It may as well have been a painting.

She sighed and pushed herself up to standing. "This is the hard part," she said, offering me a hand.

Back at her house she called for my grandfather as she opened the door. There was no reply and even though she didn't say anything I could tell she was nervous. She excused herself to check on him and went upstairs, leaving me to make myself at home in the living room.

Their living room was as unique as a hotel room: brown sofa, beige accessories, floral wallpaper that looked as though it had been put up sometime in the 1970s. It felt like a grandparents' house. There were pictures on the mantelpiece and I went over to look at them, hoping I might get a sense of who they were — she and John — and who their friends were; and when I saw them I knew why she hadn't asked me who I was.

The frames were a mix — some brass, others coloured plastic, and some just plain glass — but the person in them was the same. My face stared back at me from all the stages of my life. Some of the photos, from when I was younger, I didn't recognize; but the more recent ones were familiar. They were all taken on my birthday, in two of the really early ones you could see candles and cake. But the weird thing was that my mums weren't in any of them.

"He's fallen asleep," Martha said, from behind me.

I hadn't heard her come back downstairs and she startled me.

I picked up the picture of my last birthday, my thirteenth, when we'd had a pool party, even though Iris had hated the idea. The snapshot was a close-up of my face but you could see the edge of my swim cap across my forehead and there were the marks around my eyes from the goggles I had been wearing and which were, at the time of the pictures, around my neck. I had the stupidest look on my face, this big, goofy, toothy smile that made me look a lot younger than I was.

I held it out to her and didn't even know what to ask.

She bowed her head slightly, as though she were ashamed. "Your birthday," she said.

"I know, but you weren't there. I mean, I don't even know you."

She bit her lower lip. "Are you hungry?"

"You knew who I was this morning, when I rang the bell, didn't you?"

"I could make sandwiches?"

"Harriet doesn't talk about you or him," I said, jerking my head toward the ceiling. "She gets really, really cross when I ask about you."

"Cheese? Or we might have some chicken if you prefer."

"I don't get it. Why do you have these? Who gave them to you and why don't we ever see you?"

She went over to the sideboard and opened a small drawer, handing me an unframed photo. "This one's my favourite."

It must have been one of my first swimming lessons. I didn't seem to be that old, maybe two or three. I was in a bright orange bikini — something I would never wear now — and Harriet was holding me on my belly, swooshing me through the water.

Which was confusing — I hadn't thought Harriet could swim. She'd never been in the water as far as I'd ever seen, and anytime I wanted to go to the beach over the summer holidays she refused. She wouldn't even go for a picnic, so to see her with me in the water, even if it was just a swimming pool, didn't make any sense at all.

I looked up at my grandmother. "Why don't you ever come visit?"

Martha smiled and motioned for me to follow her into the kitchen. "I'm sure you don't want to hear about that, especially not on your birthday."

"If I didn't want to hear I wouldn't have come."

She opened the refrigerator and took out a bunch of lunch things: cheese, mayonnaise, lettuce, tomatoes, sandwich meat.

"I thought you didn't know about me," I said.

She took a loaf of bread out of the cupboard and smiled at me. "I've always known about you."

"Then why have I never met you before? Why don't you ever

come visit, or phone, or, I don't know, anything?" She was so calm about it, like she didn't see how this was a huge problem.

"It's a long, complicated story."

"Okay."

"But it's not for me to tell. You should ask your mother."

"You don't think I tried that first?"

She chuckled.

"What's so funny?"

"You're just like her."

"Who?"

"Harriet."

"How?"

"She can be quite…How should I put it? Determined?" She sliced up the cheese and tomato and said, "Mayonnaise on yours?"

I shook my head no. "Could you please just tell me what happened? What did we do wrong?"

"Nothing, dear. You did nothing wrong." She put the top slice of bread on the second sandwich and wiped her hands on her trousers. "I suppose we're all to blame. Your mother, me, John. It was one of those things that happened and we ignored it until it got so difficult that we didn't know what else to do but continue to ignore it."

"Come back with me," I said. "To dinner, tonight."

She handed me my plate and shook her head. I followed her to the table and we sat down.

"I don't think your mother would appreciate that."

"Who cares? It's my birthday."

"It's not as simple as that."

"Yes it is. You just get on a train."

"I wish it were that easy."

"It is," I pleaded. "It really is."

"Your grandfather threw your mother out of this house, years ago. Well before you were born. And he doesn't know how to apologize. It's not in him to admit that he's wrong. And your mother can't forgive him. And she can't forgive me for not standing up to him when I should have."

"Why? I mean, why did he throw her out?"

She took a bite of her sandwich and chewed slowly. "There was more than one reason."

"Okay."

"He threw her out because he didn't approve of her relationship. With Iris."

"Iris is really nice. He'd like her if he got to know her. You would, too."

"I do."

With my mouth full of shock and sandwich I said, "You do what?"

"Know her and like her. Quite a bit. She's a lovely woman."

I watched her take a bite of her sandwich as though she had just said the most ordinary thing. "What do you mean, 'know her'?"

Martha looked away, as though something terribly interesting was happening in her line of sight. Her facial expression, her body language, everything about her remained calm, still. Then, taking a long breath in, she turned back to me and said nonchalantly, "She comes to visit. At first, it felt like punishment, but…"

"But what?"

"Then I got to know her. And she does not strike me as the sort of woman who would inflict undue pain on anyone. Kindness is not always easy to give, and sometimes it's even harder to accept."

"Does she know John too?" I asked, thinking that maybe we were already halfway back together.

She shook her head. "We go out."

"But can't you do something?"

"Well, it's different now that he's..."

"Now that he's what?"

She lowered her voice to a whisper. "Now that he's getting on in years."

"I don't understand," I snapped.

"Neither did your mother."

"You're not making any sense." I didn't want to be rude because we'd only just met, but she was being so irritating. "Why can't you just tell me what happened? Maybe we can fix it."

"It's not ours to fix."

"It's our family," I said.

She looked like she was going to cry, so I tried to calm down. "It was so long ago. Doesn't he miss her?"

"In this family, Myrtle, water binds." Martha reached across the table and took my hand. "The sea holds us together."

"But we're not together!"

"We're connected, you and I. The sea did that."

"No it didn't, the train did. I did."

"It's a shame you hadn't come earlier, before John started to...unravel."

I pushed my plate of food away and stood up. "I don't understand any of this! So they had a fight. Ages ago. Can't they just get over it? Or apologize or something?"

"I wish it were as simple as that, but they're both stubborn, pig-headed, and prefer sheer bloody-mindedness to anything reasonable. John was horrible to your mother, and for her to forgive him would take something from him that he's not able to do anymore."

"You're as bad as she is. She won't talk about you, won't tell me anything about her life here. Nothing."

"I know," Martha said.

"No you don't. You had a family."

"You do too."

"It's not the same thing." I had an idea and turned toward the stairs. "Maybe you just think he won't apologize, but maybe he will if I ask him."

"Myrtle, don't," she said.

But I didn't stop. I heard her get up when I got to the bottom of the stairs and then, when I was a few steps up, I felt her hand on my arm. Her grip was strong.

"Don't. He's sleeping. Don't disturb him."

"Let go of me," I said, wrenching my arm away from her.

Her tone changed in an instant. "Please don't do this to him," she said.

I turned around and she looked upset.

"You don't know what you're doing."

"I'm going upstairs to ask my grandfather for help."

"He might not be your grandfather when you get up there."

I rolled my eyes. "What, like he's all of a sudden going to be someone else?"

"Come back to the table. I'll put the kettle on and..." She sort of slumped against the wall, looking for the first time like someone who had cancer. "The man who was shouting when you arrived. That man is not your grandfather."

I waited at the table while she made the tea and brought a plate of biscuits over.

"Myrtle," she said. "John, your grandfather, has dementia."

"Alzheimer's?"

She nodded. "Yes. At least, that's what I think he has. I can't be sure because he won't go to see the doctor." She looked at her hands and picked at one of her nails. "So, even if he were to want to apologize…" She looked up and tried to keep her composure. "Even if he wanted to, there's a good chance that he wouldn't be able to remember why he was apologizing. And I couldn't be sure he'd even remember your mother."

"Really?"

She nodded. "He's been getting worse lately. He goes through these phases, where he'll be fine for days and weeks at a time, remembering the basics — who I am, where we are, when we are — but then out of the blue, he's gone. He's been wandering, during the night sometimes. I haven't been able to do anything for him because I've been ill myself."

"Cancer?"

She nodded. "Breast cancer, but that seems to be on its way out."

I didn't know what to say.

"He came downstairs last week and saw me without my wig." She smiled that kind of smile people have when they're about to tell you something really awful. "And he didn't recognize me."

She took a biscuit from the plate and snapped it in half, dunked it in her tea, and ate it.

Later, on the train back home, I couldn't get the image out of my mind of Martha and John standing in their living room surrounded by all that boring brown furniture and the horrible Laura Ashley–type floral wallpaper, and him not being able to recognize his own wife.

I couldn't believe that my grandparents were there, all by themselves, with no one to help them because they wouldn't talk to my mum. If that had happened with Iris's parents we would've been down to Devon in a flash.

I GOT TO the bowling alley in Brick Lane just after 6 p.m. and my mums were already there, blowing up balloons.

"Hi!" Iris shouted the minute she saw me.

She was waving and doing what she did best, which was being the most enthusiastic person ever, no matter how ridiculous she looked. Which was good in this case because seeing her holding a blue balloon in one hand and waving as though she were in a crowd of hundreds and not just a nearly empty party room was the only thing that could have possibly made me smile. She looked completely out of place there, still in her primary school-teacher clothes, all floaty pastels, loose and unstructured.

Iris and Harriet looked like polar opposites. Sometimes I didn't understand how they'd even managed to meet, let alone get together. Tonight Harriet was dressed in something black on top and black on bottom, finished with a fitted leather jacket that she'd had since I could remember and was really, really worn in some parts. Iris and I hated it but Harriet wouldn't throw it away.

I went over to them and Iris nearly knocked me down with hugs and kisses.

"Happy birthday, my darling."

If she had been a dog, she would've been a Labrador. Harriet would have been a pit bull. Both loyal and protective, but in different ways.

Harriet put her arm around my shoulders and squeezed. "How was practice?"

"All right."

She brushed the hair off my face. "Everything okay?"

I shrugged, taking a balloon and stretching it. "Yeah, I guess."

Iris tied a knot at the end of the blue balloon she'd been holding when I walked in, and held it over her mouth like a moustache. I smiled half-heartedly.

"What's wrong?" she asked.

"Nothing."

"What's wrong, Myrtle?" she repeated.

"I don't want to talk about it."

"I do," she said. "What happened?"

I sat down at the table covered in birthday decorations best suited to a six-year-old and put my chin in my hand. I knew telling my parents would upset them in different ways — that it would ruin the evening for everyone. But I also didn't really feel like having a party, so I thought, why not?

"Martha," I said. "I went to see Martha today."

"Martha who?" Harriet asked, in that nervy way that meant she already knew the answer.

"Martha my grandmother."

She nearly spat her beer on the floor, and Iris put her hand over her mouth in shock.

"It's okay," Iris said.

"No it's not," Harriet said.

"She has breast cancer. And John's got Alzheimer's," I said. Then, just because it seemed better to get it all out there, I added, "They have a lot of pictures of me, in the house."

Everything stopped after that. Harriet looked like she was going to faint. She reached out to steady herself, using the back of a chair for balance. Iris sat down next to me and put her hand on my knee, resting her head on my shoulder and clinging to me in the way she had that I hated, especially in public.

"Unbelievable," Harriet said. "Fucking unbelievable."

"Harry," Iris said. "Don't."

"Why would you do that?" Harriet said.

"Because I've never met them, and I wanted to."

"You should've told us."

"You would've said no!"

"With good reason," Harriet said.

"Mum, it's not a good reason. Whatever it was that you fought about, it was ages ago, and I wanted to meet her. She's a swimmer, you know." My voice was getting wavery but I carried on. "Didn't you think I might like to at least meet her once before she dies? She's my grandmother and she has cancer. And she says that whatever it is that John did, he can't apologize for it because he might not recognize you anymore." I felt ready to burst into tears.

Harriet didn't say anything right away. She drank her beer in gulps while Iris and I watched her think about what to say. "Cancer?"

I nodded. "Breast cancer."

"How was she?" Iris asked.

"Okay. She doesn't have any hair."

Harriet closed her eyes and went really pale, even for her.

"Cancer?" she whispered.

I nodded.

"How did you find out? Did she tell you?"

"Sort of. She took her wig off before we went in the water."

"In the water?" Harriet asked.

"Yeah, she wanted to go swimming."

"You went swimming?"

"Yeah, in the sea."

"Let me understand this. You went, without asking or telling your mother and I, to Dover on your own, to meet my parents. And after you found out that my mother has cancer and my father is losing his mind, you went swimming?"

"Kind of. I found out about John when we got back."

She shook her head as though, if she did it hard enough, everything I'd just told her would go flying out her ears. "You don't go swimming in the sea."

"It was okay, actually."

"I'm not asking if you enjoyed it. I'm telling you that you're strictly forbidden from ever going in the sea like that again."

"Why?"

"Because it's dangerous and I'm your mother, that's why."

"That's not fair!"

"She's a good swimmer, Harry, and besides, I think that misses the point," Iris said calmly.

"You're right," Harriet said. Turning back to me she said, "You're grounded. You're forbidden from going to see them again. It's not up for discussion. It's a fact. You do not go there."

"Harry," Iris said, reaching out for her hand.

"What? Do you have any idea how dangerous it is, Iris? Have you ever seen someone with serious hypothermia? With her tongue so swollen from salt that she can't speak, covered in hideous welts from all the chafing? Face swollen from jelly-fish stings? Dodging boats and high seas and waves that could easily capsize that stupid fishing boat that goes with her? Have you ever seen any of that?"

"They didn't swim the Channel this afternoon, Harriet," Iris said softly. "Did you?" Iris asked me.

"No, we swam in the harbour. She didn't even talk about swimming the Channel."

"That's hard to believe. It's all she talks about," Harriet sneered.

"You guys are always saying how important family is, how much you love me, how happy you are to be my mothers. I just wanted to know them."

I got up and turned away from the table, intending to storm out of there and walk around outside by myself for a bit so Iris could tell Harriet to cool it, but when I turned around my friend Robin from swim team was there, holding out his arms ready to give me a hug.

"Hiya," he said in that way he had where he seemed shocked and embarrassed at the same time. I let him give me a big hug, and he whispered, "Is she going to coach you?"

"I didn't get a chance to ask," I whispered back. "Other things happened, tell you later."

We let go of each other and I hoped my mums hadn't noticed anything unusual.

"Am I in trouble with Coach?" I whispered, before anybody could ask any other questions.

He shook his head. "I said you weren't feeling well and he did the whole you shoulda phoned him yourself, integrity, responsibility speech."

I nodded. We got that speech at least once a week.

"So," he said, looking at my mums who were not putting a lot of effort into appearing as though nothing had happened. "Happy birthday!" he said, and he handed me a package wrapped in Christmas paper.

"Sorry," he mumbled. "We didn't have much selection at home."

I smiled at him and unwrapped it. It was a book: *Young Woman and the Sea: How Trudy Ederle Conquered the English Channel and Inspired the World.* I held it up so my mums could see.

"Perfect," Harriet said, storming away from the table.

"It is, thanks," I said.

COMING HOME

IAIN, 2013

IT WAS A surly grey English morning and the customs official asked me the reason for my visit. "Business or pleasure?" he said.

"Neither," I replied.

"You're British," he said. "This is an Australian passport."

"Yes," I said. "I'm coming home. Neither business nor pleasure. More of a requirement."

He looked puzzled.

"My mother," I said. "Cancer."

He stared at me. I knew my eyes must be red from the wine I'd consumed during the flight; I'd needed to steady my nerves, which had grown more and more strained the closer I got to home. But the way this official was looking at me felt more like he was trying to decide whether or not I was a good son or a bad one. I could have told him myself, if he'd asked.

I was a bad son trying to make up for lost time before time stopped.

"Welcome to Great Britain," he said.

I got on a train, a tube, then another train headed out of London. I wore sunglasses in the dull light — light that felt unfamiliar and familiar at the same time. I was assaulted by things from my childhood that had once been unnoticeable: middling weather, accents, and the particular smell of laundry.

The train ferried me closer to the white house with the black lacquer door, the brown sofas, and the wardrobe with the hole punched in the back — the result of an eruption of teenage frustration whose source I had long since forgotten. The house that had been home, but the twenty-three-hour flight had turned into days and months and years and it was just a house now.

It was just a house, I told myself: four walls and a roof. Carpeting, wallpaper, and a garden. It was nothing to be afraid of.

THREE DAYS BEFORE, the phone had rung late at night. I recognized my sister's voice instantly and the years since we'd spoken collapsed.

"Iain," she'd said.

"What's wrong?"

Good news arrives at reasonable hours but bad news barges in, possessing neither the restraint nor the decency to wait.

"You need to get on a flight."

"What? Why?"

Her voice was choked. "Mum. We're going out to the house."

"'We're'?"

"Me and Myrtle. And you."

"What's wrong?"

"It's not the sort of thing you say over the phone."

"Harry," I said. I pictured my sister in the tracksuit she had worn when we were teenagers: hood up and pulled tight around her head.

"We'll be there tomorrow night," my sister said.

"Harry."

"Breast cancer."

"What?"

"I don't know. She's not exactly forthcoming."

It sounded as if she was crying.

"When did this happen?"

"I don't know. You're the one who phones."

"I haven't called in a while," I said. It was true. I rationalized: I've been busy, my life is here not there, and even when we do speak, they only want to hear about the good things because those are worthy of an expensive long-distance phone call.

"How did you find out?" I asked Harriet.

"Myrtle."

"What?"

"She went to see them."

"What?"

"They went swimming."

I laughed. I couldn't help it. I pictured my mother, marching out of hospital in the midst of her treatment, the bags of chemotherapy dragging behind her. The bags themselves I pictured as poisonous jellyfish threatening to burst and sting her at any moment. And, as she had done over the course of many Channel swims, I knew she would ignore them. The sea, her answer to everything. The sea, for my mother, would make it all better.

The sun had set by the time the train pulled into Dover Priory and I had to take off my sunglasses. The only things that had changed were the billboard adverts.

The drive was shorter than I'd remembered, and in a few minutes I was standing on the pavement in front of the house. My parents' house.

The lights were on. I strained to see where everybody was, what they were doing, and what I was walking into. But it was a bad vantage point, and all I could see was my mother with her back to me, washing something in the sink.

I didn't know what to do. Ringing the bell seemed too formal; walking right in seemed too informal. I didn't even know if they'd hear me if I knocked.

My mother turned her head — toward the kitchen table or else someone standing just out of sight — and in that moment I saw her face. Her cheeks were sunken and she'd lost enough weight that her cardigan looked far too big. That she had cancer was bad enough; but to be confronted immediately by how much she had aged was more than I'd been prepared for.

Mum moved away from the sink and took a roast out of the oven. Once she'd set it on the counter I rang the bell.

I heard a bit of a scuffle, and the door opened onto my father and Myrtle.

My father looked me up and down suspiciously. "What do you want?"

Not the welcome I had imagined, even from him.

"Hi, Uncle Iain," Myrtle said, trying to push my father aside. "Perfect timing. Grandma's just putting dinner out."

Weird, too, hearing her call Mum "Grandma." Like waking up one morning to find that the Cold War had been one big misunderstanding.

My father looked at Myrtle. "Harriet, do you know this man?"

Myrtle took my father's hand in hers and dragged him to the kitchen. I heard her say, "Mum, he's doing it again."

"Hi?" I said to the empty doorway. I picked up my case and the dog charged at me the second I entered the house.

"What happened to Webb?" I shouted as the dog jumped up, licking my face. "When I left he had four legs!"

Mum nearly dropped her serving spoon when she saw me. Before she could say anything, though, Harriet ran into the foyer and wrapped her arms around me, nearly knocking me over.

"Oh my God, Iain, you're going bald!" my sister said.

Harriet's outburst seemed to give Mum a chance to gather herself. "Iain," she said quietly. "I wasn't expecting you."

I gave her a hug and a kiss. She felt frail in my arms. "It's good to see you."

"Myrtle, set another place," she said.

My father lurched into the kitchen. "Hi Dad," I said.

He looked at me dismissively and tried to put the kettle on. He fiddled with the button and it refused to switch on. "Goddamnit! Why doesn't anything in this house work?"

I looked around the table, and no one else seemed bothered by his outburst, which was unusual but I was too exhausted to ask why they were ignoring him. Perhaps it was one of the things that had changed since I'd been away.

Dad looked around wildly. "Have you all gone deaf? The bloody kettle's buggered again."

"John, stop shouting," Mum said. "Sit down at the table, please."

"Stop telling me what to do!"

I saw Mum take a deep breath. Harriet went and led him by the hand to the table, helping him into his seat.

I went over to Mum's side and offered to help with dinner. She brushed me away.

"What's going on with him?" I asked her quietly.

"He's fine," she said, not stopping in her preparations.

"No, Mum, he's not."

"Did you come all the way from Sydney to tell me that?"

She still had her sharpness, which was reassuring. "No," I said. "I came to see you."

"You should've called. We've a full house." She set the roast chicken on the table and handed me the carving knife. "Make yourself useful."

I wanted to know what was going on and why she'd kept it from me, from us. I was working to a tight schedule, my life in Australia temporarily on hold in order to tie up loose ends here. But it was obvious that wasn't what was going to happen tonight. Family was not something that could be tidied up and filed away. It continued, whether you wanted it to or not.

Mum served Dad first, as had always been our custom. He watched her, and when she put the plate in front of him he lowered his head and sniffed.

"What is this — chicken?"

Mum nodded.

"It doesn't smell right," he said, pushing the food away. He turned to Myrtle and said, "Harriet, go and put some tomato soup on."

No one moved. Mum cut a potato in half and chewed slowly. Dad waited, looking at Myrtle, and when she didn't get up he said, "You're just as wilful as your mother."

I COULDN'T SLEEP. The jet lag was punishing, but more than that, my childhood bed was claustrophobic, smothering me with the version of myself I'd left behind. My thoughts wandered back to the things that had made me want to leave in the first place: the close atmosphere of the town and the house, the way nobody ever spoke directly, and my need to reinvent myself, which was something that could only really be done by leaving everyone I knew behind. Wrapped in the same duvet that had seen me through my teenage years, I felt like that boy again, acutely aware of the whispers that lurked behind netted curtains, in queues, and in the politely banal questions of the people I had grown up with.

I walked down to the kitchen, poured myself a glass of milk, and went into the living room. I'd gone back in time.

"I'd have thought you'd be out for the count," Harriet said. "Jet lag?"

I nodded.

"What are you drinking?"

I held up my glass and she scoffed. She wrestled with the fiddly latch on the drinks cabinet, then poured us each a glass of whisky.

"Where's Iris?" I asked.

"Home," Harriet said. She leaned against the edge of the sofa and swirled the drink around in the glass. "This reminds me of the old days."

"When we'd have gone down the pub and come home steaming drunk," I said.

"Do you think they ever knew?"

"I bet Mum did." I looked at my glass. "Harry, what's going on?"

She shrugged. "Myrtle came up here last week."

"I know, you said."

"Mum took her swimming."

"'Course she did," I said.

"Right?" She shook her head, smiling. "Myrtle said that instead of putting a cap on, as one does, Mum took her wig off."

"That's a wig?"

Harriet nodded. "And when Myrtle looked — I don't know, shocked, frightened, curious — Mum told her she had cancer. Iris and I had no idea Myrtle was even coming here, that she even knew where they lived. She did it on her birthday. That evening, we're surrounded by balloons, and Myrtle's getting really moody and she just blurts out that Mum, that Grandma, has cancer. That's it. I called you, we came up here."

"Have you talked to Mum yet?"

"Yeah, but you know what she's like."

"She's fine?"

Harriet burst out laughing, then clamped her hand over her mouth. After a minute she said, "She hasn't changed a bit."

"She looks old." I looked at my drink.

"We all do. You're going bald; I have crow's feet."

I touched the top of my head sheepishly. "It's good to see you." I smiled. I hadn't realized how much I'd missed her.

She smiled back. "You too. You know, Heathrow's open pretty much all the time. You don't have to wait for cancer to come over."

"I know, it's just…" I sighed. "I'm busy." Which was true, but not the only reason.

She rolled her eyes. "Who cares? Life's short."

I finished my drink and held my glass out. She refilled it.

"Did you at least find out if the cancer's gone or what?"

"Well, she's done the chemo."

"Would've been nice to know."

"You regret coming?" I heard the same accusatory tone she'd used when I told her I was moving to Australia.

"No, it's just…" How could I say that I liked living at a distance, that the oceans that separated us made it easier to love them all? "I could've planned it properly."

"What's to plan? You pack a bag, you get on a flight."

"So she'll be okay?"

"She'll be fine."

"Right."

"Dad, on the other hand."

"What is going on there?"

"You know, for someone who phones regularly you really don't know much."

"If you think it's hard getting information out of Mum in person, try doing it over the phone. And she hasn't put him on in a while."

"I asked her about him, but she won't talk about it. At least to me. Myrtle said when she came up, Mum said it was dementia."

In the morning I heard arguing. I lay in bed and stared up at the ceiling and felt like a little boy. But this time it wasn't Mum and Dad's voices that slipped under the door and into my head, it was Mum and Harriet's.

I put my tracksuit on and went downstairs. Mum and Myrtle were standing by the door, Mum's hand on the knob. Harriet did not look happy.

"Tell her she can't go," Harriet told me.

"She's your daughter," I said.

"Not her," Harriet said. "Her," she added, pointing at Mum.

"Can't go where?"

"You have to ask?" Harriet said.

A devilish grin grew across Mum's face.

"How does your doctor feel about this?" I asked.

"I've no idea," Mum replied. "But it's my life, and today I would like to take my granddaughter swimming."

"She can't go," Harriet said.

"Why?" Myrtle whined.

"Fine," Mum said. "I'll go by myself." She opened the door and jumped back. "Henry, what are you doing here?"

"Who is Henry?" I asked my sister. I needed a coffee; the exhaustion of travelling for thirty hours was sinking in.

"Why have you got Webb?" Mum was saying. She put her bag down by the door.

"I went to get the papers and found him skulking around the bins," this Henry said, coming in after the dog.

"Who are you?" Harriet asked him.

"I live next door," the man said. "Sometimes I…" He looked at Mum, unsure of how to finish his sentence.

"He likes to walk Webb," Mum said quickly.

As if he were reminded of the purpose of his arrival, Henry said, "Martha, where is John?"

"Last I saw him, he was sleeping," she said, quickly starting up the stairs. "John? John!"

We followed the sound of Mum's footsteps as she stomped around the second floor. Then she reappeared at the top of the stairs. "He's not here."

I scratched my chest. "Maybe he's just gone for a walk." It would soon become obvious that I had never known anyone who was lost to the whims of Alzheimer's.

"Henry," Mum said.

"Pub, train station, port," he replied.

"Restaurant, bay, and lawn bowling club," she said.

Henry nodded. "Meet you back here, call if there's anything." He left.

She turned to the rest of us. "You'll have to sort out your own lunches." And then she walked out.

Harriet and I looked at each other. Webb barked. Myrtle sat at the foot of the stairs.

I went to the still-open door. "Mum!" I shouted after her. "What's happening?" I felt the distance between us so strongly, it was as though everyone else had been rehearsing for weeks and I had been pushed onstage: the last-minute addition, the unstudied understudy.

She waved, pretending not to hear.

Harriet rushed past me, following her. "Mum! Stop!" she said, as I came up behind, the paving stones cold under my bare feet.

Mum stopped walking. "It isn't the first time your father —" she said. She looked at her feet. "Has forgotten himself. Stress related, I expect. It's fine."

"It doesn't look fine from where we're standing," Harriet said.

"Then stand somewhere else," Mum replied. She walked down to the pavement, turned the opposite way Henry had, and kept going.

I looked at my sister. "What just happened?"

"Things changed," she replied.

HARRIET SENT MYRTLE for a run, and I made a coffee and we sat down at the table.

"We need doctors' names, phone numbers," she said. "Then what?"

I shrugged. "We can't do much if they don't want help."

"She has cancer, and he's losing his mind."

"I get it, but…"

"But what?"

But I came here to say goodbye, I wanted to say. Because I knew it would probably be the last time I saw them, and good-bye was easier than what faced us now. I thought it was the

right thing to do, the good son coming home. I came to spend
time with them, hear their voices, see the house. Though when
I was lying in bed upstairs, I had known that those were not
the only reasons and that none of them qualified as my main
motivation for coming back. I had come because I couldn't bear
to be known as the son who hadn't gone to see his own dying
mother. It had been guilt, pure and ugly, that had finally gotten me on an airplane.

Harriet paced. She tossed ideas at me, none of which seemed
feasible. I batted them back. I finished my coffee, I made
another. A solution seemed to require more from us, but we
didn't know what that would be.

"What if we just ask?" I said. "What if we ask them what
they want to do?"

"Get out of my house!"

I jumped at the sound of my father's shout. He stood in the
doorway, dressed in his usual waistcoat, tie, and jacket. But he
was wearing slippers, and judging by the state of them he'd gone
halfway across town and back again.

"Dad, calm down," I said. My impulse was to go over to him,
to try and comfort him, but there was something not right. His
eyes were wide open. He looked frightened.

"Whoever you are, get the hell out of my house!" He held
his fist up and I thought he was going to come after me.

"Dad!" Harriet shouted.

He shrunk back from her as she sprang toward him.

"Get away from me!" he shouted.

I tried speaking quietly, slowly, as you might to a lost child.
"Dad, it's okay. Why don't you come and sit on the sofa?"

I didn't move toward him. I kept my hands at my sides.

I caught my sister's eye and gestured for her to call Mum.

She took her phone from her pocket and I nudged her into the kitchen.

"What the hell?" I whispered.

"Just get him sitting down," Harriet said with the phone to her ear.

I didn't want to be the one to try to get him to sit down, and I didn't want to be the one who sat with him. I wanted my parents to go back to being a phone call twice a month where I was reassured that everything was, as ever, fine. Because this was not fine; this was a problem and I had no idea how to fix it.

My father sat on the couch.

"Dad," I said tentatively. "What happened? Where did you go?"

Gradually he came back to himself. He relaxed into the couch and stared out the window, ignoring me. At least I wasn't an intruder anymore.

Harriet came and sat next to me, and when she opened her mouth to speak I put my finger to my lips.

"How long?" I whispered.

"Twenty minutes."

And so we sat there, waiting for Mum to come back and sort everything out. Even though she was ill, she was still the one who would have to do the heavy lifting.

"When she gets home," I said.

"We talk," Harriet said.

When Mum returned she took one look at Dad sleeping on the sofa and I thought she was going to slap him, she looked so angry. Instead, she went into the kitchen without saying a word. Harriet and I exchanged glances, then we followed her and blocked her way out of the room. She ignored us, and set about making herself a cup of tea.

"Anything you'd like to share?" Harriet asked.

"Would you like a cup, too? There ought to be enough water." Mum opened the cupboard and took out a tin of biscuits. She took a bite and then, noticing our eyes boring holes into the side of her head, she held one up and said, "Rich Tea, my favourite."

"Mum," Harriet said. I put my hand on her shoulder; I could hear the anger growing in her voice. "Enough. We need to talk about what is going on here. With him. With you."

"He's just tired. He's having trouble sleeping." She poured the water and avoided eye contact.

"And you?" I asked. "Harry said you have cancer."

"Had," she said. "The treatment is finished now." She put the tea bag in the sink.

"That's all you have to say about it?" Harriet said.

"What more is there to say?"

"What kind of cancer? What kind of treatment? How do you know it's gone? Why are you still wearing a wig?"

"I don't see why it matters."

I thought Harriet was going to take Mum by the shoulders and shake her.

"It was breast cancer — the kind you want, is what the doctor said. It had a Latin-sounding name. They operated and I had chemotherapy. I went for a check-up last week and the doctor said everything looked fine. It made my hair fall out and it's not growing back fast." She took a sip of her tea. "All right?"

She pursed her lips and I actually thought there was a slight smirk in her expression, as if she was pleased with herself for getting away with it all, keeping it a secret.

"You didn't tell anyone you were having an operation?" Harriet said.

"I told your father and Henry."

"You should've told us," Harriet said, stabbing at her chest. "You don't keep things like that from family."

"You two have your own lives."

I could see this was going to turn into an argument none of us would win. "What about Dad?"

"He's fine, he's tired."

"He came in here and didn't know who the hell we were," I told her.

"He has Alzheimer's," Harriet said.

My mother's face turned to stone. "We don't say words like that in this house."

"Really? And how is that helpful?"

"A name isn't the same as a cure," Mum said.

"Mum, we want to help," I said.

She looked over my shoulder. "We're fine, aren't we, John?"

I turned and saw my father; his expression had not been transformed, but he was different. He was himself again, and I thought how awful, which didn't even begin to describe what it must be like; horrible, again a word lacking in the kind of agony I had heard in my father's voice only minutes ago. How unbearable it must be to never know what part of your life you might find when you walk into a room? How do you cope when your history is in a constant state of shuffle? What do you do when the repeat button in your mind gets stuck, and things skip and stutter?

"Why wouldn't we be?" Dad said.

He pushed past me, and Mum handed him her cup of tea.

HARRIET AND MYRTLE left that evening because Myrtle had to get back for school. I was due to take the evening train to

London the next day, to spend a couple of days at Harriet's before flying back to Australia.

In the morning, Mum announced she was going for a swim.

"I'll come with you," I said.

She looked surprised. "Try and keep up," she said.

We walked to the same beach where she had taught me to swim. The shoreline was closer to the cliffs than I'd remembered. There were more boats, a greater sense of activity, but it was mostly the way I remembered it. The way I'd left it.

I followed her to her usual spot and I could've done it in my sleep. It was muscle memory: my feet would always know the way across the rust-coloured pebbles to the myrtle bush where she stowed her things.

I used to hate coming here. School holidays meant swimming in the ice-cold water. The waves would crest into my face when I tried to breathe and the water would go up my nose, into my ears. And the salt stung. I would beg to get out early, I would shout and she would resist. The sea will save you, she'd say. I had my doubts then, but seeing her now, the way she was looking at the sea, the way it seemed to transform her in an instant, I wondered if I ought to reconsider.

Around the house she'd been clipped and tense. I hadn't expected a hero's welcome, but something more than irritation would have been nice. I'd wondered if it was me — if, after having moved away, having failed to visit, she'd written me off and decided I wasn't worth the effort.

I followed her to the water's edge, shivering in the mid-September breeze. I'd never been close to anyone with cancer before, and imagined such people to be frail. Though she wasn't as robust a figure as I'd remembered, she was transformed in the water. Head down, arms churning, she cut through the water for fifteen solid minutes while I followed in her slipstream as I'd done when I was a boy, letting her make it easier for me. When she stopped, I did too. She was breathing hard and my chest felt like it was on fire. I hadn't realized how unfit I was.

She trod water and let out a loud whoop. She took her goggles off and smiled at me.

"This is divine," she said. "I'm so glad you joined me."

She was a different person out here, but I was the same, and the cold burned my toes.

"Kick harder, move your arms like this," she said, reminding me how to scull.

I mimicked her movements, and though the cold water felt sharp against my skin, my muscles started to build up a bit of warmth.

"What is it, about the water?"

"Oh, you know," she said.

I shook my head, feeling the sea echoing in my eardrums. "No, I don't. Tell me."

Her smile grew broader. "It's hard to say, exactly."

"Try," I said.

"If we really wanted to, we could swim to another country from here. We could escape."

"Do you want to?"

"I've been to France."

"Escape."

"Sometimes." She rolled onto her back.

I didn't know what to make of that. "Now, or then?"

"Both." She went back to treading water and looked me in the eye.

"You're cold," she said. I was shivering visibly. "Let's go back in."

"Not yet," I said. "A few more minutes."

She laughed. "When you were a boy, you'd have never said that!"

I smiled, pleased that I was with her where she was happiest. "People change."

"Do you remember, when you were little? We used to come out here?"

"How could I forget?"

"You'd be surprised how easy it is to forget."

"We just want to help, you know."

"I do, but there isn't much that can be done."

"What's happening to him?" I knew the answer but wanted to hear her say it.

She ducked her head under water, and when she came back up she wiped her face.

"Age," she said. "We're getting old."

"Mum, please. I've come such a long way."

"Yes, you have. Grown man with a big job."

"That's not what I mean."

She dunked her head under again. When she came back up she said, "Did you know that our bodies have the same salt content as the sea? The sea is literally inside us."

"You didn't go to church yesterday."

"We haven't been in a while."

"Why?"

"This is the only church I need." She shook her head. "Besides, it's too much for him now."

"Why won't you talk about what's going on?"

"Because some things are private," she shot back. "Because I am tired of the looks and the whispers."

"What looks are you talking about? What whispers?"

"We don't go to church anymore because people started talking about your father's rather erratic behaviour. Because people talk about us, about him. They don't talk to us anymore."

"Who cares what a bunch of gossips think?"

She splashed water on my face. "I do. He does. They are, they were, our friends. They don't invite us to dinner; they don't want to come to dinner because nobody knows what your father might do. He might put his arm around Mrs. Johnstone and pretend she's his girlfriend; he might try and kiss her. He might mistake Charlie for Francis and start shouting about some petty grievance that happened thirty years ago." She spat the words out.

"What does the doctor say?"

"He won't go and there's nothing I can do about it. I can't make him do anything."

"I could've tried, I could've helped."

"Do what, exactly? A name doesn't change a thing."

"But people would be more understanding."

"No, they won't. He's frightening. He breaks my heart. I walk through town and I know people are staring. I can feel it. In the butcher, in the chemist. At the post office, at the library. Henry does most of the shopping now. I can't stand the shame."

She ducked under water again, and stayed down for longer this time. I watched as the air bubbles slowly broke the surface.

When it was time for me to leave, I didn't know what to do. I stood at the front door, my bag by my side. I considered calling off my departure, phoning my office in Australia and telling them I would be another week, saying that things were not good, not okay, that my parents needed my help.

But my mum wrapped her arms around me and said, "I'm glad you came. To see the sea."

She kissed my cheek and I could smell the sea on her skin. Nothing was okay, but she was still herself.

In the living room, my father sat in his chair, sleeping.

"You'll let us know," I said.

"Of course."

I knew she wouldn't. I knew it couldn't happen across so many miles, so much distance. That it was not her way to ask for help.

The taxi tooted its horn and she walked me down to the street. We stood there awkwardly until the driver's impatience was palpable. I hugged her again and held on longer than usual.

"Now," she said, pulling away. "That's enough. You'd best get going or you'll miss your train."

She opened the door and I put my case in the back.

"Okay then," I said.

But I didn't get in the taxi. I couldn't. As we stood on the street I regretted spending all those years away and knew I had been undeserving of her. I searched for something that would keep me with her for another minute.

"It's still flowering?" I asked, pointing to the myrtle bush.

"It's been with me since the beginning. It's a hardy thing."

"The beginning of what?"

"Have I never told you?" She ran her hand along its branches. "The day your father proposed, he didn't have an engagement ring."

"He what?"

She waved her hands as though to stop me.

"He did but it got lost. So he gave me a sprig of myrtle. The day after that, I went down to the seaside with my trowel and took a piece of the bush home. I put it in a pot on my windowsill, facing the sea. After we were married and we bought this house..." She looked away and took a deep breath. "I planted it the day after we moved in, when your father was at work."

Just before she went back inside the house, she leaned in close and whispered, "You always know how to find me, don't you?"

I shook my head, confused.

She winked and I got it. She would be where she had always been.

GROWING UP

IAIN, 2013

"WE HAVE TO DO SOMETHING," Harriet said as she helped drag my case into her flat. "Because this is not going to solve itself."

"Most people answer the door with a hi, Harry," I told her.

"We've done hi."

My sister and her family had lived at this flat in Bethnal Green for nearly eight years, and this was the first time I had crossed the threshold. I hadn't come to visit, not even once. Harriet and her family had never come to visit me either. Visiting was a thing we meant to do but never got around to.

My case safely wedged in the narrow entranceway in front of a pile of shoes, Harriet shouted, "We're going out."

She pushed past me and I stood there, wondering if I should at least go in and say hello.

"You coming?" she called from the stairwell, so I shut the door behind myself and ran down the stairs to catch up. The same way I'd done when we were children.

Years ago, when I had worked in the City, I'd have never

come to this part of east London. Back then, Bethnal Green had been rough as old boots. Now though, as I followed Harriet through the streets and alleyways, the area seemed to have got caught up in the same gentrification that felt like it was taking over. The intervening years had softened it: now there were cafés and gastropubs mixed in with the betting shops and off-licences.

We reached the high street and walked past a small supermarket crowded with after-work shoppers, queuing to buy ready meals. A few doors down, Harriet grabbed me by the elbow and dragged me into a pub that looked like every other pub in a newly gentrified place. Reclaimed wood floors, artfully peeling wallpaper, and an ironic picture of the Queen lording it over the locally made microbrews and wood-fired pizzas.

She took a seat by the window while I got the drinks.

I set the pints on the table and she reached for hers quickly, as though she had been waiting all day for it.

"Bad luck," I said as I hung my coat over the back of the chair. "We need a toast."

She glared at me.

"Harry, please."

She set the glass back on the table and I tried to think of what we could drink to. It needed to set the tone.

"To the sea," I said.

She rolled her eyes. "Really?"

I nodded.

"To the fucking sea."

We clinked glasses and drank.

"It's good to see you," I said.

"How were they last night?"

"Okay. Dad calmed down a bit after you guys left. No more walkabouts."

"I don't know why he was so upset when I was there, it's not like I brought Iris."

"I don't think he was upset, just stressed out."

"You sound like Mum. It's called Alzheimer's." Her leg bounced up and down under the table, threatening to spill the drinks.

I sighed. "Giving it a name makes it real."

"It is real."

"He doesn't care what you call it," I said.

She sat back in her chair and crossed her arms over her chest. "It's a fact, not open to interpretation or opinion."

"Harry, it was hard to leave them," I said. "All alone like that."

"She can't take care of him when it gets worse."

"If," I said.

"When," she corrected, leaning forward. "It doesn't get better."

"There have to be treatments, tablets, something."

"I think we're past that point. Most of what's available is for early-onset. Which would've been, what? Years ago?"

I looked at the head of my beer as if it were able to tell me the future.

I leaned forward, my sleeves soaking up a bit of spilt beer as I rested my elbows on the table. "Harry, do you ever feel like we've just abandoned them? Like we could've been much better children, been more involved, that sort of thing?"

She shook her head. "If they wanted help they could've asked for it."

"Don't you feel bad?"

"For not being around or for what's happening?"

"Both."

She pointed to herself. "They kicked me out —"

"Dad kicked you out."

"Mum didn't do anything to stop him. So I don't feel bad about not being around. I wasn't wanted. But do I hate that this is happening to them? Of course I do." She took a long drink of her pint. "But we're past the point of no return with Dad."

"Since when did you become the expert?"

"Since Iris's father."

"What?"

She nodded. "At first, it was little things. Like, he couldn't remember the word spaghetti. He could describe it, but he couldn't find the word. Then other things. Telling Ashley that he'd invited people round for dinner, people he was vague about, couldn't give a name, but sort of described them. She finally realized they were the old neighbours who'd moved away decades before."

"I'm so sorry. Poor Iris."

"It's hard. He didn't remember who she was, or who Ashley was, even. It was two years ago this spring that they moved him into a care home. He deteriorated pretty fast after that."

"I don't want that for Dad."

"Too bad, it's happening." She drank. "He died this spring just gone. And you know what? It was a relief. It was horrible, watching him disintegrate."

"Were they close?"

Harriet nodded. "Very."

"Are we?"

"Are we what?"

"Close."

She looked at her nearly empty glass. "You're the one who moved to Australia."

I met my sister's gaze. "This is nice. We should do this more often."

"You're moving back to the land of grey and gloom?"

I shifted in my seat. "What do you want to do?"

"We need to get him into a care home."

I shook my head. "They'll never agree to that."

She leaned across the table. "There is going to come a time when they won't have that luxury."

"What about a nurse? Someone who'll come help Mum out."

"Iain," she said, looking at me sternly. "He's going to wander off more. His personality is going to change. He's not going to remember who anyone is. Even Mum. He won't be able to eat, or bathe." She looked at her empty glass. "He won't be able to use the toilet on his own."

I felt sick.

"We can't force him. We can't force either of them to do anything," I said.

She stood up quickly. "Fine. You don't want to help, that's fine. Go back to Australia. Pretend nothing's wrong here."

She stormed out and I didn't follow her. The pub was quiet and I wanted some time to think on my own, so I got another beer.

That Harriet had been less than keen on my going away had never been a secret, but the last night I saw her before I moved halfway across the world had started off well. We had met up for dinner, Harriet's choice, at one of the curry houses on Brick Lane. She'd insisted on the location and on paying. We ordered way too much and laughed when everything arrived on the table: five metal dishes of similarly nondescript greasy, brownish sauce with lumps of meat and veg. It was a Friday night and since we were near Bishopsgate, the restaurant was crowded with young bankers, like me, all loosening their ties, preparing themselves for a weekend of debauchery and abandon before the brutal weekday regime began anew Monday morning.

We'd eaten almost all of it and the waiter had ensured our glasses were never empty. It had had the makings of a great night.

After dinner, we'd found a nearby pub with a free table in the window.

"You're brave," she told me. "To move so far away."

Harriet had this tone where she could be pointed and joking simultaneously, and even though I was used to it, it was still unsettling. Sometimes it was hard to tell where you stood with her.

"If I don't like it, I can always come back."

"You won't," she said, shaking her head. "Why would you?" A man in an Arsenal jersey stumbled into her and spilled half his pint on her jeans. She glared at him and I thought I heard her mutter "fuckwit" under her breath.

"What could you possibly miss?" she said. "You'll be raking it in, women in bikinis throwing themselves at you."

"The miserable weather, miserable food, miserable company," I said.

"Yeah, miserable company. They won't have that in Oz." Her expression said it all: cautious smile creeping over her face, eyes crinkling at the sides the way they did when she was up to something.

"Harry," I said. "Joking."

"I know," she said.

But I wasn't sure. She took her jacket and went outside to mooch a cigarette off someone, and I watched her pace back and forth in the road. It was a struggle for her: the Boxing Day disaster had made it clear the position our parents took, and though Harry knew I phoned them every couple of weeks, the fact our mother asked only if she was okay was almost worse than her not asking after her at all.

When she came back in, I got us another round of drinks. I set them on the table and she smiled.

"It's exciting. I'm really pleased for you — thrilled even. Great adventure and all that, right?

"I'll miss you," I said, reaching across the table to squeeze her hand. She drew it away and I just managed to touch her fingers.

"No you won't. We hardly see each other."

"You can visit."

"Yeah, sure. Let you get settled first."

"What's wrong?"

"Nothing," she said. "Why do you ask?"

"Harry," I said.

She downed half her pint and slammed her hands on the table. "Actually, you know what's wrong? This is a terrible send-off. Godawful. We need shots." She lurched through the crowd, elbowing her way to the front of the queue at the bar.

A few moments later she slammed two shots of whisky on the table. "Cheers!" She tapped the bottom of her glass on the top of mine and drank.

"You're not drinking?" she accused.

I tipped my glass toward her and drank.

"Wouldn't want people thinking I didn't give my little brother a proper send-off."

We continued to drink vigorously, until it began to get the better of us: Harry was propping her head up on her hand, and I wasn't sure if I'd be able to stand up when the time came. But somehow we managed to stumble out of the bar and lurched toward Liverpool Street station.

Her arm was around my waist. "I can't believe you're actually going. That you're really going to leave me here."

"Yep," I slurred. "I'm leaving you. You'll have to find a stand-in little brother to torment."

"Already got a shortlist. I'll keep you posted."

"Do tell."

"Most of them are tall, slim, well-off."

"They sound like trophy husbands."

"I have high standards — someone has to pay my bar bill. It's not like journalism pays your kind of salary."

"How will you decide the ultimate winner?"

"Easy," she said. "He'll stick around."

She had intended the comment to be funny.

"Yep," she said. "That's exactly how I'll know. My new little brother probably won't even have a passport. But if he does, and it occurs to him that he might want to leave, he'll think about all the people he'd be leaving behind," she said, hiccupping. "And how awful it would be for them."

Though her head was turned away from me, I saw her wipe her eyes, smearing her mascara. The station was up ahead, and the street was crowded with people in a similar state to us, tripping down the road with half-finished pints still in their hands. Last orders must have just been called.

"I did think about those things," I said, steering us toward a quieter corner.

"And you still decided to leave! Brilliant! That makes me feel so much better."

I leaned against a wall and propped her up next to me. "I'm not leaving you, I'm leaving England."

"You don't get it," she said. "When you leave, that's it. My family is gone."

"Mum and Dad are still here."

"They disowned me. You're it," she said. She stared, daring me to contradict her.

And, of course, I couldn't.

EVERYONE WAS SITTING down to dinner when I got back to the flat. "Just in time," Iris said, kissing my cheek.

I sat in the only empty chair, between Myrtle and my sister, who wouldn't look at me. Iris dished up salad and lentil stew and I wondered what I'd just walked into.

"Thanks," I said.

It seemed that the sound of cutlery on crockery might have to pass for dinner conversation. Harriet glared at her plate and Myrtle was distracted by her phone, which left Iris as the only person who appeared willing to participate in anything like a family meal.

I took a bite of the stew, which could only be described as healthy. "Delicious," I said.

"I'm glad you like it," Iris said. "How was your train journey?"

I nodded. "Yeah, good."

Myrtle's phone beeped and buzzed, her face cast in an unsettling shade of blue from the screen.

"Put that away," Harriet said.

"Why?" Myrtle asked.

"Because it's rude. And dinner is the only time during the day that we're all together as a family," Harriet said.

"It's not like anyone was saying anything," Myrtle said.

"That's not the point."

"How was your day, Myrtle?" I asked, hoping to cut the tension.

"Fine."

"Your uncle, who never comes to visit, would probably like to hear more than that," Harriet said. I wasn't sure who she was angrier with, her daughter or me.

Myrtle looked up. "It's a new game," she said, holding her phone out so I could see.

"I asked you to put that away," Harriet said.

Myrtle ignored her. "I'm on level three."

"Wait till you get to level five. Black holes."

"What? How do you know that?"

I shrugged. "I may have played it."

Harriet snatched the phone away from her. "No phones at the table. That's the rule."

"Leave it, Harry," Iris said.

"Do you want her to grow up like that? Thinking a computer game is more important than her family?"

"She doesn't think that," Iris said.

"Doesn't she?"

"Harry," Iris said. "If it weren't for Myrtle we'd have no idea how ill your parents are."

The room went silent. I waited for my sister to explode, but if she did it was internal. Everyone focused on eating and not drawing any attention to themselves, until Harriet gave up the charade and sulked off into the living room with the bottle of wine.

"I'm sorry about that," Iris said to me, after Harriet had left.

I shook my head. "Don't apologize. I did grow up with her."

I looked up and saw Myrtle fighting back a grin.

"Sweetheart," Iris said. "Why don't you go to your room and get started on your homework."

Myrtle cleared the table and went into the kitchen. I could see her loading the dishes into the dishwasher.

"She's fantastic," I quietly said to Iris.

"She is." Iris swirled her remaining wine around in its glass. "What about you? Any cousins on the horizon for her?"

I looked at the table, probably blushing. "I'm not really seeing anyone right now."

"Do you really just spend all your time in the office?"

"No, I mean, last month we had a barbecue."

"We?"

"The company. It was for clients, but it was social."

"Did you talk about anything not work-related?"

"Sure," I said.

"Don't take this the wrong way, but what's the point of living in a different country if you never leave your office?"

She said it delicately, and I knew it wasn't an attack, but that didn't keep it from feeling that way.

"I don't know. What's the point in coming home?"

"Your family needs you."

"They need my bank account."

Iris gave me a strange look. "We need you to give us a chance, Iain. We want to get to know you."

I sighed heavily. "I know, I'm sorry. It's hard, though."

"Make it easier, then," Iris said as she got up from the table. "You better go and see what she's sulking about while I go and sort out the washing-up."

"I think Myrtle already put everything in the dishwasher."

"Oh, she did. But she won't have rinsed anything, and I don't want my breakfast to taste like last night's dinner."

I stayed at the table and watched as Iris moved around the kitchen, retracing her daughter's steps. My mind went back to that night at the pub, before I left for Oz.

I'd thought that my sister was just angry at me for leaving, and that she'd get over it. But it was becoming clear to me that she'd spent the intervening years nursing her abandonment.

Moving back to England seemed like something I ought to do, which didn't make it any more appealing. The difference for me between working in Oz or back here was minimal: I was tied to my desk, and rarely went out. What good could I do here anyway? Mum and Dad didn't want any help, and Harriet and I would just argue over what to do anyhow. The best thing I could do was pay for it all.

Finally I went into the living room, where Harriet was stretched out on the sofa, flicking through the channels. "So what do we do?" I asked, nudging her feet in the hopes she'd make room for me.

"About what?" she said, without looking up.

"All of it."

"I thought you didn't care?"

"Move over," I said.

"Why?"

"Harry, stop it. I want to have a proper conversation with you."

She scowled. "Why? So you can go home feeling guilt-free? Back to your sunny life with your big house and flush bank account?"

I sat down on her feet.

"Iain!" she screeched, sitting up so she could punch me in the arm.

"You wouldn't move."

She pulled her knees to her chest and rested her head against the arm of the sofa. Both of us stared at the telly, then I glanced over and our eyes met and we burst into laughter.

"You're still a dick," she said.

"And you're still a twat. You know, Harry, that first year, I thought about moving back. I even went to the travel agent to see how much a ticket would cost."

"You did not."

"I did. I hated it. I had no friends, didn't even know anyone outside the office. No family, nothing. I was lonely like you wouldn't believe."

She muted the TV. "Isn't that one of the benefits? Move halfway across the world to get away from your family?"

"Not when it's Christmas and everyone else has plans. Not when you don't know a soul. Not on your birthday."

"Don't even try bullshitting me. You have friends."

"Friends aren't the same as family."

"And that means so much to you that this is the first time you've been in my house. You love us so much — it must be awful to have to stay there."

I stared straight ahead at the TV. "Come back a failure? I had to stick it out. I mean, can you just imagine what they would've thought if I'd given up after a year?"

She chuckled. "Mum would've said you hadn't committed."

"Right. And Dad?"

"He wouldn't have said anything," she said, sitting up and wrapping her arms around her legs. "He would've just shaken his head and despaired because you would've been as disappointing — if not more — than me." She sighed. "And now we have to take care of them."

"How do we do it? How do we get him into a care home?"

"It's not easy. There are good ones and bad ones."

"Private or National Health Service?"

"Private, all the way. And you're paying."

"He gets the best."

"Agreed," she said.

I looked at her. "I would've thought you wouldn't be that bothered if he didn't get the best." I braced myself for an explosive reaction.

She leaned back against the couch and was quiet.

"I'm sorry, I didn't mean to imply —"

"No, no, you're all right. I'm not offended. I probably deserve that," she said. "Just because he was a crap father doesn't mean he deserves to suffer. Even I have a hard time staying mad at him when he's like this."

"He wasn't always a crap father."

"No, he wasn't." She leaned forward and refilled her glass of wine. "Do you want some?" I nodded and she went to get me a glass.

As I scanned the room I noticed there was evidence of Iris's calming influence everywhere, from the candles to the soft throw pillows and even the colour scheme — earthy and woodsy — as opposed to what I imagined Harry would have chosen on her own. It was nice to see that someone had managed to smooth some of her sharper edges over the years.

There were pictures, too. Family photos, of Iris's family, I assumed, since I didn't recognize their faces. But when I got up to take a closer look, wedged in the back was a picture of our family, on the beach at Dover: Mum in her swimsuit, Harriet with her arm around her, smiling proudly, Dad with his arm around me and Mum, and all of us looking, in our own way, every bit the content, close family we had been in the beginning.

I took the picture off the shelf and brought it back to the couch; when Harriet returned with a glass and another bottle of wine I held it up to her.

She seemed embarrassed to be the sort of person who would keep such a sentimental thing.

"Why do you keep it?" I asked.

"Still family, right?"

"For someone who hates them, it's an odd thing to have in the living room."

She sighed. "I don't hate them anymore. Hate's too strong. I don't understand them, but . . ." She took the picture from me and looked at it. "Myrtle changed things for me. It's hard — you know, you try to do your best . . . They aren't the best parents, but they're the only ones we've got."

"But you never went to visit either, until now."

She shook her head. "My daughter changed things, but she didn't make me perfect. Anyhow," she said, running her hand over the frame, "I'm trying to get over the bad bits by remembering the good bits."

"Is it working?"

"It's not easy." She handed me my glass.

"Are we terrible?" I asked.

"Generally or more specifically?"

"Both, maybe? I dunno, it's just . . . it took this" — I swept my arms open, hoping to encompass everything that had happened — "to get us to notice them. They've been up there ticking away, all these years, and we haven't noticed they were getting old and needed help."

"We probably are terrible, but they don't make it easy."

"I hate that this is happening to them."

She nodded. "I hate that it happens."

THAT NIGHT I slept on a blow-up mattress in Myrtle's room and I thought about how strange it was that my parents were the ones who needed my help now. I had known it would happen, but the difference was in the details.

I thought of my father, who had helped me with my multiplication tables in school. Who had taught me to polish my shoes, and to always walk on the outside of the pavement when I was with a woman. Who had spent a long time teaching me how to whistle. I pictured his face when I graduated from university, filled with pride and astonishment, and that cheeky wink he'd given me when Daphne Rogers — a girl who was completely out of my league — agreed to go out with me, even though it was only to irritate her ex-boyfriend, who hated me. I tried to fill in the blanks of the years I'd been away.

It occurred to me quite suddenly that even though I knew a lot about my father, I didn't know everything — I didn't know anywhere near the full picture. And that the time in which to learn it, to find out who he was, was slipping away.

"Uncle Iain?" Myrtle whispered.

"Yeah?" I rolled onto my side and saw her face, still lit up by the glow of her phone. "You still playing that game?"

"No," she said, holding it out for me to see. "Have you seen this?"

I looked at the website and smiled. "No, but that's your grandmother."

My mother's picture was there, next to a list of all her Channel swims.

"I made it because she didn't have a Wikipedia page and I thought, you know, she should."

"Did you show it to her?"

"No."

"I'm sure she'll love it."

"How come Mum doesn't talk about her?"

"That's a long story."

"So?"

"What did your mum say when you asked her?"

"Nothing really. Iris said Grandpa didn't like them, but…"

"You want to know them, don't you?"

"Yeah."

"They're a strange old pair, and whatever Harriet tells you about what happened, just remember this: they love her."

"You didn't answer my question."

I chuckled. "It's not my question to answer." I looked at her, and her face was so young and curious. "Do you know why your grandmother was able to swim the Channel?"

"She's a good swimmer."

"No. She is, but that's not how she did it. She's strong-willed. Stubborn, even."

"So?"

"She said to me once that when you get in the water you have to know that you're not getting out until you reach the other side. Simple as that."

"I wish I could've known her better."

"She'll be around for a while longer."

"It makes them fight," Myrtle said.

"Who?"

"My mums. Iris thinks we should visit more often."

"She's stubborn. Both your mums are. And you are too, I think. In a good way."

"What was she like when you were growing up?"

"Who? Harriet?"

She nodded.

"Not a whole lot different than she is now. But her hair was different. She got the world's worst perm once."

"No!"

I laughed, remembering how much she'd looked like a clown. "It was horrible. She's probably burned all the pictures. She'd begged our parents for that perm, though. Did chores around the house, big ones: painting, cleaning, gardening. Washed Dad's car so many times we joked the paint would come off. Then one Saturday afternoon, when she finally had enough money saved up, off she went. And when she came back a few hours later she was inconsolable. Absolutely sobbing, saying things like she wasn't going out until it washed out, that she wanted to shave it all off. Mum tried to calm her down, told her it wasn't the end of the world, but Harry wasn't having any of it."

Myrtle was leaning over the edge of her bed, loving it, and I made myself a promise that I would get Harriet to tell her daughter more stories about back home. Not everything that had happened was awful.

"So two days later, she cut it off and it looked even worse. Your mother does not suit short hair. It looked like ... boy bedhead, sticking up all over the place. Mum took pity on her and they went back to the hairdresser together to see if there was anything that could be done. But, of course, there was nothing. Your mum bought a hat in a charity shop on her way back and refused to take it off. At first our mum insisted she take it off at the dinner table, but Harry was so mortified that Mum made an exception. In fact," I smiled, remembering, picturing how silly we'd all looked, "our mum got up and came back in

a few minutes with a hat for each of us. We must've eaten dinner with hats on for a week."

I hadn't thought of that in years. The way we had all sat
there, trying to continue as though everything were perfectly
normal, struck me as particularly sweet.

In the morning, Myrtle got up for practice before it was
light. She stumbled over my mattress and I mumbled something
about seeing her later. When I heard Iris and Harriet moving
around I got up as well, but as I was about to open the door I
paused. I heard them talking and I listened, not for the words
but for something else — the timbre of their voices, maybe, just
to have it as a memory later on, to prove to myself that I did
know them in their hidden moments.

I stood like that, listening to them, remembering weekend
mornings in front of the telly with Harry, and I wished for
those days to come back. When the most difficult questions
we had faced had been who would make the bacon sandwiches
and who would get the first crack at a hot shower. Back when
we had had no real problems to solve.

UNWITNESSING

MARTHA, 2009

THAT MORNING, as we sat in our usual spot — third pew from the front, on the right-hand side of the aisle — I took comfort in the feeling of community that the congregation afforded us. As the gulf between us and our children grew wider, and John's mind became nearer to an unravelling ball of string, the familiarity of the faces I saw stood in for the things we had lost.

As we listened to the sermon, it was the buttons on John's waistcoat that were flummoxing him. He buttoned them and unbuttoned them: part nervous twitch and part something else. Sometimes he got them done up properly; other times the buttons missed their corresponding holes and he had to start all over again. I tried to focus on the priest as his voice filled the old stone building. It reminded me of a time when I — and by extension John — had been the beneficiaries of the sort of kindness and generosity that the Church attempts to inspire in people.

After my first unsuccessful swim I had promised myself that I would try again and that I would not fail. Swimming the Channel required extreme amounts of training and dedication, which I had or could muster. But it also needed funding: a thousand pounds at least, per swim, for the pilot, the petrol, the boat, the Federation official, the food. It was money we could not afford, and every day, as I swam, I thought of how I could raise it. I thought of getting a job, but I wanted to be there for the children when they were younger, and John, I knew, wanted to be the breadwinner. Besides, I had nothing beyond swimming and mediocre housewifery skills. France had seemed further away than ever.

One Sunday morning after the service, Edward, the priest, asked if I could stay behind, so I left John to talk with our friends outside and went to the office in the back of the church. I sat opposite him across a large oak desk — the same desk John and I had sat at over fifteen years before, when we had come to discuss getting married.

"Martha," Edward said. "I wonder if you might be able to help."

I nodded, expecting him to ask me to volunteer to organize a bake sale or an outing for the children.

"I need an assistant, a secretary of sorts, someone who would be available for a few hours during the day."

"I'm sure someone like that shouldn't be hard to find. You might mention it next week before the service."

He leaned forward, his perfunctory black-framed glasses slowly sliding down his rather obvious nose, and lowered his voice. "I had someone in mind, but it might be difficult to convince her. I was hoping you might be able to help me with that."

"Of course, I'll do what I can. Who do you have in mind?" I couldn't guess who he was thinking of — his vague description did not make me think it would be difficult to find such a person, given that most of the congregation was made up of housewives like myself.

"I have you in mind, Martha."

"Me?" I unconsciously sat up straighter.

"Yes," he said, hesitantly.

"I don't mean to be rude, but why?"

"I need someone with tenacity."

"I'm quite sure I'm not the only person with that."

"Martha, I'm offering you a job."

"Yes, thank you, I understand. But I'm not clear on exactly what it is that you need my help with."

"The accounts, mainly. Dealing with the builders — the boiler is on its last legs."

"Edward, the boiler gave up months ago. Have you not noticed everyone keeps their coats on? It's not out of respect, you know."

"You're already aware of some of the challenges I'm facing."

"Everyone is aware of the boiler issue, Edward."

He sighed as he leaned back in his chair. "Martha, I understand you want to swim the Channel."

"What has that got to do with this?"

"I understand it's an expensive proposition."

"It's certainly not inexpensive."

"I've seen you swimming in the harbour."

"I expect most people have."

"You're there every day."

"I am. I'm training."

"But you can't afford to make the swim."

I looked at him sternly. "Thank you for reminding me. I don't remember the church's remit extending to parishioners' finances before."

"I've seen the way you look at the water, Martha."

"And how is that?"

"Like a woman possessed."

"Are you going to stage some kind of exorcism?"

He laughed. "No, no. Of course not. We're not Catholic. Perhaps a better word is devotion."

"Yes, perhaps it is."

"I'd like to see you swim the Channel, Martha."

"As would I."

"I'm offering a way for you to be able to do that."

I tried very hard to retain my composure but my face, I'm certain, was a dead giveaway because Edward smiled; I believe he knew he had me at that point.

"It would be good for the community. Give everyone something to get behind."

"Quite," I said.

"Would you be ready to go at the end of the summer? Physically, I mean."

"Yes."

"The role I'm offering would allow you to meet that goal."

"How do you know how much it will cost?"

"Beg pardon?"

I looked him straight in the eye. He pushed his glasses up nervously. "You've spoken to John, haven't you?"

"He is part of my congregation."

"Yes, he is. And I don't expect he was particularly keen on you indicating you had a rather intimate understanding of how unable we are to pay for the swim ourselves."

"Martha," he said, his frustration growing. "I am trying to help."

I crossed my arms over my chest.

"It would be clerical work, as I said — the accounts, ordering in whatever the church needs, managing basic repairs and the like."

"And I would be able to swim in September?"

"You would be able to afford to, yes. As to your ability, I leave that for you to judge."

"I'll be ready."

He smiled. "Then I'll see you tomorrow. Shall we say ten o'clock?"

I stood up to leave. "Half past eleven. I train in the mornings."

I never thought I would wish for those days to come back, but as I sat on the pew next to my husband, I wondered if he longed for the days when there were solutions to our problems. We were halfway through the service, and John's fidgetiness was becoming increasingly troublesome. I knew he was getting away from himself. His hands couldn't stay still and they were moving beyond the buttons: he was pointing at something only he could see, somewhere up in the rafters, and his mouth was moving as though searching for the right words. This was punctuated with bouts of him looking around as though he'd never been in the church a day in his life.

He turned to his right and whispered something to Harold, who ran a B & B up near the castle, and who we had known for over twenty years. Though I didn't hear what he'd said, the look on Harold's face told me it wasn't good.

John whipped his head around to me and said, "Get that one's phone number." He gestured to Harold's side of the pew. His voice was several notches above a whisper.

I put my hand on his knee and tried to calm him.

"Isn't she in your year at school, Molly? You must know her."

I was shocked to hear him say his sister's name. A name he'd not spoken in years. "I'm not Molly," I said, putting my hand on his arm. "Calm down."

"She's a real looker. That one, in the blue dress."

Harold's wife was wearing a blue dress and bright red cheeks.

"Don't be daft," I said, wondering how we were going to get out of there without any further embarrassment.

There was something in his expression that frightened me. It wasn't aggressive, and to look at him, you wouldn't think he was confused. But what was happening for him and what was happening for the rest of us were plainly out of step. And that he'd mistaken me for his sister Molly spoke of darker things.

I picked up my purse from the pew, but before we could leave the priest asked everyone to stand and sing and I took it as a gift; we could excuse ourselves without any undue commotion. But then John did something I had never known him to do, even when we were much younger. He reached around behind Harold, shoving him out of the way, and tried to pinch his wife's bottom. I managed to grab his hand and wrench it away before he touched her, but the damage was done. Everyone had seen it.

The voices picked up and the familiar lyrics filled the room as I dragged John down the aisle toward our car.

I, the Lord of sea and sky,
I have heard My people cry.

Getting him into the car was tricky, but somehow we managed to make it home, where I shut the door on the rest of the world. I could only hope that whatever had set him off was out there and that we could go back to what passed as normal, for at least a few hours. But he sat down at the table, still insisting I was Molly.

"I don't see why you wouldn't even introduce us," he said. "I think she fancied me, she couldn't stop looking at me."

I clenched my jaw and wondered where to even start.

"We could double-date, Molly. Think of it. Pictures next weekend, maybe. See if she'll come along."

"John," I said, trying and probably failing at keeping my voice calm and measured. "I am your wife. We have been married for over fifty years."

He rolled his eyes. "Stop fooling around."

"I'm not Molly. I'm Martha. Your wife."

A cloud came over his face, as though something in the recesses of his brain was willing to go looking for the memory that would solve this riddle.

"No, you're my sister — otherwise, why would you be living here?"

"We live here because this is our house."

"Yes, our parents' house."

"No, ours. We bought it. Or rather, you did."

"I don't know what you're playing at."

I bit my lip, determined to not let him see me cry. "Molly passed away when you were young. Before we met."

"No, you're right here."

I gripped his shoulders. "I'm your wife. Martha. We were married in the church where we were this morning."

The look in his eyes was the most horrible thing I have ever seen. It was blank. In that moment he didn't know who I was; couldn't remember any of the things that made him him, and me me.

"Molly's passed?"

I turned away and wiped my eyes. "Polio. She was just a girl."

His mouth fumbled as his fingers found his buttons and I didn't know which was worse: to tell him again that she'd passed or go along with it.

"Why don't you lie down, just for a bit?" I suggested.

He nodded but didn't move, so I took his hand and led him upstairs. He sat on the edge of the bed and when I reached out to help him with his buttons, he batted my hand away like an angry cat.

"I'm not a child," he bellowed. "I can do it myself."

I left him to it and pretended to busy myself with straightening the already tidy room. I moved things around on the dresser, I closed the curtains, and I refolded his trousers that hung on the back of the chair in the corner, all the while keeping an eye on his progress. When he was undressed and under the covers I sat on the edge of the bed and promised myself I would not cry.

I bent forward, brushed a few stray hairs from his forehead, and kissed his cheek as I always did.

"Sleep well," I said, hoping he didn't hear my voice catch on the tears that I knew were coming.

I went downstairs and put the kettle on, trying to steady myself by doing the most routine thing I could think of. I put the teabag in the cup and listened as the water came to a boil, and then I couldn't. I just couldn't.

Without thinking, I grabbed my swimming bag and set off for the bay, where my Channel swims had technically begun. I didn't go to the harbour, where I had usually trained, because I wanted to be alone.

Shakespeare's Bay is where the pilots — and for me it was always Charlie because he knew the Channel better than anyone — dropped the swimmers off at the start of our swims. Charlie picked me up in the harbour, and we'd scoot around to the bay. It was a routine that still held up after all these years: I'd jump off the boat and swim to shore, and then I'd wave and that was the formal start. The official in the boat would start his watch and so would Charlie. The time made little difference to me, but to have the swim recorded, to have it marked down in the record books, one needed an official from the Federation, and a time.

When I got to the beach I changed in full view, which was fine because it was empty. But even if the beach had been covered in sunbathers I would've changed right there, regardless. I was past decency for appearance's sake. I got my swimsuit on quickly and didn't bother stowing my things. All I wanted to do was get in the water. I ran into the sea, dove under quickly, and swam as though my life depended on it.

My elbows came high out of the water, arms stretching out past my head, and then, plunging in, I accelerated through the water as I pulled myself forward. My hands brushed past my hips with a flourish as my arms circled back out of the water to repeat the process. My feet — pointed ever so slightly inward — kicked hard, the force coming from my hips and thighs.

But the physical exertion did nothing to relieve me, as I had hoped. John kept rolling back into my mind like the waves I swam through. That look of utter confusion, as though I had been speaking a language he did not understand. The way his face had been able to convey, through a complex mixture of muscle movements, the fact that he knew it was wrong and upsetting that he did not recognize me. It was comforting — at least — that he knew I was someone close to him, and that I was someone he loved. But it didn't change anything. I still needed him to remember all the days we had spent together — because if he couldn't, then what had been the point of it all? I had always imagined us growing old together and reminiscing about the old days. But that was not a luxury we were going to have.

The most difficult thing to understand was the way in which he had forgotten me. I had not been erased completely, but the route to those memories was broken, constantly changing. Some days we were lucky, and walked down the same road toward each other — meeting was a happy accident. Other days, though, we wandered in search of one another through the fog that had moved in from the sea, clouded the cliffs, and seeped into his mind. I knew that as the disease progressed he would forget me for longer periods, that I would not be the woman who had shared a life with him, borne him children, and been by his side for more than fifty years.

My chest burned and I stopped swimming. Flipping onto my back quickly, I tried to slow my breathing. The sky was beautiful: hazy with the sun high above, warming my face.

I wondered how frequently John was going to forget; whether this was going to be a series of blips, or a more sustained unwitnessing. Would he recognize me when I got home? Would he be able to hold that thought tight enough to remember me through the afternoon and on into dinner? Or would he dine with a stranger?

I propelled myself underwater as deep as I could go and then I screamed. I used up all the air in my lungs and howled at the indescribable unfairness of it. I surfaced reluctantly. Looking around I saw the water stretching for miles and miles, the beach, the town in the distance, and the train tracks. I turned my back to the town and looked ahead to France.

The most important things in my life had happened here in the salt water. But the sea was not a witness to the parts of my husband's mind that had become lost like so many messages in bottles, forever drifting away on the currents.

I bobbed in the small waves and let the sea support me as it had always done.

"Do you remember when he proposed?" I said aloud. "When I brought our children here? When he and I first met?"

I hit the water with my hand, splashing no one but myself.

"And do you remember how much time I've spent here, with you, while he's looked on? Do you remember the way the moon hung heavy in the sky when you carried me back from France? What about the way you inched toward us, under the pier, before he and I were married?"

I pounded both fists as hard as I could onto the water's surface, and they slipped under as though there was nothing in their way.

My arms railed against the sea, and if someone had seen me from shore I imagine they would have thought I was drowning.

"He is forgetting! He is forgetting me!"

I dove down under water and let myself cry. Salt water into salt water. I came up for air, sobbing, gasping, and went down again. The waves gently ferried me back to shore, and left me to go and see my John, who was unravelling beyond all repair.

ON THE MONDAY that I started work at the church, I had dropped the children off at school and gone to the sea for my swim. Early spring meant that the water was still very cold, but I'd managed a few minutes, enough to begin preparing myself for the twenty-one-mile swim.

It was a strange feeling to have to fit my swim into my life. My training sessions that early in the season had a minimum duration — thirty minutes — but never before had I had to make sure I was out of the water by a certain time. Swimming was the thing I looked forward to most and the thing I did without restriction. I always swam until I couldn't swim any longer and then, to bolster my endurance, I forced myself to swim fifty more strokes. Motivation was easy: I pictured being pulled out again as I had on my first attempt; I remembered being sick on the boat ride back. I reminded myself that this was my last chance. After this, I would either be a Channel swimmer or a failure.

I don't think Edward knew quite what to make of me when I arrived at the church. There I stood, hair dripping, wet towel and swimsuit in my bag, water seeping through the cloth to create a puddle at my feet. He let me hang my things over the radiator that hardly worked; by the time I finished that afternoon, my swimsuit would be cold and clammy, but not completely wet. It wouldn't matter, though; I'd put it on again. The children were old enough to see themselves home from school.

Edward shook his head in mock disbelief at the wet clothes, then we sat down and he showed me what he needed help with.

It was far more than I had imagined. Edward didn't have a head for figures and the church accounts were a shambles: envelopes full of receipts, no weekly totals for the collection, no idea of how much money was in any given place at any one time.

"How have you managed?" I asked.

"An act of God," he said.

I shook my head in exasperation.

Little by little, week by week, I worked through the mess,

until a month later, when I had everything up to date, and I sat down with him to go over it.

"Edward," I said. "It's not good news."

"I should think having everything in order is very good news."

"You have been counting on a fairly steady collection each week."

"Yes," he said.

"I'm afraid that's not the reality." I pointed to the column in the ledger. "The collection has been going down steadily over the years. People are leaving the congregation, and those who have stayed don't have as much money as they once did."

"I see," he said. His tone indicated otherwise.

"What I'm trying to tell you is that you have a lot less money than you thought you did."

"We're a church, Martha. We're not in the business of making money."

"No, but you do need to cover your costs."

"And we will."

"I'm afraid you might not. The cost of heating has gone up dramatically, and the boiler is on its last legs. You're in arrears with the heating bills."

"No, I paid those. I'm sure I did."

"The heating company disagrees."

He nodded glumly and I continued, going over every item, rhyming off numbers and bills. When I was finished I turned to him and said, "And to be quite honest with you, you haven't got the money to keep me on, either."

Edward looked at me then with an air utterly devoid of hope. His job was to minister to his flock and provide spiritual guidance. Accounting was not in the job description.

"We could start an appeal," I said, trying to cushion the blow. "Get volunteers, ask for time and assistance. Not money."

He nodded.

"And you'll stop paying me."

"No. I hired you to do a job."

"You can't afford to pay me."

He straightened his posture. "I'll find a way even if I have to pay you myself."

I shook my head. "The strongest leaders are the ones who lead by example."

The following Sunday I stood in front of the congregation and explained the situation. We appealed to the community's generous nature. I asked for nothing; I simply told them that the church needed their support and that I was doing my bit, and asked for them to join me. After the service I stood at the door with Edward and a sign-up sheet. People put their names down, adding whatever skills they had and whatever else could be of use.

John stood next to me. At one point I overheard him talking to the butcher.

"Quite the woman you have there, John," the butcher was saying. "A force to be reckoned with. Galvanized the whole community. You're a lucky man."

I glanced over and saw John beaming.

"I am," he said. "Quite lucky indeed."

Remembering that moment now, it felt so close I almost forgot the present, almost forgot to worry about what would be waiting for me inside the house when I returned from my swim. I had no idea if John would even still be there. It had been irresponsible of me to go out and leave him on his own. Anything could have happened.

I stood on my front doorstep and I thought about running away. I thought about leaving Dover and going to another town, or another country, and starting over by myself. But I opened the door, because he was my husband and I had promised in sickness and in health — though when I had agreed to that, the sickness I had imagined amounted to nothing more than a bad flu. I had never dared picture anything like this.

I stood in the foyer and listened for sounds that would give me an indication of what to expect, what would be waiting for me further inside the house.

Everything was silent. In the kitchen was the unmade cup of tea, and no sign that John had woken.

I crept upstairs, worried that I wouldn't find him in bed, but he was there — fast asleep on his side, with his back to me. I watched the duvet as it rose and fell with his breathing. I went round to my side of the bed and saw his hand stretched out, curling around my pillow. We had slept like that since the beginning. He liked to trace the tan lines across my back, the outline of my swimming costume. My other skin, he called it.

I took off my shoes and slid into bed next to him. I moved his arm gently, hoping I wouldn't wake him, and then I put his arm over my shoulder, pulling myself tightly against his chest. He murmured softly as though he was about to wake, and I kissed his hand.

I did not know if he was dreaming, and if he was, what was happening in the dream, but he looked calm. In that moment he was the man I loved, the man I had married, and the man he had always been. He was my John and if this was the only place I could find him, if this was the last place where he was himself, then this is where I would come. I lay next to him, my wet hair dampening the pillow, and I wondered if he could smell the sea on me, if it permeated his dreams.

I HADN'T MANAGED to earn enough money working for the church to pay for my swim, and with two young children, John and I couldn't afford to spare anything. It would have to wait another year, and I would have to find another job. I resigned myself to it. The sea would still be there when I was finally ready.

Then, one Sunday in mid-August, Edward stood in front of the congregation and spoke. Over the months that we had been working together he had asked about my swimming in a way that no one else had, curious about all the tiniest details. I had thought it was unusual, but I enjoyed the chance to talk about it.

I had told him about my training: how many miles I'd logged over a month, how I went about getting used to the temperature, how I gained weight to insulate me from the cold. I'd showed him the sores on my shoulders from where the straps and the salt had chafed and burned my skin. I'd let him smell the horrible sheep grease I used in an effort to protect my skin. And I had told him about the myrtle bush.

That Sunday morning, Edward began the service by mentioning the plants in the Bible.

"The myrtle is a sort of shrub, with evergreen leaves, and small flowers that bloom in the height of summer. Like so many other plants in the Bible, the myrtle is the only representative of its family in Israel. It is not mentioned in the Bible until the time of the captivity. The first mention is Nehemiah 8:15, in reference to the celebration of the Feast of Tabernacles. But I want to draw your attention to the references to myrtle in Isaiah 41:19 and 55:13. They refer to the divine establishment of the people in the land in subjection to Jehovah. As an evergreen, fragrant shrub associated with water, the myrtle is a fitting symbol of the recovery and establishment of God's promises."

He paused briefly, looking out into the congregation, letting his words settle in. From the back pews, I heard a mother hush her child, followed by the crinkling of a sweet being unwrapped.

Edward continued. "And so it is here, for us, that the myrtle is also a fitting symbol for recovery. Many of you have contributed to the recovery of our church, offering your help, assistance, and expertise. I mention the myrtle because a member of our congregation, Mrs. Martha Roberts, has been volunteering to help us with this recovery. She has also been training to swim the Channel. Each day, twice a day, she goes to the harbour and swims. On the shore there is a myrtle shrub where she keeps her towel while she's in the sea. Mrs. Roberts has the opportunity to make an attempt on the Channel this year, and as we could not have recovered the church without her help, so too can she not make this extraordinary attempt without ours. She does not know this, but I have been working with some of you to ensure that she is able to try this year, this September. Her pilot, Charlie Rose, has volunteered his services. As a congregation we have raised enough money to pay the Federation's fees, so that her swim may be officially recorded. I hope you will join me in seeing Mrs. Roberts off when she takes this challenge on."

I turned to John, who was barely able to contain his glee.

WRITING ON THE WALLS

IRIS, 2014

OUR HOME PHONE RANG, which was unusual.

"Hello?" I said, on what had been until then a perfectly ordinary early Tuesday evening in late January.

I had come home from teaching and was indulging in my secret, guilty pleasure of chocolate biscuits and one of Flashman's historical adventures.

The person on the other end of the line didn't answer immediately and I wondered if it was a sales call, some random computer trained to dial endlessly, hoping to find someone willing to talk.

"Iris, is Harriet available?" It was Martha.

"Have you tried her mobile?"

There was another pause. "No."

"You should be able to reach her on that number," I said.

"Iris?"

The tone of her voice, tentative and unsure, was completely unlike the Martha I had secretly gotten to know over the years.

"What's wrong?" I said, instantly aware that something awful was upon us.

"It's John," she said.

My hands went weak.

"What about him?" I asked.

"He's in hospital."

"Martha," I said. "We're coming."

An hour later I had gathered up my two best girls and we were all packed into the car, driving along the motorway as Harriet spoke to Iain somewhere deep in the early hours of the Australian morning, and Myrtle distracted herself by working her way to the next level in a game on her phone.

The car was silent and I was left with my own private thoughts. It was not unlike the annual pilgrimages I'd been making in secret along this same stretch of road for years, to share something of our life with Harriet's mother.

Each visit had been the same. I would pull up to their house, park the car, and ring the bell. Martha would answer and invite me in for a couple of hours. Or, in recent years, we'd meet in the tea house on the pier. Over tea, I would dash through the highlights of the year, focusing mostly on Myrtle and glossing over anything that might be in the least bit provocative.

The first time I'd visited, I'd gone shortly after Myrtle's first birthday and it had been difficult to get away, but I had seen how overjoyed my parents were to meet our gurgling daughter and I could not deny Harriet's parents the pleasure of at least knowing about her. And part of me believed a granddaughter would soften them. I had pressed the bell with hesitation, and when Martha answered the door my hesitation began to turn into regret.

"Yes?" Martha had said with her typical curtness.

I wasn't sure she remembered me. We had met only once before and that had been over a year previously.

"I'm Iris," I said.

"I know who you are," she'd said, pulling her cardigan tightly around herself against the beginnings of autumn.

I looked at my feet, ashamed that I'd wanted to include her in our world when she so obviously did not want to be included. I didn't know quite what to say so I showed her a picture of Harriet holding Myrtle in the hospital.

Martha took it and squinted at it in the bright daylight. I watched her face change when she realized what she was seeing.

"Come in," she'd said.

It wasn't a formal arrangement, but in time she came to expect me. I believe she looked forward to these clandestine visits that were equal parts wonderful and heartbreaking. It was only an afternoon once a year and I knew they weren't capable of changing everything, but I thought they might slowly eke out a space in which our family might fit into theirs.

I told Martha about Myrtle's swimming, school, likes and dislikes. I told her the stories that Harriet and I told each other, remembering Myrtle's first steps, first words, and first days: at nursery, school, and swimming. I provided the details that make up a life. Myrtle loved strawberries, hated bananas; loved asparagus, refused to eat mushrooms. I said that our daughter smelled like chlorine. That whenever I smelled bleach, I thought of her.

The first year I went to visit, when it was time to leave, Martha had hugged me tightly and said, "Thank you."

Because I'd been making this trip in secret every year, I'd learned the route, and I worried that Harriet would notice that I was making good progress without the help of directions.

Things between my wife and her parents had been inching slowly forward — cancer had a way of softening hard feelings — but Harriet had suffered enough shock for one day. Finding out about my secret visits could easily undo the progress she had made. But she was too wrapped up in the logistical nightmare of pulling her family together over miles and miles of distance to notice.

"I'll let you know," Harriet said into the phone as she unfastened her seat belt. "I'll phone again when I know more."

She bolted out of the car and burst into the house. And Myrtle shot me a look of confusion.

"She might not like them," I said, putting my hand on her shoulder. "But she does love them."

Inside, Martha was on the sofa and Harriet sat at her side. The tension that filled the room was suffocating.

"Why? Why did you wait so long?" Harriet demanded. "We could've done something."

"What could you have done?"

"Helped."

"Helped to keep him from falling? How would you have done that, exactly? And from London, no less."

"Would you have even accepted it? You didn't seem to need anything when Iain and I were here in September. You had everything under control."

Myrtle whispered to me, "Do something."

"Tea?" I suggested with too much enthusiasm. "Would anyone like tea?" My chipper tone palpably grated against their strain.

Martha and Harriet glared at me. They were intent on having a fight and I was powerless to intervene.

"Are they keeping John in hospital overnight?" I asked.

"Yes," Martha said.

"Myrtle, why don't you and I go and see if we can't cheer him up?" I said. "Bring him dinner or something."

"They won't let you bring in food," Harriet snapped.

"Why not?"

"Against the rules, remember that article I did last year?" Harriet said.

"Well, we'll just go along for a visit then."

"It's past time now," Martha said. "They won't let you in."

"Then Myrtle and I will go and have a drink. We'll stop at the Chinese and pick up a takeaway. Is that all right? Because quite frankly I don't want to listen to the two of you do this and you need to get it out of your systems. So go. You have one hour." I grabbed my daughter's hand and we stormed back to the car.

I drove through the streets that I had grown familiar with over the years, searching for somewhere to go. But the lights in the tea room on the pier were off, and it seemed that most of Dover had given up and gone to bed on this dreary, rainy evening. Myrtle was silently staring out the window, and I despaired that we would ever find anywhere we could sit until I saw the lights of a pub glowing through the gloom.

We went inside and found a table easily. I prayed they wouldn't make an issue of Myrtle being underage and they didn't, which I put down to either the look on my face when we walked through the door or the tone of desperation in my voice when I ordered a glass of wine.

Uninterested in her fizzy drink, Myrtle looked around for something in the way of entertainment. She found it almost immediately.

"Mum, look!" she said, pointing to the wall. "What is that?"

On the wall next to our table was a name, date, and time: 10 September 1982, Jules Russell, 9:32. Next to it was another: Omar Amon, 31 July 1981, 8:14. The pub was covered in them. The handwriting was different but they were all essentially the same.

"What is it?" Myrtle asked.

I shrugged, so she went to ask the barman and though I didn't hear his answer I expected it was good because I heard her clap her hands excitedly. She rushed back to me, nearly tripping over a chair as she did.

"It's swims," she said, her face lit up. "We have to find Grandma's name."

"I don't know if this is the sort of place your grandmother would have come," I said.

"He said everyone does it," she replied, pointing to the barman.

She went back to the bar and I watched as she described Martha. The barman, who must have had excitable teenagers himself, listened patiently and then led her to a spot near the door. Myrtle took a picture on her phone and tapped away furiously. I hoped she wasn't sending it to Harriet.

The barman waited for her to finish her message and then showed her the next spot, and the next. Her reaction was the same for each: picture then message. The only difference was the size of her smile, which continued to grow. She nodded enthusiastically at whatever he was telling her, tucking her brown hair behind her ears in a way that reminded me of Martha: all speed and efficiency.

Had I ever told her grandmother about that tic? Not for the first time, I marvelled at their similarity. They hardly knew one another at all, and yet there was something that drew them together, a commonality of spirit or character that drew them both to the water.

"Look!" Myrtle said, shoving her phone in my face.

I blinked and moved the screen further away in order to focus. "I had no idea these were here," I said.

"This was two days before I was born!"

She sunk into the chair next to me, satisfied to have had her curiosity piqued in a direction I knew Harriet would disapprove of. I patted her knee.

"The barman said she came in here after. Each time. The lady in the harbour, that's what they call her. She's famous here."

"Is that so?"

She nodded and turned to me conspiratorially. "He asked if I was going to do it."

"Do what?"

"Mum," she said, tilting her head to one side, looking at me as though I were daft.

"Are you?" I asked.

She looked as though she was unsure of how to take the question, though I didn't need a reply to know her answer. It was written all over her face.

"Don't tell your mother," I said.

She did a little fist pump the way she did when she won a race and went back to her phone, no doubt alerting her friends on the swim team to the plan.

IN THE MORNING we all piled into the car and went to see John. His ankle was broken, but because he had been disoriented when they found him — out for a walk or a wander, depending on who you believed — the decision had been taken to keep him overnight. Propped up in bed, he seemed to be in a decent humour and smiled when he saw Martha.

She, however, was not best pleased. "All these years, and nothing. You wait until now to break something?"

He held out his hand for her and she took it.

"They said to rest, but how am I meant to do that if they come in every hour and ask how I'm doing?" he said.

"Where's your doctor?" Harriet asked.

He eyed her and I wasn't sure, but I didn't think he recognized her.

"Dad," she said.

His face changed, the furrow in his brow returned, and it looked like he was coming back to us.

"The doctor," Harriet said. "What did he say?"

"She," he replied. "He's a she. The doctor."

"Then what did *she* say?"

"That I was lucky."

She turned to me. "I'm going to see if I can find out more."

I squeezed Harriet's elbow and saw how scared she was. She would never say as much, but seeing him there in a hospital bed, hooked up to machines, his frame bonier than she had expected — she was struggling with it. I knew exactly how that felt, and that it would be harder for her: that she was battling herself, too, to see which Harriet would emerge — the one who loved the father she'd grown up with or the one who hated him.

She left the room quickly and I followed her into the corridor.

"Harry," I said.

She started to run so I chased her, down the stairs, through another corridor, until we were outside and finally she stopped. When I put my hand on her shoulder she turned around and her eyes were red and swollen, her nose snotty and runny, so I wrapped my arms around her and held her as tightly as I could, her hands — balled up into fists — jutting into my chest.

"I can't," she sputtered. "I don't, I don't know what to do."

I smoothed her hair and held on as tightly as I could. Her chest shook as she sobbed and then she grew calm enough to speak.

"There are things that can be done, but they won't. They won't have any of it."

I thought of the last time I had come to see Martha, how I had presumed her loss of appetite was due to old age. It had been the previous summer, before Myrtle had shown us what we had been missing in Dover, before she had proven herself to be braver than Harriet and I combined. Seeing Martha's ease and familiarity with the doctors and nurses, just seeing her in the hospital made it clear, and I was upset with myself for not noticing.

Over the past several years, Martha had developed a preference for meeting me in the tea room at the end of the pier, and I hadn't thought much of it. Perhaps it upset John, or perhaps she wanted to keep our visits private. But last year I found myself at loose ends a bit earlier than September and so I took a chance, showing up unannounced.

I rang the bell and waited for her to answer, and when she did a look I had not seen in some time crossed her face. It was a similar expression to when I had driven Harry up there against her express wishes. Over the years I had grown to feel welcomed by Martha, but now I felt as though I was once again the last person she wanted to see.

She hesitated, looking over her shoulder at something I couldn't see, and with a heavy sigh, opened the door.

"I wasn't expecting you," Martha said.

"If now's not a good time…" I said.

I saw her take a breath, but before she spoke she seemed to reconsider, and smiled. "I'll put the kettle on."

But before the water had boiled John had ambled down the stairs. His shirt was buttoned wrong and there were dark shadows under his eyes. He looked wild and was moving erratically, jerking about as though his legs weren't entirely under his control.

"What is the problem, John?" Martha said.

He ignored her, throwing open the cupboard doors then slamming them shut. "Why do you insist on moving everything around? How am I meant to find anything in this mess!"

"I'm sorry," she said to me. "He should calm down eventually, or at least he'll run out of steam. Either way, he'll sleep soon." She looked at the clock that hung on the wall over the sideboard.

"Sleep?" It was only just past eleven in the morning.

"He's become a night owl in his old age. He spends most nights shuffling around the house. I hear him take the swimming case out, lay the things on the table. Sometimes he puts them back, other times I come down to a disaster. The maps have been quite troublesome recently. He crumples them up and stuffs them in strange places — cupboards, behind the sideboard."

I thought I was going to be sick. I thought of my mother's face when she had told me of my own father's disordered behaviour. "That's not good, Martha. What if he goes out during the night?"

She looked at me as though to say, what can I do? And I saw how tired she was, the black circles under her eyes a matching set to her husband's.

"If he goes out, all I can do is hope he comes back."

"Martha," I said. "He needs help. So do you. What has the doctor said?"

She shook her head. "He refuses to go. Shouts bloody murder if I even mention it."

"Martha," I said again, because there was nothing else I could say. Sorry wasn't anywhere near enough. "I should tell Harriet, Iain. We can help."

Again, she shook her head. "You can't help a man who doesn't want help," she said firmly.

"Goddamnit!"

John's voice came from the foyer, followed shortly after by a crash. We rushed to see what had happened and found him covered in coats, clutching the case.

"What is wrong with you?" Martha hissed.

"I couldn't find it," John said.

"Find what?" I asked.

Martha pointed. "The damned case."

"I don't see why your nose is out of joint," he snarled. "This case doesn't do me any good, I've only brought it for you."

"Then why were you so desperate to find it?" she asked him.

"I'm looking for something."

She crouched down next to him. "What?"

He looked at her like a puppy that had just been kicked.

"The pebbles."

Martha put her hand on his arm and they stayed like that for a moment.

Standing behind her, I waited for what he had said to become clear. John felt through the mess until his hand found an old jam jar with a faded label that I would later learn had once held Britain's best strawberry jam. He struggled with the lid and Martha didn't move to help him. When he got it open, he closed his eyes and inhaled deeply.

And then, she knelt beside him and placed her hand on his shoulder. John passed her the jar and then she, too, smelled its contents.

"Pass me the lid, please," she said tenderly. "We don't want to wear them out."

He did as she asked and she replaced the lid before helping him to his feet.

"John, dear, I think you might be tired," she said.

"Yes," he said. "Tired."

"Maybe it's time for a lie down?"

She helped him upstairs, as one might do a small child, leaving me standing in the mess — unsure of what to do but certain that they were both losing something important.

After a while Martha came back downstairs and smiled weakly.

"It sounds foolish, but these pebbles do have a certain smell. Now and then, on a bad day, it lifts the spirits." She placed the jar on the table as if it held the most delicate eggs. "At the start of each of my swims he would pick one off the beach. A souvenir, I suppose. But really more for good luck." Her eyes were filling with tears.

"Martha," I said, reaching out for her.

"No, don't." She looked around. "I haven't got anything in the house. Would you like to go out for an early lunch?"

"Are you sure?"

She nodded. "He'll be all right for a while. I'll just pop in to tell Henry."

I waited at my car while she went to the neighbour's and spoke to a middle-aged man who waved to me. After a short discussion, she got in the car and suggested we go to the pier.

It was a nice day, hazy but not raining, and full of the weather's last gasp of summer. We sat outside with sandwiches and builder's tea, looking at the sea.

"I'm sorry," I said.

"He comes and goes," she said.

"What will you do?"

"What can I do? My GP suggested a care home, but…" She picked at the crust of her sandwich. "I know John doesn't want that. Not that I can really discuss it with him."

I didn't know what to say.

"That's the strange thing. Not being able to talk about it with him. He wants to carry on as though nothing has changed."

"But it has."

"Of course it has."

"You should tell Harriet and Iain. You could talk about it with them. They could help. Martha, we could help." I didn't allow myself to say more than that. I wasn't sure I would be able to keep the worst bits of my father's deterioration to myself if I started talking.

"We don't want to be a burden." She stared out at the water. "I should have brought my swimsuit."

"We could do some research, help find a place for him to go."

"I can't imagine living in that house without him."

"You don't have to," I said.

She looked surprised. "Where would I go?"

"You could sell the house, move into a smaller flat. You could move nearer the sea. That would be nice, don't you think?"

"What would I do with our things? All that furniture. There's no way it would fit into a pokey little flat."

"You could sell it."

"I don't think so," she said. She pulled the tomato slices out of the sandwich and placed them on the bench. "Never cared for tomato. Terrible texture."

"You don't have to do this by yourself."

"It's my life," Martha said. "Who else is going to do it?"

OUTSIDE THE HOSPITAL, Harriet kissed me and I wiped the tears off her cheeks. The mascara that had run made her look like she'd been out for a very rainy Halloween. She took my hand and we went back inside.

The doctor was in John's room when we arrived, talking to Martha near the door in hushed tones. John was holding Myrtle's phone, looking at the pictures she had taken in the pub the night before. Harriet went up to the doctor and asked how her father was.

"The break was a clean one," she said. "He was very lucky." She looked down at his chart and then back at Harriet. "But that's not what I'm worried about."

We all knew what was coming next.

"His cognition is declining. This is going to happen with greater frequency. It's in his best interests to be moved to a facility where they can provide him with the care he needs, around the clock. There's a very good —"

Martha cut her off. "Thank you, but we won't be needing any of that."

"Mum, what are you talking about? He needs help."

"Your daughter is right. Treatments are advancing every day. A good care home can make sure his needs are met."

I stared at the doctor as she spoke and wondered how old she was and if she had ever had any personal experience with dementia. She didn't look old enough to drive a car.

"I'm his wife," Martha said. "I've been taking care of him almost his entire life."

"Yes, of course," the doctor said.

I was certain this doctor had heard it all before — pleas from patients and their families for her to join in the group delusion that everything would soon be back to normal, that there was nothing wrong, and that any minor change to routine could be managed at home without outside interference. And I knew that the moment John was put into a care home, his condition would deteriorate quickly. No amount of medical care could compensate for the familiar comforts of routine.

"But," she continued, "there are going to be things you won't be able to do for him. He'll need help eating, washing, and going to the toilet." She managed to rhyme off the list without flinching.

"I understand that," Martha said. "And he'll be coming home with us today unless there's anything more that can be done for his ankle."

The room was quiet except for the dull hum of the fluorescent lights overhead. The doctor looked at Harriet, who seemed ready to throttle Martha; Martha looked to me for something — help, sympathy, kind words, I wasn't sure; and I looked at our daughter, who was just getting to know her grandfather.

"Is there a nurse who could come?" I said. "To help out. Just for a few hours, here and there."

The doctor pursed her lips. "Yes, but round-the-clock care —"

"Send a nurse," Martha said. "I've made up my mind."

"Mum!" Harriet said, unable to contain herself any longer. "How can you not see this is for the best? He can't even get up the stairs with that ankle."

"I'll figure something out," Martha said. "The important thing is for us to go home now. All of us."

"Mum," Harriet pleaded.

"Do you remember when I swam from France?"

"Everything is not about swimming!" Harriet screamed.

Martha ignored her. "I got in the sea that day knowing that I was swimming home. Do you know what I thought about? For twenty-one hours and seventeen minutes I thought about my family, about you, your brother, your father, and our house. And I swam for that."

"Dad has Alzheimer's! This has nothing to do with fucking swimming!"

I put my hand on Harriet's shoulder, but she shrugged it off.

Martha looked Harriet dead in the eye, and with calmness and strength she said, "It has everything to do with swimming. It's about commitment and keeping your promises. In sickness and in health, Harriet. You've promised the same, and I expect Iris will hold you to it."

"His life is at stake!"

"So is mine." She turned to John and smiled. "We always made it home, didn't we?"

John looked confused.

"In the boat," she said. "I always swam home to you, didn't I?"

A cloud of recognition passed over his face. "The boat," he said. "Ten pebbles for ten swims."

REPEATER

MARTHA, 2014

IT WAS APRIL and time for my twice-yearly doctor's appointment. Henry knocked on the door and Webb barked a welcome.

"Come on, John, time to go," I said.

It was morning and my husband was nearing the end of his day, which now encompassed most of the night. Dinner had become breakfast, and in some ways I didn't mind. At least eggs were easier to cook.

John shuffled to the door, eyes heavy with sleep.

Yawning, he said, "I don't know why you can't schedule these appointments at a more reasonable hour."

"I thought we might go for a bite after," Henry said.

I looked at John. "Depends on how long the doctor takes."

"Just a check-up?"

I nodded. "Shouldn't take long. He'll need to eat anyway, before bed."

Henry drove us to the clinic, and through the rooftops and trees I caught a glimpse of the sea, shimmering blue and calling my name. We motored past the White Horse Inn and I turned to John in the back seat, pointing to the pub.

"We used to go in there," I said.

He followed the direction of my finger and I watched as he stumbled through his memories, hunting for the right one. His mouth moved soundlessly and I wondered if it was somehow an integral part of his thought process, helping him to get to where he wanted to go, steering him like the keel on a ship.

"One night, after a swim. There was a band, fiddles maybe. They played our request," he said, when the White Horse was well behind us.

I whistled the tune a bit and sang a few lines.

There'll be bluebirds over the white cliffs of Dover,
there'll be love and laughter and peace ever after, tomorrow,
just you wait and see

His face lit up. "We danced."

"We did."

He reached out to me, as though touching might turn up the volume of his memories. "I sang it to you, on the boat, coming back, once?"

"Did you?"

He nodded, unsure of himself.

Henry pulled into the car park and we all got out. It was strange to think that where we were once two, now we were three, with Henry our helper, lifeline, and chauffeur.

The medical centre was a dull little building, modern, with an impersonal air of efficiency. We marched in, single file, like schoolchildren on a day out.

In the waiting area there were chairs that looked deceptively comfortable, but they were arranged in a single row that reinforced a clinical atmosphere, which was further heightened by the smell of industrial cleaning solution and the briskness of the staff.

We didn't have to wait long before my name was called. Both John and Henry, according to the manners that had been drilled into them from a young age, stood when I did.

"I'll be fine," I said, relieving them of their obligation. "Won't be long at all. Wait here."

In the examination room I put on the horrible crinkly gown. I felt like a paper doll, the tabs folded over my shoulders holding the gown in place while doctors moved me around at will. I crinkled as I sat down in the chair, trying to preserve at least a shred of dignity.

Dr. Davies knocked before she entered and when she came into the room she was swift and professional, reading my chart as we exchanged the usual greetings.

We repeated the questions and answers as we always did.

"How are you feeling?"

"Fine," I said.

"Have you noticed any changes to either breast?"

"No, but then you did remove one of them."

She never acknowledged the fact that I had undergone a mastectomy — at her request — in these initial interrogations, and I wondered why: was it because she simply forgot, or was it because some government mandate required her to ask the same questions of every patient? Either way, the question grated.

"Have you noticed any lumps?"

"No."

"Have you had your blood checked?"

"Yes, they told me they would send the results through, as usual."

She looked at me over the rim of her glasses, as though to make sure I was telling the truth.

"Yes," she said. She flipped through the chart and then went to her computer and clicked away for a few moments. "They've not arrived."

She picked up the phone and spoke with the receptionist, her expression changing from bored disinterest to concern.

"Have them phone back right away," she said.

"Is there a problem?"

She looked up, and it was the first time during the appointment that she actually made eye contact with me. We moved to the examination table and she began the sequence I had learned from previous trips: she probed my chest, armpits, and groin. That last part was new.

"Do you feel any tenderness?" she asked.

I shook my head. "Nothing new."

"But there has been tenderness?"

"After a swim, yes, of course. The shoulders. Under the arms."

She frowned. "You haven't mentioned this in the past."

"It's not new."

"When did you last swim?"

"Autumn, the end of October."

"And the tenderness? When did you last experience that?"

"I'm not a young woman, Dr. Davies. I've worn all my joints out. I'm tender and stiff most days."

She went to answer the ringing phone. I watched her nod and scowl as I changed into my clothes again.

"Martha, the lab is double-checking your bloods. I'd like you to come back this afternoon."

"I'm afraid I can't," I lied. It was warm and the sea was flat.

"It's important. I can see you at half past four."

I had learned, through the course of my chemotherapy treatment, that it was best to humour doctors and so I agreed to return.

Dr. Davies paused as she was walking through the door and said, "Bring someone with you, Martha."

And that told me everything I needed to know.

I WENT TO collect my men and Henry suggested lunch.

"Change of plans," I said. "We're going for a swim."

"'We're'?" he said.

I nodded. "Yes, all of us. Right now."

"Martha," Henry said.

"To the sea," I said.

"How was the doctor?"

"Fine," I said firmly.

"Everything's all right?"

"Not the harbour," I said, pointing in the direction I wanted to go. "We're going to the bay today."

Bless him, he didn't argue with me. John was dozing in the back seat, it was a lovely day, and I wanted to do something fun because it had suddenly dawned on me that fun had been in very short supply of late. And if time was escaping me then I wanted to spend some of it with those I loved the most.

When we got to the shore, John looked around and started fiddling with his buttons.

"Why am I here?" he asked, a nervy edge to his voice. He looked around, his hair, thinning now but generally holding its own against his increasing age, flying helter-skelter in the breeze.

A gull passed overhead and cried, a sound so familiar I sometimes felt I understood what it was meant to communicate. I wanted to answer it back in the same sharp tone but, like so many other things, it wasn't to be.

"To see," I said to John.

I looked over my shoulder and Henry was leaning against the car.

"Come down," I called to him, but he shook his head.

"Leave you to it," he said.

John stumbled over to the myrtle bush where I had been leaving my clothes for so long it wouldn't have surprised me to find a stray sock, left behind years ago, having sprouted roots. The pebbles shifting underneath John's already unsteady legs made him appear as though he were drunk, which gave his confusion a comedic shadow. He plopped himself down and the stones cascaded away from him, making the distinctive sound that anyone who has ever swum the Channel knows better than their own voice. It sounded like breaking glass.

He looked around and then settled his gaze on me.

"To see?" he said.

"Yes," I said.

"The sea," he said, repeating the only answer I was ever able to give him as to what I was doing out here.

I went over to him, crouched down, and kissed his cheek. Then I pulled my top off, followed by my trousers, and walked into the sea clad only in my bra and knickers. It was cold and it had been too long.

Without my usual armour of goggles, cap, earplugs, and swimsuit it felt so natural — a better, clearer connection with the water. It was difficult to have a proper swim without those things, though, which was just as well. I didn't want to swim.

After breaststroking out a ways, I turned around and looked at the scene on the shore: my husband coming undone while picking at the fresh pink blossoms on the myrtle in the sunshine.

I flipped over onto my back and floated, letting the sea support me. As the water trickled into my ears it was as though all the memories the water and I shared rushed back to me in an instant.

The moment John forced me to come out of the water on my first try; and the second swim, where I saw heads of lettuce, lost from a passing container ship, bobbing in the Channel on my way back to England. The nausea that had plagued the third swim through the chop and waves, slowing me down so I spent more time than ever being scrubbed raw by the salt and sand. The moon reflected on the inky black expanse of water on the fourth or fifth. The swim when my timing was perfect and I captured the speed and motion of the changing tides to complete the distance in — for me — a record time.

Funny, of course, that I had no recollection of what that time had actually been. That swim was around when my granddaughter was born, unbeknownst to me, in London, that girl with a name that had shocked and delighted me. Her name that I took as proof that my own daughter didn't hate me.

Every swim had ended with my tongue too swollen to speak properly, my skin covered in sores, and my body cold and aching in a way I had come to crave because it reminded me I was strong.

The last swim, which I had not known then would be the last, was completed a year before the cancer diagnosis. I had just passed into my seventies, making me almost the oldest to have ever swum the Channel. And then driving to my doctor for what I expected to be an uneventful appointment, I remembered so clearly wondering if I had it in me to do one more crossing.

I saw motion from the corner of my eye, and flipped myself upright to see John moving toward the water's edge. I swam in quickly, and when it was shallow enough I stood and walked, my hand stretching out to him.

He reached forward and, fully dressed, waded in up to his knees. It was one of only a handful of times he and I had been in the water together. We stood there — I shivered and he wrapped his arms around me as I soaked through his suit — and we looked at the sea.

"I can't swim," he said.

I looked up at his face and saw his cheeky smile.

"That's because you never let me teach you."

He took a couple of tentative steps further into the water. "Now," he said.

"Now what?"

"Teach me now," he said.

He gripped my hand tightly as he kept moving forward, for once unaware of or uninterested in the fact that he was fully dressed. We walked a bit further out and though his teeth were chattering he refused to turn back.

"Is it always this cold?"

I nodded.

"How on earth do you manage it?"

I burst out laughing and so did he. It was such an absurd thing to have said after all these years.

"Come on then," I said. "You can at least float." I held my arms out. "Lie back, I'll hold you."

He did as I said, letting himself go. He was no longer getting the better of himself. His strict need for proper behaviour had utterly vanished.

He lay back and I held him as he half floated, half sank due to the lack of fat on his wrinkly old body. I remembered how he had looked when he was younger: his skin had approached a Scottish whiteness and he had been slim and wiry, but his muscles had been there. What I had liked most were his hips — the way they jutted out, subtly highlighting the muscles in his torso.

John didn't float well, but for a few moments I thought he understood something.

We went back to the shore and sat in Henry's car as he turned up the heat to warm our freezing, dripping bodies. We grinned like teenagers and Henry was good enough to not mention that the water was ruining the seats. The salt dried on my skin and the smell of the sea filled the car, that kelpy, fishy scent that was so familiar it sometimes came to me in my sleep.

JOHN SLEPT THAT afternoon and I elected not to go back to the doctor after all. And so, shortly before five o'clock, the ringing phone roused me from my light sleep on the sofa. The doctor was, understandably, upset that I had missed our last-minute appointment.

"Tell me what you need to tell me," I said. "Being there in person won't make a bit of difference, will it?"

"It's that we prefer to say these things in person," she said.

I pictured her in her white lab coat, at her desk with her degrees on the wall behind her, focused on business as ever.

"I won't file a complaint," I said.

"That's not it."

"Doctor," I said. "What is it that you need to tell me?"

There was a pause and I wondered if she was uncomfortable having to say what I expected her to say.

"Martha, the bloods came back. I'm sorry to say you have cancer."

"In the breast?"

"No, it's in your blood now."

"What does that mean?"

"We'll start you on a course of chemotherapy immediately, and radiotherapy. In eight weeks, we'll check your bloods again."

"Tell me what is most likely," I said, looking at the pictures of my granddaughter on the mantel. "Tell me what you expect to happen."

Her tone was matter of fact, which I appreciated. "It's quite advanced. There is a chance that chemotherapy can extend your life."

"By how long?"

"An additional three months, maybe four."

"And without?"

"Without what?"

"Without treatment."

"Eight months, if you're lucky. I've had patients who have lived as long as ten."

"Thank you," I said.

"The nurse will phone you to set up an appointment, so we can make sure you're well enough to begin treatment."

"Tell her not to bother. I won't be starting any treatment."

Before she had a chance to try to convince me otherwise, I hung up the phone. I settled back into the sofa and thought of John's face that afternoon as he was looking up at me. He had been so happy.

As the afternoon sun set behind the garden wall, I hoped I would go first so I didn't have to lose any more of John than I already had.

THE LAST WET

MARTHA, 2014

THE RAIN HAD been howling for days, lashing against the windows and blurring the tiny porthole I had on the world, though because I couldn't see the sea from my bed it hardly mattered. All I wanted was a sea view but that was not to be, so I let my eyes close and listened, hoping for a message from the salt water through the rain. But if the water had sent word I didn't catch it; the constant drumbeat of the raindrops drowned out all else and I was forced to resign myself to the fact that I was marooned on dry land now for the rest of my days.

I tried to think of other, happier things. Fragments bobbed like driftwood through my mind: the sound of the stormy waves against the pebbles, mimicking broken glass; the way Harriet shrieked with delight the first time I took her into the sea; lying in the fishing nets of Charlie's boat on the way back from Cap Gris Nez with John, looking up at the stars. The horrible taste of chicken broth in a mouth swollen by salt, the smell of petrol from the boat's motor, the heavy quiet that could only

335

be found under water. And the feeling of having returned to my natural place when I dove under the water and started to swim.

How long had I been held captive in this bed? My ascent to this high, dry ground had happened gradually: over a series of months, I had gone from the sea to the shore and then into the house, until finally I had reached my final location, the bed. This transition had been punctuated with short bouts of remission where I was able to regain some territory from the cancer, but never enough for me to make a lasting comeback.

"Martha?" John said as he came into our room.

My ears pricked up — he had used the right name.

"Pass me the water, please," I said. He held it as I struggled to lift my head, helping me ease my head forward as mouth stumbled for straw.

"Thank you," I said, letting my head fall back onto the pillows.

He returned the glass to the side table and sat on the edge of the bed, looking at his hands, searching through his thoughts for the reason he had come upstairs.

"Did you call for me?" he asked.

"No."

He looked around, hoping, I imagined, to see whatever it was he had come for. He had managed to dress himself that morning, though he'd gotten a bit turned around — he was wearing the same shirt he'd worn the day before, and his fly was undone — but he was dressed and that was enough. His hair stood up on end and for a moment I worried that he hadn't washed recently; the black filth under his nails was visible. But it was the least of our problems.

John stood up and took a few shaky steps forward, paused, turned around, looked at me, and shoved his hands in his pockets.

"Molly," he said. "You weren't at school today."

How quickly things could change.

"I'm Martha," I said.

"Who?"

I tried to let it pass.

"Your wife."

"I'm not married, sweetheart."

"Of course," I said. "How silly of me." I didn't have the energy to correct him.

"You're always playing games with me, aren't you?"

"What are sisters for?"

"Are we going to see Grandmother for the summer holidays?"

"I don't think so."

"We always do," he said.

"Not this year."

"Father must be busy," he said.

"Yes, that must be it."

"Will I go and see what Mother has made for tea?"

"No, I don't feel much like eating."

He shook his head. "Molly, you need to get your strength up."

"Maybe tomorrow."

"No, I'll go and make you a Bovril, will I?"

"Fine," I said. "A cup of Bovril would be lovely."

"We'll have you on your feet soon enough."

He stared at me for quite some time and I hoped my face was coming into focus for him, but he left the room without saying anything else. What would I have done if I had the strength? Continued to correct him? Force-fed him memories? Would I have shouted at him? Got angry with whatever it was that was indiscriminately eating him up piece by piece? Probably, even though I knew that making him return to his old self was not possible.

I shut my eyes, and again remembered being in the boat with him, coming back on that clear night. We lay in the fishing nets, which were as comfortable to me then as any bed in a fancy hotel, and John asked Charlie to cut the motor for a few minutes so we could enjoy the moment. I was covered in sheep grease and very much worse for wear, and John wrapped his arms around me, not at all bothered about the nice suit and tie he had insisted on wearing. Funny, I couldn't remember ever asking him why he always dressed like that, whatever the occasion. It was just who he was. Formal, buttoned-up. The wind off the water had snaked around us and I'd nuzzled into the crook of his arm.

Sometime later, I awoke to the sound of clattering in the kitchen. Immediately I worried that he might inadvertently set something on fire; the gas burner that had once been the source of so many dinners had turned into a death trap. I wondered how much time had passed and out of habit turned to my right to check for the small clock that had always been at my bedside. It wasn't there, of course, because I'd asked John or Henry to move it — the incessant ticking had grated my last nerve and in my increasingly delicate state all I wanted was comfort. Besides, time didn't matter so much anymore.

I heard the front door open and the tone of John's pottering changed instantly. I smiled. The time was three o'clock because Henry was here.

Henry was a good man. He was slightly too pushy for my tastes, but he'd proven himself to be exactly the sort of man you'd want living next door.

Straining to hear, I focused on Henry's voice, knowing that the majority of John's communication with him would be done

through a series of glares, grunts, and grimaces. I couldn't make
out what he was saying, but John seemed to be holding off on
his usual torrent of shouting, which I took as a good sign.

A few minutes later, Henry knocked on the door and
stepped into the room.

"You're lucky you don't have anywhere to go," he said.
"Biblical rains out there. In fact, I might see if I can get any
interest going in building an ark."

I smiled. "Hello, Henry."

"How are you feeling?"

"Fine."

He raised an eyebrow.

"Fine enough."

He pulled the duvet up around my shoulders and adjusted
the pillows.

"Really, I'm fine."

"Of course you are."

I looked at the door and he caught my meaning, closing it
before pulling the armchair in the corner up to the bedside.

"How is he?" I asked.

"You spend more time with him than I do."

"I'm bedridden. I only see what he does up here."

"Kitchen's in an utter state."

"Of course it is," I replied.

"I'll see what I can do before I'm off."

"You're too good to us."

He ignored me and looked at the window.

"How are things, then?" I said.

"Same as ever. Trying to get into the garden, but what with
the weather, it might be spring before I do." He reached out
and put his hand on my arm. "How are you?"

"Which way is the wind blowing?"

"Is that some kind of riddle?"

"Inland or offshore?"

He paused. "Inland, I think."

"Open the window."

"It's blowing a gale."

"Henry."

"All right," he said, and went to the window. "You're sure? What if you get cold?"

"Open it."

That's the only good thing about dying: people humour you because every request could be your last. The wind gusted into the room with such force that it blew over the framed photographs on the dresser. Henry closed it quickly but I begged him to open it again.

He did and I breathed in deeply. It was faint but it was the smell of my life. The temperature in the room dropped quickly and I started to shiver so Henry closed the window.

"I never thought it would be my last swim," I said.

"You might have another one in you yet."

I pointed to the chamber pot. "I can't get to the toilet. I don't think I can make it to France."

"Never say never."

"Henry," I said.

He shrugged. I knew he would not accept it until the last possible moment and, even then, I wondered if he might be tempted to go to extraordinary lengths to keep me alive.

"Now," he said. "What have you eaten today? Tomato soup?"

I chuckled; John's steadfast refusal to eat anything but tomato soup was one of the few constants in his life.

"No, no soup."

"Can I bring you anything?"

"No. Just go and make sure he's all right. He's going to burn the house down one day with his soup."

"You're sure? Tea? Toast?"

I shuddered. Even the thought of food was too much. I pulled the duvet up to my chin and let my eyes close, able to overlook the usual formalities.

Once he'd gone I drifted in and out of sleep for a while, and when I was able to open my eyes again the room had grown dark, and I felt different. Over the years, the training had taught me how to listen to my body. I'd learned what it needed and wanted: cramps meant insufficient potassium, getting cold too easily meant a lack of iron. I could tell the difference between a sprain and a strain better than my doctor. But this was something different. Though I knew it would be painful, I had not imagined this.

They had given me pain medication, of course, though I had tried to avoid taking it because it made everything fuzzy; I needed to hold on to my memories as tightly as possible because I was remembering for two. But now — my elbows hurt, feeling as though they were bruised and beaten deep inside. My ankles and shoulders throbbed and my back ached profoundly.

"John," I called.

I listened for the sound of him moving, but the house was still.

"John!" I shouted, but nothing. Maybe he had gone out, taken the dog for a short constitutional. Or maybe he'd finally wandered off.

"John," I pleaded with the dark room.

My medication was on the far edge of the table and it took all my strength to prop myself up and reach for it, but I was shaky and my hand bumped the glass of water, spilling it all over the floor. If I'd had the energy, I would have wept.

I considered trying to dry-swallow the tablets, but knew that would only make matters worse when they inevitably got stuck going down. I had a choice: live with the pain until such time that John got home, which could be in anything from ten minutes to several hours, or go downstairs and get a glass of water. Eyes closed, I tried to get past the pain.

Using my aching elbow I pushed myself up and dragged my legs over the side of the bed. When my feet touched the floor it was one mile, when I pushed myself up to standing that was another. I paused when I was on my feet, waiting for the dizziness to pass, because I could not afford to faint. I took a deep breath and shuffled forward, careful not to take my feet off the floor any more than necessary. Every muscle, tendon, and joint felt as if it were breaking and burning.

After what seemed like ages, I made it to the door and pushed it open. The corridor was cold and dark and I wondered if John had switched off the heating everywhere else in the house so that I could have a warm room. It was a lovely gesture but it made me wish I had thought to get my dressing gown. I could have gone back for it but retracing my steps would take energy I didn't have to spare.

My hand felt for the wall and I used it to guide me toward the top of the stairs, where I called his name again and got the same empty reply. I fumbled for the light switch and put the overheads on so I could at least see where I was going as I eased myself down the stairs. Each stair felt like much longer than a mile in the sea, possibly because I was supporting myself completely, missing the water's generous embrace holding me up as I made my way through it. I moved with extreme caution: the thought of the pain I would experience if I were to fall slowed me down.

Shaking, I clutched the blister pack of tablets in one hand and gripped the banister with the other. When I got to the bottom I leaned against the wall and wished, prayed, and hoped that John would come home. I caught my breath and watched the door, waiting and counting, trying to take my focus back to the water where everything was always okay in the end.

When I made it into the kitchen, John's state of mind became obvious: the sink was overflowing with dishes, pots and pans, and endless bowls of half-eaten tomato soup, half-eaten crusts of bread, and half-drunk cups of tea. Every mug, cup, and bowl we had was on the counter. Had Henry seen this? He must have, it was unavoidable. If I'd had the strength I would have phoned him up and demanded to know why he hadn't told me the full extent of it.

As it was, it took all my energy to find what I hoped was a recently used mug and fill it with water. Getting to the tap was nearly impossible but I managed. I pushed four tablets — double the dose — out of the packet and swallowed them greedily.

I leaned against the counter and caught a glimpse of myself in the window. An old, haggard woman stared back at me and I didn't recognize myself. My skin hung off my face, my jowls drooped, the skin underneath my chin and on my neck was paper thin and really did look like a turkey neck. My complexion was so pale as to be ghastly and ghostly, and my freckles had been washed away. I looked skeletal. I knew I was dying, but I had never seen up close what that looked like. Now I knew.

I surveyed the damage in the kitchen as I waited for the tablets to get to work. On the kitchen table, amidst the detritus of John's disordered mind, was a glass full of water with a small brown twig in it. I thought he must really have been losing his mind if he was using a stick as a table decoration, but when I looked closer I saw the buds and recognized it instantly. And in that moment, as I reached out for it, I felt the ground give way, and my head spin, and I knew that a part of him still remembered that he loved me. As my head hit the table I thought that there was hope yet for us.

"Martha!" John shouted.

His voice sounded far away, as if it were under water. I felt as though I were floating away from him and tried to claw my way back.

"Martha," he said, softer, and I felt his breath on my cheek.

I struggled to open my eyes, which felt like they were glued together from sleep, and when I prised them apart, he was there. He put his arms around me and cradled me to his chest. He didn't ask what had happened.

"John," I said. "The bath. I'm drying up."

He helped me into the bathroom and sat me against the wall as he turned the taps on, and when I heard the running water I felt as though I had just breached the surface and could breathe again.

"Not too warm," I said.

He lifted me up. I had forgotten that I wasn't the only one with strength in our house. My husband helped me to undress and it reminded me of a night early on in our marriage when he had tugged at the sash of my dress.

The tub was full and he lowered me into it gently. I had lost so much muscle, so much weight, that it felt like my bones were scraping against the bottom of the porcelain tub, but the water felt good.

John sat on the floor and put his hand in the water.

"It's a bit warmer than you're used to."

"It's okay."

I reached out for him, cupping his chin in my hand.

"Thank you," I said.

"For what?"

"All of it."

"Ten pebbles," he said.

"Ten pebbles, two children, sixty years."

He kissed my hand. "It was my pleasure."

I smiled. "Mine, too."

He put my hand to his cheek and held it there. I didn't know when his moments of lucidity would arrive or how long they might last, but I was glad he was with me.

"Salt, John. Can you get the salt?"

He didn't question it, didn't even flinch. He went into the kitchen and returned with the box.

"Maldon sea salt," he said.

"I'll make do."

He sprinkled it over me and it looked like snow. When the box was empty he sat down again and I took a deep breath, sliding under the water. When it poured into my ears and I was fully immersed, I exhaled slowly.

I could sleep here, I thought. I wanted to stay in for as long as I could, to be held by the water and stay forever.

I must have started to drift off because I heard the sound of the bathwater going down the plughole.

"You're getting cold," John said.

"I don't care."

"I do," he said.

He took a towel from the rack and wrapped me in it, and somehow he managed to get me upstairs and into bed. He opened the dresser, looking for pyjamas, but I told him to stop.

"Come here," I said.

He got into bed with me and I rested my head on his chest.

"I'm sorry it wasn't the sea," he said.

SOUL MASS

HARRIET, 2014

"SHE WANTED TO BE CREMATED," I said to the man at the funeral parlour.

"Yes," he said, his suit as plain and quiet as the room itself.

"A pine casket will be fine," Iain said.

"Very good," he replied.

"I don't know what I pictured," I said to my brother.

"I imagined she'd go back into the sea," he said.

"Like a mermaid?"

Iain's ears reddened and he stared at his shoes. "Sort of."

The phone had rung at breakfast while I was eating yogourt. Iris was in the shower and Myrtle at practice. It was a Tuesday. The phone's piercing tone had startled me and I remembered scowling at it, thinking it was probably another sales call. It had rung and I had eaten another spoonful of yogourt, right from the container. The phone wouldn't stop so I gave in.

"What?" I demanded.

"This is Henry."

"I don't want whatever you're selling."

"Your parents' neighbour, Henry."

"Oh," I said. "Sorry."

It was early and my mind had been halfway between the night before and the day ahead.

Casually, I asked, "Is everything all right?"

The moment I said it, it dawned on me that the answer was obvious. Henry had never phoned before.

I heard him take a breath. "She's passed, your mum."

She's passed. Your mum. My mum. Mum.

It had been coming, but there had been no way of predicting when, and no opportunity to gather around her as a family during her last days. It could've been sooner or later that Henry would pick up the phone and give me the news. I had thought about it obsessively since she'd invited us up to the house — all of us — to tell us that her health had taken an irrevocable turn for the worse.

"When?" I said.

"Last night."

I didn't know what to say. What was there to say? She was dead and gone.

"John's not coping too badly, considering."

My father. His dislocating mind. What must it have been like for him? Had he known or understood?

"I'll keep an eye on him until you can get here," Henry said.

"Yes, good, thank you," I said. I was absorbing the news physically — my hands began to shake and I felt a tidal surge sweeping toward me. "How did you find out?"

"I went over in the morning. For tea and to check. He was in the kitchen with his tomato soup. I went upstairs and there she was. In their bed."

I put the phone to my chest, pressed it against my ribs and tried to push it through me to distract myself from the image of my father, unwinding, next to my mother's body in bed.

"I've called emergency services. And the funeral home. They'll need to speak with you."

"She's still there?"

"They're coming. Within an hour or so."

My father in the kitchen eating soup first thing in the morning because for him it was dinnertime. My mother's body upstairs, getting colder and stiffer. The scene in my mind was grotesque. But what else could be done? The living keep on living and the dead stay dead.

"Harriet?" he said.

"Yes?"

"I'm sorry."

Now my brother and I sat together on one side of a dark wood desk, hedged in by dark wood panelling and surrounded by plush red carpets. If the mood had been slightly cheerier it could've been a pub in a tiny village, but instead of a barman there was the funeral director and he handed us a catalogue of urns.

Iain flipped through the pages and I thought about the person who had to write the copy for the brochure, to quietly and sombrely extol the virtues of a gold-plated urn over simple and understated white china. The final resting place for your loved one, but something that would still look nice on the mantelpiece or on the sideboard next to the good whisky and crystal cut glasses. It was absurd.

"What about this one?" Iain said, as he pointed to a blue cloisonné urn with gold trim.

I leaned over and whispered, "We're scattering her ashes in the sea."

"I think the blue is nice, like the sea."

"Not her sea."

He turned to me. There were black circles under his eyes and he was pale — he hadn't had time to get over his jet lag. Our parents' house was chaotic, full of neighbours who probably hadn't darkened their door in years, put off by my father's constantly changing mental state. Now people I hadn't met were bringing casseroles in lieu of apologies.

Such is the way of small towns: no one wanted to be seen as unsympathetic in the face of tragic circumstances, even though most had all but shunned my mother and father in recent years. It was kind of them to stop by, and I tried to be appreciative. But the constant flow of people was having an adverse effect on Dad, who needed constant reminding that Mum had died, which in turn led to frequent shouting and the slamming of doors and Dad's hiding out over at Henry's.

"The blue one?" I said.

Iain nodded.

"Fine."

Everyone was struggling: Iain spent the evenings listlessly staring at the television next to Dad, and I wondered how on earth we were ever going to get through any of this.

AFTER HENRY HAD said what needed to be said, after he had broken the news I had expected but was still unprepared for, I dropped the phone and ran into the bathroom, grateful that Iris and I had agreed at the outset not to lock any doors in our home. I flung back the shower curtain and Iris jumped in shock.

She stared at me, hand on her chest, shampoo in her hair, soap on her legs.

"What?" she'd said. "What's happened?"

I burst into tears, sobbing uncontrollably, and she pulled me close. I pressed my face into her body as we stood there, half in and half out of the shower, the room filling with steam. Iris smoothed my hair down as I wept for myself, my loss, and my Mum.

An hour later and I was in the car driving to Dover. Iris hadn't wanted me to drive in my state but the train schedule was uncompromising and made no exceptions for the fact that I needed to be there immediately. She would join me later, after picking Myrtle up from school.

Then there was the problem of getting Iain home. My phone call had woken him up; it would take the better part of three days and I would have to manage things on my own until then.

But at first, it was just me driving, going home alone, and I didn't know what to expect and what would be expected of me. It was the first death I'd had to manage. There would be the details to sort out, the funeral, the burial, and a reception of some kind, but who would be invited and where would we have it? More importantly, what would we do about Dad?

I had enjoyed the luxury of putting his needs out of my mind on the premise that we would deal with them later, when they became more pressing, because I could count on Mum to take care of him. But now that she was gone...

I pulled into the drive and was surprised to see no outward reflection of what was happening inside. I found myself wanting the house to show the loss by somehow looking as though it were in mourning, too, but of course it didn't. It was just a house. Just four walls and a roof. The sky, though, the sky was grey and looked like the winter sea: cold and ugly.

I went inside and called hello, which felt too cheery — I

realized I had no idea how to act in these circumstances. My father was sitting on the sofa, staring at the wall, and Henry was at the table, staring at his tea.

Everything was about how I had expected it to be — except for the extent of the mess. I was not prepared for the pots and pans piled high in the sink and the overwhelming smell of rotting tomato soup.

I should have been more aware of the degree of her deterioration. We had promised to visit on weekends, and we had promised regular phone calls, and we had slowly failed. The daily phone calls turned into weekly ones and then, when there hadn't been much to report beyond that things were the same, when the conversations were just repetitions of the same four words: sick, horrible, and not yet, we had all but stopped. The intention was strong and so was the guilt.

"Hi Dad," I said. He was listless and made no reply.

Henry and I hugged stiffly before I took a seat next to him.

"How long has he been like that?" I asked.

"That's where he was when I came round this morning," Henry said.

"He hasn't moved?"

Henry shook his head.

I lowered my voice. "He knows, though, doesn't he?"

"Somewhere in there he does."

"How has he been recently?" I asked.

Henry looked at the mess in the kitchen and I understood. "But he'll surprise you when you're least expecting it."

My father seemed far away, as though the couch he was on were in a different world and a different time.

"Nights are better," Henry said. "Mornings are the worst. Time's backwards."

"Thank you," I said. "For everything. I...we..." I turned away from him, tears rolling down my cheeks.

"Right," he said awkwardly. "The funeral home said they'll be in touch."

"Yes, good."

"I'm going to go."

"Yes, of course."

"I'm only just there," Henry said, pointing toward his house.

The day before her body was to be cremated, I went into their bedroom and stood in front of the wardrobe. It seemed unnecessary and impractical to pick out her favourite dress only to have it incinerated. No one would know what she'd been wearing; why make the effort? Why go through the agony of trying to figure out which outfit she would have preferred when I couldn't picture her in any of them?

I put all the dresses she had on the bed: navy, red, and green. They were old and out of fashion, the fabric frayed around the hems. I was staring at them, hoping that an image of her wearing one of them might come to mind, when Dad came into the room and stood next to me. He admired the dresses, running his fingers over the thin wool as if he had a clear picture in his mind of her wearing them.

"This one," he said slowly. "She wore this on the ferry." He picked up the navy dress and laid it across his lap. "I waved her off to France."

I was silent, having learned that it was best to let him speak uninterrupted in these moments. He turned the dress over and ran his fingers along the shoulder seams, smiling. He held it up to me, pointing at a faint mark.

"A bird," he said. His lips fumbled, as though by making a chewing motion he could help himself remember the right word. "A...By the shore. Terrible things. White..." His mouth searched for the proper word and then he shouted, "A gull!"

I looked closer, but didn't quite follow.

"For good luck," he said.

And then I understood: a bird had messed on the shoulder of her dress.

He put the navy dress back on the bed and smoothed it out, and as he did his expression changed, as though he had remembered anew that she would not be wearing it ever again. Fully dressed, he lay down and I helped him off with his slippers. He rolled onto his side, crushing the navy dress along with the others, and stretched out his arm, but he couldn't settle. His arm hunted for the right position as I watched, tempted to offer help but knowing it was better to let him work whatever it was out on his own. With his eyes closed, he drew my mother's pillow near his face and inhaled deeply and then his face contorted into an angry scowl. He felt for the dresses and pulled the green one over the pillow, inhaling again until his face relaxed.

"WILL YOU BE holding the service here?" the man asked now, snapping me back to the task of our mother's funeral. "We can make all the necessary arrangements. Many people find it's easier."

I looked at Iain. He nodded.

"I can show you to the room where the service will be held, if you like," the man said. "There's an adjoining room for a reception afterwards."

We followed him through to another room with dark wood panelling, and everything was so hushed and proper that it felt rude to speak in anything above a whisper.

I took Iain aside. "We can't say goodbye to her in here."

He nodded. "She would've hated it."

"Decadent," I said.

"What would people think?"

"I can't breathe in here."

"What about the church?" he suggested.

And so we left the funeral home and drove to the church, but the priest that Mum had worked for when we were children had either moved on or retired. The priest who had taken his place wasn't much older than Iain and me; but even though he didn't know us, he welcomed us into his office.

"My deepest sympathies," he said.

"Thank you," I replied.

"We'll remember her in the service this Sunday."

"Yes, thank you," Iain said.

"And how is your father coping with the news?"

"As well as can be expected," I said.

"It's a pity, a real shame." The priest nodded solemnly.

"Yes," I said. "I'm sure he'll take comfort in coming here more than ever now."

The priest's expression changed suddenly and he shifted uncomfortably in his seat. "Will he be joining us again?"

"I expect so, yes."

"Did your mother not mention this?"

"Mention what?" I said, looking at Iain who shrugged in reply.

"Ah," the priest said, putting his fingertips together. "It's terribly unfortunate what's happened to your father."

"Happening," I corrected.

"Yes, happening."

"He has always drawn strength from the services here," I said.

"It's been a while now, since he's been able to attend."

"With my mother's illness," I said.

"Of course," he said. "It had been a while, though, before that."

"I'm sure his attendance will improve in the near future."

"I'm sorry," the priest said. "There's no delicate way to put this, but we'd prefer he didn't attend. Anymore."

"Sorry?" I said.

The priest didn't look me in the eye, focusing instead on some invisible mark on his desk, picking at it with his index finger. "There were some outbursts, some behaviour that made some of the other parishioners uncomfortable, which is to be expected in his condition, but even so . . ."

I looked at Iain in disbelief.

"Such as?" I said.

The priest was flustered. "He forgets himself, interrupts the service. Generally inappropriate behaviour. I have to think of the greater good, you understand."

I shoved my hands into my pockets, balling them into fists. "Surely the church is meant to provide a place for every member of the congregation? Surely the church doesn't discrimin-ate against members who are suffering and need to feel they are part of their community?"

"As I explained to your dearly departed mother, it is inappro-priate for your father . . . and certainly now — if I'm honest —"

"Oh yes, please. Do be honest," I said.

Iain put his hand on my arm and I shrugged it off.

The priest gave me a placating smile. "I doubt very much that he gets anything from the service. In his condition."

"His condition? His condition is that of a bereft widower."

"I mean his medical condition."

I stood abruptly, unable to tolerate his lack of decency and charity, and Iain followed my lead.

"I'm sorry," the priest said. "What was it that you wanted to speak with me about?"

But Iain took me by the hand before I could say something I might later regret and dragged me out the door.

Once we were in the car I couldn't contain myself. "That's been their church, our church, since before I can even remember," I said.

"She said to me, a while back, that some of their friends had been a bit standoffish, that she didn't like doing the shopping anymore. Whispers, stares."

"Typical small town," I hissed. "Small-minded and completely incapable of understanding."

"I didn't think to this extent, though," Iain said. I saw him grip the steering wheel tightly. "Who gets kicked out of church?"

"What do you think Dad did?"

"I hope he ran through the place naked," Iain said.

I laughed. "Serves them right. After all the time and energy they put into that place."

Iain sighed and rested his chin on the steering wheel. "Now what?"

We went home to regroup and to see how Iris and Myrtle were faring with Dad, who, it transpired, had spent most of the morning sleeping, rousing himself sometime after lunch to take up his place on the sofa, from which he'd been staring off into space ever since. He seemed hollow sitting there, as though he were just a shell now, waiting for something to happen — though I couldn't bring myself to acknowledge what that might be.

I wondered how Mum had coped with it. The practicalities were exhausting: making sure he'd eaten, helping him get dressed, helping him bathe — which was a job Iain took on without having to be asked. In all this time Mum hadn't once reached out for help, preferring to go on as they had always done. Iris thought it was sheer stubbornness but I disagreed, because there was a part of me that understood it. If Mum had asked for help with Dad it would have made his condition completely real; by not asking, by keeping it confined, I suppose she let the rest of us keep him for as long as we could. She bore the brunt of his disease to save us from it. It was heroic and it was selfish and it was exactly the sort of thing that only she would have done.

Dad seemed to be caught up in the pictures Iris had brought over the years — on trips I had only just learned about. But the day had exhausted me, and I had run out of the energy required to be angry with her, too. Instead I thought of how she had given my mother the things I hadn't, and in those moments of regret I was pleased that my wife had been able to do to what I could not.

My parents had always kept themselves to themselves, and I wondered what had happened here, in their world built for two. What had taken place that Iain and I hadn't seen? Those evenings spent watching television or reading, eating dinner together — what were they like? There was so much I didn't — and couldn't — know about them; it felt as if they were destined to remain strangers. And it wasn't possible now to talk about that awful Boxing Day dinner all those years ago.

"Dad," I said, sitting next to him on the sofa.

He didn't move or appear to have heard me. I looked at how he'd aged: the skin around his eyes had grown paper thin, there were age spots on his neck and cheeks, and his posture, which had always been so rigid and formal, was so lax that he appeared to be retreating back into the fetal position. He looked helpless, pathetic, and lost. I looked up at the ceiling and caught my breath.

"Dad," I said again, placing my hand on his knee.

He turned to me, his eyes cloudy and rheumy, and stared at me as a smile slowly grew over his face.

"Martha," he said.

I smiled as I felt the tears hot in my eyes.

"No, Dad, it's me, Harry."

"Did you see the sea today?" His wrinkled hands with the long fingernails that needed cutting reached out for my face.

I took his hands in mine and said, "Dad, it's me, your daughter."

He took the information in slowly.

"Where's Martha?" he asked.

I looked over at Iris who was sitting at the kitchen table, hoping that she would know what to do, desperate for her — or anyone — to fix this, but she didn't say anything.

I took a chance and said, "I love you, Dad."

They had spent their last days together like this, I imagined. When he couldn't be counted on to be in the right time or place, and she had been lying and dying in their bed upstairs, and the whole thing was so cruel I couldn't stand it. I wanted to scream.

AFTER IAIN AND I left the church, without discussing it he drove us to the sea, to the place where my mother had always started her swims. We went out and sat on the cold, damp pebbles. The sea was flat and grey, with a cloud cover hanging low as though the water had joined us in mourning.

"Let's skip it," I said.

"Skip what?"

"Let's not have a service. Why can't we just do it ourselves?"

"What about her friends?" he said.

"The women bearing casseroles?" I asked.

Iain nodded. "We'll never hear the end of it. Disgraceful children. Leaving her all alone to cope with John in this state."

"That's what they're saying?"

He nodded again.

"They say that in our house?"

"Yep."

I picked up a handful of pebbles and flung them at the sea. "Are we?"

"Are we what?" he asked.

"Disgraceful."

He ran his fingers through the pebbles. "Maybe. A bit."

"Here," I said, holding out my arms. "Why can't we have it here? If she wants the ashes scattered in the sea."

"And the reception? Late October's not really picnicking weather."

I looked around, and then, at the very far end of the promenade that skirted the shore, I saw it. "The White Horse Inn."

"That's disgraceful! A common public house," he said, mocking the tone of the women who had invaded our home.

"I don't really care what a bunch of gossipy old ladies think," I said.

"She told me before — the last time — she told me that some of them wouldn't come to visit anymore. Because of Dad."

I shook my head, looking out at the water. "This place fits."

"It does."

I thought about what he had said earlier. "Did you really think she would just go back in? Like a mermaid?"

"I was a kid."

I looked at him in disbelief.

He looked back out at the sea, and threw a couple of pebbles in. "The first memory I really have of her is watching her walk into the sea. It was hazy — you couldn't tell where the water stopped and the sky started. I thought she was swimming off the edge of the world."

THE MORNING FINALLY came when we officially said goodbye to our mother. It was a miserable late October day — windy, cold, bleak — and when we got to the water's edge the sea was in a frothing rage, all rollers and white horses.

We had decided to hold the service right next to the water — but what we hadn't counted on was the tide being in, covering the small beach. We had been forced to relocate to the outcropping on the cliff above, distancing ourselves from the water.

Our family, including Henry, formed a circle, huddling in close to keep out as much of the weather as possible. We had planned to take turns speaking, but no one knew what to say so we were a silent circle. The few phrases that we managed to mutter were short of the mark — but then, how could we possibly sum up her life in a few words? There was no way to adequately describe her or her life or what she had meant to us.

My father was holding the urn. When it was his turn he was ushered into the middle of the circle, but he refused to speak. Shoving a hand in his pocket, he looked to the ground, avoiding all eye contact with the rest of us. After a few moments he looked up, but it was only to stare at the sea, his feet shuffling in the way I had come to learn meant that he was anxious and that his brain was trying to tell him something important. Abruptly, he turned toward the footpath that sloped gently down to the water's edge and set off, still carrying the urn. When Iain raced after him to bring him back, Dad shoved him away and kept moving forward.

There was nothing to do but follow him. When he reached the shoreline and the waves were lapping at his feet, the water covering his shoes, he paused and bowed slightly. Worried that something might happen — that he might lose his balance and fall, or worse, that he might keep walking — we all followed him into the water. Everyone's shoes got wet — which, I thought, must have pleased my mother a great deal.

Dad took the lid off the urn and waited for a wave to come close — and then he flung the ashes out, and as the wave retreated it took my mother out to sea. Iain had been right: though she hadn't walked into the water herself, she had returned to it in the end.

BAPTISM

MYRTLE, PRESENT DAY

AT THE END of August, just as I was getting up to clear the plates, my mum asked me what I wanted to do for my birthday.

"Sixteen is a special birthday," Iris said.

And in my mind, I said: Yeah, I know — because it means I'm legally allowed to swim the Channel and all this training won't be for nothing.

Instead, I said, "You say that about every birthday."

"We can go to a nice restaurant? Somewhere in town maybe? You can invite Robin if you like," Harriet said.

I had to give them credit: they hadn't mentioned my newfound chubbiness. I had always been slim, verging on ropy, and I was sure the change in my body had not gone unnoticed.

"Actually, I was thinking it might be nice to go and visit Granddad."

Harriet poured herself another glass of wine. "That's sweet, honey, but is it really what you want to do? I know you love him, and we do too, but if you don't want to go out for dinner, maybe you could have a party here?"

I shook my head. "I want to go to Dover for the weekend."

"You're sure?"

I saw them exchange concerned looks, as though they couldn't understand why a normal teenager would want to spend her birthday with her grandfather. Maybe they thought I was making up for what had been lost.

So we agreed, and one day before my birthday we went to go and see Granddad.

His care home was up near the castle, and from the dining room there was a view of the port where and he would sit for hours, watching the boats and ferries come and go.

We didn't leave London until after rush hour, so it was too late to visit Granddad by the time we arrived. But we did manage to meet Henry at the White Horse Inn. He was waiting for us when we walked in, and after a round of hugs and hellos he asked me to help him bring the drinks over from the bar.

"You haven't told them, have you?" he said while we waited for the pints to be poured.

"What?" I said.

"Myrtle, you promised."

"What makes you think I haven't?"

"Because I haven't had any angry phone calls."

The barman smiled at me as he placed a glass of wine on the tray.

"It'll be fine."

Henry frowned at me.

"I'm telling them tonight."

"Oh Lord," he said. "They're going to hate me."

"No they won't. I've been preparing them for it." Which was a total lie.

"How?"

"Easing them into the idea, you know?"

"No, I don't."

"Just leaving hints and stuff."

"This was part of our deal. You are not getting in that water unless they approve."

I picked up the tray of drinks, and as I walked back to the table, I said over my shoulder, "Don't worry, Henry."

One Saturday last November, I'd told my mums I was spending the day at a friend's and took the train to Dover. I went to the only place I knew besides my grandparents' house and knocked on Henry's door.

"Myrtle," he said. "Is everything okay? Is John not answering the door? Do you need the key?"

I shook my head. "I haven't been over yet." I looked next door and then back to Henry. "Can I come in?"

"Of course," he said, stepping aside.

He led me through to the living room, which was a bit of a mess, but a bunch of old newspapers and magazines scattered all over the place didn't bother me. I sat on his couch and he brought me a cup of tea before sitting down on the other end of the sofa.

"So, how are you?" he asked.

"Yeah, fine." I stared at my drink.

"Harriet and Iris?"

"Yeah, they're good."

"School?"

"'Sfine."

"Swimming?"

I nodded and blew on the hot tea.

Henry leaned forward, resting his elbows on his legs. "Myrtle?"

"You know how my grandma was a swimmer?"

He nodded slowly.

"Well, it's like, I was thinking…"

Henry looked at me and I could tell he knew where I was going with this.

He shook his head. "Not a good idea."

"You don't even know what it is!"

He scowled at me. "I don't need to hear you say the words; I can see it on your face."

"Because I look like her?"

"No, because you look like you're about to do something stupid." He set his tea on the coffee table and rubbed the back of his neck. "Have you spoken to your parents about this?"

"Not yet."

"I see. Have you started training?"

"I swim six days a week, Henry."

"Yes, I hear the currents in a pool can be quite treacherous." He looked at me, and I must have seemed really disappointed.

"I'm a strong swimmer."

"You need to get used to the cold water."

"I've swum in the sea before."

"You need to be prepared. It's dangerous."

"I want to do it for her. In her honour."

"I know, sweetheart, I know. But it's dangerous."

We drank our tea in silence and I wanted to go — Henry was as bad as my mothers, though in a totally different way.

"You don't understand. Why would you? What'd you ever do that was extraordinary?"

I got up and stormed to the door. I grabbed my bag, and when my hand was on the door handle, Henry put his hand on my shoulder.

I turned around. "What?"

"Clear it with your parents, and I'll see what I can do to help you on this end," he said.

Now Henry hung his head as he watched the barman pour the drinks. "I wanted to have a nice birthday meal with you and your parents. And they're going to be in no mood for it once you've told them."

"So I'll wait until after dinner."

"No," he said firmly. "You'll do it now."

He took the tray of drinks from me and I had no choice but to follow him back to the table.

Iris held up her glass of wine after we'd all sat down again and said, "To our lovely, wonderful daughter, Myrtle. Happy birthday, my darling. Your mother and I love you very much."

We clinked glasses, and just as the conversation had turned to Henry and catching up with him, the bartender brought over half a pint of cider. He set it on the table in front of me and said, "For good luck tomorrow."

"What's happening tomorrow?" Harriet asked.

Henry kicked me under the table, and I glared at the barman.

"She hasn't told them?" the barman said.

Henry shook his head and I stared at the half pint of cider.

"Hasn't told us what?" Iris asked.

I took a drink, gulping it down in the hope it would give me courage. "I'm going to swim the Channel tomorrow," I blurted out.

Harriet nearly choked on her beer. She coughed and her cheeks went red and Iris patted her on the back.

"Sorry, I don't think I heard you right," Harriet said.

Henry stood up. "This is obviously a family discussion. I'll be at the bar."

"Sit," Harriet barked. He did as he was told.

"Explain," she said to me. Iris put her hand on Harriet's shoulder and squeezed.

"What's to explain?" I said. "I'm going to swim the Channel."

"Over my dead body," Harriet said. Iris kneaded her shoulder.

"It's already sorted."

"What is?" Iris said.

"Everything," I said. "Charlie, the boat. Henry got the Federation to waive their fee, and Charlie's waiving his too. In honour of Grandma."

"Henry did?" Harriet said, as her eyes bored a hole into Henry's face.

Henry blushed and took several gulps of his ale.

"That's why you wanted to come up here and visit your grandfather?" Harriet said to me.

I nodded.

She turned her attention back to Henry. "And you," she said. "You organized this whole thing? And didn't think that maybe it was worth a phone call to let us know our daughter was about to throw herself into the sea, intent on certain death?"

"Mum, you're being way too dramatic."

"Am I? Am I really?"

I curled my hands into fists, and just as I was about to start shouting, Henry put his hand on my shoulder.

"I understand you're upset," he said to my parents. "But let me tell you about what she's done."

"Oh yes, do tell us," Harriet said.

"She's worked incredibly hard. She's come up here every weekend to train in the harbour. She's done the requisite open-water swim, eighteen miles with no wetsuit."

"Sorry?" Iris said. "Every weekend?"

Everyone turned their attention to me.

"I took the train, first thing on a Saturday. Henry picked me up and brought me to the harbour and I did what Charlie told me to do."

"She's done everything that's been asked of her," Henry said.

"The open-water swim?" Iris asked.

"You know how me and Robin went to Lanzarote for training camp in March?"

She nodded.

I scrunched up my nose. "Well, we were training, but in Jersey. With a woman named Sal."

Iris whipped her head around to Henry. "You knew about this? Two underage children going to Jersey on their own?"

Henry held up his index finger as though to highlight his point. "That, I found out about after the fact."

Harriet took a deep breath and laid her hands on the table. "Let me try and understand this. You took the train up here every weekend and swam in that freezing cold harbour with an old fisherman as your coach? After having got on an airplane on your own and stayed on Jersey for a week?"

I nodded.

"How could you lie to us?" Iris said. "Haven't we always told you that you can tell us anything?"

"There's anything and then there's this."

"All this sneaking around," Iris tutted. "All this lying." She folded her hands over her chest.

"I had to! You wouldn't have let me otherwise."

"Who says we're letting you now?" Harriet demanded.

"But you have to. It's too late not to — everyone's ready. Charlie says the weather looks good and so we're going. Before dawn tomorrow morning. You can't stop me."

"The hell I can't," Harriet said.

"Mum!" I half whined, half shouted. "I've trained harder for this than anything. I learned to swim in the sea. I got used to the cold water. I gained a stone and a half! I just want to honour Grandma, to follow in her footsteps."

Harriet shook her head.

And so I said something I knew would hurt her, but I felt it was my last hope. "You kept me away from her. If it wasn't for swimming, I would've never met her. She would've died up here, alone, without anyone. Everyone here has gone out of their way to help me. Charlie's even agreed for Granddad to come along on the boat. And I want you — both of you — to be there too." I stood up. "You don't have to come, but you can't stop me. I'm old enough to do it without your permission."

My mum's face went pale and she turned toward the wall.

"Myrtle," Iris cautioned.

"What?" I said to her. I had completely lost my patience. "For years, all she said about them was that they were horrible, awful people. I get that they hurt her, I do. But they're my grandparents, and I barely even got to know Martha. I want to do this. I've trained, it's all organized, and I'm ready."

Harriet wouldn't look at me.

"You're as bad as you say they were!" I shouted. I'm sure the entire pub heard me. I stumbled over my chair and ran outside.

A few minutes later, Iris came to find me. She sat on the curb next to me and didn't say anything, which was what she always did when she wanted me to talk.

"I can do it," I said.

"I've no doubt you can," she said.

The street was empty and it felt like we were in a ghost town. In the distance, I heard the horn of the ferry arriving from Calais.

"Then why won't she let me?"

Iris sighed. "It's been a hard year."

"No, really?"

She put her hand on my knee and squeezed. "I know it's been hard for you too. But try and see it from her point of view. She's already lost her mother — and her father, for the most part. She couldn't bear losing you too."

"She's not going to," I said. "You've seen me swim. So has she. I'm strong enough to do this. Why can't she trust me?"

"It's not you she doesn't trust. When she was a girl, she almost lost your grandmother on her first swim."

"I know, but that wasn't the sea's fault. That was Grandma's. She told me. She wasn't ready. But I am."

I looked at my mum and didn't know what else I could say to convince her, to convince both of them. "Everyone here has gone out of their way. Charlie, he retired last year, but he's going back out just for me. I'm not letting everything they've done go to waste."

Iris sighed as she stood up. "You're just as stubborn as she is."

"Who?"

She smiled. "Why have I surrounded myself with such stubborn women?"

I took her hand and she pulled me up.

"But I have." She put her arm around my shoulders. "Okay. I'll work on Harriet if you promise me something."

"Anything."

"If, at any time, you start to struggle, you come out. No ifs, ands, or buts about it. If there's even a whiff of danger, you get out of the water."

"Okay."

"I mean it."

"Okay," I said. "Oh, and one more thing."

I saw her brace herself.

"Granddad comes in the boat."

"I don't think that's a good idea, Myrtle — he's so frail."

"He always comes on the swims. He's like a good luck charm."

Iris laughed, shaking her head. "I'll leave the bit about John being good luck out of it when I talk to your mother."

LAST WINTER AFTER my grandmother died, Granddad was still in his house on Shakespeare Road. There were only two care homes in Dover and it turned out they both had waiting lists, so for a few months he would have to stay where he was. A carer came to see him a few times a week, to make sure he was okay, and Henry kept an eye on him. In the meantime, Uncle Iain and my mum spent hours and hours fighting with each other on Skype about what to do with him. I'd gotten used to the sight of her shouting at the computer.

Iain and my parents agreed, though, that we would all come back to Dover so my grandfather could have one more Christmas in his own house before he was moved into the care home in the new year. But as the holiday together wore on, I began to think they were more interested in arguing than spending time with Granddad.

It bothered me that they talked about him when he was in the room. I knew he had dementia and that he didn't always understand what was going on, but it still felt wrong. And mean. They used to say that sort of thing to me when I was younger. They'd say that I didn't understand, or that I couldn't understand, and even though that may have been true, I knew that they were talking about me and that I wasn't going to have any say in what happened.

"We're abandoning him. He won't know anyone there," Iain said.

I glared at them from the sofa but they didn't notice.

"He doesn't know us anymore," Harriet said.

"It doesn't feel right, dumping him somewhere."

"What's the alternative? Are you going to quit your job and move back? To watch him all day, every day?"

I found an old episode of *Doctor Who* — a Christmas special I'd seen before — and turned up the volume, wishing the Doctor and his Tardis would come and take Granddad and me away with him.

"He needs his family, Harry. He needs us."

My mum slammed her hands on the table and it sounded the same as when someone intentionally did a belly flop off the starting blocks: a crack and a slap at the same time.

"He doesn't know who the hell we are!"

My mum's voice overwhelmed even the Daleks.

"Look around you," she said. "He's not our father anymore. Moving back here to take care of him is not going to change any of that. It won't do anything for your guilt."

"But we haven't even tried."

I turned my head and saw her wiping her eyes with the back of her hand, and Iris rubbing her back.

"We've done the best thing we could do for him by getting him into this place. It's the right thing to do, Iain."

"We should've done more," Iain said.

"You can't focus on what you didn't do," Iris said. "You can't change the past."

On Boxing Day, Henry joined us for lunch and when he offered to take out the rubbish, I offered to help. My mum was shouting at Iain again so I figured no one was listening to us anyway.

"So?" I said quietly. "Did you talk to Charlie?"

"I did. He'll do it, but there's a problem. Well, there are a few. You need to complete one open-water swim before they'll let you try the Channel. And technically you won't be old enough."

"How am I going to do an open-water swim before summer?"

"You have cleared this with your mothers, right?"

"Yeah, totally. I just want it to be a surprise for everyone else."

He looked skeptical but didn't ask any more questions. "Come by my house later. Charlie gave me the number of a woman down in Jersey who might be able to help."

I WAS LUCKY because spring came early, and March came in like a lamb and left as one, too. As the warm air pushed in from the Continent, the water in the harbour at Dover warmed slightly, which was good news because I had traded chlorine for salt.

The first Saturday in April, I got on a train out of Charing Cross and headed to Dover. I arrived at the station, where Henry had come to meet me.

He hugged me and then asked, "Are you sure about this?"

I nodded and he shook his head in a way that I took to mean I was a frustration, but in a good way, and we drove down to the harbour, which wasn't crowded with other swimmers because it was too early in the season. But I had to make up for lost time.

We stood next to the car and surveyed the sea, which was glassy and calm, but also a foreboding grey. Henry reached into the back seat and handed me a wetsuit.

"Charlie says you're to wear this until further notice."

"I've been training outdoors. In the lido."

"What did we agree?" Henry said in his schoolteacher voice.

"That I was to do exactly as Charlie says."

He looked at me with raised eyebrows. I picked up the wetsuit.

"Fine," I said.

And so I developed a rhythm. Saturday mornings I took an early train and arrived in Dover around 10 a.m. I would swim until lunch, when Henry would drive us up to my grandfather's care home. We got Granddad bundled into the car, which was no easy feat because his ankle had never really healed and so he walked with a limp and a stick, which could be used as a weapon if the moment took him, and together we went to the White Horse Inn for lunch.

In the morning, Charlie picked us up at five in the morning and we all got on his boat together: my mums, Henry, and Granddad. Iris had calmed Harriet down after dinner and convinced her — somehow — that it was my choice and that the right thing to do was to support me.

We motored out of the harbour and over to Shakespeare's Bay. The weather was good and the water was calm. The sun hadn't quite peeked over the horizon yet, but even though I felt nervous, I was more excited than anything. Charlie got as close to the shore as he could and went over the rules with me once more as the official from the Federation nodded along.

"Rule number one: you cannot touch the boat, anyone in it, or the feeding pole. Understood?" he said.

I stood on the deck of his fishing boat with my family around me and nodded my head.

"Number two," he said. "Feedings start after the first two hours. From then, it's every forty-five minutes. I don't care if you're not hungry."

"Okay," I said.

There was a gentle breeze that curled around me and I shivered slightly, standing there in only my swimsuit.

"The last and most important rule is this: if you're struggling, if your stroke rate goes down, if the sea gets too choppy, if you get cold, if anything happens — and I mean anything — that I think puts you in jeopardy, then you are getting out. Getting. Out. Do you understand?"

I nodded.

"Say it," he said, in this gruff voice that I used to be scared of but had come to learn was just his way of being kind.

"I understand. I will come out if I'm in danger."

He turned to my mums and said, "I would've liked her to have had more experience in the open water." He shoved his hands in his jacket pockets and looked at the water. "You two are going to have to watch for signs that she's getting cold. Some of them will be hard to see, so to check her mental state you'll have to ask questions. Simple ones. If she struggles to answer, if her speech is slurred — even if you just think it sounds slurred — she comes out."

Iris held Harriet's hand tightly and said, "Okay."

He crossed his arms over his chest and looked me up and down. "Are you ready?"

"I'm ready."

He pointed into the distance. "That's France," he said. "That's where we're headed. The tide's on its way, so you should have the luck of the currents. Stay close to the boat. Pay attention. Conditions can change quickly."

"Charlie?" I said.

"What?"

"It's time to get in the water."

He smiled and kissed my forehead. "Do Martha proud," he said, before going to the controls. He turned and added, "What are you waiting for? Sea's ready for you."

My belly did flip-flops and I was so hyped I thought I might be sick, but I held it together.

Before I slipped off the back of the boat and into the water, I took Granddad's hand. He looked totally ridiculous with a bright orange lifejacket strapped to him, but he didn't seem to mind. He was sitting next to the edge so he could watch me swim, and at his feet was the worn leather case he'd brought each time Martha had crossed the Channel.

"Granddad," I said. "Is there anything you want me to tell her when I see her?"

He looked at me and I knew he was in between times, searching for the right place to steady himself, trying to make connections with the past and present. I took his hand and placed a pebble I'd taken from the beach in his palm. "Here," I said. "I'll tell her you came to see."

"To see the sea," he repeated.

"To see her in the sea," I said.

I squeezed his hand shut and gave him a kiss on the cheek, and then I hugged Iris, who was tearing up.

Harriet wrapped her arms around me next and held me for ages, until I struggled to get out of her embrace. "You know how proud we are of you, don't you?" she whispered. She let me go and I saw that she'd got grease on her cheek from holding me so tightly. I reached out to wipe it away but she stopped me.

"I don't mind the smell as much as I used to," she said.

I smiled at her and gave Henry a fast hug before slipping into the water.

I sprinted to shore, and once I had walked ten metres from the water I turned around and waved my arms. Henry waved back and I knew that my swim had started. Slowly, I walked toward the sea and wondered what my grandmother had thought about when she'd done this very same thing. Had she thought about my grandfather, my mum, my uncle, or the water?

When my feet were covered in the foamy surf, I paused to take one more look. The Channel was beautiful. The sun was a warm blip on the horizon, filling the sky with pink and purple hues. The water reflected those colours and dampened them slightly; it would take more than a hint of light to warm even the surface of the water. A shiver went through my body. Standing there, wet and exposed to the air, I was cooling down already. I didn't have time to dawdle. I licked the inside of my goggles and pulled my cap down over my ears. And then I started moving quickly, running into the waves until it was deep enough for me to dive forward and swim.

My body felt good. The extra weight I'd gained made me a bit more buoyant and that was helpful. My skin felt slick, and as I moved through the water I felt close to my grandmother and wished that she could have been here with me.

The water burned and made me feel stiff, but I knew from my training that once I'd worked up enough sweat my muscles and joints would ease up and the going would be easier. But my instinct was to sprint, and after maybe half an hour, when

I turned to breathe, I saw Henry waving his arms at me.

I trod water nearer the boat so I could hear what he was saying.

"Too fast. Slow down."

I shook my head. "I have to get warmed up."

"Charlie says you're going to run out of steam. You need to pace yourself."

I nodded — but when I was horizontal in the water again, I ignored him. I was losing feeling in my hands and feet, and I knew the only way to keep going was to move faster. People had completed the swim in as little as six hours, and though I knew I couldn't go at a full-on sprint speed for that long, I was confident I could keep a faster pace than Charlie had planned for me. He had a lot of experience, but he wasn't a swimmer. He would never know what this actually felt like. It was contrary to what we'd agreed, but I knew my body and knew that I needed to push myself into high gear to warm up.

I kicked harder, pulled faster, while telling myself that I was still warming up. My hands and feet stung from the cold, a strange sensation that felt like burning, but I pushed that out of my mind. I thought about my grandma, my grandad, and getting to France.

At the two-hour point, Charlie slowed the boat and I trod water, waiting for the feeding pole. John stood next to Henry as he leaned over the edge, trying to get the cup of broth close enough for me to grab hold of.

The change in direction, going from horizontal to vertical, made me dizzy, and it was difficult to focus on the boat and the cup. I took my goggles off and rubbed my eyes.

"Myrtle," Henry called.

I looked up at him, maybe eight feet away. Iris waved but

I didn't wave back. The water was still calm and the sun had come up over the horizon. I smelled the petrol from the boat and felt queasy.

"What's your home address?" Iris shouted through cupped hands.

"London," I replied.

"Charlie wants you to give the full address, sweetheart," she said.

"Flat four, Pott Street," I said. It was tricky to say the words right because my mouth was swollen from the salt.

I saw Iris look at Henry. The currents were making it hard to keep myself steady.

"What are your grandparents' names?" Henry shouted.

"Martha and John."

"Surname?"

"Roberts," I said.

I looked away from the boat, out to the open water, and wished I hadn't stopped. The loss of momentum made me realize how tired I was. They probably had more questions for me, but I needed to keep moving, so I put my goggles back on, flipped to my stomach, and started to swim. Whereas before I'd felt like a seal, like my body was gliding through the water, now I felt like I was swimming through mud.

Turning my head to breathe, I saw them all standing on the side of the boat, waving at me. I ignored them and kept swimming until I heard the boat's horn toot. Charlie wanted a word and I knew I would have to stop. I got myself upright in the water and waited for them to tell me whatever it was they needed to.

"Myrtle," Charlie shouted.

My head was barely above the water; doing the egg-beater kick was hard and I could feel myself losing heat.

"Come closer," he said.

I pulled myself a few strokes closer to the boat.

"How do you feel?" he demanded.

"Tired, but I want to keep going." My words must have sounded funny because I tripped over my tongue.

All of a sudden, my legs gave out and I bobbed under water. Sculling with my arms, I came back up, coughing. Though my goggles were fogging up, I could still see everyone on the boat rushing around in some kind of panic. I shook my head and assumed it was something to do with Granddad. They looked busy and I didn't want to waste any more energy treading water, so I started to swim again. A lazy freestyle, but at least I was moving.

I thought I had hit a wall and that I needed to just push through it. I counted off my strokes: one, two, three, breathe. When I turned my head to the left, I saw the boat. My grandfather, in his bright orange life vest, wasn't where he ought to have been. I kept kicking, holding one arm out front — a drill we did a lot at practice — so I could look for him, but I couldn't see him. Everyone else seemed to be freaking out and I was worried — what if something had happened to him?

I saw Henry waving his arms frantically at me, so I moved a bit closer. The wind was picking up and whipping the surface water into froth. I tried to tread water again as I scanned the deck for Granddad, but it was harder than it should have been and that's when I knew something was wrong. I felt my body slipping under the water and when I kicked my legs, they didn't move the way I wanted them to, which made it hard to get above water.

Somewhere in front of me I heard, or maybe felt, a splash. I made the effort to push my head up with the strength of my arms and I caught a breath but as I was inhaling, I took in a mouthful of water that I spat and coughed out.

Then all I could see was the bright orange of my grand-father's life vest. But that was weird, because why would he be in the water? He'd never even learned how to swim.

"Martha!" I heard him shout.

"Granddad," I said, water rushing up my nose and into my mouth. "Get back on the boat!"

I didn't know what was happening on Charlie's boat, but if Granddad was in the water then everything was going wrong. The orange vest came closer. I tried to kick hard, even just twice, so I could push my head up and get a lungful of air, but my legs weren't working. I couldn't feel my feet, they were so cold, and when I looked down I saw the skin on my legs was pale instead of red.

I slipped under again but managed to draw myself up in time to see Harriet jump off the edge of the boat.

"Hang in there, sweetie!" Iris shouted. "Harry's coming to get you!"

I knew then that I was in trouble. And even though I wanted to keep going, I knew I couldn't. I tried to move in the direction of the boat but I didn't have the energy.

I went under water again and it was funny how calm and quiet it was. Just me and the deep, dark sea.

I felt something scraping against my shoulder, then it got brighter, and then my head was above water. My grandfather in his lifejacket, suit, and shoes, was grabbing for me, dog-paddling, clawing his way through the water.

"Martha," he cried out. "I'm here. I'm right here."

"Myrtle," I said. "I'm Myrtle."

"It's all right, my love. I'm here now. I'm here with you," he said.

ACKNOWLEDGEMENTS

THERE ARE A great many people in my life to whom I owe a debt of gratitude, and it would be impossible to list them all here. But there are some who must be named, in no particular order: my first readers, Kimmy, Ursula, Richard, Ailsa, Helen, Derek, Jena, Silvana, Liz, Frase, and Ann. Antanas Sileika, a tremendous writer and mentor. Team Ph.D. and the Bankhouse Massive for unwavering support and belief. Neil and Kes, for encouragement and a home away from home. The York U Crew who somehow, some twenty-odd years later, will still drink with me, especially Drew and Glaze. My Bristol girls, Kate and Helen. And to anyone else not mentioned by name who stood me a round, bought me dinner, put me in a taxi, and generally helped me keep my shit together over the years. Though we may not have lived in the same city while I wrote this book, believe me, your support helped me put these words down.

And finally, a big thank you to Melanie for her editing, as well as Janie, Sarah, and the rest of the team at Anansi for bringing this book across the pond.

Author photograph: Laura Waddell

GILLIAN BEST is a writer, swimmer, and seaside enthusiast. She won the Bronwen Wallace Award for Emerging Writers and was a finalist for the Bridport Prize International Creative Writing Competition and the Wasafiri New Writing Prize. She was also longlisted for the Writeidea Prize Short Story Competition. She has studied at York University, University College Falmouth, and the University of Glasgow. Originally from Waterloo, Canada, she now lives in Bristol, U.K.